How Dark the
NIGHT

How Dark the NIGHT

A NOVEL BY

WILLIAM C. HAMMOND

NAVAL INSTITUTE PRESS
Annapolis, Maryland

Naval Institute Press
291 Wood Road
Annapolis, MD 21402

Library of Congress Cataloging-in-Publication Data

Hammond, William C., 1947–
  How dark the night : a novel / by William C. Hammond.
    pages cm
  Summary: "How Dark the Night continues the seafaring adventures of the Cutler family by picking up the action where the fourth volume, A Call to Arms, ends in 1805. The years leading up to the War of 1812 were devastating ones for the young republic. The life-and-death struggle between Great Britain and France caught the United States in a web of financial and political chaos as President Jefferson and Secretary of State Madison labored to keep the unprepared United States out of the conflict without compromising the nation's honor. On the home front, Jefferson's embargo threatened the livelihood of the Cutlers and other New England shipping families as merchant ships rotted on their moorings and sailors sat on the beach, penniless"— Provided by publisher.
    ISBN 978-1-61251-467-3 (hardback) — ISBN 978-1-61251-466-6 (epub) — ISBN 978-1-61251-466-6 (pdf) 1. United States. Navy—History—19th century—Fiction. 2. United States—History, Naval—To 1900—Fiction. 3. United States—History—1801–1809—Fiction. 4. New England—Commerce—History—19th century—Fiction. I. Title.
  PS3608.A69586H69 2014
  813'.6—dc23

                                                         2013049999

22 21 20 19 18 17 16 15 14   9 8 7 6 5 4 3 2 1
First printing

In loving memory of my uncle
LANSING V. HAMMOND
Lance always encouraged me to write.

Death be not proud, though some have called thee
Mighty and dreadful, thou art not so . . .
One short sleepe, we wake eternally,
And death shall be no more; death, thou shalt die.

THOMAS DONNE

Prologue

SOON AFTER the turn of the nineteenth century, as the opening salvoes in the war against Tripoli thundered along the Barbary Coast, the United States became increasingly embroiled in the Napoleonic Wars, an epic struggle for national survival fought between Great Britain and its ancient enemy, France. By 1805 the conflict had become a world war, having slogged its way across the globe since its French Revolution genesis in 1793—with only a brief fourteen-month interval of peace provided by the Treaty of Amiens in 1802. Napoléon Bonaparte's ego and determination were every bit as strong and unrelenting as his armies; all that stood between him and his dream of global domination was the sea power of the Royal Navy, the much-heralded "wooden wall of England." By the summer of 1805 the war had consumed nearly every corner and byway of Europe, and its funeral pyres blazed as far away as the West Indies, Latin America, South Africa, and the Orient. And now Napoléon was threatening to up the ante by dispatching his Armée de l'Angleterre to northern France in preparation for invading Great Britain.

In this conflict the United States remained neutral. In truth, it had no choice: it had no viable army, and its fledgling navy was otherwise engaged in the Mediterranean. Further, the young republic had no vested interest in the war's outcome; it did not take sides, at least in theory. Because the nation supported the principle of free trade, one customer was just as desirable as another, regardless of what language that customer spoke or what political theory he espoused. But to the two great leviathans slugging it out in Europe, the upstart Americans posed a serious threat. Yankee sea captains were out to turn a profit at every opportunity, and the scourge of war in Europe provided a potential windfall for American ship owners and their crews.

In lockstep with high potential rewards, of course, come high potential risks. Peril lurked on every horizon and in every port of call. France
might rule the Continent, but the Royal Navy ruled the world's sea-lanes.
And because America's merchant fleet was the world's largest neutral carrier of food and supplies, the British Admiralty had stated publicly and
repeatedly that it would do whatever was necessary to keep those ships
and their cargoes out of enemy hands.

While the entrepreneurial Federalists in the northeastern states wres-
tled with such transnational issues, the Republicans, most of whom lived
in the southern and western states, looked inside their own country for
their rewards. In 1803, with the purchase of the enormous Louisiana Territory, the United States had doubled in size. In that same year the state
of Ohio had been admitted to the Union and the Indiana Territory orga-
nized. In 1804 President Jefferson had given his blessing to the expedition
proposed by two Virginians of his acquaintance: Meriwether Lewis and
William Clark. Newspapers carried electrifying reports and detailed maps
of their exploration route, which wound northwestward across the hills
and hollows of the Louisiana Purchase before snaking westward through
the high mountains on a course between British possessions to the north
and Spanish possessions to the south and west of Great Salt Lake. Their
ultimate destination was the Oregon Territory, which belonged formally
to no nation but was richly coveted by all: Great Britain, Spain, and the
United States—and Russia, whose traders and pioneers had migrated
southward from their base in Alaska to the mouth of the Columbia River.

It was not exports or new overseas markets that the Republicans
craved; it was raw land that they could purchase for pennies and then earn
dollars by farming the land and selling its produce. Native Indians posed
a constant threat along the frontier, and British agents in the Northwest
Territories and agents of Spain working the border between Spanish-held
Florida and Georgia were doing their best to stir up trouble.

Thomas Jefferson, recently reelected to a second term in office, was
again caught in a geopolitical bind. Republican to his core—for Americans of every political and social stripe he embodied the Republican
ideals of states' rights, agrarianism, and limited government spending,
especially on the military—Jefferson's back-and-forth positions on issues
of national defense and national honor had often left both politicians and
citizens scratching their heads in bewildered confusion. He professed to
oppose a strong navy and preferred the construction of gunboats to frigates; yet during the war against Tripoli he had, without hesitation and
without consulting Congress, dispatched four naval squadrons across the

Atlantic and had stayed the course until the United States had secured what to his mind was an honorable peace. Even now, USS *Constitution*, arguably the most powerful frigate ever to sail the seas, remained on station in the Mediterranean to safeguard America's interests there. Further, whereas President Jefferson advocated the virtues of the yeoman farmer over those of merchants, bankers, and investors, he also espoused the principle that free ships made free goods. The primary beneficiaries of that policy were the wealthy New England shipping families—who had voted against him in the last two presidential elections.

Napoléon, it was reported, guffawed when informed of Jefferson's stance. The British were less amused. In an attempt to prevent America from capitalizing on Europe's depleted merchant fleets by shipping directly from French, Spanish, and Dutch colonies in the West Indies to their mother countries, Britain imposed the "Rule of 1756." Under that rule, trade that had been closed in time of peace could not be opened in time of war; certainly Holland, for example, had never allowed direct shipments of goods from Saint Eustatius to Rotterdam (or vice versa) in American merchant vessels. Undaunted, American shippers responded with the principle of the "broken voyage," a tactic that brought produce bound for Europe from the West Indies to an American port where it was offloaded and then reloaded for re-export to Europe. Perhaps as a result of the rapprochement that had existed between Great Britain and the United States since the signing of John Jay's treaty in 1795, the British Admiralty Court at first upheld the legitimacy of the broken voyage. In the *Polly* case, it ruled that produce imported to an America port ipso facto became the property of the carrier, and the carrier could do with it whatever the carrier wished.

Great Britain was not, however, entirely amenable to American interests. With the lapse of the Jay Treaty in 1803, Great Britain applied with a vengeance its long-held right to board American vessels to capture Royal Navy seamen suspected of jumping ship and signing on with an American merchant vessel or man-of-war. Any British citizen, in fact, could be forced into service. Although maritime Americans viewed impressment as nothing less than kidnapping on the high seas, it was not an issue subject to adjudication in British courts, as was, for example, the disposition of American merchant vessels and cargoes seized by the British. The right of impressment was considered a prerogative of the Crown. The Royal Navy desperately needed sailors to man its thousand-plus warships and was determined to take them wherever it could find them, regardless of such diplomatic niceties as naturalization papers, which could easily be, and often were, forged. If in the process of exercising the king's prerogative American citizens were impressed into the Royal Navy either by mistake or on purpose, no one in Great Britain was inclined to give it much thought.

These events and outcomes abroad were vastly unsettling to New England shipping families such as the Crowninshields and Endicotts. The golden goose that was their carrying trade depended on good relations with the former mother country. Britain was America's chief trading partner, accounting for nearly 80 percent of all imports into the United States and a healthy percentage of its exports. What would become of this country, they asked, if the artery conveying its lifeblood was blocked or severed? More important to many of them was the question of what would become of the families. In the fall of 1805, no merchant or trader or politician had a ready answer.

As ominous as the dark clouds beginning to gather over the eastern horizon might be, one New England shipping family—the Cutlers of Hingham, Massachusetts—had a more immediate and pressing concern to address, one that was at once both life-defining and life-threatening.

One

Hingham, Massachusetts
September–October 1805

"RICHARD? I'M SORRY to wake you, but it's almost nine o'clock." The voice seemed to come from a faraway place, a different dimension, yet it was a sound familiar since his earliest childhood. His eyelids fluttered open, then his gaze shot to his wife lying on the bed next to the wingback chair that for the last three days and nights had been his watch post. To his relief he found her peacefully asleep, her chest rising and falling steadily, the ship-shape bedsheet and blanket across her chest attesting to serene dreams. He had seen the same sight throughout the night, at least until the wee hours when exhaustion had finally claimed him.

He glanced up at his sister. "Nine o'clock you say, Anne?"

"Yes. Dr. Prescott just arrived. The family is gathering in the parlor."

"Right. Give me a minute. I want to tidy up a bit and stoke up the fire."

"Take whatever time you need," Anne Cutler Seymour said. She squeezed her brother's shoulder before walking quietly out of the room.

Richard leaned forward in his chair and stared intently at his wife. He longed to touch her, to take her hand or caress her bare lower arm, but he did not want to wake her. As if reading his thoughts, she stirred slightly and turned her face toward him. But still she slept.

He rose and stretched out the soreness in his legs and back and neck. He realized that such would not have been necessary had he followed the advice of his siblings and children and gone upstairs to sleep in one of the spare bedrooms, perhaps the one he and his brother Will had shared as boys. But Richard would not, could not, leave his wife's bedside. The downstairs study, which had once been the purview of his father and was now that of his brother Caleb, was hardly large enough to accommodate the bed and other extra furniture it held. But it was on the first floor, in the quietest part of the house; and it was off the kitchen, where boiling water was quickly available to sterilize sheets and bandages and surgical instruments. Caleb had insisted that for the procedure Katherine be brought here to the family seat on Main Street where he and his wife, Joan, and their infant son, Thomas, resided. Richard had not argued. This house was considerably larger than Richard and Katherine's home on South Street, and it contained more amenities.

He tucked in his shirt, buttoned his brown cotton waistcoat, and rolled up his sleeves. From a pitcher set on a table before a mirror he poured water into a porcelain basin. After splashing some onto his face, he smoothed back strands of near-shoulder-length blond hair that retained a youthful thickness and luster belying his forty-five years. Late last evening he had shaved with soap and razor in anticipation of this morning's gathering. As he ran his fingers back and forth across his chin he felt no residual stubble, although he did note, more with passing interest than concern, the bloodshot eyes looking back at him in the mirror and the puffy gray skin around them. He dried his face with a towel and, turning around, found to his surprise and delight that his wife was watching him.

"Well, good morning, my lady," he said cheerfully as he walked over to her. He sat down on the edge of the bed and took her left hand in both of his. "Sleeping in a little, are we?"

A faint smile graced her chapped lips.

His tone turned serious. "How do you feel, Katherine? Is there anything I can get for you? Water? Soup?"

She shook her head and glanced down at her chest, which was covered by layers of bandages, a sheet, and a blanket. She lifted her gaze slowly back to his. "It's over, isn't it?"

"Yes. It's been over for nearly a day. You've been drifting in and out of consciousness, so I doubt you remember much. Dr. Prescott has been in to see you and gave you a dose of laudanum for the pain. He's here right now, in fact, in the parlor. He wants to meet with the family to explain things. After that, he'll be in to check on you."

"Then you must be going," she rasped. "You must not keep the good doctor waiting."

"I won't. But I won't be gone long. Rest now. We need to get your strength back, and I must tell the family the good news that you are awake." He raised her hand to his lips. As he kissed the warm, silken flesh, emotion whirled within him. "In fact," he added with a broad grin, "it seems I must tell the entire town, for most of Hingham has been keeping vigil outside along Main Street for the last two days. Some people stood in the street all night holding candles. Many of them are still out there."

"Dear God," she murmured. "How very, very kind."

"They love you, Katherine. You have touched many lives during our twenty-three years in Hingham." He forced himself to stop there, although there was more, much more, that he ached to say to her. But he dared not continue lest his emotions overcome him. He had resolved to remain upbeat in her presence during the early days following the procedure. They both knew that her reluctance to admit to her condition and seek treatment had made matters worse than they might have been, but he was determined not to mention that. And there was, after all, no reason *not* to be upbeat. What he had been told privately by Dr. Prescott—and what he would no doubt hear repeated in a few minutes—was that there was every reason to be hopeful. Holding that blessed thought in mind, he placed his hand on her forehead and looked deep into her hazel eyes, "I love you," he said softly and leaned down to kiss her lips.

She lifted her hand to touch the side of his face and mouthed the same words back at him. Then the opiate took hold again and she drifted back to sleep.

Richard stood, walked over to the hearth, and placed thin sticks of white birch on the hot embers. When the flames blazed up, he added a slab of heavy oak to keep the fire going. Then he slipped away through the kitchen and down the front hallway to the parlor near the entrance of the house.

Most of his family was waiting, seated on sofas and chairs. His younger son, James, was not present—he remained on station off the Barbary Coast in *Constitution*—and Agreen Crabtree, Richard's closest friend and his first officer in *Portsmouth*, was still at the naval base in Hampton Roads, Virginia, attending to the peacetime disposition of the 36-gun frigate that had been their command during the war against Tripoli.

The subdued conversation ceased abruptly as Richard entered the room. All eyes followed him as he walked over to where Dr. Prescott stood in the middle of the gathering—dressed entirely in black save for the silver buckles on his shoes and the blood-red buttons of his waistcoat.

"She is resting peacefully," Richard said to the doctor in a voice loud enough for all to hear. "She awoke for a few minutes and spoke. She says she is comfortable and in no pain."

"That is most encouraging, Richard," Prescott said. "We can all take comfort in that news." He motioned Richard to a seat on a sofa next to his younger sister, Lavinia, and her husband, Stephen Starbuck, up from Duxbury. Lavinia took Richard's hand and gave it a brief squeeze of sympathy.

Prescott cleared his throat. "Thank you for the gift of your family," he started in. "That may seem an odd thing to say at this moment, but you are the key to Katherine's recovery. Never in my many years of practicing medicine have I encountered another family so beloved by each other and by an entire community. Have you looked outside? Those good people, waiting there, your friends and neighbors, reflect that. They stand there for Mrs. Cutler, of course; but in truth they stand for you all."

Diana Cutler, the mirror image of her mother when she was seventeen, gave a wrenching sob, overcome by her fear and despair. Adele Endicott Cutler, who was sitting beside her, raised a hand and began gently kneading the nape of Diana's neck. Adele's husband, Will Cutler, could only gaze helplessly at his distraught sister.

Dr. Prescott addressed Diana directly. "It is good to weep," he comforted. "Tears express love and they cleanse the soul. Your mother's travails in this process have been many, and they have been difficult, as they have been for you all. But I assure you that the worst is over now, certainly for the time being. As I have told Captain Cutler, we have every reason to be hopeful."

Diana nodded and hid her face in her hands, grateful for his comfort but unable to utter a word.

"Then in your estimation the surgery was a success, Doctor?" That question came from Frederick Seymour, Anne's husband. Everyone in the room had expected him to ask that most vital question. Direct and candid language was not only at the root of his nature, it also was at the root of his own medical practice in Cambridge.

"In my opinion, yes it was, Doctor," Prescott stated. "My assistant Dr. Thorndike and I removed Mrs. Cutler's left breast without complication or compromise. I do not believe the surgery could have gone better."

Joan Cutler was about to ask the inevitable follow-up question when Lizzy Cutler Crabtree, Katherine's closest friend since their childhood together in England, asked it instead. She had been the first person in whom Katherine had confided back in April, when Richard was off waging war in the Mediterranean, and had borne the secret alone until he had returned. "Were you able to remove all the cancer?"

Prescott hooked his thumbs in the pockets of his waistcoat and stared solemnly at the floor for a moment, as if to contemplate his answer or to underscore its significance. "Regretfully, we cannot determine that, Mrs. Crabtree. It's really anyone's guess. Medical science knows very little about this dreadful disease. For now, everything is in God's hands. But as I said, we have every reason to be hopeful. You are aware, of course, that President Adams' daughter had the same procedure for the same reason and is now living a normal life."

"When will we know for certain if the cancer is gone?" Lizzy persisted.

"Again, I cannot tell you *when* we will know, or even *if*. The cancer may return, but in the meantime she may have months—even years—of a perfectly normal life. We'll just have to take each day as it comes and be grateful for that day. I realize that you want specifics, but those I cannot give you. Certainly we can all pray for her full recovery. I can assure you that I will do so." What remained unsaid—that Katherine's prognosis would likely have been better had she agreed to the surgery earlier—was best left unsaid. The family understood what lay behind that decision, and nothing would be gained by reexamining it now.

"But my mother *will* get better, at least for a while?" Diana threw out her question as a plea, her delicate features a study of desperate hope. Yesterday there had been no consoling her; neither her father nor anyone else had been able to ease her pain. She had soldiered on nonetheless, determined to keep her dark fears and anguish bottled up to the extent possible, waiting in agonized suspense for this moment.

Prescott smiled at her. "Yes, Diana, your mother *will* get better. *That* much I can promise you. She was living a normal life *before* the surgery, was she not? So why not *after* the surgery? I daresay that if this splendid weather holds, in a few weeks' time you and she will be riding your customary route at World's End. At a walk or a canter, mind you," he added, wagging a finger at her in mock sternness, "*not* at a hard gallop."

With that, the dike burst. "Thank you, Doctor!" Diana sobbed. "You could not have said anything to make me happier." As if to belie those words she leaned forward, buried her face in her hands, and wept great heaving sobs, giving vent to the unspoken emotions felt by everyone present. Richard bit his lip and dabbed at his eyes with a handkerchief as his brother Caleb stood up to stand beside Dr. Prescott.

"Thank you, Doctor," he said, pressing Prescott's hand. "The Cutler family is most indebted to you for your excellent care of our dear sister and mother."

Prescott bowed. "It is my honor, Mr. Cutler."

"Can we see her now?" Diana begged, swiping at tears.

Prescott nodded. "Soon, Diana. I will see her now, along with your father. But this afternoon, you and Will may go in to her. Please keep your visits brief during the next several days and present cheerful faces. She needs your encouragement. She also needs to rest, so don't tire her, and she needs to slowly start eating something of substance."

"You need have no concerns about that, Doctor," Caleb pointed out good-naturedly. "Not in this house."

Everyone in the room, including Dr. Prescott, understood that Caleb was referring to Edna Stowe, the tireless housekeeper who had devoted most of her adult life in service to the Cutler family and was at that moment upstairs tending to little Thomas Cutler and eight-year-old Zeke Crabtree. Her reputation as a cook and as a woman who brooked no nonsense from those in her charge—and that included every member of the extended Cutler family—was well established in Hingham. And on that positive note the family gathering ended.

DR. PRESCOTT'S prediction was correct. Katherine Cutler did show rapid improvement. Another week would pass, however, before she judged herself well enough to leave Caleb's house on Main Street for her own home a quarter mile away on South Street. Richard supported the move wholeheartedly, certain that her return to the house so full of happy memories would expedite her return to health. But the rest of the family and Edna had first to be convinced that it was safe. Although Diana wanted her mother home more than anything, she was concerned that something would go wrong were her mother to be moved prematurely from the room that had become a sanctuary of recovery.

"I am hardly a dish of china that will shatter the moment I stumble," a frustrated Katherine said one day amid the clatter of opinions and warnings. That outburst settled the matter. The move was made on a day in early October when the lingering summer sun warmed the multicolored splendor of the New England fall.

It was not a carefree transition from one house to another, however. Katherine's soul clearly remained troubled even as her body healed, and during the first several weeks in her own home she was able to walk outside to take the air only for brief periods. As out of character as her quick temper and swings of mood may have been, they were not, according to Dr. Prescott, out of order. Consider, he counseled Richard in particular, the mental and physical suffering that she had endured alone for long months before admitting that she was ill, and the pain of the surgery and its aftermath. It was a cross, he stressed, that few people would have the emotional or physical stamina to bear.

During that first week and into the second, Richard remained in Hingham, leaving the day-to-day operations of the Boston-based family shipping business to Caleb, the proprietor of Cutler & Sons, and to his son Will, who was being groomed to someday take over the business, together with the family's 50 percent interest in a considerably larger commercial enterprise administered in alliance with the Endicott family of Boston. On days when Caleb and Will were thus occupied in Boston, and when his wife was at rest, Richard busied himself with correspondence to his son Jamie in the Mediterranean, to the Navy Department in Washington, and to his English cousins John and Robin Cutler, who managed the family-owned sugar plantation on the West Indian island of Barbados. They and their wives were dear friends as well as cousins, and they were most keen to be kept current on Katherine's recovery.

On Katherine's first night back at home, Richard had asked his daughter to stay the night with Will and Adele at their home on Ship Street. He wanted this time alone with her mother, he told Diana, who was quick to understand.

Supper options that evening had been many. Enough food had been left on their front door step, Richard had laughingly informed Katherine as they slowly walked along South Street arm in arm amid the autumn brilliance, to feed a five-ship naval squadron. But there was no decision to be made. To mark the occasion, Edna Stowe had prepared their favorite meal: creamed codfish, peas, and whipped potatoes. After setting out the Wedgwood platters and dishes on the oval teakwood table in the dining alcove and lighting the candles in the silver candelabra, she announced her intention to depart and to return early in the morning to do the dishes. Unless, of course, Katherine and Richard needed her to remain?

"Thank you, no, Edna," Katherine smiled. "We can manage quite nicely from here. You have been more than helpful and kind."

Edna nodded her acknowledgment. "Very well, then. If there is nothing else." She turned to leave and then turned back. "Richard, you *will* mind the hearth, won't you? You mustn't let the fire go out!"

"The fire *always* goes out, Edna," Richard said, grinning, "the moment you leave our company."

Edna snorted and stomped out of the room. A minute later they heard the front door creak open and then click shut.

Alone at last with his wife, Richard poured two half glasses of Bordeaux and offered one to his wife, then held out his own glass up in a toast. "To us," he said meaningfully. "To being home together again. And to your swift and full recovery."

She clinked her glass against his, and their eyes met and held.

"You look lovely tonight, my lady," he said, and as always when he said that, there was truth in his words. Katherine Hardcastle Cutler had been endowed with an unusual grace and beauty that even at age forty-six could stir desire in men and envy in women. Tonight, however, she had done little to enhance her natural charms. Her rich chestnut hair was pulled back into a simple plait; her light blue dress was of homespun cloth and unadorned; only a faint scent of jasmine bespoke any attention to feminine detail.

She set her glass on the table, folded her hands in her lap, and looked down at them. After several awkward moments, Richard asked hesitantly, "What is it, Katherine? Aren't you happy to be home?"

"Of course I'm happy to be home," she said quietly. She continued to look down at her lap.

"Well, then, what's bothering you? Whatever it is, we need to talk it through. Is it something I've done?"

She glanced up in amazement. "Don't be ridiculous, Richard. *You* have done nothing wrong. I do want to tell you, but I find it difficult to explain, and I fear you will not understand if I try."

"I understand more than you realize, Katherine." He paused for a moment to marshal his thoughts. "I think you're feeling guilt for hiding your illness and then refusing to allow Dr. Prescott to treat it, and for the pain all of us have suffered as a result." He placed one finger across her lips to stop her from speaking. "In fact, my darling, I feel just as much guilt for what I have done to you and to our family. And it's a loathsome burden."

"Guilt? *You?*"

"Yes. Me."

"What *sort* of guilt, in heaven's name?"

"Guilt for not being here when you needed me the most, when our children needed me the most. I have left you alone far too often in our marriage, from the very beginning in Barbados."

She held his gaze for several moments, as if seeking a clue as to what lay behind what she considered a shockingly unfair assertion. "God's mercy, Richard," she said finally, "you can't be serious. When you went to sea, you were not going off on a lark. You were doing your duty, either to your family or to your country—or to both."

"But at what price," he insisted, "when the one I love more than my own life suffered for months without me here to offer comfort." He took another healthy swig of wine.

Katherine did not follow suit. "Richard," she said crossly, "that is utter nonsense. You are saying it only to make me feel better about my own guilt. There is not a shred of logic or reason behind your words. You have been—you are—a wonderful husband and a wonderful provider, and you have made us all very happy and proud. You have done your duty, a hundred times over, and your wife and children are the beneficiaries of that." She leaned in toward him. "Please let me say what I need to say," she whispered, her voice beginning to crack. "The guilt we are discussing tonight is *entirely* mine. For too many weeks I realized something bad was going on inside me and I did nothing about it. I could have. Lizzy urged me to, begged me to. But I did nothing. *Nothing*, Richard. *That* is a guilt I can never dismiss, nor ever come to terms with."

Richard shook his head in denial. "I know perfectly well why you chose to do nothing, Katherine. Lizzy told me what you said when you first confided in her. You said that under no circumstances would you allow your husband to return home from war to a mangled wife. Is that not true?"

Katherine's silence suggested that it was, at least in part.

"Please God, Katherine, as misguided as I believe you were, I understand. All of us understand. I only wish that you had understood that the loss of your breast would have done nothing—has done nothing—to affect my love and desire for you. You are still the most beautiful woman I have ever known."

"I was afraid," Katherine went on, as if she had not heard his words, her voice soft and distant. "I was scared of the disease. And I was scared even more of the surgery. Dr. Prescott says that I am healing as well as can be expected a week after the procedure. That is all well and good, but every time I look at myself in the mirror, I feel sick to my stomach. No matter what you say, Richard—and I love you for saying it—I *am* mangled. No longer completely a woman." She looked down at her tightly clasped hands.

Richard did not hesitate. "Look at me, Katherine. Please. Now take my hand." When she slowly, reluctantly, offered her hand, he took it and brought it to his lips. "Do you remember our last night together in

Tobago?" he asked. "When you told me you were pregnant with Will, and how happy you were?"

"I remember," she whispered.

"And yet, despite our joy and the love we felt for each other at that moment, you urged me to join the French fleet the next day and sail with Admiral de Grasse to Yorktown. Remember?" She nodded. "You knew that if I didn't go, if I followed my heart and remained with you, I would forever regret not doing everything in my power to avenge the death of my brother."

"Yes," she said. Tears began coursing down her cheeks, but she made no effort to wipe them away.

"And do you remember what I said when you told me to go? I asked God to tell me what I had done in my life to deserve a gift such as you." He squeezed her hand, the tears welling, threatening to undo him. "Nothing has changed, Katherine. Nothing could *ever* change the way I feel about you. I could just as well ask that very same question tonight."

"As could I," she whispered. She took a deep breath, winced a bit, and then smiled at him. "I think it is time we were in bed, my lord. I want to feel your arms around me. But just that," she added quickly. "Later—well, later we'll see. For tonight I just want to sleep in your arms, to feel them around me the entire night through. Can we do that?"

He furrowed his brow and began thrumming his fingers on the table as if collecting his thoughts. In truth, he was collecting his emotions. Then: "I will grant my lady's wish on the condition that she grant this poor pilgrim two small boons in return."

"Hmm. Based on previous conditions you have imposed on me, I am rather afraid to ask. . . . What are they?"

"The first is that we finish our supper. Else we'll have Edna's wrath to contend with in the morning."

She nodded. "And the other?"

"The other is that you sleep late tomorrow."

She gave his hand a squeeze in return as her smile broadened. "Your boons are granted, good pilgrim."

Two

Boston, Massachusetts
November–December 1805

WITH KATHERINE CUTLER'S prospects gradually return-ing to a semblance of nor-malcy, the Cutler family turned its attention to other serious concerns. Although the West Indian rum and sugar production that defined the heart and history of Cutler & Sons was thriving, dark clouds were gath-ering on the eastern horizon. The Orient trade that governed the substan-tial cargoes and profits of C&E Enterprises—in which the Cutler family held a 50 percent share—was facing new threats. C&E ships were increas-ingly being openly harassed on several oceans and several continents. Matters came to a head on a day in early November when a messenger from Boston delivered a note to Richard Cutler in Hingham. The note, signed jointly by his brother Caleb and by Jack Endicott, requested Rich-ard to sail to Long Wharf the next morning to discuss a "matter of utmost importance." Richard sent a note in reply stating that he planned to be there by eleven o'clock.

The day dawned typically for November: raw, overcast, and squally. On the cruise in to Boston from Hingham, the single-masted sloop had to battle whitecaps and spindrift whipped up by stiff headwinds that forced the sturdy fifty-foot vessel to stay within the lee of the pearl-like string of Boston Harbor islands that formed the northern boundary of Hingham Bay. By the time the sloop had skimmed into the relative calm of Boston's inner harbor and doused her wings of snapping canvas, a bluster of rain and sleet dotted with flakes of wet snow was howling along the half-mile length of Long Wharf.

Thaddeus Hobbes, the sloop's helmsman, grabbed hold of a bollard and jumped up from the sloop's bulwark onto the wharf next to his mate, Tom Johnson, who had been first off the boat with the bow mooring line. Hobbes reached down toward the sloop to offer Richard a hand. "Mind your footing, Captain Cutler," he cautioned. "It's a mite slippery."

When Richard was up and standing close to him, Hobbes said over the moan of wind, his soaked oilskins flapping, "Foul weather to be sure, Captain. Tom and I would have been hard-pressed out there had you not taken command of the heads'l sheets. My apologies for the inconvenience, but I thank ye most kindly for your assistance."

"Think nothing of it, Hobbes," Richard shouted back. "You and Johnson did fine. And I must say, it felt good to feel wind on my face again."

Hobbes grinned. "If ye say so, sir. Do ye still want to sail back to Hingham on the morrow?"

"Yes. Let's keep it at ten o'clock. I suspect we'll have the company of my brother on the voyage home."

"Very good, Captain. Ten o'clock it is. Tom and I will be standing by."

Richard took his leave and began picking his way down the massive wood-and-stone wharf to his family's countinghouse located at midwharf between another company's warehouse and a sail loft. Along the way he dodged ship owners and ship's masters, clerks and sailors striding purposefully, in and out of buildings built one against the other along the wharf's north side, and off and on merchant vessels of various rigs nested one against the other along the south side. These people went about their business as though oblivious to the inclement weather, and for good reason. During the past ten years Long Wharf had grown into a commercial juggernaut. The armada of merchant ships tied up there or anchored out in the harbor—a number of them Cutler & Sons vessels—defined the essence of a national merchant fleet that by now had blossomed into the world's largest neutral carrier of merchant goods.

As he opened the door to the countinghouse and stepped inside, Richard took a moment to enjoy the blessing of dry warmth provided by the large room's three cast iron wood-burning stoves. Caleb and Jack Endicott were engaged in a lively conversation at the far side of the square chamber, beyond the clusters of desks where clerks busily scratched out the numbers and correspondence attached to the various comings-in and goings-out of both Cutler & Sons and C&E Enterprises, careful to keep separate accounts of the two shipping firms. Richard waved to the two men and began to unbutton his oilskins. As he did so, he heard a familiar voice behind him.

"Nasty weather, is it not, Mr. Cutler. Fit for a fish or a gull perhaps, but hardly for a man with any sense about him."

Richard turned to find George Hunt, the longtime administrator of the Boston office of Cutler & Sons, standing before him. Approaching eighty years now, Hunt was evincing ever-clearer signs of his advanced age. His stooped posture, wrinkled and spotted skin, and cloud-white whiskers and hair marked him as an old man, but a fire of acumen and vitality still burned within his clear, dark blue eyes. Every member of the Cutler family knew and was grateful that, whatever the circumstances, George Hunt would remain in the employ of Cutler & Sons until the day he drew his last breath.

"Good morning, George," Richard replied. "It is indeed nasty out there."

"And your voyage from Hingham? That must have been a treat, on a day like this." Hunt helped Richard out of his dripping oilskins and hung them from a peg.

"Quite the treat, George. It's why I'm so late."

"Not to worry, Mr. Cutler. We assumed you would be delayed. Might I offer you a bite to eat? We've had dinner brought in from the Bunch of Grapes tavern. Your brother and Mr. Endicott have just finished eating theirs."

"I'll wait on the food, but a cup of tea would do nicely. The hotter the better."

"I shall bring it right over."

"Thank you, George." As Richard walked across the room between the clusters of desks, clerks paused their goose-quill pens to acknowledge him with a nod or a wave. Several of them stood as he passed in what he knew to be a silent tribute to Katherine. Richard acknowledged each of them in turn, last of all Jack Endicott, who heaved himself to his feet at Richard's approach.

"Welcome, Richard," he said, shaking hands. "A pleasure, as always, to see you. Allow me to say how terribly sorry I was to hear of Katherine's illness, and how delighted I am to learn of her excellent recovery. Adele has kept us in the know now that Will is off to Baltimore and we have the pleasure of her company for a few days. Truly, I am so very pleased that Katherine is on the mend. Anne-Marie is too, of course. You both continue to be in our thoughts and prayers."

"Thank you, Jack," Richard said, genuinely moved but grinning inwardly at the mental image of plump Jack Endicott on his knees in prayer. "That is most kind of you."

"Not at all, my dear man. Not at all. Now then, you *will* drop by the house later this afternoon, won't you? Caleb tells me that you and he are taking supper with the Cabots this evening. That is all well and good, but surely you can accommodate a glass of Madeira with us on your way there? Anne-Marie will be most disappointed if you do not."

Richard glanced at his brother, who gave him a quick grin in reply.

"Of course, Jack. Shall we say five o'clock?"

"Five o'clock is excellent. We shall expect you then. Lest I forget, Caleb," he added, "please do remember to send my best regards this evening to George," referring to George Cabot, Joan Cabot Cutler's father and a Boston patriarch of consequence. "I hear he has not been himself lately, and I want to wish him well. He is a dear friend. Now, please sit down and make yourself comfortable, Richard. Ah, here comes George with your beverage. Thank you, George. If you will take a seat as well, we shall get started."

Richard settled in on a sofa facing the north wall of the building while George sat primly upright in a chair. Through the paned window Richard could see the white steeple of Old North Church standing tall and bold in the far gray distance. He took a sip of tea, savoring the delicious warmth that coursed down his throat into his stomach.

"The news today, I'm afraid, is not good," Endicott began soberly. "Then again, when *has* it been good lately? By all accounts the situation is worsening by the day." His plump face reddened in anger. "We *now* have to contend with a recent ruling by the British Admiralty Court. According to a report I have received from our agent in London, the court has reversed the *Polly* decision. The new *Essex* ruling states that the 'broken voyage' tactic we have so successfully employed in the past is no longer valid, the court having concluded—no doubt with considerable urging from Parliament and British mercantile interests—that because the *intent* of the 'broken voyage' is to circumvent the Rule of 1756, it is therefore illegal. Pay no mind to the fact that it *has* been legal for the past five years. Henceforth, all cargoes we carry from colonies of European nations to the United States must remain in the United States for our own consumption. We are no longer permitted to re-export these cargoes to Europe, at least as far as Great Britain is concerned." His breathing quickened as his anger grew. "As you well know, of course, if we are not allowed to re-export these goods to Europe, we forgo most of our profits. Indeed, it hardly makes business sense for us to continue to engage in this trade at all."

Endicott paused a moment to dab at his brow and allow Richard to digest this information. As was true for many New England shipping families, a small but still healthy portion of Cutler & Sons' revenues came from carrying the trade of West Indian colonies to their mother countries in Europe, after first conveying them to the United States. Most European maritime countries no longer retained the merchant fleets they once had boasted, especially in the West Indies. So they relied heavily on American merchant vessels to transport their goods for them—at a healthy fee. England now seemed determined to stop that trade.

Caleb spoke next. "We have been discussing the possibility of something like this happening, Richard, although we have not wanted to add to your recent worries. George here has been an important part of those discussions. John and Robin have also shared their thoughts on the matter. So we're not caught entirely off guard. Still, the questions remain: What do we do in response to this ruling? And how will the ruling affect shipments of sugar and rum from Barbados to anywhere? The legal ramifications are profound, it would seem, and the financial ramifications are much more so. It's just as Jack says."

Richard Cutler offered no immediate comment, his mind laboring to fit together the pieces of the complex international puzzle. Then: "I'm not sure I agree," he said to no one in particular. "We can still ship produce from the Indies to America. And we can sell our produce to the interior of the country. Admittedly, our revenues would be less without the European trade, but so would our costs. We should still show a healthy profit. And the risk would be far lower than reshipping goods to Europe." He nodded, convinced of his own argument. "Father's gamble of opening a shipping office in Baltimore will pay off, although perhaps not for the reasons he envisioned." He looked at Endicott. "The language of this ruling affects Cutler & Sons more than C&E Enterprises, Jack. C&E has never engaged heavily in the re-export trade, has it?"

"We do our fair share," Endicott replied, "out of necessity. You were out of the loop whilst in the Mediterranean, but the war in Europe has interfered with our spice trade and we have had to find new sources of revenues. Herr Van der Heyden," referring to the director of C&E Enterprises' Far Eastern headquarters in Batavia, on the island of Java, "confirms that many wealthy Europeans, in particular the French, now find it unseemly, if not unpatriotic, to purchase luxuries and indulge in extravagances of any kind while their country is at war and so many of their people are starving. Never forget that just a decade ago French aristocrats who flouted their wealth were deemed enemies of the state and lost their heads to the guillotine. Today, Frenchmen with means are being extremely discreet. Exotic spices from the Orient are not high on their list of desired purchases.

"Our main entry ports in Europe are, of course, in Holland," he added. "With this new *Essex* ruling the British can now block *this* trade as well, should they have a mind to do so. Hitherto they have chosen to look the other way, but I doubt that will continue. The Batavian Republic," Holland's name under France's dominion, "is nothing more than a puppet state of France, and many islands in the East Indies are considered its dependencies. So the *Essex* ruling most likely applies."

George Hunt interjected a comment into the ensuing silence: "As I see it, Richard, the issue is not how the ruling is worded. Rather, it's how we can expect it to be enforced."

"Hear, hear," Endicott agreed.

"And how do you expect the British to act, George?" Richard said.

Richard was startled by Hunt's reply.

"The United States is involved in a war," he said. It is not a shooting war for us, not yet, and God forbid it should become so. But it's a war nonetheless—an economic war. America has the means to supply most of Europe. We have the ships and crews, and we can secure the necessary goods. But we can rest assured that from here on, England will do everything in its power to keep our trade out of Napoléon's hands through stiffer blockades of European ports. We can also rest assured that Napoléon will return the favor by doing everything *he* can to harass our trade, either by preventing it from reaching a British port or by somehow punishing American ships that *do* reach a British port and then sail on to Europe from there."

Hunt paused for a moment. "But I do not see the French as a major problem for us. Napoléon may control most of mainland Europe, but the Royal Navy continues to control the seas. Great Britain is our primary concern. Her economy is in danger now that her trade with other European nations has vanished. England simply cannot afford to allow American ships to carry cargoes to and from Europe. And then there is the subject of impressment. *That* issue, to Jefferson and Madison, is paramount because it ignites the greatest public outcry. Citizens of Tennessee or Kentucky or Georgia care little if the French seize a C&E ship in Rotterdam. A wealthy New England shipping family, they think, can well afford the loss. But let the English dare to board an American ship and drag off sailors sailing under the American flag—*that* is an entirely different matter. That is a matter of national honor," he concluded. "And as we all know only too well, matters of national honor can lead to war."

No one could argue with that perspective.

"We mustn't forget," Caleb pointed out, "the most important consideration of all, that Great Britain is our main trading partner. More than 80 percent of America's imports come from Britain, and most of what America produces is exported to Britain. How can we ever expect to prevail in this economic war, as George correctly refers to it, if England is acting as our enemy?"

It was a rhetorical question. No one expected an answer. Jack Endicott, nevertheless, had a comment to tag onto it.

"And yet Jefferson is doing everything in his power to turn England *into* our enemy," he stated categorically. "Dam*nation,* that man is an enigma. He touts free trade—and for that, I must applaud him—but then he trots out legislation and policies that are directly intended to rile up the British against us. Clearly he favors the French in this conflict. The *French,* by God! What has Napoléon ever done for us? Not a blasted thing! How a president so willing to sell out his country managed to be reelected to a second term is utterly beyond me."

Jefferson was reelected, Richard thought to himself, because there are many more Republicans in the southern and western states than Federalists in the northeastern states, and Republicans everywhere continue to revere Jefferson as an icon of American idealism. As he listened to Jack Endicott, two people came to mind: his father-in-law, the recently deceased Henry Makepeace Hardcastle, a salty Royal Navy post captain who often spouted off the way Endicott had just done; and Alexander Hamilton, a longtime family friend who was one of the most intelligent and articulate statesmen to espouse Federalist ideals, including the crucial importance of the young republic maintaining strong relations with England. A year ago last July he had been shot and killed in a "duel of honor" with Aaron Burr, Jefferson's vice president at the time. His sound mind and wise counsel would be sorely missed, Richard suspected, in the upcoming regional and national debates.

"What would you have us do, Jack?" Richard asked quietly into the silence that followed the tirade. Outside, rain and sleet still pelted the window glass, although with less intensity than earlier. Inside, in the center of the large room, clerks kept up their busy pen work, seemingly oblivious to the animated conversation taking place not twenty feet from their desks.

Endicott shrugged. "I doubt there is anything we *can* do," he said with resignation, "beyond waiting for developments to unfold and keeping ourselves informed. But mark my words: George is right: the *Essex* case marks only the first broadside aimed at us since the Peace of Amiens dissolved. Every time Britain steps up its blockade of Europe, Napoléon will step up his retaliation. And each time *that* happens, our country's prosperity and the prosperity of our families will be further jeopardized. Who knows where this all might end?"

"It would seem we're caught between the proverbial hammer and anvil," Caleb observed gloomily, and no one could gainsay his summation.

BY 1805 THE BEACON HILL area of Boston rivaled Philadelphia and Charleston as the epicenter of high society in America. From the 1740s into the 1780s, most of Boston Neck, save for the commercial hub near Long Wharf and Faneuil Hall, was a sparsely settled backwater community kept low by the ravages of war and continuing economic stagnation. Visionaries saw the potential, however, and as New England merchant fleets took to the seas in the 1780s and 1790s, they put that potential into action. Among those spearheading the social transformation was Charles Bulfinch, who designed the gilded-domed state house and oversaw its construction in 1795 on property once owned by another visionary, John Singleton Copley. Bulfinch moved his family to Beacon Hill and formed Mount Vernon Proprietors, a group of wealthy landowners determined to develop the area in exquisite good taste. First step: raze the old wooden buildings on Beacon Hill and replace them with elegant red brick residences of Federalist and Greek Revival design. Even the towering beacon that for generations had warned Boston and neighboring communities of enemy attacks was dismantled and carted away to make way for progress. By year-end of 1805 the population of Boston had swelled to nearly thirty thousand souls. Included in its social registry, up on Beacon Hill, were some of the wealthiest and most renowned families in Massachusetts, many of them, including the Endicott family, made rich by the burgeoning overseas carrying trade.

Richard had been to the Endicott residence on Belknap Street on numerous occasions, both alone and in company with Katherine. The Endicotts were, after all, the in-laws of his son Will, and it was Will's wife, Adele, who bobbed him a respectful curtsey as she met him at the front door at the appointed hour of five o'clock.

"How very nice of you to drop by this evening," she said, opening the door wide. "Please do come in out of the cold and damp."

A servant dressed in fine English-style livery stepped forward. Richard handed him his bicorne hat and then shrugged out of his coat, thankful that he had swapped his well-worn oilskins for something more stylish before leaving Cutler & Sons. Arriving at the Endicott residence wearing a sailor's foul-weather gear would simply not do.

"Thank you, Adele," Richard said as the servant closed the front door and imperiously conveyed his hat and outer garment elsewhere. He studied her for a moment. "My Lord, daughter, how lovely you look this evening. You are the very image of a Greek goddess," he added, not without cause. Her curly ebony hair cascaded down fetchingly over the purple taffeta dress that perfectly fit the contours of her slender frame. Nor could he help but notice the sea blue of the eyes that gazed affectionately upon him. They were exactly like those of her mother, a beautiful aristocrat whom Richard had come to know intimately while serving as aide-de-camp to Capt. John Paul Jones in Paris during the war with England almost thirty years earlier. "I pity my poor son, to be called away from such beauty."

"On family business," she reminded him, smiling. "Nonetheless, I do so look forward to his return next week."

Richard returned her smile and gave her a brief, appreciative once-over. "I have no doubt that he does as well," he said. As she blushed prettily he offered his arm, and together they walked slowly down the grand hallway to the sitting room located off the far end.

"How is Frances?" he asked. "I have not seen your younger sister in a while."

"She is doing very well these days. You will be pleased to learn that she has several beaux. One of them is becoming quite ardent in his pursuit of her. You may know him. His name is Robert Pepperell. He lives not far away, at Louisburg Square."

Although Richard did not know the young man, he certainly was acquainted with his family. In 1745, during the War of the Austrian Succession, Robert's grandfather William Pepperell had served as commander in chief of a New England colonial militia unit that, with help from a British naval squadron, had captured the French colonial capital of Louisburg on Cape Breton Island in Canada. For services rendered to the Crown, Sir William was awarded the first American baronetcy, and Louisburg Square, where the Pepperell family still lived, was named in commemoration of the momentous victory.

"Good for Frances," he said, then lowered his voice and whispered conspiratorially, "Do you think Jamie will be jealous?"

"I suspect he will be delighted," she whispered back. Frances Endicott's long-standing interest in Jamie Cutler had by now become a subject of good-natured banter between Richard and his daughter-in-law.

"What are you two discussing in such secrecy?" Jack Endicott's voice boomed out into the hallway. "I trust it has nothing to do with me!"

"It *always* has something to do with you, Papa," Adele assured him. She gave her stepfather a peck on the cheek and disappeared inside the sitting room. Endicott motioned to Richard to follow her. "I have summoned a bottle of our best Madeira," he said, clapping a hand on Richard's shoulder, "as I do whenever you honor us with your company. I only wish your dear wife could be with us this evening."

"As do I, Jack," Richard agreed.

"Richard, my dear, how wonderful to see you." Without hesitation, Anne-Marie Endicott walked up and put her arms around Richard. As was normally the case, even in Katherine's presence, she allowed her embrace and the kiss on the side of his face to linger longer than propriety might deem appropriate. As usual, Richard returned her greeting chastely. Although he realized that Katherine had long ago made peace with the affection Anne-Marie still harbored for him, her open sentiments made him uncomfortable, in part because it flouted normal social conventions, but in greater part because feeling her supple body pressed close against him inflamed memories best left forgotten. After giving her a brief kiss in kind, he backed away a half step.

Anne-Marie backed away as well but kept hold of his hands. "I am so very sorry, Richard, about Katherine. I can't imagine how terribly difficult this must have been for her, confronting such a cruel disease with you away in the Mediterranean. I wish there was something I could have done for her."

"You did do something, Anne-Marie," Richard said. "The very kind letter you wrote meant a lot to her. She keeps it on the table by her bedside."

"Along with many others, I should imagine. So many people care so much about her—and with good cause. She is a warm and loving woman."

"She *is* blessed with many friends," Richard agreed.

Just then a servant entered the room bearing a tray and four glasses brimming with rich amber liquid. Jack Endicott distributed the glasses and raised his. "To Katherine Cutler," he said.

"To Katherine Cutler," the other three said in unison, and four glasses clinked together.

Two weeks later, as the chill of November yielded to the cold of December, stirring reports headlined the front pages of American newspapers. A British naval fleet under the command of Admiral Horatio Lord Nelson had achieved a stunning victory against a considerably larger French and Spanish fleet under the combined command of French admiral Pierre-Charles Villeneuve and Spanish admiral Federico Gravina. For weeks the two massive fleets had been jockeying for position off the coast of Spain and across the Atlantic in the West Indies. On the twenty-first of October, Villeneuve and Gravina ventured out from the Spanish naval base at Cádiz and made a dash eastward toward the Mediterranean. Lord Nelson, however, caught wind of their intentions and was lying in wait for them off Cape Trafalgar near the entrance to the Strait of Gibraltar.

Dividing his twenty-seven battle cruisers into two parallel columns— the weather column led by him in *Victory,* the lee column by Vice Admiral Cuthbert Collingwood in *Royal Sovereign*—Nelson had cast aside time-honored battle tactics by sailing his two columns at right angles against an enemy fleet strung out in traditional line-of-battle formation. Nelson's unexpected tactic shattered the enemy line and tore into 100-gun ships of the line, raking them bow and stern, pulverizing one battle cruiser after another at point-blank range while the eight ships cut off in the van struggled to come about in the fluky northwesterly breeze and bring their guns to bear on the English. Unable to do so—or perhaps despairing of their chances based on the devastation taking place behind them—the eight ships disengaged entirely and sailed off to leeward.

Reports in Boston newspapers numbered the French and Spanish ships captured or destroyed at twenty-two, or two-thirds of the entire allied fleet. The British, by contrast, lost not a single ship. The initial reports did not specify the exact number of casualties suffered by the British; but whatever the number was, the *Boston Traveler* speculated, it paled in contrast to the many thousands of casualties suffered by the French and Spanish. Editorial writers and military spokesmen alike were already calling Trafalgar "a most decisive and glorious victory," and for good reason. The French defeat at Trafalgar ended Napoléon's dream of invading England. The French fleet that was to escort his invasion barges across the Channel had been rendered impotent. Of greater significance, the victory at Trafalgar ensured Britannia's rule of the waves for many years to come.

Richard Cutler pored over every account of the battle he could lay his hands on, and not just because of his standing as an American naval officer. A man he greatly admired had died in that battle, a victim of a sniper's bullet fired from a French fighting top as *Victory* sailed past a French ship with her starboard guns blasting. When Richard first met Horatio Nelson as a teenager, the two young men—boys, really—had been vying for the heart of Katherine Hardcastle. Over the years, Richard's jealousy toward Nelson, which continued even after Richard had won Katherine's hand, had matured into a deep and abiding respect, both for the man and for his gifts as a brilliant naval strategist. The last time Richard had seen Nelson, on the island of Malta during America's war with Tripoli, the two men, once rivals, had met as friends.

"Poor Horatio," Katherine mused quietly as she and her husband sat together on a sofa before the fire in their home on South Street. They were alone that evening; Diana, the only child still living with them, was having supper at the Sprague residence nearby. The joy Diana had radiated when her beau, Peter Sprague, arrived to walk her to his parents' home helped to offset Katherine's sadness over the loss of a man she too held in the highest regard.

"This must be so terribly hard on Emma," she said. "I could never approve of their affair, of course, even though I understood why a beautiful young woman would leave a husband twice her age for a living legend who adored her. It crushed Fanny Nelson. She'll never recover from the humiliation and loss." Indeed, the passionate affair had been the subject of extensive coverage by the scandalized British press, although the British people were willing to forgive their hero anything—even open adultery, especially after it became known that the cuckolded Lord Hamilton also regarded Nelson as a hero and even set up house with Nelson and Emma, the three of them living together in luxury for a spell.

"His death is hard on the entire British nation," Richard said. "I heard that when word of Nelson's death reached England, men and women wept openly in the streets. As my Uncle William used to say, England loves its naval heroes. And England has never had a naval hero quite like Horatio Nelson. It likely never will again."

"No," Katherine agreed. For several moments she sat quietly staring at the flames crackling in the hearth, her mind drifting back fondly to an earlier age in Burnham Thorpe, in East Anglia, when she had been the light in Nelson's eyes. As his fame mounted, she had sometimes idly wondered how different her life would have been had she chosen him over Richard. Her conclusion was always the same: no man could have been a better husband than the one she married. "Have you heard what the funeral arrangements are to be?" she asked, taking Richard's hand. "I saw nothing about them in the newspaper."

"I do know, but only because of the dispatch I received today. Apparently, our Navy Department is as saddened by Horatio's death as the British Admiralty. The tradition is to bury the body of a dead sailor at sea, of course, whatever his rank. But both Admiral Collingwood and Captain Hardy understood that England would wish to honor his remains, so they preserved his body in a barrel of brandy and brought it back to England.

She smiled ruefully. "Horatio would have approved of that decision. He ever did enjoy his brandy."

Richard went on, "The funeral is set for early January. As you can imagine, it will be quite the affair of state. Horatio's remains are to be interred at the crypt in St. Paul's Cathedral."

"How appropriate," Katherine said, then sat silently for several minutes. She continued to stare at the flames in the hearth, remembering the fine young man she had known so long ago. Then, in a half-whisper, "I do *so* wish I could be there."

"Jeremy will be there," Richard consoled her. Katherine's older brother had been a close friend of Horatio Nelson since the early days of their naval careers. "Hugh will be there too," he added, referring to Katherine's other brother, also a Royal Navy post captain and personal friend of Horatio Nelson. "And don't forget that Hugh and Phoebe will be visiting us this summer. They can tell us all about the service then."

The reminder that her brother and his wife would soon be emigrating from England to Boston lifted Katherine's mood considerably. On an impulse, Richard sought to reinforce that mood.

"No doubt we'll be home from our voyage long before Hugh and Phoebe get here," he said offhandedly.

She gave him a puzzled look. "Voyage? What voyage?"

"The voyage we are taking together."

"Where are we going?"

"Barbados."

"Barbados? Richard, what are you talking about? Have you taken leave of your senses?"

"To the contrary. I have been in contact with John and Robin. There are serious business matters we need to discuss, and we all agree that we need to discuss them in person. Caleb suggested I be the one to go, and I had thought you might care to join me."

"Care to join you? Of *course* I would care to join you. But . . . but . . . I don't see how it will be possible."

"Why not?"

"Well, Diana for one thing."

"Diana will stay with Caleb and Joan while we're gone. Joan is delighted to have her help with young Thomas."

"They are in on this?"

"Of course."

"What about your commission?"

"I'm on the beach at half pay for God only knows how long. I have notified the Navy Department of my intentions, and there is no problem from their perspective. What's more, Agee writes that because *Portsmouth* is well settled, he'll be sailing home in a fortnight or so, and he'll be here to look after things too. I'm sure Lizzy is beside herself over *that* welcome piece of news."

She shook her head slightly. "My health, Richard. It's long past time that I be concerned about it . . ."

"As are we all. So of course I have consulted Dr. Prescott."

"Does he approve?"

"Not only does he approve, he strongly encourages it. He thinks the sea air and tropical sun will work wonders on you."

She gave him a look that was a blend of bewilderment and amusement. "And Robin and John? What do they have to say about all this?"

"John assures me that he and Cynthia will have the West Room done up good and proper for our visit, and Robin writes that Julia already has the horses saddled. So, what further concerns might you have?"

"That everyone has been in on this secret except me," she said dryly.

"Well, it has taken some doing to keep it from you. Your ability to sniff things out is legendary."

"How long has this secret been going on?"

"For several months. I had planned to tell you next week, as a gift on Christmas Day. But somehow it seemed appropriate to tell you tonight."

"When do you propose we depart?"

"In the early spring, if you're willing. . . . So what do you think, my lady? *Are* you willing?"

She raised his hand and brushed her lips against it. As he lowered it, she lifted her gaze to his. "What do *you* think, my lord?" she asked quietly.

He put his arm around her shoulders and drew her close. "Methinks this ship's master has found himself a mate."

"I believe he has," she agreed. "I believe he has."

Three

Hingham, Massachusetts, and Barbados
Winter 1806

KATHERINE CUTLER ladled out a healthy portion of hot porridge into a bowl, sprinkled a dash of Ceylon cinnamon on it, and brought the steaming gruel over to the oval wooden table. After she put a plate of toasted bread next to it, she sat down across from her daughter, near the fire that warmed the kitchen. Outside, the sun was inching up above the trees, spreading tentacles of feeble blue light across a frozen landscape carpeted with freshly fallen snow that seemed studded with diamonds.

"Aren't you having any, Mother?" Diana asked as she poured cream into the bowl from a chinaware server. "You mustn't just have coffee for breakfast."

"I ate earlier. I've been up awhile."

"Are you feeling all right?"

"I'm feeling fine," her mother assured her, adding with a note of sternness, "and please stop treating me like I'm some sort of wounded bird. Please God, there's a dance in this old girl yet."

Diana looked chastened. "Yes, of course there is. I'm sorry, Mother."

Katherine smiled. "Right, now; out with it. You've been near to bursting at the seams ever since you came home last evening. I heard you prancing about your room during the wee hours of the morning, and I have a strong suspicion that Peter is somehow responsible."

"He is!" Diana burst out in an explosion of joy. "I couldn't tell you last evening, Mother," she explained rapidly. "Oh, how I wanted to, but I couldn't, not with your friend Mrs. Preston here so late. Peter has asked for my hand. He has asked me to marry him!"

"Aha. So my suspicions were correct. And you said what?"

"I said, 'Oh dear lord yes, of course I'll marry you, Peter! I love you! There is nothing on this earth I wouldn't do for you!'"

"How very ladylike. You didn't pounce on him like a cat, did you?"

Diana laughed delightedly. "No, Mother. I wanted to, but I restrained myself."

"Well, good. I am relieved to learn that your parents and your Derby education instilled *some* sense of modesty in you. Did you say anything else to him?"

Diana came abruptly down to earth. "I told him that he will have to speak to Father."

"That was wise of you."

"He *will* speak to him, Mother," she said earnestly, "either tomorrow or the next day, as soon as Father comes home. Peter is very traditional. He insists on receiving Father's permission. And yours, of course."

"He already has mine, which can come as no surprise to you. Peter is a fine young man from a good Hingham family. And he has excellent prospects, both at Harvard and in the practice of law afterward. More to the point, his feelings for you clearly match yours for him. What mother would stand in the way of such happiness and security for her daughter?"

"So, you think Father will acquiesce as well?" Diana asked eagerly.

"Yes, but not right away, all else being equal. He'll want to ask you and Peter to wait awhile. He'll say you're too young to get married."

"For heaven's sake, Mother, I'm eighteen . . . almost."

Katherine laughed softly. "No matter *what* your age, your father would still think you too young. You will always be his little girl, even after you have your own little girls. He's perfectly aware of your feelings for Peter. And I assure you he holds Peter in as high regard as I do. But he'll want to defer the inevitable for as long as possible because he doesn't want you ever to leave us, even though he knows you must."

Diana nodded ruefully. "I had feared as much."

"Now, now, not to worry," her mother soothed. "You just heard me say, 'all else being equal.' But all else is *not* equal. You and I are allies in this matter, and we have two secret weapons in our arsenal that cannot fail to persuade him."

"We do?"

"Yes, we do. The first weapon," she announced, "is me."

Diana gave her mother a quizzical look. "You? I'm afraid I don't understand."

"It's quite simple, really. Ever since I met your father I have been, by his own admission, both his greatest source of strength and his greatest weakness. If there is something I truly want, he loves me too much, and respects my judgment too much, to say no to me. Of course, to ensure that I don't ever overplay my hand, I never ask for anything that is unreasonable. Being entirely committed to your happiness, I am now prepared to draw this weapon on your behalf." She did not add that given the uncertainty of her medical condition, the last thing Richard would ever deny her was the joy and satisfaction of seeing her only daughter properly wed.

"Thank you, Mother," Diana said sincerely. "I would expect nothing less of you, but still, it makes me happy to know. What is the other weapon?"

"The other weapon is your father's past. When he and I met, he was about the same age as Peter was when you two met. And when we were married, he was about Peter's age, and I yours. So it would be rather hypocritical of him to claim that you and Peter are too young to get married when he and I were not. And I daresay that regardless of our ages when we wed, our marriage has turned out rather well."

"Oh, it has, Mother," Diana readily agreed. "Everyone says so. And Peter recognizes it as well. He speaks of you and Father with the highest affection and praise. Last evening, when he asked for my hand, he said that your marriage is one that he and I should try to replicate throughout our life together. I obviously agree with him."

"That was kind of Peter, but as you two will discover for yourselves, no marriage is perfect. All have their ups and downs. But here's what I want you never to forget: through all the years I have been with your father, there has not been a single moment—not one—when I questioned why I married him. Nor was there a single moment—not one single moment—when I wished I hadn't. If you can say the same thing at my age, then you will have had a successful and loving marriage. I hope you will be able to say the same thing to your own children, as I pray Will and Jamie can to theirs someday." Katherine paused, stabbed by the realization that she might not live long enough to see her grandchildren. She fought back a surge of regret. "So," she said with forced gaiety, "have you and Peter settled on a date for the ceremony?"

"Not the actual date," Diana said, the flower of her joy returning to full bloom, "but we are thinking of September. Jamie writes that he will be relieved of duty in *Constitution* in early summer, so he should be home long before then. Uncle Agreen will be here, and Uncle Hugh and Aunt Phoebe are planning to arrive in Boston sometime in June or July. You and Father will be home from Barbados in May, so that gives us the entire summer to plan the wedding. Peter says that he sees no reason why his family can't all be here in September. It seems the ideal time."

"It does indeed. Fall is a beautiful time in Hingham, and I'm happy to think that you'll be married in the same month as your father and I were. I say we get right to it and start making a list. Those from far away will need plenty of time to plan their travel. I'll get pen and paper." She made to rise.

"Shouldn't we wait on that, Mother?" Diana said, she the one now offering a cautionary note. "Might that not be pressing our luck? Perhaps after Peter has talked to Father and everything is official . . . I do *so* worry that something will go wrong. It's not that I don't believe every word you've told me. I do. But too often things go wrong just when it seems they shouldn't."

Katherine smiled. "Perhaps, my dear. But not this time."

FOUR DAYS LATER, two days after Richard Cutler returned home from business in Boston, formal word was sent to Cutler family members in Massachusetts, England, and Barbados announcing the betrothal of Diana Cutler to Peter Archibald Sprague. Two weeks after that, details of the proposed wedding were sent to the society pages of local and city newspapers. The ceremony was set for Saturday, September 20, and would take place at First Parish, the Cutler family church in Hingham where Will Cutler and Adele Endicott had been married. Wedding banns would be published in the church for three consecutive Sundays beginning on August 10.

All of Hingham rejoiced over the announcement; the Cutlers and the Spragues were among the village's oldest and most admired families. But if there was one person whose joy might have eclipsed even that of the newly betrothed couple, it was Lizzy Cutler Crabtree, whose husband returned home from sea at last on a crisp sunny day in mid-February.

Other than a brief conversation on the afternoon of Agreen's arrival, Richard allowed thirty-six hours to pass before paying his first officer a formal visit, understanding Agreen's need to be alone with Lizzy and Zeke. "Welcome home again, Lieutenant," he said as the two sat in the snug little parlor of the Crabtree home on Pleasant Street.

"It's damn good t' *be* home, Richard," the wiry and wizened man of forty-five years replied. He and Richard had become fast friends during the war with England while serving together in the Continental navy, first as midshipmen in the sloop of war *Ranger* and then, after their escape from Old Mill Prison in England, as acting lieutenants in *Bonhomme Richard,* both vessels under the command of Capt. John Paul Jones. Their friendship continued after the Peace of Paris in 1783. Richard had hired Agreen as sailing master in the Cutler & Sons vessel *Falcon* to accompany him to North Africa to try to ransom Caleb Cutler and his shipmates from an Algerian prison. At the onset of the Quasi-War with France almost a decade ago, Agreen, now married to Richard's first cousin Lizzy Cutler, had joined the fledgling U.S. Navy as a lieutenant in *Constitution* at the same time Richard was serving in a similar capacity in *Constellation.* Together they had spearheaded an attack against a privateer base on the French West Indies island of Marie-Galante. When war with Tripoli erupted two years later and Richard was given command of the 36-gun frigate *Portsmouth,* he never considered anyone other than Agreen as his first officer.

"I'd almost forgotten the simple pleasure of just sittin' in this room," Agreen said with a contented sigh.

"While being waited on hand and foot by a beautiful woman."

Agreen grinned. "You've got that right, matey. And it's a damn sight more than my hand and foot that's bein' waited on."

Richard grinned back at him. As if on cue, Lizzy Crabtree entered the room bearing a tray with two mugs of coffee and slices of sweet bread she had baked for the occasion. As she bent forward to place the tray on a table set between the two chairs, Agreen touched her hip and began gently massaging it. She carefully set the tray on the table and then turned her head to meet his gaze, holding it as silent messages flew between them, back and forth like a pendulum. Then she straightened, kissed him on the forehead, smiled at both men, and left the parlor.

Agreen watched her go. "You've got that right," he repeated softly. After Lizzy closed the door behind her, he shifted his eyes back to Richard.

"Tell me about Katherine," he said. "Liz tells me she's feelin' like her old self again."

"Very nearly," Richard acknowledged. "Dr. Prescott tells us her recovery is really quite remarkable."

Richard summarized the details of his wife's ordeal, going back to before the surgery. Although he had related much of this information in letters to Agreen, as had Lizzy, Agreen was hungry for details. When Richard finished talking, Agreen said ruefully, "Damn, Richard, I wish I could have been here to help. For her and you and your children. And for Lizzy. She was devastated, and I felt so helpless down there in Virginia."

Richard shrugged. "You're here now. And Katherine and Lizzy understand that duty to country comes first."

"So despite what the good doctor says, there's no real prognosis?"

"No. He really can't offer predictions. All we can do is make every day count. And we can pray."

"This may come as a shock t' you, but I've been doin' quite a bit of that lately." After a pause Agreen added, "and I've been givin' some serious thought t' another matter you and I need t' discuss."

"Oh? What's that?"

"I've made a decision, Richard, and it's not been an easy one t'make. I haven't even told Lizzy about it yet, so you're the first t' know. I owe you that courtesy as my commanding officer. Not t' mention my closest friend."

Richard braced himself for what he sensed was coming. "Pray continue," he said. "I'm all ears."

Agreen did not blink. "I'm resignin' my commission in the Navy."

Richard allowed several moments to elapse. Then: "Why, Agee?"

Agreen pointed across the room. "You just saw one reason walkin' out that door. The other reason is upstairs in his room. I'm not gettin' any younger, Richard, and bein' away at sea for such long periods has finally gotten t' me. Hell's bells, you and I have fought side by side in three wars over three decades. An' that don't count our little escapade to Algiers and France. In this last war we were away for comin' on three years. Three years is a mighty long time, my friend.

"Now don't get me wrong," he was quick to add, "I'm not complainin'. Not by a long shot. I love the Navy and I love my country. But you an' I have had enough gut-swigglin' adventures t' last us both two lifetimes. Servin' as your first in *Portsmouth* will always be the greatest honor and thrill of my life. But it's time for me t' step down. I want t' watch Zeke grow up. And I want t' make love t' my wife on a far more regular basis. I know you understand. We talked about it often enough of a night in your after cabin."

Richard did understand. He understood and sympathized far more than Agreen realized. But he decided that this was neither the time nor the place to confess his own doubts about his future as a captain in the U.S.

Navy. Katherine's illness had sparked those doubts. He could not possibly deny that, nor would he ever wish to; but his doubts were also tied
to what he had said to Horatio Nelson in the San Anton Palace in Malta
two years earlier. George Hunt was correct: war drums were once again
pounding out their ugly beat. And if war were to come, Richard had long
ago concluded, it would be fought for control of the seas, and it would
be fought against England. Even before Trafalgar, France had lacked the
means to effectively challenge U.S. neutrality at sea. And war could not
be far in the future. The war hawks in Congress were already demanding
satisfaction against England, but for what Richard considered to be relatively minor issues. Impressment, Indian raids on the frontier fomented
by British agents, and American merchant vessels detained in British
ports were violations of neutrality, treaties, and maritime law, and might
be viewed as egregious acts. Richard himself had been a reluctant eyewit-
ness to several such violations. Britain was fighting for its very survival
in a global war that was not of its making. In any case, such trespasses
did not justify a war that in all probability would be an act of suicide
for the young republic. He had also told Lord Nelson that if such a war
were to come about, he would have no role in it. He would never again
fight against his own family; nor would he fight against men like Nelson,
whatever the matters of national honor or political expediency involved.
His resolve remained unchanged.

Aloud he said, "I was hoping you might want to step *up,* Agee, not
down. You know that I have put in your name for promotion. Lord knows
you have earned your own command. I am quite certain that Mr. Smith
concurs."

"I do know you did that for me, Richard, and I thank you. From the
bottom of my heart I thank you. But whether or not the secretary of the
Navy and the Navy Department concur, it doesn't change anything. Five,
ten years ago, I would have jumped at the opportunity. But not today. Sure
as hell I can sit here as merry as you please and draw half pay until I'm
recalled; but because I will not accept that call when it comes, such a thing
just don't sit right with me." He took a drink of coffee and then broke
into a grin. "Besides, if I resign now, I'll not only have a clear conscience,
I'll make out a lot better in the long run. Unless, of course, you've promised my former position in Cutler & Sons t' that highfalutin' ex–Royal
Navy post captain brother-in-law of yours."

"That would be Caleb's decision, not mine," Richard said, smiling
back at him. "But I wouldn't fret if I were you, Agee. Cutler & Sons will

certainly welcome you back, assuming you're rock-hard in your decision to resign your commission in the Navy."

"I am, Richard. Rock-hard."

RICHARD SPENT the latter part of February and into March catching up with family business and disposing of his ship and crew. With peace declared, *Portsmouth* was to be laid up in ordinary, meaning that she would be taken out of service and her guns, stores, and masts would be removed, leaving only her shell intact until the clarion call to duty forced her reactivation. The petty officers and topmen who had been employees of Cutler & Sons and had signed on for the duration of the war against Tripoli to serve under Richard Cutler returned comfortably to their former civilian jobs, as did most of their shipmates. George Lee, the second lieutenant, volunteered to go on half pay and sailed home to Cape Ann. Eric Meyers, *Portsmouth*'s third lieutenant, did no such thing, however. He was, as Agreen put it, "a Navy man from the hair on his head t' the tip of his toenails," and Richard had been pleased to recommend his services to Navy Secretary Smith. Two days earlier, Smith had replied in a dispatch sent by a military packet boat to Boston and delivered to Hingham by the newly introduced "flying coach" mail stage operating between Boston and Plymouth. Smith's message confirmed that he had secured a second lieutenant's berth for Meyers in USS *Chesapeake,* Capt. Charles Gordon in command.

"Well, *that* sure as hell should please the lad," Agreen commented when informed of the promotion and of the ship to which Meyers had been assigned. "I heard rumors in Virginia that Barron's up for command of the Mediterranean Squadron. As I recall, both his father and his brother served as commodores too. That'd make three commodores in one family. Can you imagine that? Jamie may have occasion to meet with Barron over there if that appointment goes through anytime soon— Excuse me. I forget myself. I should have said, *Lieutenant Cutler* may have occasion to meet with him over there."

Richard shook his head in mock dismay. "An understandable error, Lieutenant, but don't let it happen again." Confirmation of his son's promotion from senior midshipman to lieutenant had accompanied the same dispatch from Washington. By now word of the promotion had spread throughout Hingham.

Other, more disturbing dispatches were soon to follow. As Jack Endicott had feared, the British had impounded one of his ships. The Royal Navy had intercepted *Orient,* a C&E Enterprises merchantman bound to

Rotterdam from Java with her hold laden with spices, as she stood into the English Channel between Finistère on the Breton coast and Land's End in Cornwall. Details were slow to reach Boston, but it appeared that *Orient* was not only being detained, but her cargo had been impounded as well. It had been off-loaded and was being thoroughly examined for contraband. C&E Enterprises' agent and legal representative in London warned that the British Admiralty Court had become involved, a sure sign that the situation would not be quickly resolved. Even if the Court ultimately ruled in *Orient*'s favor, which it most likely would, it could take months to have all the legal issues sorted out and the ship, crew, and cargo restored.

"And by then," Endicott groused in his office on Long Wharf, "we will have lost the entire cargo." He pounded his desk in frustration. "Hell, we've *already* lost our cargo. It's stacked up on a quay somewhere and will rot long before this matter is settled. In God's name, what do they think we're doing? Smuggling weapons to France in barrels of nutmeg and ginger?" Answering his own question, he roared, "No, that's not it at all. *Orient* is nothing more than a sacrificial lamb to underscore Britain's determination to block all American trade to the Continent. *All* trade! *All* of it! Jesus *Christ*, what an abomination! We stand to lose everything. *Everything*, do you hear?

Caleb Cutler and George Hunt had no difficulty hearing Endicott. Neither man put any stock in Endicott's prediction of a pending financial catastrophe; annual revenues and profits for both Cutler & Sons and C&E Enterprises were climbing toward record levels. Yet Endicott refused to be consoled.

THE VESSEL assigned to convey Richard and Katherine Cutler from Boston to Barbados had joined the Cutler fleet just two months earlier following sea trials under the watchful eye of her captain, Frank Bennett, a burly, no-nonsense Hingham native whose services had recently been acquired by Cutler & Sons. Launched at Fell's Shipyard in Baltimore— the same shipyard that gave birth to the superfrigate *Constellation*, in which Richard had served as second lieutenant in the war with France— she belonged to a new breed of two-masted schooners and brigantines called "Baltimore clippers," both because of their Maryland heritage and because many of them were actually built in Baltimore. Prized for their exceptional speed with or against the wind, they were normally 100 feet at the waterline and featured a heart-shaped midsection with a short keel and strongly raked stem, stern post, and masts. The low-sided, sharp-lined, sharp-bowed hull permitted minimum freeboard. Typically, these sleek, jaunty vessels boasted no figurehead, headboard, or trailboard, and most were painted black.

The schooner *Dove* carried no square topsail on her mainmast as some clippers did. Instead she carried a large quadrilateral fore-and-aft sail on her taller mainmast and a larger quadrilateral sail on her taller mainmast. Adding in her three headsails, her sail plan was designed for maximum maneuverability and sail-handling efficiency. She also carried four 6-pounder guns, two on each side on her weather deck, plus six 3-foot swivel guns mounted three to a side on Y-shaped brackets bolted to the outside of her hull—all there to ward off pirates and other maritime miscreants.

Speed was a clipper's primary asset, but it was also a bit of a liability. Because of their speed and maneuverability, Baltimore clippers were fast becoming the vessels of choice for pirates, privateers, and slavers. Thus the need for *Dove*'s naval-style guns, the cost of which, though not insignificant, was minimized thanks to a long-standing business relationship between Cutler & Sons and the Cecil Iron Works of Havre de Grace, Maryland. It was a relationship first forged by John Rodgers, who had served with Richard in the French West Indies and whose father was a close friend of Stephen Hughes, the proprietor of Cecil Iron Works. Hughes had supplied the guns for *Constellation* at government expense, but he had subsequently agreed to a generous discount on the cost of guns supplied to vessels of Cutler & Sons and C&E Enterprises that were paid for from family funds. It was the promise of such steep discounts that had prompted Jack Endicott, who had supplied the majority of the startup capital for C&E Enterprises, to offer the Cutler family a 50 percent share in the Far East business venture.

Leave-taking for Richard and Katherine came on a cloudless and unusually warm day for the third week of March. At the docks in Hingham to see them off were Diana and her fiancé, Peter Sprague; Agreen and Lizzy Crabtree; Peter's parents; and a host of Hingham residents, many of them the same friends who had stood vigil on Main Street during the night immediately following Katherine Cutler's surgery. Everyone agreed it was God's blessing to see her looking so hale and hearty, and so clearly excited by what lay ahead.

"See you in May, Richard," Agreen said soberly to Richard as they clasped hands at dockside. In years gone by, he would have offered an off-color remark regarding the loose morals and insatiable sexual appetites of the scantily clad minxes awaiting Richard's arrival in the exotic Windward Islands. Today he did not.

"In May," Richard acknowledged, and then stepped down into the packet boat that was to take them to Boston, where *Dove* and the remainder of his family were waiting to say farewell. He helped Katherine on board and then helped stow their luggage for the brief trip. At the command of her master, the mainsail was raised, the jib set, and the mooring lines cast free, and the packet boat edged away from the quay, the southwesterly breeze quickly filling her sails on a beam reach.

In Boston, the transfer to *Dove* was made quickly and comfortably. After another round of farewells to family members and friends, *Dove* nosed out of Boston Harbor under jib and mainsail, sailing before the wind with a handpicked crew of nine sailors—five of whom had served in *Portsmouth* during the war with Tripoli—Captain Bennett, and mate Bob Jordan. Once clear of the lighthouse on Little Brewster Island, Captain Bennett ordered the clipper's foresail, fore staysail and flying jib set. With the extra press of canvas and a fifteen-knot offshore breeze kicking in, *Dove* leapt forward like a living being, her sails taut and thrumming at the leech. Foam creamed out from her stem as she drove through a light chop of cresting waves. Long past Provincetown she hauled her wind and headed southward on a close haul. Off the coast of Cape Cod and Nantucket—and the dangerous shoals lurking beneath those waters—*Dove* passed by a number of vessels bound for Georges Bank—named in honor of England's patron saint—and the rich harvests of cod and halibut there for the taking.

Since the beginning of the cruise, Katherine had stood either amidships, when the spray was active, or at the clipper's very bow, exhilarating in the splendor of the sun-drenched sea sparkling around her. Richard was concerned, for the sea air was cool, but he was loath to call her away and diminish her obvious joy. Plus, he knew from long experience that gainsaying Katherine when she was determined to do something was at best an act of futility.

"Very well, my lady," he said to her late in the afternoon as he stood on her windward side amidships with an arm wrapped around her waist. "If you're going to remain topside, allow me at least to go below and get you another layer. I can see your breath, it's so cold, and the wind is not wont to show mercy even to you."

She leaned her head against his shoulder. "As you wish," she said happily. "But I promise you, I am not cold." She looked up into his face, placed a hand on each side of his mouth, and kissed him hard on the lips, her mouth open. "Thank you," she said softly, when reluctantly she pulled away from him.

"For what?" he asked.

"For this," she answered, gesturing with both arms. "It has been a long time since I have felt so alive!"

Richard went below to the locker in the after cabin and took out a fleeced coat lined with goose down, the warmest he had brought. Back up on the weather deck, he walked aft along the flush deck to speak to Captain Bennett at the helm. "What are we making, Frank? Good Lord, it must be fifteen knots!"

"More like eighteen, Captain," Bennett replied, allowing a rare glint of satisfaction to shine through, "last we threw over the chip log. We'll have a hundred fifty sea miles behind us by nightfall, another hundred by morning. If this wind holds, I daresay the crew and I will be taking supper Sunday night at Gleason's Pub in Bridgetown."

"I doubt that," Richard said, grinning, "but I appreciate your optimism." He clapped Bennett on the shoulder and made to walk forward with the coat.

A word from Bennett stopped him. "Captain?"

"Yes, Frank?"

Bennett chewed his lower lip and pushed back the black hair blowing across his forehead. "I'm a bit concerned about your missus, sir," he said finally. "Never in my life have I seen a woman so pleased to stand on a rolling deck. It's a marvel to watch, I admit, but I can't help being worried. In her state and all," he added uncomfortably.

Richard nodded as a smile played across his lips. "I appreciate your concern, Frank. In fact, I suggest that you go up there and advise her to go below. But be forewarned: she tends to set her own mind on things, and it can be the very devil to change it. You're welcome to try, however. You have my blessing and I wish you the best of luck. I'll take the helm in the meanwhile."

Bennett continued chewing his lip as he mulled the implications of Richard's suggestion. "That's all right, Captain," he said eventually. "I'd be a fool to think I would have better luck than you. If it's all the same to you, I believe I'll just stay put."

"A wise decision, Frank."

WITH RICHARD'S APPROVAL, Bennett had shaped a course for the Caribbean that, once free of Cape Cod and the islands, took them southwestward and then south along the coast to North Carolina. Off the Outer Banks they pushed out to sea until they lay within easy reach of the highly predictable trade winds. Now comfortably within the warm caress of these northeasterly breezes, *Dove* kept the wind two points abaft her beam on a course that, without unforeseen interference, her crew would likely not have to alter until they approached Barbados. This sailing plan involved considerably more sea miles than a more direct southerly approach into the Caribbean through the New Bahama Channel or the Mona Passage between Hispañola and Puerto Rico, but it also kept *Dove* clear of the pirate lairs that infested many of the more remote islands of the Bahamas, the Caymans, and the Greater Antilles.

Every day that conditions permitted it, Richard called out the crew for an hour to exercise the guns. Since each 6-pounder gun required three men to service it, Richard rotated the crew into two groups of four, with himself acting as the third gunner for each of the two guns exercised on a given day. The drills were intended to keep the men highly skilled in their gun assignments, but they were hardly necessary: every member of the crew save one had hands-on experience with naval gunnery, and each sailor respected Richard's own experience as commander of the gun deck in *Constellation*. On that deck he had outranked everyone, including, at Captain Truxtun's insistence, Captain Truxtun himself.

It was during such a drill on a cloudless, soporific day in early April, with *Dove* swaying lazily back and forth in the gentle Atlantic swells, that an urgent call came down from a lookout high in the foremast.

"On deck, there!"

Richard shaded his eyes and glanced up. Because they had crossed the latitude of the Tropic of Cancer at daybreak, he assumed that the young lookout had raised the British-held island of Anguilla. "Deck, aye! What is it, Walsh?"

"A ship-rigged vessel, sir," Walsh yelled down with more than a note of worry in his voice. "She's showing all plain sails to royals."

"Where away?"

"Broad on our larboard bow. She's following a reciprocal course, sir."

Richard frowned. A ship-rigged vessel, signifying that she carried square sails on all three of her masts, was a vessel of consequence. The fact that she was showing all plain sails to royals strongly suggested that she was a man-of-war. To his surprise and disgust, he could already make out the white head of the foremast royal on the distant horizon ahead. She was, he calculated, only about five or six miles from them, and closing fast on a starboard tack.

Richard cursed under his breath. "Can you make out her ensign?" he shouted up through cupped hands.

"No sir. Not yet."

"Stand by, Walsh. I'm coming up." To Bennett at the helm: "Bring the wind to two points on her quarter, Mr. Bennett." Bringing the wind onto her larboard quarter on a broad reach would shift *Dove* from a fast point of sail to her fastest point of sail. It would also set her on a course obliquely away from the oncoming vessel.

"Two points on her quarter, aye, Mr. Cutler," Bennett acknowledged. To his mate he said: "Stand by to loose sheets!"

"Stand by to loose sheets!" Jordan shouted through a speaking trumpet. Instantly the crew responded by leaving the guns and assuming their sailing stations. At the mate's subsequent command, the sheets on all standing sails were eased out. *Dove*'s jib-boom swung to starboard. When she had veered a full twenty degrees on the compass rose, Bennett ordered the sails sheeted home.

Richard stole a glance at his wife watching him intently by the bulwark amidships before clambering up the larboard ratlines on the mainmast shrouds, using the ship's heel to starboard to facilitate his climb. At the first crosstree he met Walsh, who offered a hand up. Richard ignored the hand and secured himself within the hempen cords, then took Walsh's long glass from him and brought it to his eye. He could make out little detail on the deck of the oncoming ship, although he would bet his life on the pedigree of those three towering pyramids of white canvas.

"Sorry, sir, I should have spotted her sooner. She came up sudden-like."

Richard was too angry to trust himself to reply. Walsh was right. He *should* have spotted her sooner. A ship of that size does not appear "sudden-like" on a clear horizon on a relatively calm ocean. Walsh had been caught daydreaming, Richard concluded, a dereliction of duty that in the Navy would earn him twelve lashes at the grate even in peacetime. He felt the fury rise within him. Damn this youth for putting his wife and vessel in jeopardy! He rued the day he had agreed to sign on the eager young topman, the one sailor on board who lacked naval experience. He did have excellent vision and a thorough knowledge of ship design, which was why his primary responsibility on this cruise had been as a lookout. But daydreaming on watch!

"Can you make her out, sir?" Walsh asked cautiously. Richard continued to study the oncoming vessel. "She's a warship, sure enough," he said to himself rather than Walsh. "A frigate, I'd wager. In these waters and with those lines, she has to be British."

"That's exactly what I thought, sir," Walsh said, in an ingratiating tone. "Is she likely to give chase, do you think?" Whether the anxiety in his voice was due to guilt or trepidation, Richard could not determine.

An incident off the coast of Bermuda four years earlier came to mind. The British frigate *Temptress* had intercepted his schooner *Barbara D* on her northward cruise from Barbados to Boston and had forced her to lie to. Royal Marines had come on deck and dragged off a newly signed-on seaman named Cooper who claimed to be an American but had lost his papers.

Richard lowered the long glass and examined the oncoming man-of-war with his naked eye, pondering Walsh's question. "Who can tell," he said, unable to hide his anger. "We'll just have to wait and see, won't we, Walsh."

THIRTY MINUTES before Seaman Walsh reported the approach of an unknown ship, a lookout high in the foremast of that ship had shouted down a sighting to the midshipman stationed on the starboard gangway near the point where the mast disappeared below into the partially open gun deck and beyond to its step on the keelson.

"Can you identify her, Sawyer?" the tall, lean, ruddy-complexioned midshipman called up.

Sawyer shouted down what details he could.

"Very well. I shall inform the captain."

The midshipman strode purposefully aft and down the companionway ladder located between the mainmast and the rise of the quarterdeck from the weather deck. At the base of the companionway, on the gun deck, he turned aft and returned the crisp salute of the Royal Marine posted on sentry duty before the captain's cabin holding a gleaming, bronze-butted musket horizontally at his side. Two chevrons on the lower sleeve of his flawless red uniform jacket indicated his rank of corporal.

"Message for Captain Humphreys," the midshipman announced.

The Marine pivoted and rapped gently on the shuttered door. When a gruff voice answered on the other side, the Marine cracked open the door and announced the visitor, then opened the door wide, nodded to the midshipman to enter, and closed the door after him.

"Yes? What is it?" the British captain inquired of the midshipman after he had removed his bicorne hat, tucked it under his arm, and saluted. Although the young man had served five years as a midshipman in His Britannic Majesty's Navy, and had spent much of his childhood before that at sea, he remained awestruck, as did even seasoned veterans, by the magnificence of a post captain's after cabin. And this captain clearly possessed the financial wherewithal to adorn his living space with lavish and elegant accoutrements, from the oil paintings hanging all around him to the thick Persian carpet underfoot. The cabin's opulence made a mockery of the midshipman's damp and dreary quarters down on the orlop.

The midshipman stiffened. "Seaman Sawyer's duty, Captain Humphreys, and he has sighted a schooner northeast of us following a southerly course. She's flying the American ensign. Sawyer believes she's a clipper."

"Indeed. How very interesting . . . and how very tempting."

Salusbury Pryce Humphreys pondered that piece of information while the midshipman stood by awaiting orders, his eyes glued to the front of the desk at which the captain was sitting.

"No," Humphreys ruled at length. "If she's a clipper, and I trust Sawyer's judgment on that, we would be hard-put to catch her. Besides, if there were British sailors on board the schooner, she would more likely be heading north than south. No, we shall maintain present course. Once we're on station we shall have ample opportunities to snatch and hang deserters. Is that understood?"

"It is, sir. Very good, sir." The midshipman saluted and made to leave.

"Incidentally . . ."

The midshipman turned back. "Aye, sir?"

Humphreys settled back in his chair, folded his arms, and studied the young midshipman intently. "I am hearing rather encouraging reports about you from my officers, including Mr. Bryant," referring to his first lieutenant, the man most responsible for the proper disposition of the ship's officers and crew. "Clearly you come from good stock and know your way around a ship. More important to me, you apparently run a *taut* ship." He smiled at his turn of phrase. "The men in your division clearly respect you, because it has one of the highest ratings of any division. I am a stickler for such things, as every jackanapes on this ship is painfully aware, so I must commend you for your achievements. How long have you been going to sea?"

"Eight years, sir," the midshipman replied, "since I was twelve. I joined the Navy when I was fifteen. My father was opposed at first but has since come around."

"Not an uncommon state of affairs. Have you considered taking your lieutenant's exam?"

"Oh, yes, sir. I've been studying for it at every opportunity."

"Good. Very good. When the time comes, I shall be delighted to put in a good word on your behalf."

"Why, thank you, sir," the midshipman said, blushing with pride and embarrassment. Captain Humphreys was not normally one to offer compliments. "That is most generous of you."

"I did not mean to be generous," Humphreys stated gruffly. "I offer only what you have earned."

"Yes sir. Thank you, sir."

Humphreys began rummaging in the papers he had been sifting through when the midshipman entered his cabin. "Ah, here we are," he said with satisfaction. Then he glanced up, as if surprised to find the midshipman still standing at attention. "That is all, Mr. Cutler. Please carry on."

"Aye, aye, sir." Midshipman Seth Cutler saluted stiffly and left the cabin.

Four

Barbados, Windward Islands
Spring 1806

ARLISLE BAY was just as Katherine remembered it. Although nearly a quarter century had elapsed since she and Richard and baby Will had departed Bridgetown for Boston in the Cutler & Sons brig *Eagle*, precious little seemed to have changed. The harbor was still alive with seagoing vessels and crews. On the eastern side of the vast crescent-shaped bay, brigs, brigantines, and other merchant rigs flying the flags of many nations were moored fast to the finger-like quays jutting out along Front Street. On the western side, beneath Government House perched high above the fray and surrounded by royal palms and a riot of multicolored flora, lay at anchor the frigates, schooners, and sloops of war that comprised the Windward Squadron of the Royal Navy's West Indian Station.

Richard noted, not to his surprise, that there were considerably fewer ships in that squadron than he had counted on previous visits to the island. Everywhere, nonetheless, was the hustle and bustle of empire, from the lighters and hoys supplying ships of the squadron with fresh water and provisions to the commercial on-loading and off-loading at quayside orchestrated by bare-chested dockers toiling in the hot sun as cultured gentlemen and gentlewomen in the latest European fashions strolled arm-in-arm nearby. The contrast between the rich white planters and the poorly clad dark-skinned workers was striking. The former were in town for the day from the sugar plantations that formed the basis of the island's economy and enriched those who gained handsomely from what those plantations produced—the sugar, molasses, and rum whose vast profits lined the pockets of English planters, of shippers who conveyed their "white gold" to markets worldwide, of tax collectors in service to the British Exchequer, and of a host of intermediaries and beneficiaries clogging the routes from the cane fields to the banks.

"Do you think John or Robin is here in Bridgetown?" Katherine inquired of her husband as she took in the splendor of what seemed at this distance a tropical paradise blooming with the blissful memories of young love. They were standing near the bow to make room for sailors preparing to douse the foresail. Each wore a straw hat and a long-sleeved cotton shirt as protection from the searing sun.

Richard shook his head. "I doubt it. If either of them were here it would be pure luck. We'll likely need to hire a coach to take us to the plantation. But first we'll need to hail a wherryman to take us ashore." He gave her an amused look. "Let's hope he commands a stout boat. *Dove*'s little boat would sink under the weight of all you brought with you. Indeed, I'm amazed *Dove* herself remains afloat."

She smiled. "A woman needs her comforts, my dear," she said. "And don't forget, we're carrying gifts for everyone." Then she sighed quietly as Captain Bennett brought the helm alee and *Dove* nosed her bow into the wind; her canvas went slack and her anchor plunged into the turquoise depths. The outbound cruise was over, and despite the anticipation of what lay ahead, that realization saddened her.

"I suppose I should go below and make certain those comforts are all packed," she said as the anchor line chuntered out through the hawse-hole. They lingered a moment to watch a large black bird with a bright scarlet throat pouch swoop down on a hapless tern, seize hold of it, and shake it until it disgorged its last meal, which the predator snatched up and swallowed before releasing the tern and flying off.

"Not very neighborly of the bugger, was it?" Richard observed.

"It's called it a man-of-war bird, isn't it?" Katherine remarked. "I remember them being quite common when we were here before. Hugh once told me it's also called a pirate bird," she added.

"We just saw why."

Below, involved in last-minute packing in the comfortable after cabin that had been their home for nearly three weeks, they heard a hail from nearby and an answering call from Bob Jordan, the mate. Richard gave it scant attention until he heard the thump of a boat against the larboard side of the schooner and then a stamp of boots walking on the deck above him. A glance through an open porthole revealed a flash of scarlet ascending from a ship's cutter in which a coxswain and two oarsmen stood by. Several minutes later there came a rap on the cabin door.

Richard glanced toward it. "Enter."

Robert Jordan opened the door and peeked in. "Sorry to disturb, Captain," he said, "but we have visitors. It's the British, sir. Captain Bennett asked me to bid you topsides."

"I'll be right up, Jordan."

"Very good, sir."

Katherine arched her eyebrows. "What is this about, Richard?"

"I'll soon find out. Perhaps the natives have sent a welcoming committee, just as they do on Tahiti and other South Sea islands." His smirk suggested the desirability of such a scenario. "However, in my experience," he added, "welcoming committees do not wear British military uniforms and carry weapons. In fact, as best I recall, they wear very little at all."

On deck, Richard found that four visitors had come on board through the larboard entry port. The one dressed in a blue-and-white uniform jacket, spotless white breeches, and a gilt-lined bicorn hat was clearly a Royal Navy officer. The other three wore the scarlet uniform coat with white cross-belts of the Royal Marines. Two of them wielded sea-service muskets. The fourth man was a Marine noncom, a sergeant or a corporal. Richard walked over to where the Royal Navy officer was engaged in animated conversation with Frank Bennett. Their conversation ended as he drew near.

After nodding at the visitors he addressed the ship's captain. "What do we have, Frank?"

"Good morning, Captain," Bennett said. He indicated the British naval officer. "The lieutenant here has requested permission to search our vessel and examine our manifest. He also wishes to review our crew's papers."

Richard shifted his gaze to the lieutenant. "On what authority do you make such a request?"

The officer ignored the question. He removed his hat and bowed from the waist. "Neil Dunbar, first lieutenant of His Majesty's frigate *Redoubtable*, at your service," he offered politely. "May I ask whom I have the honor of addressing?"

"My name is Richard Cutler," Richard replied curtly. "I hold the rank of captain in the United States Navy. I therefore outrank you, Lieutenant. So, again I ask: On what authority do you make such a request on an American merchant vessel?"

The British officer stiffened. "On the authority of a recent order in council of His Britannic Majesty's government. And it is not a request, sir. Your Captain Bennett was incorrect on that point. Duty compels me to insist upon such an inspection, your rank notwithstanding. We will not detain you longer than is necessary."

"Your order in council be damned," Richard spat. "Your government issues a new one of those every week. It's impossible for those of us engaged in honest trade to keep up with such orders, let alone understand them. I doubt *you* understand them."

"I understand them well enough, thank you, Captain Cutler. Now if you will please allow me to go about my business."

Richard forced down his anger, realizing that this officer was simply doing what he had been ordered to do. A lieutenant did not formulate policy; he implemented it. "Lieutenant," he tried again, "every sailor on this schooner has been in the employ of my family's company, Cutler & Sons, for many years. They are all American citizens. On that you have my word as an officer. As to our cargo, we carry none beyond provisions for our cruise and barrel staves. You have my word on that as well. I am here in Barbados to confer with my English cousins, John and Robin Cutler. Perhaps you have heard of them? Or perhaps you have met them. They can certainly vouch for me and my crew."

The officer's hesitation suggested that he at least knew of John and Robin Cutler. His tone, nevertheless, remained adamant. "If what you say is true, Captain—and I assure you I do not doubt your word—then we can conclude our business here quickly. But as I have indicated, I must proceed, with or without your cooperation. Sergeant Russell!"

The Marine sergeant snapped to. "Sah!"

"You may carry out your orders."

"Sah!"

"If you will kindly step aside, Captain Cutler," Dunbar requested in a low but firm voice, "and let my men through."

Richard did not step aside. He advanced forward one step, placed his hands on his hips, and was about to offer a further protest when a female voice intervened.

"Just a moment, if you please, Lieutenant Dunbar."

All eyes shifted to the elegant woman in the ivory dress and wide-brimmed straw hat who was approaching the entry port. Lieutenant Dunbar bowed again, this time with added flair.

"Madam," he said. "You are . . . ?"

"I am Katherine Cutler, the wife of Captain Cutler," she answered

him. "My maiden name is Hardcastle. Does that name by chance reso-
nate with you?"

Dunbar started. "Why, yes, madam, it does. There was a Captain
Hugh Hardcastle attached to the Windward Squadron for many years.
He served on the very ship in which I now serve. His name is legendary in these waters. Is he by chance a relative? I believe I do see a family
resemblance."

"Captain Hardcastle is my brother. He is recently retired from the
service and is soon to join my husband's company in Boston. I have one
other brother. His name is Jeremy Hardcastle and he is currently a senior
post captain attached to the Mediterranean Squadron. Both of my brothers were dear friends of Admiral Lord Nelson—as was I. As they both
have meaningful connections in Whitehall, it would surprise me indeed
if My Lords of the Admiralty would not be disturbed to learn that a
British lieutenant attached to the Windward Squadron had unduly incon-
venienced a vessel of such heritage and ownership, their order in council
notwithstanding. Do you not agree, Lieutenant?" she asked, when silence
prevailed.

Dunbar narrowed his eyes. His squint went from Katherine to her husband, then to Frank Bennett and the schooner's crew standing in a cluster
amidships, many of them with their arms folded across their chests. Not
a single pair of eyes wavered. Then: "Sergeant!"

"Sah!"

"Belay that last order. I have determined that this vessel is as much
British as she is American. We have troubled these good people long
enough. We shall return to our ship."

"Sah!"

As the Marines wheeled about and waited for Lieutenant Dunbar to
descend first into the cutter, as naval protocol demanded, Dunbar bowed
a third and final time, showing a leg and holding his bicorne hat out at
his side. "Madam," he said, straightening, "it has been an honor. Captain
Cutler and Captain Bennett, if there is anything I might do for either of
you whilst you are here in Barbados, you need only ask. You know my
ship, so you know where to find me. I wish you and your crew a most
pleasant good day."

As Dunbar made his way down into the cutter, followed by the Marine
sergeant and then the two privates, Richard glanced at his wife. In reply,
she gave him a mischievous smile. "And now you know why I have often
been referred to as 'a daughter of the Royal Navy,'" she said before turning about and making for the aft companionway. The crew of nine sailors

quickly made room for her, several of them offering a half-salute as she strode by.

BRIDGETOWN, THE colonial capital of Barbados, may have seemed a tropical paradise when viewed from the deck of a vessel entering Carlisle Bay. But as was true of many West Indian ports, Bridgetown's luster and sheen cracked and peeled on closer inspection. The rank odors of rotting fish and animal waste assailed the senses, the putrid stench fortified by the effects of the hot sun and by the pungent odor of the sweat glistening on the faces, arms, and bare torsos of dockers loading hogsheads of sugar, rum, and molasses onto ships or into warehouses. Then there was the assault to the eyes: African slaves dressed in ragged clothing intermingled with the refuse of colonial society on the cobblestone streets, many of them half seas over even at this early hour, eager to pick a fight or a florin from an unsuspecting passer-by. And finally there was the assault to the ears: shouts, curses, and exhortations in several languages seethed along the quays while inland a few feet, along Front Street, garishly dressed and gaudily painted prostitutes brazenly hawked their wares, leaving in their wake no need for the imagination to contemplate the full menu of services they were prepared to provide—either à la carte or as a complete meal.

Bridgetown, to Richard, represented a bizarre and intriguing blend of the best and worst of the human condition. Over the years it had become one of his favorite ports of call, and not just because he had family living on the island. To his surprise, he discovered today that his wife had always found it equally intriguing. She seemed mesmerized as she stood on the docks taking it all in, and it was with some reluctance that she took her husband's arm and walked beside him—trying to walk a straight line on legs more accustomed to the lurch and pitch of a rolling deck—to the waiting coach-and-two, its aft compartment stuffed with baggage and with additional baggage lashed securely to its top.

Richard opened the door to the coach. "Shall we, my lady?" he asked. "Or do you prefer to take a room at a local inn and savor all this"—he swept his arm across the riotous panorama of Bridgetown—"for a day or two. I will understand if you do. A woman with your beauty and elegance fits right in here."

"Thank you, no. I believe I've had my fill." She stepped up and inside the coach.

Once he had followed her in and settled himself beside her, Richard thumped twice on the side of the coach. The liveried Negro driver flicked the reins, and the carriage lurched forward. As the coach rolled slowly past the gleaming white stucco buildings on Front Street and the warrens of shadowy byways and alleyways leading away from it, Katherine stared out the open window on her side, her mind drifting back to earlier occasions when she had traveled these streets. When Richard sailed to Yorktown in 1781 as an American lieutenant serving in a French frigate, she had stayed at the home of John and Cynthia Cutler on the family plantation in the island's interior. And it was in that home, in January 1782, that their first son, Will, was born, several weeks after Richard returned from the war. During the intervening years, busy raising a family in Massachusetts, she had seldom traveled beyond the confines of greater Boston, where the rigid social norms and expectations were very different from those in Bridgetown. She felt a freedom, a lightening of her being, barely remembered from those early years.

Richard sat in silence, leaving her to her thoughts even as the coach veered off Front Street and dove into the island's interior on a well-maintained dirt road. Here the scenery was considerably more cultivated and relaxing, save for the spectacle of black African men and women toiling in the sugarcane fields, severing the ten-foot-high stalks at ground level with machetes or cane knives and dragging them in bunches over to carts drawn by mules. Under the watchful eye of white overseers armed with pistols and whips, the slaves brought the stalks to the mill, boiling house, and curing house complex that defined the core business of a typical plantation. Overall responsibility for the production process fell to the plantation's agent, a man highly trusted by the plantation's owner. The agent's foremost duty, in league with the boatswain who ran the windmills and rolling presses, was to turn a handsome annual profit for the owner, whatever the monthly maintenance costs and daily toll in human suffering.

To his surprise, Richard had been fascinated by the evolution of sugar and rum production from the day he was introduced to the process, and he had joined those welcoming the 1781 innovation in rolling presses that allowed more juice to be squeezed out of the cane in the mill, and thus higher profits to be squeezed out of the end products. Katherine, he realized, was less enthralled, in large part because of her aversion to slavery. A movement afoot in Parliament to abolish the slave trade throughout the British Empire pleased her no end, just as it worried those who saw it as yet another threat to an old order already shaken to its core by the slave rebellion that had established the free and independent nation of Haiti. That the Cutler family treated its Negroes better than most planters on Barbados mattered little to her, despite the open hostility it aroused on other plantations. Such a policy, to her mind, was based more on economics than on humanitarian concerns. To some extent that was true: John and Robin Cutler had long ago determined that well-fed and well-treated workers were less likely to fall ill, shirk their work, or engage in sabotage. The end result was a higher number of man-hours in the fields and a higher daily output per man-hour, a combination of factors that year after year yielded considerably higher annual profits than the other plantations produced.

While agreeing with his wife in principle on the evils of slavery, Richard saw no practical way to end an institution so embedded in the culture and economy of Barbados. He therefore tended to avoid the subject with her whenever possible.

As the coach gathered speed, Katherine settled back in the cushioned seat, stretched out her legs, and closed her eyes to revel in the clean tropical air streaming in through the open windows and tousling her thick chestnut hair. "This is heavenly," she murmured. "I daresay it's snowing or sleeting in Boston."

"You're not going to sleep, are you?" he chided her.

"Heavens, no," she laughed. "You hardly need worry about that, my love. I'm much too excited to sleep. I was just wondering when we might talk to Joseph. The news about him has been so good, but I want to see for myself that he is really better. And, of course, to offer our proposition."

The son of John and Cynthia Cutler, now a young man of twenty-two years, had been a silent and withdrawn child, unwilling, or unable, to interact normally with others—even his own family. Seven years ago his parents had taken him to England to consult the best medical minds in the Royal College of Physicians. Neither they nor anyone else had been able to put a name to Joseph's symptoms or to propose a remedy. In recent years, to his parents' infinite relief, he had begun to emerge from his shell.

"I say the sooner the better," Richard said. "He will need time to consider it. Actually, I'm more interested in how his parents will react. Joseph is their only child, and he has never been apart from them. It will not be easy for them to watch him sail away with us."

"No indeed," Katherine had to agree. "We'll speak to them first, of course. Perhaps we should have written them when we first had the idea. Well, too late for that now."

Thirty minutes later the coach-and-two rumbled down a pebble drive and shivered to a halt inside an oval area that formed the center of a complex of buildings and gardens. As the driver secured the reins, Richard looked about him. He had last visited this inner compound six years ago, toward the end of the war with France when he was recovering from an injury incurred during the engagement between *Constellation* and the 40-gun frigate *L'Insurgente*. Everything appeared very much as it had back then. Two large one-story houses of brick and coral stone construction anchored the compound, one on the north side of the wide oval, the other directly opposite on its south side. Mahogany, tamarind, and myriad other kinds of trees and flowering shrubs provided abundant shade. Where sunlight was allowed to filter through, and on the periphery of the circle, well-groomed gardens of brightly colored plants pleased the eye. North of the compound sat the considerably smaller but still attractive homes of the plantation's administrators, and beyond those, clusters of wood-and-stone dwellings for Negro and Creole slaves. Each cluster of dwellings was located near fruit and vegetable plots, the produce of which was shared among the slave families living there. Now, in the early afternoon, the able-bodied workers were out in the field; only the very young and very old were present, along with a smattering of teenage girls who were attending to them. Within the compound itself serenity reigned, save for the rustle of wind in the trees, the chirping of birds, and occasional snorts from the two horses that had pulled the carriage from Bridgetown.

Before Richard and Katherine could dismount, the front door of the mansion on the south arc of the circle flew open and a woman's voice cried out, "Oh, thank the Lord you're here! You're really here!"

Katherine pushed open the door on her side of the coach, saw herself out, and flew toward the woman rushing toward her. They came together under the glossy green leaves of a banyan tree, falling into each other's arms, laughing, pulling apart to look at each other, and then clasping each other tightly again. Richard, meanwhile, paid the driver and began arranging the baggage in several piles. Julia Cutler motioned him over with her hand. When he came up to her, grinning hugely, she released Katherine and wrapped her arms around his neck, drawing him in close. As her face touched his, he felt damp tears on her cheek.

"Welcome," she said, smiling. She swiped at her eyes with her sleeve. "Welcome indeed! You both look absolutely tip-top. My goodness, Katherine, I can't believe that after all these years and all you've been through, you still look the radiant bride!"

"For the joy of seeing you again," Katherine said, stepping back for a long look at Julia. "And you're still 'the voluptuous belle of Barbados,' as Robin used to call you."

"Oh, posh," Julia laughed, her Scottish brogue bursting through. "Enough of that! We must get you properly settled right away. You will be staying in the West Room in John and Cynthia's house. I'm sure you remember it fondly," she added with a meaningful laugh.

Katherine sighed with happiness at the thought of being once again in the room where she and Richard had stayed as newlyweds and where Richard had stayed during every visit to Barbados since.

"I do so wish you could stay with Robin and me," Julia continued, "but John insists, and as the elder brother he always gets his way. We shall be seeing each other often throughout the day, of course, and every evening we shall all gather for supper. Katherine, you and I will take our first ride just as soon as you unpack and change. There is so much to show you! I've been planning our route for months! Charles will see to your baggage, so please leave everything just where it is and come inside." Richard looked back at the luggage and saw that the compound's major domo was already directing servants to carry it inside. Julia's joyous laugh brought his attention back to her. "Oh, how wonderful this is! How very, very wonderful!" She beamed at Katherine and embraced her again.

"Is Robin here?" Richard asked as they walked toward John and Cynthia's house on the north arc.

"Not at the moment," Julia told him. "He and John are at my parents' home," referring to the ancestral home of the Fletcher family, among the oldest of the Mount Gay rum families on the island. "They took Joseph with them."

"How is Joseph?" Richard put in.

"Doing so much better," Julia assured him. She could not stop smiling. "Mary, Benjamin, and Peter are somewhere about," she added, referring to her three youngest children. "I'll round them up. Seth is off at sea with the navy, alas, so you won't be seeing him this visit. Come now," she urged. "Let's get you two tucked away so that we can start the festivities!"

THE ADULT Cutlers dined alone the following evening at John and Cynthia's home, the younger children being in the care of Anna Odegaard, a Norwegian woman of thirty years who fulfilled a similar function for the Cutler family in Barbados as Edna Stowe did in Hingham. Joseph Cutler, however, was at the table, and not only because he was the oldest of the children.

After two servants dressed in white had removed the soup dishes and had replaced the silver tureen with platters of sautéed pompano and fresh vegetables, Cynthia turned to her son. "Joseph, your aunt and uncle have something they would like to discuss with you."

A second bottle of red Bordeaux was making the rounds as Robin Cutler did the honors of serving the meal. He was casually dressed in tan trousers and a lemon-yellow shirt open at the neck that he had purchased from a local merchant. His brother John was, as always, dressed more formally in a blue-and-white-checkered waistcoat, white linen neck stock, and an elegant deep purple dinner jacket that had been tailored to his specifications in London. Their wives wore fashionable empire gowns: low-cut muslin dresses that fit closely under the bust and flowed in simple elegance to the ankles.

Joseph's russet-brown eyes shifted to Richard and Katherine, seated across from him, as his parents stole a glance at each other and at Robin and Julia. "Oh? What is it?" he asked tentatively, mindful of the silent messages being transmitted around the table. Although he was no longer the emotionally remote child he once had been, even when in the bosom of his family he became edgy when attention was focused strictly on him.

"Listen carefully now, son," his father said unnecessarily, adding to Joseph's unease.

"Joseph," Katherine launched in quickly, before the young man could become even more nervous, "your Uncle Richard and I have a proposition for you."

"A proposition?"

"Yes, one we believe, and hope, will be of interest to you."

Confused, Joseph looked first at his mother and then at his father. He could draw nothing from their blank expressions. He took a deep breath and looked back across the table. "What is your proposition, Aunt Katherine?"

Katherine's kind eyes held his. "When your Uncle Caleb was here a few years ago, he told you quite a bit about where we live in Massachusetts, didn't he?"

"He did," Joseph said. He smiled, clearly recollecting those six months Caleb Cutler had stayed with his family back in '99. At his own father's urging, Caleb had sailed to Barbados to learn everything he could about the family sugar business, and Richard had joined him during his period of convalescence from his war injury. John and Cynthia had long credited both men, but especially Caleb, for doing more to help their son than the combined efforts of the Royal College of Physicians in England. Joseph had wept when Caleb left the island, and that by itself gave his parents ground for hope: it was one of the few times that their son had ever revealed his emotions. "I feel as though I know Hingham quite well from what everyone has told me and the descriptions you have written to me. It seems a special place."

"It *is* a special place, Joseph," Katherine said, "and we would like you to know it better. In fact, we would like you to see it for yourself. We are inviting you to sail home with us next month and live with us in Hingham for a while."

Joseph's jaw dropped. "Live in America? Would I live with you?"

"We would like that very much, and so would our children. But your Uncle Caleb and Aunt Joan want you to stay with them. Theirs is a much larger home than ours—as large as your home here—so there is plenty of room. And it's quite near where Uncle Richard and I live. You could stay there as long as you please, at least until you have settled into your new position and found a place for yourself."

"New position?" Joseph was at sea. "Excuse me, Aunt Katherine, but I am terribly confused. *What* new position?"

"Why, your position as teacher of mathematics at Derby Academy. You've heard of Derby in my letters. All three of our children went there. It's a private school for *both* boys and girls, one of the first of its kind in America. And it's located just down the street from where Caleb and his family live. You can walk there in a couple of minutes."

Joseph blinked, then ranged his gaze about the dining area, focusing on no object or person in particular. Julia Fletcher Cutler, seated beside him, patted his knee. "It seems a perfect opportunity for you, dear boy."

Richard said, "Aunt Katherine is the mastermind behind all this, Joseph. It was her idea. She went to see the headmistress of the school, and lo and behold, she discovered that there is an opening for a mathematics teacher starting in September. The headmistress agreed to hold open that position for you, based on what Katherine told her about your love of mathematics and your skills in the subject. Apparently you are just the man Derby is seeking. The headmistress and trustees of the school are most anxious to welcome you, as are the students and other teachers."

A significant pause, then: "I don't know what to say . . ."

"You needn't say anything yet," Katherine assured him. "We have put a lot on your shoulders this evening, and you need time to consider it and to discuss it with your parents. Just let us know your decision. And know this, too: whatever you decide, your Uncle Richard and I will support you. So will your Uncle Caleb. So will *all* your family. We love you and we want only the best for you."

"Thank you so very much, Aunt Katherine," Joseph said, his emotions choking his words.

AS JOSEPH CUTLER mulled over his future, the other members of the Cutler family on Barbados mulled over theirs. Most planters on the island agreed that their livelihood was fraught with uncertainty. Several key issues added to that uncertainty, the future of slavery first among them. Highly placed sources in Parliament had indicated to John Cutler that the movement to abolish the slave trade was gaining momentum. So much so, these sources speculated, that the ban on buying and selling slaves was likely to be enacted into law within the year. If that were to happen, John Cutler said during an afternoon discussion with Richard and Robin, they could expect the law to be vigorously enforced by the Royal Navy, especially on British-held islands such as Barbados where the Navy maintained a base. The abolition of the slave trade, John said, affirming the obvious, would eventually mean the abolition of slavery itself. What effect, he wondered, would *that* have on the family business?

Robin Cutler took his time before answering, looking up as if seeking inspiration in the eighty-foot breadfruit tree that shaded the men sitting on cool stone benches beneath it. Whereas many people, Robin reminded his brother and cousin, believed that the institution of slavery provided free labor to plantation owners, slavery was in fact a very expensive mode of production. The initial investment involved a large cash outlay—a healthy African man or woman typically cost the plantation owner between fifty and seventy pounds—to which must then be added the costs of feeding, housing, and maintaining such a large labor force, not to mention the maintenance of those responsible for overseeing the slaves. The cultivation of tobacco, the staple of most West Indian islands in the 1600s, had not been able to absorb these expenses sufficiently to yield the plantation owners a satisfactory return on their investments. Sugarcane was a different proposition. Given the worldwide demand for sugar, molasses, and rum, cane production could easily absorb both operational and capital costs—while building a handsome contingency fund to protect against hurricanes and other unforeseen calamities—as long as the African slave trade provided the necessary labor to slash and haul the cane. Robin, however, had long seen a serious flaw in the perspectives of most planters that connected the handsome financial returns they were realizing to the institution of slavery. Consider the facts, he urged. Should Parliament abolish slavery, the capital costs associated with slavery would disappear, as would the operational costs, which would be replaced by an hourly wage paid to workers responsible for their own living expenses. And because these individuals would be working voluntarily with the added incentive of possibly earning a higher hourly wage, logic dictated that they would produce more per man-hour in the fields than slaves working with no incentive beyond surviving another day. No doubt the transition from a slave economy would involve outlays of capital. But those outlays, whatever their amount, would ultimately be covered by the higher annual profits that a "free" economy could be expected to generate.

"So what you're telling us," Richard said after his cousin finished speaking, "is that the abolition of slavery would actually *increase* Cutler & Sons profits?"

"Perhaps not right away," Robin warned. "But in the long term, yes, I believe it would. In no circumstance do I foresee a scenario in which the loss in revenues and profits in a free economy is as catastrophic as most planters would have us believe. Such speculations defy the laws of economics and are just plain nonsense."

John Cutler visibly bristled at that remark but said nothing.

"And remember," Robin went on, "our family is somewhat protected by the rum we produce and sell. As John can confirm, the demand for our rum continues to grow: here, in America, and in Europe. If conditions here should happen to deteriorate in the future, we can always move rum production off the island and charge a higher price per bottle to cover our expenses. John and I believe that raising our prices would not result in a significant drop in sales. In fact, the *opposite* has occurred where we have tested a higher price. In those instances demand has actually *increased*, we believe because of the increase in perceived value in the mind of the customer. It's a lesson your father taught us, Richard. As long as we don't compromise the quality of the rum we produce, we will always find customers willing to pay an extra shilling or two for the best."

Richard nodded his head thoughtfully. "That was well spoken, Robin," he said. "I'm curious, however: do your in-laws agree with your theories on slavery?" Most of the other planters on the island held the Fletcher family in the highest esteem, not least because they were sharp businessmen. If the Fletchers were on board, the rest would follow.

"Not only do they agree," Robin replied, "they have tested the hypothesis. They have allowed free Negroes paid an hourly wage to work side by side in the fields with Negro slaves. In virtually every instance, the daily output of the free Negroes outpaced that of Negroes held in bondage. So yes, they most definitely agree with my theories."

Richard's gaze swung to his other cousin. "But you do not, John, I take it?"

John shrugged. "Let's just say I am yet to be convinced."

THE OTHER matter weighing heavily on the Cutlers involved a new order in council from London, the very one to which Richard had been introduced on his arrival in Barbados. The order instituted an eight-hundred-mile blockade of the northern European coastline by the Royal Navy, covering the coast from the Elbe River in Germany to the city of Brest in Brittany. And as Lieutenant Dunbar had amply demonstrated on *Dove*'s weather deck, the order authorized the British to search neutral vessels for deserters from the British navy as well as possible contraband being shipped illegally, as defined by British law, to France or to a French colonial port such as Basse-Terre on the island of Guadeloupe.

"So, with regard to our products, we're damned if we do and damned if we don't," John Cutler said on another occasion. "If we ship to America, our cargoes must remain in America, no matter what flag we sail under. We are forbidden to re-ship them to Europe without first passing through a British port. And there is considerable risk in trying to defy the order, although I grant you, there is profit in doing that as well. Our countrymen are prepared to pay a fair price for the goods we sell, but not nearly as good a price as the French or the Dutch or the Spanish are prepared to pay.

"And even if our intention is indeed to ship directly to England and thus avoid any possible violation of the broken voyage rule," he continued, "our vessels in the Caribbean often run into French privateers eager to claim them as a prize. In all my years on this island I have never seen such rampant piracy go unpunished. The Royal Navy has always escorted our merchantmen until they were well clear of these islands and out of danger. But thanks to Napoléon, it no longer has the ships to do that. The Windward Squadron is a far cry from what it used to be—here and on Antigua, Saint Kitts, and Port Royal. Whitehall has called many of our protectors home to England, and we are left to look after ourselves."

"It would seem so," Richard had to agree.

"Nor is that the worst of it," John Cutler added, his dander up now. "Not by half. The worst part is what is happening with those warships *not* being recalled to England. Rather than remaining here in the Indies to protect British trade from French privateers, they are instead being dispatched, one by one, to the North American Station to harass American merchantmen and to make the bloody point that those poor blighters must obey the mandates of the British government. It is as though Britain is trying to reduce America back to colonial status!" He laughed bitterly. "What folly! What utter nonsense!

"I am proud that my nephew is willing to join in the fight against England's enemies. But *which* enemies, by God? France and Spain? No sir! Seth's squadron has been ordered to intercept neutral merchant vessels whose only act of war is trying to scratch out a decent living for themselves and their families, just as *we* are trying to do. Yes, I agree that Europe is in a bloody awful mess. And who knows into what black abyss Napoléon might take us? But that is all the more reason for England and America to forge an *alliance* with each other in this war. Whitehall turning everything topsy-turvy makes no bloody sense. It is downright preposterous!"

As John ranted on, Richard stole a glance at Robin, whom he knew from earlier conversations agreed with everything his brother was saying, however differently he might express his opinions. He too held serious reservations about the wisdom of deploying British warships off the American coastline. Those tactics of search and seizure were clear violations of a country's neutrality and sovereignty. And the outright blockade of New York Harbor by the British frigates *Cambrian* and *Leander* was, to Robin's mind, tantamount to a declaration of war.

"While these practices continue," he had quoted from an article that appeared in the *Bridgetown Gazette,* "America cannot consider itself an independent nation." The quote was from a leading member of the Foreign Relations Committee of the U.S. House of Representatives. Robin feared where Britain's current policies might eventually lead not only his country and his company, but also his eldest son, currently serving as a midshipman in HMS *Leopard,* one of several British frigates out on patrol off the Virginia Capes and Chesapeake Bay.

"What is more important to Whitehall?" John demanded more quietly, his fiery passion finally expending itself. "Nipping a few British deserters and impounding a bale of cotton or protecting the economy of an island whose bloody high taxes are *paying* for its campaign against Napoléon?"

It was a rhetorical question, but one for which there was only one rational answer.

SPRINGTIME ON Barbados offered an intoxicating mélange of warm sunshine, gentle sea breezes, and sweet-smelling flowers, each delicate bud the start of a new life. For the Cutlers, one day flowed appealingly into another until the summer-like days of May signified the time for Richard and Katherine Cutler to return home to America. During a last ride together, Katherine and Julia plodded along an unspoiled stretch of seashore on the Caribbean side of the island, where as newlyweds Richard and Katherine had loped and laughed and loved during the early-morning hours as the sun peeked above the deep blue Atlantic to spread its golden warmth across glistening white sands and the dewy jade of sugarcane fields.

The two women dismounted near a patch of grass up where the sand ended and the rich foliage of the interior began. As the horses grazed, Julia and Katherine gazed out across the glistening sea, each absorbed in her own thoughts. At the water's edge, perhaps thirty feet away, sandpipers scurried about in search of sand fleas and other morsels hidden within the scattered clumps of sargasso and other refuse washed ashore during the last high tide. As she looked out upon sweet memories, Katherine smiled. She could almost see Richard in the surf, her young husband of not yet twenty years trudging toward her, holding in one hand a rock lobster he had plucked off a reef and wiping the stinging salt from his eyes with the other. The sight of his strong, lean, sunburned body had never failed to ignite her passion. They had known such hunger for each other back then, she mused, a raging appetite that seemed impossible to sate. The fires of youth had subsided to a warm, comfortable blaze, but the abiding love that had sustained them through twenty-five years of marriage lived on, deeper today than it had been even during those first glorious years of discovery and delight. The images of their entwined bodies vanished as Julia asked a simple and not unexpected question.

"Will I ever see you again, Katherine?"

Katherine looked at Julia, trying to think of a reassuring response.

"I cannot bear the thought of not seeing you again," Julia said as tears welled in her eyes. "I realize that we promised beforehand not to talk about this, but I simply must. I hate what has happened to you, what you have had to endure. No matter how little we have seen each other over the years, you remain my very dearest friend. These past few weeks have been among the happiest of my life."

"Of mine too, Julia," she quietly agreed.

"And so you must agree," Julia said firmly, "that we cannot just say good-bye. I plan to come to see you in Hingham. I have already talked to Robin about it, and he is in complete agreement. Cynthia is too. We have, in fact, agreed to come together. We both want to see Hingham, especially now that Joseph will be there." She clasped Katherine's hands tightly. "It is so very kind of you to invite him, and such a splendid opportunity for him! I have never seen him so thrilled about anything! You have given him a wonderful gift."

Katherine shook her head. "The gift is from Joseph to us, Julia. As for you and Cynthia coming to Hingham, I can't imagine anything that would please me and my family more."

"It's settled, then," Julia said. "We shall do it."

LEAVING BARBADOS had never been easy—emotionally or logistically—and Friday, May 16, was no exception. During the three days prior, Richard had busied himself with the myriad details of the voyage home, first by having Frank Bennett recall *Dove*'s nine-man crew from other work they were performing on Cutler vessels and in Cutler warehouses in Bridgetown, and then by reviewing the sail plan with *Dove*'s master and mate. Richard endorsed Bennett's suggestion that *Dove* sail westward from Barbados and across the Caribbean, taking a sailor's advantage of the easterly trades until they hauled their wind near the western tip of Cuba and sailed around the island into the Strait of Florida. From there the Florida Current would carry the ship north to the point where it merged with the five-knot northerly flow of the sixty-mile-wide Gulf Stream. Such a course, assuming fair winds, could lop days off the three weeks or so normally required for a fast vessel to sail the twenty-five hundred sea miles between Boston and Barbados. The only significant danger in shaping such a course, aside from the possibility of running into extreme weather, which was unlikely during the spring, was the threat of piracy. Richard intended to significantly reduce that threat by stationing two lookouts throughout the day and night, and by keeping the four 6-pounder guns run out and loaded with grapeshot until they reached American waters off the coast of Georgia. Until then, he would also rotate watches every four hours, as in the Navy, rather than every six hours as had been the norm during the southbound cruise. Four-hour watches were more demanding, but over the short term they kept every man jack more alert.

Julia and Robin and their three youngest children were at the dock to see them off. John and Cynthia were there as well, of course, and despite their propensity to keep chin up whatever the circumstance, they were having a difficult time saying good-bye to their only child. It was Joseph who broke the embrace with his mother. He gently coaxed away her arms and slid his hands down to take hers. "I will see you soon, Mother," he promised. "You are coming next spring—less than a year from now. Please do not worry about me. I'll be fine."

"Of course you will, my dearest love," Cynthia managed, "Of course you will." Beside her, Katherine and Julia embraced for a final time.

"Good-bye," Julia managed, ignoring the tears blinding her vision. "Godspeed."

Katherine shook her head. "À bientôt, my sweet friend. I will see you again soon." She turned toward the boat as Julia gave way to sobs.

Within less than an hour *Dove* was sailing westbound on a broad reach. The three Cutlers standing at her stern waved at those watching them from the dock, never stopping until the stretch of sea separating them became too great to distinguish one human form on shore from another.

Five

Grand Terre, Louisiana Territory
May 1806

RICHARD CUTLER awoke with a start and stared up through the open skylight in the deckhead, listening intently. He heard nothing beyond the squeak of blocks, the hum of wind in the rigging, and the gurgle of water running along the clipper's hull. Uncertain what had roused him from a deep sleep, he reached out for the waistcoat watch that he kept during the night in an open compartment secured to the lower bulkhead. The feeble light of a guttering candle encased in a glass lantern allowed him to read the time: 3:50. Falling back on the double bunk that had been specially constructed for this voyage, he listened again—and again he heard nothing but the small sounds of a vessel rigged for night sailing. *Dove* was heeling slightly to larboard, which meant that earlier in the night she had hauled her wind and was now heading east on a starboard tack. Mentally calculating elapsed time and approximate speed, he estimated their position to be somewhere within the southern reaches of the Gulf of Mexico, northwest of Havana and approaching the Dry Tortugas, a group of sparsely vegetated islands located six hours or so, assuming fair winds, due west from an island the Spanish called Cayo Huesco. Legend held that the island, located at the extreme end of a hundred-mile-long coral archipelago stretching southwestward in an arc from mainland Florida, was an Indian burial ground. Not a particularly pleasing thought in the dark early-morning hours.

From long experience, Richard realized that sleep would not return once a sea sense had tolled its silent alarm. He tossed aside the light blan-

ket and sat up at the edge of the bunk, rubbing his eyes and stretching
out his arms. When he reached forward for the shirt and trousers draped
across a heavy wooden chair, he felt the warmth of his wife's hand on his
naked back.

"What is it, Richard?" she asked groggily. "Why up so early? Is something the matter?"

He turned to her and took her hand. "No, nothing's the matter. I
couldn't sleep, is all. I'm going topside for a few minutes." He kissed her
forehead. "Go back to sleep, darling. It's hardly four o'clock."

"I will, if you're sure nothing's wrong."

"I'm sure."

As Richard's head emerged through the aft companionway, the gentle
caress of a southeasterly breeze ruffled his hair and loose-fitting cotton
shirt. His eyes swept the deck. *Dove*'s mainsail and two of her jib sails
were set; overhead, a cloud-covered sky was just barely coming to light.
Afore her mainmast, at deck level, two lookouts kept station, one to larboard and one to starboard. At the first spread of dawn they would climb
aloft to more than double their range of vision across the slight chop of
the Florida Strait.

Richard pulled himself up through the square hole at the top of the
companionway and strode aft to where Robert Jordan was writing on a
chalkboard, recording the four o'clock readings of wind direction, present course, and speed as indicated by the log line. Next to him, the helmsman of the watch kept a steady eye on the compass rose illuminated by a
lanthorn secured to the binnacle.

Jordan glanced up as Richard approached the helm. "Good morning, Mr. Cutler," he said, his voice registering no surprise at seeing his
employer on deck during the graveyard watch. "A pleasant morning, it
would seem."

"Good morning, Bob," Richard returned. "Yes, so it would seem."

Richard glanced at the binnacle; the compass arrow was floating
between 85 and 95 degrees. To the south and southeast lay the Spanish-
held island of Cuba. Ahead to the east-northeast lay the Spanish-held
territory of Florida. Due north was the Gulf of Mexico and, beyond
it, the vast territory of Louisiana recently purchased for $15 million by
the United States from Napoléon, who desperately needed the money to
finance his war in Europe. Although Louisiana was now a U.S. possession,
its southern reaches, particularly in and around the port city of New
Orleans, remained predominantly French. That population had recently
been fortified by an influx of French men and women who had fled the civil

war on Haiti and its aftermath. Toussaint L'Ouverture, a self-educated former slave, had waged a brilliant campaign against the French and won independence for his country in 1801. Soon afterward, Napoléon betrayed him and had him taken to France, where he languished in prison for two years before dying from neglect and starvation. When word of Toussaint's death reached the Haitian capital city of Port-au-Prince, the last remnants of the former French settlement on the island—both the whites and the mulattoes, the *gens de couleur*—decided to get out, and quickly, especially after an 1802 expedition led by Napoléon's brother to reclaim Haiti as a French colony ended in humiliation for France.

Many of Haiti's French population had fled first to Cuba, bringing with them their knowledge of sugarcane cultivation. But when Napoléon invaded Spain, the Cuban colonial government ordered everyone of French pedigree off the island on pain of death. From Cuba these émigrés fled to Louisiana, a land born to French culture and named in honor of the French Sun King, Louis XIV.

If trouble was brewing, as his sea sense told him it was, Richard suspected that it would more likely come from the French than the Spanish. Peering into the still-dark sky to larboard, he could make out little beyond the few feet illuminated by the cutter's lanterns. He was not surprised when an image of Agreen Crabtree sprang to mind. He would have been glad indeed to have his old friend and shipmate by his side this morning. No one was more reliable in a tight spot. He found himself wondering if Agreen's tender of resignation had wended its way through the Navy Department. Odds were that it had. I won't be far behind you, Agee, he thought.

"Good morning, Mr. Cutler," a voice greeted him at the railing. Richard was relieved to see Frank Bennett looming in the darkness. Frank wasn't Agreen, but he was a reliable and competent sea officer who demanded much from himself and his crew—which is why Caleb had been so eager to sign him on at Cutler & Sons. Plus, he was pleasant to talk to and in general a good man to have around.

"We should have light in another thirty minutes or so. Dawn comes early in these latitudes. If there's anyone out there," Bennett added, reading Richard's mind, "we'll spot him soon enough. Shall I send below for some coffee? The water's hot, and I could use a cup myself. I had Turner stoke up the stove before the start of the watch."

"Yes, do, Frank. And a long glass, if you please. I'm going aloft with the lookouts. And Frank," he added, "at first light have the men standing by the guns."

A half hour later Richard climbed the ratlines, secured himself within the hempen cords attached to the mainmast crosstrees, and trained his glass northward across a mottled sea quickly transforming from ebony black to pewter gray. There was indeed a vessel out there, just as his instinct had told him. She was a good distance downwind of *Dove*—perhaps five or six hundred yards—on a parallel course and closing. He lowered the glass, studied her with his naked eye, and then raised the glass anew, focusing the lens in and out until the image grew clear and unmistakable. "Damn!" Richard cursed under his breath. Captured in the lens of his glass was a single-masted vessel boasting a triangular fore-and-aft sail on her single raked mast with a square topsail above, still furled to its yard. At her bow, three large triangular foresails were set on a jibboom that was perhaps twice the length of *Dove*'s. It was the exceptional length of that boom—in alliance with her trim lines, deep hull, and narrow beam—that pegged her provenance.

And what a provenance it was. The speed of a Baltimore clipper such as *Dove* was legendary, but if any other type of vessel could outsail a clipper, it was a Bermuda sloop. Like the one he was looking at now. The Royal Navy's respect for these Bermuda-built vessels was such that it had commissioned large numbers of them into the service. They were ideal for reconnoitering and for chasing smugglers. They were also ideal for communicating important information to other ships both distant and near—and to shore, as HMS *Pickle* aptly demonstrated when she raced from Gibraltar back to England in record time to report the stupendous victory at Trafalgar and the untimely death of Horatio Nelson.

Richard could not immediately determine the sloop's nationality; she flew no ensign. But he noticed that she had six guns run out on her starboard side and three-man gun crews standing by each of them. He climbed down to the weather deck and was about to speak to Frank Bennett when a lookout above called down that the sloop had fired a blank charge to windward. The heavy thud of the discharge washed over *Dove* several seconds later.

"That should dispel any doubt," Richard muttered, "if ever we had any." A gun fired to windward was an international signal of malice.

"Fucking pirates," Bennett snarled. "They must have spotted us late yesterday and shadowed us through the night. You were right, sir: we should have doused our lanterns."

"It's too late to worry about that now," Richard said. "We don't know who these people are yet, and we don't know their intentions. Besides, as you correctly pointed out, dousing our lanterns would have exposed us to other sorts of dangers." He squeezed Bennett's arm. "Chastising ourselves serves no purpose, Frank. The question is what we do now."

Bennett nodded grimly. "I say we set all sail and show them our heels," he stated emphatically. "The wind is freshening and the men are ready."

Richard set his jaw and considered his limited options. In this stretch of water there was not a friendly port for hundreds of miles, and there was virtually no possibility of outrunning the sloop over such a distance. His only other option, beyond immediate surrender, was to stand and fight. Although his training as a naval commander demanded he take such action, he was hesitant to fire on a vessel that heavily outgunned and outmanned his own, especially with his wife and nephew on board. But he had to make a decision, and he had to make it now. The sloop was closing fast.

He summoned Robert Jordan, who had yielded the helm to another sailor and was standing by for orders, and looked at Captain Bennett. "I want you at the helm, Frank," Richard said. "We'll come off the wind and bear up. When the sloop shadows our move, I'll give her a broadside. I'll aim for her mast and rigging—and who knows, we may get lucky. As soon as our aft gun is fired, we'll come off the wind, clap on all sail, and resume our present course. If we do that smartly, Bob, we can put some distance between them and us while they're trying to get back on course. Have the men stand by to dump everything portable overboard, and that includes our guns and supplies. Understood?"

Both men saluted in crisp naval fashion. "Aye, aye, sir," they said in unison.

Richard hurried below to warn Katherine and Joseph to remain in their cabins. He gave his wife a quick summary of what was happening. "We can expect a return volley or two," he said in conclusion. "But not to worry. I've never known a pirate who can shoot straight at a hundred yards. If it turns out we can't outrun them, then so be it. I will not put you and Joseph in further jeopardy."

Katherine nodded her understanding. "What are the odds?"

"Slim, I'm afraid."

"Be careful, Richard," she pleaded.

Richard nodded and closed the door.

Topside, the Bermuda sloop continued to close as *Dove* bore off the wind and her three larboard guns were run out. The gun crews looked expectantly at Richard, who was on a knee by the forward larboard gun, peering through its sight, waiting for the sloop to bear up. Two hundred yards narrowed to a hundred yards, and still the sloop continued to come at them bow-on. A sickening feeling washed over Richard as he realized that she had no intention of turning. He was losing valuable time—and distance. He had to shoot now, and pray to hit a pole a hundred yards away.

The sloop drew into *Dove*'s sights, dead-on to her single mast.

Richard stood up and to the side. "Firing!" he cried out, and jerked the gun's firing lanyard.

The gun carriage screeched inboard as a 6-pound ball exploded from the gun's muzzle through a viper's tongue of orange flame and white sparks. Richard was already at the mid-ship gun when the gun captain of the first gun reported a miss.

"Firing!" Richard shouted again, and the process was repeated, and then once again at the aft gun.

He snatched a long glass and surveyed the arena of battle. Nothing of significance caught his eye. The sloop's flying jib had a hole torn through it, but apparently the shot had not struck the mast behind it. The mast did not wobble and the sloop did not lose speed. White foam continued to cream off both sides of her cutwater.

Richard understood the futility of his position. Because the sloop had not presented her broadside to return fire, and had instead kept coming straight at them, the advantages he had hoped to gain from superior gunnery and seamanship were gone. The sloop was only fifty yards downwind. Were *Dove* to show her heels now, the race would soon be over and the victor declared.

"Strike our colors and heave to," he called to Frank Bennett standing by the helm.

"Captain?"

"You heard me," Richard said hoarsely. "Heave to. That's an order!" Despite himself, he could not keep outrage and disgust from his voice. He had gambled and lost, and now he *had* put his wife and nephew in danger. Whoever these pirates turned out to be, he suspected they would be none too pleased to have been fired upon.

"Aye, Captain," Bennett said reluctantly. He ordered *Dove*'s sails set to counteract each other, and in short order the clipper was hove to and bobbing up and down on the sea in a lazy drift. The sloop, meanwhile, had tacked across the clipper's stern and had come up parallel on her windward side, the maws of her six larboard guns trained point-blank on *Dove*'s hull. The sloop's spokesman, standing amidships, wasted no time getting down to business.

"American *vaisseau*," he shouted through a speaking trumpet, "I am sending over a boat with a *pilote* and four men. These men are armed. You will send me, in return, your *capitaine* and four of your sailors. *Comprenez-vous?*"

"*Je comprends très bien*," Richard muttered. He looked at Bennett. "So be it," he said. "I'll go." But when he made to answer through his own speaking trumpet, Bennett clamped a hand on Richard's arm and forced the trumpet down.

"By your leave, Captain Cutler," he said. He held out his hand, and Richard slowly surrendered the trumpet.

Bennett raised the trumpet to his lips. "I am the captain of this vessel," he shouted back. "I understand your message. Four of my crew and I shall come on board as you requested. May I assume that my vessel is then to follow yours?"

"*Oui*," was the curt response.

"Thank you, Frank," Richard said as he watched a boat being lowered away beside the sloop. Seven men jumped nimbly down into it. "You didn't have to do that."

"With respect, Captain, I did," Bennett responded. "I will not see you separated from Mrs. Cutler. Besides," he added with a sketchy grin, "I *am* the master of this vessel."

The exchange was made and soon both vessels were sailing north on a broad reach, the still unidentified sloop in the lead. Not only did she show no flag, Richard noted, she bore no name.

"I'm sorry I got you into this," he said to his wife, who, with Joseph, had joined him on deck at the first exchange of words between the sloop and cutter.

Katherine brushed away his remark with a flick of her hand. "Nonsense, my dear. Neither you nor anyone else is to blame for getting us into whatever 'this' turns out to be. I *am* curious, though: what do you think they intend to do with us?"

"Your guess is as good as mine," Richard said. "If it's our cargo they're after, they will be sorely disappointed. Our hold carries only ballast."

"But they didn't even look below," she pointed out, "to see what cargo we *might* be carrying. Why wouldn't they at least do that?"

"It's a mystery," Richard agreed. In the back of his mind, however, a notion was festering that this was no mystery at all. But he dared not share that notion with his wife.

As the two ships cruised northward, Richard had plenty of time to take stock of their situation. The four French sailors—if indeed they were sailors—stood in pairs at each end of the cutter, each with a cutlass and pistol held at the ready or tucked into the waistband of his trousers. The pilot, dressed like his comrades in homespun cloth, manned the helm. To Richard's surprise, however, they seemed quite relaxed, as though intercepting an American merchant vessel was nothing out of the ordinary for them.

Late the next afternoon, lookouts aloft raised tufts of land on the horizon. Except for the uncertainty about what awaited them at the conclusion, *Dove*'s voyage through the Gulf of Mexico had been rather a pleasant interlude for the Cutlers. Although the four French guards had done little to help sail the vessel, in truth there had been little for them to do. The southeasterly breezes held steady, and without the need to adjust the sails, Robert Jordan saw fit to divide the five remaining American sailors into two six-hour watches of three men, with himself serving as the sixth sailor. The French pilot had even allowed Richard—to his knowledge merely a passenger—to take a turn at the wheel, but only under the scrutiny of a French guard. Not one of the five Frenchmen offered a clue about why *Dove* had been detained, where they were going, or what they might expect when they arrived there, despite Richard's frequent attempts to ferret out bits of information. But they had behaved pleasantly enough. They had even joked around with Joseph and applauded his attempts to test his command of French on them.

"*Mais ne vous inquiétez pas,*" one of them said to Katherine on one occasion. "*Aucun mal ne vous viendrá.*" The Frenchman's assertion that no harm would come to any of them eased their anxiety at the same time it piqued their curiosity.

ALTHOUGH NO American in *Dove,* including Richard Cutler, had ever set foot on the Louisiana coast, its reputation as a hotbed for pirates, smugglers, slave traders, gold hunters, gold diggers, and other social misfits was by now well established. American justice—*any* sort of justice—was far from being established in the nation's newest territory. As *Dove* glided between the first frail outer islands scattered along the seacoast, it was easy to understand why. As far as the eye could see, the place was a confused morass of interlocking lakes, swamps, mangroves, bays, and bayous that served as a lush breeding ground for alligators, mosquitoes, yellow fever, malaria, smallpox, and miscreants seeking to escape the long arm of the law. For decades, ownership of Louisiana had teetered back and forth between France and Spain until Napoléon sold it to the United States. Based on what he had seen so far, Richard wondered out loud why on earth Jefferson had sent Governor James Monroe of Virginia, erstwhile U.S. minister to France, to Paris with diplomat Robert Livingston to negotiate the deal.

"Louisiana is said to be a vast territory," Katherine said idly as she too took in the eerily fascinating scenery of muddy water, tangled undergrowth, and moss-hung cypress trees. Eager to escape the heat and humidity belowdecks, which had intensified now that the cutter had sailed within the lee of the outer islands, she had come topside to join Richard and Joseph. Even with her hair gathered into a knot at the back of her neck, beads of sweat formed anew on her forehead moments after she blotted it with a handkerchief. "It stretches clear up to Canada. Surely this must be the worst of it."

"One can only hope," Richard replied, mopping his own brow.

Ahead, the Bermuda sloop, sailing under a double-reefed mainsail and narrow jib, slipped between two substantial islands and rounded eastward into what appeared to be a sizable bay. Here and there Richard spotted armed men sitting in canoe-like boats partially hidden in the pungent-smelling reeds and marsh grass. Most of them wore an air of grim duty; aside from a red bandana covering the top of their heads, they were dressed in the same homespun cloth as the Frenchmen in *Dove*. Richard glanced down at the chart he held flat on the cutter's starboard railing. Although neither of the two islands was named on the chart, the large body of water they had entered was labeled Barataria Bay, and it stretched well beyond the eastern tip of the island off to starboard that apparently was their destination.

Robert Jordan ordered his crew to round *Dove* into the wind and drop anchor in a wide-mouthed cove, following the evolutions of the Bermuda sloop. Richard noted that the water was deep here, as measured by the length of anchor line paying out, and that the complex of islands surrounding them would offer safe harbor even to a large naval vessel. But shelter was about all it could offer. A square-rigged frigate such as *Portsmouth* would be sorely confined whatever the direction of the wind. It would be nigh impossible to bring her guns to bear against a force of the smaller, well-armed, fore-and-aft-rigged vessels that pirates favored. *Portsmouth* would be chewed to pieces in this bay, whatever her advantage in firepower. An image came to his mind of a stricken shark, its tailfin shorn, being ripped to shreds by a school of dagger-toothed barracudas.

After both vessels were secured at anchor, a rowboat conveyed two individuals, whose attire and mannerisms marked them as men of influence, to the sloop. Richard watched them climb on board and then turned his attention back to the cove and the shore.

He counted eight vessels of various lengths and rigs anchored nearby. All except one, a brig, were relatively small single- or double-masted affairs, and all appeared to carry guns on their weather deck. He could see few buildings on the island. A warehouse-style structure located near the waterfront dominated the few smaller buildings around it. It was long and narrow and constructed mostly of stone; overlapping sheets of thin, rusted metal covered the steeply pitched wooden roof. To the right, at the western tip of the island, stood a modest but seemingly sturdy fort constructed of red brick. Black barrels of sizable cannon stuck out through embrasures on the single circular gun tier that covered all approaches to the fort, including those by land.

"*Quel est le nom de cette île?*" Richard asked the French pilot.

"Grand Terre," the pilot replied tersely.

At length, the boat that had been rowed out to the sloop was rowed over to the cutter. The same two men Richard had observed earlier came on board. First on deck was the leader of the fortress-like complex, at least judging by the quality of his colorful silk garments and stylish felt hat; indeed, he looked more like a French *chevalier* than a local magnate. He was tall, matching Richard's six feet, and his pale skin contrasted sharply with his shoulder-length curly black hair. A long and well-groomed mustache in the shape of an inverted v fell to a finely chiseled jaw. Those were Richard's immediate impressions of the man, although he quickly detected a depth and intelligence that went beyond shallow pretenses or false pride. He was a handsome man, extraordinarily so—the sort of man that enflamed women's fantasies. No doubt many people were drawn to him for that reason alone. But Richard was far more impressed by the easy and cocky manner in which the man boarded *Dove* and took charge simply by his presence, without having to utter a word. It was as though he were a medieval lord and this his fiefdom, loyal vassals expected to obey his every command. As the Frenchman continued to take careful note of every aspect of the cutter, Richard wondered how many honest men he had seduced into corruption—and how many chaste women into his bed.

His inspection finished, the man stopped a few feet short of Richard and placed his hands on his hips. "You are the captain of this vessel?" he asked in nearly perfect English, with just a trace of a French accent. "I sense there is some confusion here."

"My family owns this vessel," Richard informed him. "Captain Bennett, whom you are holding captive over there"—he jabbed his finger toward the sloop—"is her master."

The man ignored that. "So you are this vessel's *owner*, Monsieur Cutler? *Tant mieux*. But you too hold the rank of captain, *oui?*"

"I hold the rank of captain in the United States Navy."

"*Bien, c'est vrai*," the man said delightedly. "Monsieur Bennett speaks true. *La Marine des États-Únis! Mon Dieux. Je suis impressionné, monsieur!*" He glanced at his companion, who rolled his eyes and chuckled, for what reason Richard failed to grasp.

"And who are these two?" the man asked, pointing at Katherine and Joseph standing behind Richard by the mainmast. He studied them more thoroughly. "*Cette femme, elle est très belle, je crois.*"

Richard did not appreciate the man's tone. "*Cette femme*," he snapped, "is my wife. The young man is my nephew. We were bound for Boston from Barbados when your sloop intercepted us and forced us here. You are aware, monsieur, that you have committed a blatant act of piracy."

The man advanced one step, his brown eyes boring into Richard's blue ones. "Be very careful, *mon ami*," he said, his voice turning low and dangerous. "Be very, very careful. You are sailing, as they say, in shallow waters, and there is no safe harbor for you or any of your passengers and crew without my permission. You may have authority in your Navy ship, *capitaine*, but you have no authority here. None. *Zéro*."

Richard merely stared at him.

"*Bien*," the man snapped. "You will wait here until I send for you. We have a matter to discuss, you and I."

"You know my name, monsieur," Richard said to the Frenchman as he climbed adroitly down into the boat. "May I know yours?"

The man stepped over a thwart and sat down in the stern sheets. As the oarsmen pushed off and the coxswain steered for shore, the man glanced up. "My name is Jean Lafitte," he said.

THE SUMMONS came two hours later as dark clouds gathered and rain threatened, intensifying the already insufferable humidity. It was now Richard's turn to climb down into the boat sent out for him.

"Be careful, Richard," Katherine pleaded, adding, more as an admonishment, "and whatever you do, don't antagonize him. Diplomacy is what is called for, not your foul temper. We have no friends here, and don't forget we have Joseph in our charge."

"I won't forget," Richard promised.

He was met on the beach by two armed guards who escorted him into the warehouse. Just inside the entrance Richard noted four desks on which papers were neatly arranged next to quills and ink bowls and other accoutrements of business administration such as one might find in his own family's countinghouse on Long Wharf. One guard ordered him to wait and stayed with him while the other walked toward a private office off to the side. As he waited under the watchful eye of his guard, Richard studied the interior of the warehouse. There was not much to see. A wooden wall with double doors at its center separated the administrative area from the much larger back area, which Richard assumed was used for storage. When someone opened one of the doors and stepped through it, he managed to catch a glimpse inside. Stacks of hogsheads and barrels and burlap sacks flashed into view before the door clicked shut.

The second guard returned and motioned Richard into the private office. Richard's gaze swept the room as he entered. It was richly appointed in a fashion that even Jack Endicott in Boston would have found appealing. His gaze settled on Jean Lafitte seated casually behind a deep red mahogany desk of intricate design. On the other side of the desk, facing the Frenchman, were three upholstered chairs. A peal of thunder echoed through the office, followed by the not unpleasant sound of rain pattering on the metal roof above.

Lafitte made a show of checking his waistcoat watch. "*Comme d'habitude*," he said, shaking his head in theatrical disbelief. "You can set your watch by the rain storms each day." He grinned at Richard. "May I offer you a drink, *capitaine*? As you can see"—he gestured toward the decorative sideboard behind him, on top of which was set an array of fine crystal decanters, each containing a spirit of a different color—"I am well stocked." He raised a glass for Richard's inspection. "I am having a glass of bourbon whiskey, the best that the great state of Kentucky has to offer. It was a gift from the Williams family, who distill the best bourbon in the entire state." He took a sip, smacked his lips, then: "Did you know that this spirit is named in honor of a French royal family? *Ah, oui*. The House of Bourbon. So it is *approprié* for the occasion." When Richard remained stone-faced, Lafitte again raised his glass. "Indulge me?"

"Thank you, no."

"*Vraiment?*" Lafitte shrugged. "*Encore*, since you choose not to be friendly, be seated and we shall discuss our business matter." Lafitte waved his hand at the three chairs facing him.

"I prefer to stand, monsieur, if you have no objection."

Lafitte squinted at Richard while tapping the fingers of his right hand on the table. Then: "*Allez-y.* Suit yourself," he translated in a less than cordial voice. He picked up his glass and swirled its contents. "I am curious to know," he said reflectively, "if you have heard of me."

"No. Should I have?"

Lafitte made a dismissive gesture. "*Peu d'importance.* Since that is the case, however, perhaps you should know a little about me. I would not want you to misunderstand my character." Lafitte spoke to the glass, not to Richard. "I was born in France but lived much of my boyhood on Saint-Domingue—the land we now call Haiti. I learned very little in the few years of schooling that my family could afford. A little English, but even that I had to teach myself. I did, *pourtant*, manage to learn much about the lessons of life. I am referring to the *harsh* lessons of life, monsieur, the ones that teachers do not teach and that men born to privilege"—he nodded sardonically toward Richard—"rarely understand." He downed a shot of whiskey and poured out another. "Since that time," he went on in the same tone, "I have made good use of what I learned. I was not yet twenty when my older brother, Pierre, and I started a business. We are equal partners in this business, and we each have an important role. He procures the goods, and I store them on Grande Terre. From here I ship them to merchants in New Orleans and to merchants . . . *bien*, let us just say to merchants who may live quite far away. Of course, the best of these items I keep for Pierre and myself to sell in our store in New Orleans, on Royal Street. I receive quite a nice price for them."

And make quite a nice profit too, Richard thought. Yet, oddly, as the Frenchman's grin broadened into a wide smile Richard found himself drawn to the man. Aloud he said, "Tell me, Monsieur Lafitte, how does Pierre manage to procure these items you sell? Does he pay for them? Or does he simply take them?"

A storm cloud passed over Lafitte's face. "I do not like your insinuation, monsieur," he said, the tone of his voice matching the dark glint in his eyes. "I am telling you these things because I see in you a quality I admire. We are men of the world, you and I. But do not think that you can insult me. Again I warn you: be very careful with your choice of words. I will not be called a pirate by you or by anyone else."

"Perhaps 'smuggler' is a more accurate word?"

"*Assez!*" Lafitte banged his fist on the table, upsetting the glass of bourbon and sending it crashing onto the stone floor. "It is one and the same, monsieur!" he shouted. "I tell you, I am *not* a pirate! Men who

have dared call me that lie dead in their graves. I have challenged many
to a duel, and as you can see for yourself, monsieur, I remain very much
alive. Do you too wish to challenge me? If so, I shall oblige you, at your
pleasure. My sole regret will be making your lovely wife a widow!"

Richard remained as stiff as a marlinspike. He did, however, moderate
his tone. "I do not wish to test your skill with the pistol, monsieur," he
said. "I can clearly see that you are a man of many talents. But if you are
not a pirate or a smuggler, then what are you?"

Lafitte leaned back in his chair. "I am a privateer," he said firmly.

"Operating under whose letter of marque?"

"Guadeloupe's."

"Guadaloupe? Then I suspect you are soon to be disappointed, monsieur. The British have Guadeloupe and Martinique under siege. If they
take those islands—I should say, *when* they take those islands—they will
revoke your letter.

"Yes, I quite agree," Lafitte said casually.

"What will you do then?"

Lafitte offered a wisp of a smile. "*Then* I shall go elsewhere for a letter
of marque."

"But where? There are no other French colonies in the Indies."

Lafitte selected another glass and splashed bourbon into it. "It is
rumored that Spain's colonies in South America will soon gain their independence," he said. "I have no doubt that they will issue letters of marque.
In any case, Spain is an ally of France in the war against England. So, even
as a colony of Spain, the government in Bogotá, *par exemple,* is most
eager to issue letters of marque to men like me."

"For a handsome price."

Lafitte nodded. "*Naturellement.* But whatever that price is, I will pay
it gladly. A letter of marque keeps my business legitimate, *non?*"

Richard blinked, realizing that under international law what Lafitte
had just said was correct. In effect, a letter of marque legitimized piracy
while in theory protecting its holder and his crew from punishment befit-
ting pirates. As corrupt and contemptible as the system might be, it was
a system long recognized by all civilized nations, and there was nothing
he could do or say against it. He had one last card to play, and he chose
his words carefully.

"I concede your point, monsieur," he said. "However, privateering is
considered a legal activity only when the country that issues the letter
is at war with the country whose ships are taken. To the best of my

knowledge, the United States is not at war with either France or Spain—
or with the government in Bogotá."

To Richard's surprise, Lafitte laughed. "You have the balls to stand
before me and talk of legalities? *Mon Dieu*, are you really so naïve? What
have legalities to do with *anything*? British warships and French privateers alike have been seizing your merchant ships at a rate to outrage your
government. But what does your government *do* about it? What does your
president do? He does nothing. *Rien de tout.* One of life's lessons I have
learned, monsieur, is that in dealing with one's enemies, real and presumed, fear is a potent weapon. My enemies fear me and the force of my
will. Those who have the will to win *will* win. Everyone else suffers. Your
president has not the will to win, so his people suffer. You and your family
suffer. Regrettable? *Peut-être. Mais c'est la vie, monsieur, n'est-ce pas?*"

Richard's shoulders sagged. Feeling the wind knocked out of him, he
sat down in one of the three chairs facing Lafitte. "If the offer still stands,
monsieur," he said, "I will join you in a glass of whiskey now."

"*Bon.*" Lafitte took another glass from the sideboard behind him,
filled it to the brim, and handed it to Richard. "*Santé,*" he said before
downing a hearty slug.

"*Santé,*" Richard said before downing one of his own.

"And so, Monsieur Lafitte," Richard said after the bourbon had settled his nerves, "where do we go from here? Exactly what do you intend
to do with us?"

Lafitte raised his eyebrows. "With *you,* monsieur? Nothing whatso-
ever. You and those in your ship's company are free to depart this island
any time you wish."

"Free to depart?" Richard said as calmly as he was able. "In my own
vessel, I presume?"

Lafitte smiled. "You may presume whatever you wish, *mon ami.* I
never wish to deny a man what he might presume."

"Can we get to the point, monsieur?" Richard asked curtly before
uttering the words he dreaded saying. "I believe that the business matter
we are here to discuss concerns my ship. Am I correct?"

Lafitte clapped his hands in applause. "*Exactement,*" he said happily.
"She is a Baltimore clipper! A sweet and very fast vessel." He leaned in
and spoke softly, as if offering a confidence. "You may be interested to
know that Pierre and I have eighty ships. Those out there in the cove are
just a few of them. The rest are away at sea. They are all fine ships, but we
do not have a clipper in our fleet. That is, we did not have one until today."

And an armed one, at that." He grinned. "The *capitaine* of my sloop did well by me, *non*? And he did well by himself and his crew. They will be handsomely rewarded, I can assure you. It is another of life's lessons, one that every successful businessman understands: to keep men loyal and working hard—those men you *choose* to keep loyal and working hard— you must pay them well for work well done. Unless I am mistaken, this is a lesson you yourself have learned. *C'est vrai, mon ami?*"

Richard's brain spun between relief, on the one hand, and outrage, on the other. How could he return home without his vessel? It was not just the ignominy of losing the newly minted crown jewel of the Cutler & Sons merchant fleet to a French pirate. As embarrassing and appalling as that loss was, he was powerless to prevent it. But how, without his vessel, would he get his family and crew home from Grande Terre? He put that question to Jean Lafitte.

"Ah, *mon ami*, you are in luck," Lafitte replied magnanimously. "It happens that I have business in Saint Augustine. An important but rather impudent client there is angry with me over certain terms of sale. I must therefore go and help him understand my perception of things. So if you are willing—if you will accept my hospitality—I will take you in my brig to one of the islands off the coast of Savannah. I shall have to keep your crew under lock and key during the voyage, you understand, but you and Madame Cutler will be free to stroll the deck and to dine with me at your pleasure. You will all be treated well; you have my word on it. *Encore*, from Savannah it will be an easy matter for you to book passage to Boston. *C'est ça?* Are such terms acceptable to you?"

Richard exhaled slowly. "What choices do I have?"

"I regret to inform you, *Capitaine* Cutler," Lafitte replied with a grin, "that you have *no* choices."

For a brief instant Richard considered the possibility of spotting a U.S. Navy warship out on patrol off the coast of Georgia. He quickly dismissed that forlorn hope: the odds were ridiculously small. Even if they did happen upon one, how could he signal her to interfere with what would look like, with her guns rolled in and her gun ports camouflaged, an innocent merchant brig? And even if he did see a Navy ship and could signal her, that would again place his wife, nephew, and crew in serious jeopardy. Lafitte was correct. He had Richard checkmated.

"Such terms are acceptable," Richard said, determined to make the best of this horrible turn of events.

"*Eh bien*," Lafitte said with a broad grin. He raised his glass. "*À un bon voyage, mon ami.*"

Six

Savannah, Georgia, and Hingham, Massachusetts
Summer 1806

FROM A DISTANCE, the vast flat marshlands along the Georgia coastline seemed very much like those that dominated the Louisiana coast. Here, though, nestled a short way up the Savannah River and within easy sail for a hired sloop, was a city of substance—indeed, the first colonial capital of Georgia and its first state capital. Off to the east of Savannah was yet another beacon of civilization: a lighthouse erected on what the sloop's master identified as Tybee Island. Tybee Light, originally constructed in 1736, was the first lighthouse to grace America's southern waters. It had been destroyed by fire and rebuilt twice, the sloop's captain told Richard, and today rose one hundred feet above its base. Richard and the others sailing with him across the eighty-five miles separating Sea Island from Savannah had found the gradual emergence of Tybee Light on the northern horizon a most welcome sight.

Richard had no difficulty booking passage northward once he made it known along the waterfront that he was a U.S. Navy captain seeking passage to the naval base at Portsmouth, Virginia. After he had submitted a written report to naval authorities at the Gosport Shipyard, to be forwarded up the Potomac to the Navy Department in Washington, the company would continue on to Boston. Although he realized there was little the Navy would or could do about Jean Lafitte—and in truth, the cruise from Grand Terre to the Sea Islands had tempered his and Katherine's initial impressions of the man—he felt it his duty to more clearly define the threat to American commerce in the Gulf of Mexico. Plus, it was just possible that Navy secretary Robert Smith might be in Portsmouth, which would suit Richard's purposes all the better.

As it turned out, the seizure of *Dove* on Grand Terre and subsequent layovers in Georgia and Virginia delayed their arrival in Boston to a hot and breezy morning in early July—a full month behind schedule. Those waiting for them to return home from Barbados had felt every hour of that extra month, their anxiety at the outset gradually deepening into despair each day that a Baltimore clipper failed to materialize to those watching high on a widow's walk or some other tall structure. When the master of a Cutler & Sons packet boat dispatched by George Hunt on Long Wharf announced to the Cutler family in Hingham that a U.S. Navy sloop of war carrying Richard and Katherine Cutler, their nephew, and *Dove*'s captain and crew had arrived in Boston from Portsmouth, word spread quickly about town that the prodigals would be sailing for Hingham later that same day.

By mid-afternoon a sizable crowd had gathered near the quays at Crow Point. The safe return of *Dove*'s passengers and crew was reason enough for many Hingham residents to be there; but what truly swelled the crowd were the rumors concerning the circumstances of their delay. Imagine! Pirates and cutthroats boarding a Cutler & Sons vessel and seizing it! The terror— the unspeakable brutality—of it all! Imagine Katherine Cutler— that dear, frail woman—falling into the hands of the most vile and unprincipled men sailing the seas! Well! People came streaming in toward the quays from every direction and pushed in closer for a better view.

Diana Cutler and Peter Sprague stood in the vanguard of that crowd, in company with Agreen and Lizzy Crabtree, Adele Cutler, Carol Bennett, and two other Cutler family members recently arrived. Excited chatter filled the air as eager eyes scanned the waters of West Gut between Peddock's Island and Hough's Neck for telltale glints of white sail and jib on a single-masted packet boat.

"There!" someone shouted, pointing. "That looks like the one!"

"Thar she blows, my friends!" Agreen shouted out a moment later. His vision was sharp, and his knowledge of Cutler & Sons packet boats thorough.

Spontaneous cheers broke out. Diana beamed at Peter. When she wrapped her arm around his waist and leaned against him, Peter put his hand on her shoulder and drew her in tight. Agreen was bolder. With a whoop of joy, he placed his hands on Lizzy's hips and lifted her high into the air, grinning as he held her above his head.

"Agee!" she shrieked. "Put me down this instant! What will people think?"

"They'll think that I love you," he shouted out for all to hear, and all loved hearing it. Cheers erupted as he lowered her gradually, bringing her lips ever closer to his, ending in a public kiss for which she would excoriate him later but which she could not resist now. Another round of cheers broke out as he set his wife on solid ground.

"So much for Puritan Hingham," Agreen chuckled.

"Agee, you are incorrigible!" she muttered indignantly, smoothing the wrinkles in her dress. "Look at me. What on earth got into you?"

Agreen just stood there grinning.

The westerly breeze brought the packet in on a broad reach, and the high tide allowed the boat to pass Crow Point under reduced canvas and glide in under the lee of Button Island before wheeling about and feathering up to a berth cleared for her along the easternmost quay. As one sailor stood by to douse her last shreds of canvas, another sailor in her bow heaved a coiled line to a dockhand on the quay. A second line was heaved from her stern to another dockhand. Each line was looped thrice around a bollard, and the two dockhands stood by, holding the bitter end of their lines until the rope stretched and groaned, taking the full strain of the packet's forward momentum. Gradually the 50-foot vessel slowed to a standstill. Deckhands then freed the two lines from the bollards and began warping her in toward the quay.

"So, Joseph," Katherine said to her nephew, who was watching from amidships as the larboard side of the hull began inching in toward the dock. "What do you think thus far?"

Joseph stared at the crowed, rendered speechless by their shouts and applause; many were waving their hats in the air. "I think, Aunt Katherine," he finally said quietly, "that you are much beloved here."

"It's not me, Joseph," she said, squeezing his shoulder. "It's our family, of which you are a member. Those people are welcoming you, too."

"I hope so. . . . Is that Diana waving at us? The young lady in the yellow dress? It must be; she looks just like you. She looks excited too."

"Yes!" Katherine had spotted Diana earlier and again waved back happily at her. "That's her fiancé, Peter, beside her. To their left is Adele, the wife of my son Will, whom you just met in Boston. To their right is Mr. Crabtree—does he not look the same as when you met him in Barbados?—and next to him is his wife, Elizabeth, my very dearest friend. You have heard me speak of her often. Now, let me see; next to them—"

She paused, shaded her eyes with a hand, and squinted. "Oh my dearest Lord," she gasped. "It *can't* be. But it *is!*"

"Is what, Katherine?" Richard asked, walking up beside her and ready to hand her ashore now that the packet boat lay snug against the wharf. A sailor had opened the packet's larboard entry port and seized hold of a gangplank thrust up from the dock.

"Richard, it's Hugh," she exclaimed. She pointed in the general direction. "It's my brother Hugh! And Phoebe!"

Richard searched the crowd and then broke into a broad grin. "Well call me a son of a bitch!" he exclaimed. Then, in a quieter voice: "Please excuse my language, Joseph."

Joseph didn't hear him above his own gleeful laughter—a sound heard ever more frequently since he had left Barbados.

"YOU GAVE us quite a scare, my dear," Hugh Hardcastle said to his sister, summing up the feelings of everyone present. All of the Cutler family members in America—save for Caleb, who was in Baltimore, and Will, in Boston for the week—were seated on chairs and sofas in the spacious parlor of the family seat on Main Street, sated by the homecoming supper. Edna Stowe had been nominally in charge of the meal, but the infirmities associated with advancing age had reduced her role in the kitchen to supervisor. Nevertheless, she had supervised a magnificent feast.

"I cannot say that I care for the welcome you tendered Phoebe and me when we arrived," Hugh continued. "We come to Hingham at last, crossing an ocean to get here, and what do we find? No sister, no brother-in-law, because *they*, it seems, preferred to have a jolly old time in a pirate ship whilst their poor shipmates languished below in the ship's brig. These two poor ladies"—referring to Diana and Adele, who had done yeoman's work in preparing and serving the meal—"hardly knew what to say when they opened the door to us. 'Who *are* these ragamuffins?' I distinctly recall Diana saying to Adele after we introduced ourselves and they agreed to let us into the house. 'Through what black hole in the wall did *they* waltz?'"

"You distinctly heard incorrectly, Uncle," Diana said, smiling. "We knew to expect you, and we were delighted to see you." Her tone grew somber. "In truth, though, we did not give you the welcome you deserved. Adele and I were hardly the best of hosts; we were so very worried. But we are ever so grateful that you were here to lend your support. It's wonderful having you here, and we hope you will stay with us forever. I know my mother would be pleased." She glanced at her mother, who gave an approving nod. "And my father. He has told us a little about your adventures together, and I hope to hear more about them from you. Peter demands to be here when you do. He already admires you greatly."

"Well, at least your beau has excellent taste," Hugh rejoined, at which his wife groaned aloud. "Of course," Hugh went right on, as if he had not heard her, "in saying that I was referring to you, Diana, not to me. Seriously, now, Peter is a fine young man, and a most fortunate one. Further, your hospitality these last ten days has been superb considering your worries. Phoebe and I were happy to share your burdens—and would share them again, tenfold, in order to share in the joy of this day."

"Caleb should be returning in a day or two," Richard said, filling the pause that followed Hugh's remarks, "and when he does, he'll bring Joan and Thomas down with him from Boston. I understand that they intend to be here at least through Diana's wedding. And of course Caleb will welcome you in this house for as long as you wish to stay." His gaze wandered around the parlor as his mind wandered through memories. "It's comforting to see the house full again," he said wistfully. "With you two in my old room, and Joseph in my sisters' room, it will be like old times. May they last . . ."

"You needn't worry about that, old boy," Hugh Hardcastle interjected. "Phoebe and I have given the matter considerable thought, and you will be pleased to learn that we intend to stay right where we are, in this house, until young Thomas grows up, takes over the business and the house, and kicks us out. When he does, we will move in with Will and Adele on Ship Street. Adding my generous wages from Cutler & Sons to my Navy savings, and without having to worry about living expenses, we should be quite comfortable in Hingham, wouldn't you say, my dear?"

Phoebe Clausen Hardcastle was a lovely and charming woman, as one might expect of the wife of a Royal Navy post captain born to the manor and to the best English schools—and thus to the fantasies of many young women of society, and their mothers. She was several inches shorter than Hugh and nine years younger, and her lithe body retained a youthful allure. Although not of noble blood, she carried herself as regally as any marchioness. Equally important for a happy marriage, her sense of humor, when called for, and her sense of decorum, when required, matched Hugh's own—which was one reason, Katherine had observed, why they complimented each other so well. She had immediately loved Phoebe six years ago when she and Lizzy Crabtree had sailed with their children to England to visit with their parents one last time and to attend Hugh and Phoebe's wedding at the family church in Fareham.

"My husband's wit," Phoebe said, taking Hugh's hand without looking at him, "sometimes gets the better of him. I must apologize on his behalf. The truth is, I very much doubt that Will and Adele will have us when we're 'kicked out of here,' as my husband has it. By that time they will doubtless be living in splendor on Beacon Hill near Adele's parents." She dropped her mock seriousness to add, "Oh, they are such fine people, Adele. I especially admire your mother. She is beautiful and gracious, just as you are, and clearly she cares very much about you all. I can only imagine her relief this evening. Joseph told me that when *Dove*'s company sailed from Boston this afternoon, Will was on his way to Belknap Street to inform your parents of everyone's safe return. She will be overjoyed."

"Indeed she will," Katherine said, so softly that only her husband heard her.

"Thank you, Mrs. Hardcastle," Adele said. She started to add something, hesitated, thought better about what she was going to say, and then thought better about not saying it. "Will and I would love to have you and Captain Hardcastle stay with us on Ship Street," she said. "That goes without saying. But the truth is, that is not going to be possible. And not because of any future move to Boston."

Everyone in the parlor cast her a curious look, more so when her cheeks flushed bright pink. "You see," she explained, "we have only one extra bedroom in our house. And that room is no longer available as a guest room. We are turning it into a nursery."

Silence, and then Katherine asked cautiously, "Adele, are you telling us . . ."

Adele beamed at her mother-in-law. "*Oui, maman,*" she said, reverting to her native French for this delicate announcement. "*Je suis enceinte.* Will asked me not to say anything about it until he could be here, but I could not stop myself. Tonight seems so perfect!"

Katherine was up in an instant to take Adele in her arms, trying through her tears to express her joy. The others gathered round to give their own hugs and kisses of congratulations.

The evening ended with more laughter when Hugh Hardcastle, flush with drink, proclaimed loudly to his wife, "My God, my dear. These young people are showing us up. I say it's time you and I get cracking!" In truth, there was an element of poignancy in the amusement. Everyone in the room was aware that more than two years earlier Phoebe had given birth to an infant daughter who had died in the womb, and that she and her husband had been unable to conceive again.

As JULY slipped warmly into August and the first inklings of autumn chilled the night air, the Cutlers became increasingly engrossed in family matters. In addition to Will and Adele's welcomed announcement, which ignited a profusion of back-and-forth visits between the Cutler family in Hingham and the Endicott family in Boston, the final details of Diana's wedding required attention. Early in the month, a Navy dispatch announced that Jamie Cutler should be home in time for the wedding. Although *Constitution* remained on station in the Mediterranean, some of her officers who had been on duty for more than three years were being rotated off and granted extended shore leave. *Chesapeake* was due to relieve *Constitution* as flagship of the Mediterranean Squadron in several months. The official dispatch, signed by Lyle Pearson, clerk of the Navy Department, went on to request that Richard Cutler reconsider his decision to resign his commission. Impressments and ship seizures at sea were on the increase now that the proposed Monroe-Pinkney Treaty, which was to have repaired relations with England, had come undone. Certain U.S. Navy warships currently held in ordinary would soon be recalled to active service, and the Navy Department was most anxious to have Capt. Richard Cutler reassume command of *Portsmouth*. A personal note scrawled at the bottom of the dispatch in the hand of Secretary Robert Smith appealed to Richard's patriotism, and to his sense of honor and duty.

"Why did negotiations break down?" Hugh Hardcastle asked the morning after Richard received the dispatch. He and Agreen Crabtree were talking with Richard in the original Cutler & Sons shipping office at Baker's Yard near Hingham Harbor. It was tight quarters compared with the family's spacious countinghouse on Long Wharf in Boston, but the family kept the office nevertheless. It carried great sentimental value while providing space for family members in Hingham to discuss business affairs in quiet and familiar surroundings. Both men already knew that Richard had tendered his resignation from the Navy; they had, after all, made the same decision. But Richard had sworn them to secrecy until he felt the circumstances right to tell Katherine and other family members. Specifically, he wanted to wait until Jamie returned home.

"I'm rather out of the loop these days," Hugh admitted. "I was aware that Mr. Monroe, your minister to Great Britain, was negotiating a treaty with Lord Holland and Lord Auckland on behalf of Mr. Grenville," referring to the leader of what had come to be known as the 'Ministry of All the Talents.' "But I hadn't realized that the negotiations had broken down. More's the pity that William Pitt died in January. I daresay the outcome would have been quite different had he been around to direct things. Not only was he a strong advocate of American rights, he actually *liked* you chaps in the colonies."

"*Us* chaps in the colonies, you mean," Richard corrected him. "You're one of us now, Hugh. From what I understand," he continued, "negotiations didn't break down. Secretary of State Madison received the full draft of the treaty from Mr. Monroe and found it acceptable. But President Jefferson rejected it outright and refused to send it on to Congress for approval."

"Why, in heaven's name?"

"I believe he found the treaty lacking on the issue of impressment. It may have adequately addressed trading rights between the two countries, but to Jefferson, impressment is the predominant issue and is nonnegotiable. He has made it clear, time and again, that he will not tolerate British seizures of American ships and citizens at sea."

"Nor should he," Agreen put in. "How long d'you think King George would tolerate havin' *his* ships and sailors seized? I'd wager about as much time as a half-cocked rooster would last in a sex-starved hen house."

"I agree with you," Hugh said, "although I would not have put it quite that way. It *is* an abominable practice, however much the Royal Navy may require additional hands to man its ships. Precious few Englishmen are volunteering these days in spite of the French threat. However poorly that fact may speak to English patriotism, the question on the table is what your president intends to do now. Without a treaty of sorts, we're back to sailing in stormy waters. So . . . what do *you* think Jefferson will do, Richard? What *can* he do?"

The voice was his brother-in-law's, but the words were those of Jean Lafitte, and Richard still had no idea how to answer. "I don't know," he said, "but he'll have to do something. Congress and the American public will demand action. As will the president's own conscience. Nevertheless, I fear that whatever he does decide to do will have grave consequences."

"Count on it," Agreen said.

THAT SAME evening, for a reason he could not explain even to himself, Richard cast aside his resolution to wait and read the dispatch from the Navy Department aloud to his wife. They were sitting side by side on a sofa before a crackling fire in the parlor of their home on South Street, in what had become a nightly ritual for them, whatever the weather. This was their time together, their sanctuary from the cares and concerns of the outside world. A glass or two of red Bordeaux helped to keep those cares and concerns in proper perspective.

"You resigned your commission?" Katherine asked incredulously. "Why would you do such a thing? *When* did you do such a thing?"

"During our layover in Portsmouth. I included a personal letter to Secretary Smith in the dispatch I sent to the Navy Department. I had hoped Mr. Smith might be in Portsmouth—he often is—but it turned out he was in Washington. I wanted to tell you at the time, but I feared you would try to dissuade me."

"I would most certainly have tried to dissuade you, Richard. The Navy is your life. You love the Navy. Why did you do it?"

He stared into the fire. "I'm getting on, Katherine. I'm not the young man I used to be. Command is best given to younger sea officers, and our Navy is fortunate to have a boatload of them who have been battle-tested in the Mediterranean. 'Preble's boys' are the Navy's future. Jamie is one of them, I'm happy to say. You've heard me speak of some of the others: Stephen Decatur and James Lawrence, for example. And of course Eric Meyers."

"I have heard you speak of them often, and indeed they sound like exemplary officers. Now tell me the *real* reason you resigned your commission."

Her inquiring eyes seemed always to see through to his very core. "You're right about one thing, Katherine," he said. "I *do* love the Navy. I am honored to have been given the opportunity to serve my country in the way I have. But you're wrong when you say that the Navy is my life. *You* are my life. Our children, our family: *this* is my life. The whole truth is that I no longer have either the ability or the desire to sail away from you for months or years on end. That part of my life I have cherished, but that part of my life is now over, as it should be. There is plenty for me to do right here in Hingham and Boston. It's where I want to be and where I *need* to be."

"You are doing this for me, then," she said softly.

"No," he said, "I'm doing it for myself. I love you, Katherine. Neither of us knows what the future holds for us. But whatever it holds, we will face it together. Not separated by thousands of miles, but here, together, where we have lived and loved for so many years."

Katherine said nothing further. She rested her head on Richard's shoulder and felt his arm adjusting to make her more comfortable. She stared blankly into the dying flames in the hearth until she heard her hus-

band drift off to sleep. Then, finally, she too succumbed to the blissful
dark, safe for the moment within the tender embrace of her husband.
Safe, too, for yet another day, from the terrible secret she was carrying
silently within her, and that she dared not speak of, whatever the consequences, until the inevitable day of reckoning.

Seven

Hingham, Massachusetts
Fall 1806

THE CEREMONY uniting Peter Sprague and Diana Cutler was mostly a South Shore affair. Relatives and close friends from away were invited, of course, and those able to attend filled First Parish Church to beyond capacity, forcing many of the male attendees to stand in the back of the church and in the narthex. But there was little of the pomp and ceremony that had marked the wedding of Will Cutler and Adele Endicott in this same church four years earlier. Today, the cream of Boston society remained in Boston—with one notable exception. As Jack and Anne-Marie Endicott, in company with their daughter Frances and Frances' fiancé, Robert Pepperell, approached the center of town along North Street, they caused many heads to turn and tongues to wag. Many, perhaps most, citizens of Hingham had never before seen a coach-and-eight replete with English-style coachman, footman, and postilion dressed in full livery.

After the Reverend Henry Ware conferred God's blessings on yet another Cutler wedding, the entourage and invited guests—who included most of the population of Hingham—repaired to Caleb and Joan Cutler's home on Main Street for the traditional post-ceremony fun, fiddling, and feasting. The air was crisp, and thick, leaden clouds covered the sky. When shards of sunshine managed to break through, a golden brilliance highlighted the nascent splendor of autumn colors against the backdrop of dark, brooding pewter. The clash of seasons posed a constant threat of quick-soaking squalls, and the more devout among the guests cast their eyes skyward and prayed that the rain would hold off for several more hours.

Diana Cutler Sprague was not among those who did. She paid scant attention to the weather as she, arm-in-arm with Peter, made the rounds outside and inside the house. Tradition suggested that the bride and groom need not linger long at such an event, and the newlyweds wished to pay their respects to as many people as possible before departing for Stockbridge. That picturesque village, nestled at the foot of the Berkshire Mountains of western Massachusetts, was renowned for its English missionary roots, its magnificent scenery, and the Red Lion Inn, a hostelry with a well-established reputation for hospitality, fine cuisine, and discretion. The honeymooners would be gone for ten days, giving them a solid week together in Stockbridge to explore the wonders of Man and Nature.

"My dears," Katherine Cutler said as she bade them good-bye near the stage and hired driver waiting on Main Street. "You have given me one of the happiest days of my life. Thank you for that gift." She embraced first Peter and then her only daughter.

As she withdrew from their embrace, Diana looked deep into her mother's hazel eyes, mirror images of her own. "Thank you for all you have done for me, Mother—every day of my life." She clasped her mother to her again, harder this time.

"Go now, my darling," Katherine whispered to her. "Go with God; go with your husband; and go with my love forever."

Diana, swiping at tears, embraced her father and Peter's parents in turn and then let Peter hand her up into the stage. At the crack of the driver's whip the coach lurched forward, clattering down Main Street and across South Street before taking a sharp left on North Street at Albert Fearing's house.

After the stage had disappeared, Richard gently pulled his wife against his side. "Will you come back into the house with me, Katherine?"

"You go along," Katherine said, still staring at the spot where the carriage had disappeared. "I'll join you in a minute."

"Very well," Richard said reluctantly. "I'll have a glass of Madeira waiting for you in the parlor. We could both use a glass of that, I think."

Katherine gave him the inkling of a smile. "I think we could both use a *lot* of that."

As he made his way back across the fairground-like lawn, where merriment was backsliding into raucous and rowdy behavior, Richard noticed Anne-Marie Endicott approaching him. She was elegantly attired, as was her wont in public, and the sight of her took his breath away, as it had every time he had seen her since he had spirited her out of Paris on the eve of the French Revolution. Her husband at the time, Marquis Bernard-René de Launay, the last royal governor of the Bastille, had been seized when that bastion fell and was summarily decapitated by a mob hell-bent on revenge for the marquis' stoic defense of King Louis and the *ancien régime*. Richard had first met Anne-Marie Helvétian a decade earlier in Paris, during the high noon of the American Revolution, when she, an alluring young woman of savoir faire and Swiss heritage, had been a protégé of Benjamin Franklin, and he, a young, sexually naïve midshipman, had served as aide-de-camp to Capt. John Paul Jones. They had danced the minuet together at Versailles; they had attended a performance of *The Barber of Seville* together at the Tuilleries Palace; and they had fallen head over heels into bed together at the Helvétian residence in Passy. The memories of those few idyllic days had continued to tantalize them both, long after Richard had risked all in 1789 to snatch the beautiful marquise and her two young daughters from the holocaust consuming Paris and spirit them away to America in his sloop *Falcon*. Since arriving in Boston, Anne-Marie Helvétian de Launay had regained her former wealth and social status by marrying Jack Endicott.

She came up to him and said in a concerned voice, "Is Katherine all right?"

"I think so," Richard replied. "I suspect she's feeling as I do: a little down despite the joy of the day."

Anne-Marie nodded knowingly. "Let me talk to her."

Anne-Marie joined Katherine on Main Street and followed her longing gaze. "Four years ago," she said softly, "I watched from this very spot as a carriage took Adele and Will to the Hingham docks. I was so very happy for her, to have married such a fine young man as your son. And yet, do you know what I remember most about that moment? It was the pain of loss. My beloved daughter had left my home and my side to live with someone else; and in truth, at that moment, it didn't matter to me who that someone else was or how right he might be for her. She was with him, not me, and I knew that would never change. One of the hardest things for a mother to do is watch a daughter ride off with her prince, especially a daughter with whom you have been so close. I never bore a son; but I imagine it is easier for a mother to watch a son ride off than a daughter."

"Perhaps a little easier," Katherine acknowledged.

"Trust me, my dear," Anne-Marie went on, "your heartache will ease. You won't see Diana as often as you once did, but when you do see her, a new relationship will open up to you and the ties will be stronger than ever, in ways you cannot appreciate today.

"And," she added conclusively, "you have the great comfort of having Richard at your side. He knows your heart, and he loves you very much. My Jack, bless him, is a wonderful provider, but he does *not* understand much about personal feelings. Nor does he understand what it means to truly love someone else. He loves his business, but if a matter has no bearing on making money, he is likely to pay it scant attention. When my dear Frances marries in June, I will be left quite alone for much of the time. I will still have Jack, of course; but I'll be alone nonetheless."

JAMIE CUTLER was standing in the parlor when he noticed his father in the front hall conversing with a couple he did not recognize. But then again, he had been away at sea for three and a half years, and there were many people in attendance who were either unfamiliar to him or whose names he could not recall. He was turning his attention back to his conversation with his cousin Joseph and Frances Endicott when a tall, svelte figure across the room caught his eye. Although her back was to him, he had no trouble recognizing the blond curls flowing fetchingly across her shoulders and down the back of her elegant white empire gown. Jamie had known Melinda Conner since both were children. She had been his sister's closest friend since their earliest recollections, and as such she had been an attendant to the bride, as he and Will had been to the groom. During the ceremony, as Reverend Ware cited Scripture and conferred the blessings of God, the Son, and the Holy Ghost upon this most sacred union and sanctuary, she and Jamie had cast furtive glances at one another. After the ceremony Jamie had been so besieged by friends and well-wishers that he had lost sight of her until this moment.

"You were *saying*, Jamie," Frances said brightly when it became clear that Jamie's attention had not returned to her.

"Sorry," Jamie said, returning his eyes front and center. To his surprise, he felt himself blushing. "Forgive me, Frances, but I just saw an old friend whom I need to greet. Will you two please excuse me?"

"Of course," Frances said, her disappointment evident. "As I must soon return to Boston, perhaps I won't see you again until June, at my own wedding. Assuming, of course, that all the forces of good on this earth can persuade you to attend."

During the awkward pause that ensued while Jamie tried to formulate a reply, Joseph put in chivalrously: "Go with my gratitude, cousin. I am delighted to have this lovely young lady's company to myself until her fiancé returns."

"Thank you, Joseph," Frances said, without taking her eyes off Jamie. "That was gallant of you. How very grateful I am to be in the presence of a gentleman."

"Joseph is certainly that," Jamie agreed cheerfully, adding: "If duty and circumstance allow me to attend your wedding, Frances, of course I will be there. It will be my great pleasure to see you married." He leaned forward to give her a quick buss on the cheek. As he did, she turned her head toward him and brushed her lips against his.

Blushing even more furiously now, Jamie bowed to her and turned away toward the group that included Diana's childhood friend. He held back until he deemed the moment right. Then, clearing his throat, he approached her from behind.

"Excuse me . . . Melinda?"

She turned and smiled brilliantly at the boy whose presence had once reduced her to shy giggles. She saw a man now, with her own brown eyes and tall height, his thick chestnut hair, coursing right to left across his forehead and falling below his ear, framing clean-shaven, finely chiseled facial features that marked his Anglo-Saxon descent.

"Yes, of course . . . James?"

He grinned. "How are you, Mindy? It's been a while and you have . . ." His voice faltered as his gaze swept appreciatively over her. " . . . *blossomed* since I last saw you."

"I'm glad you think so," she said evenly. "And I could say the same thing about you. How dashing you look in that sea officer's uniform! Not that I am the only one to notice. All the ladies in church had their eyes on you. Really, it was quite scandalous. So . . . how am I to address you? 'Lieutenant?' 'Commander?' 'Friend?' How?"

His response, "'Your Grace' will do nicely," made her laugh. "Very well then, Your Grace! It *was* a lovely wedding, wasn't it?" she continued. "Didn't Diana sparkle! She looked so beautiful standing at the altar, so much like your mother. Thank heaven she and Peter will be living in Hingham, at least for the foreseeable future. I don't know what I would do were she to move away. I think I would have to follow her."

"I should hate for that to happen," Jamie said quickly. "But you two have been friends for a long time. We Cutlers consider you a member of our family."

"Now *that* is a compliment I shall forever treasure."

She waited while a family acquaintance stopped to welcome Jamie home. Jamie thanked him and, as he watched him depart, noticed through a window that a burst of rain had sent the merry-makers outside scurrying for home or shelter.

"Nice man, Mr. Guild," Jamie commented.

"Nice, yes, but he can act rather oddly at times. How Mrs. Guild puts up with all of his shenanigans is really quite beyond me. She's such a gracious and lovely lady."

"Oh? What sort of shenanigans?"

Mindy laughed. "I daresay you have a lot of catching up to do when it comes to Hingham gossip, Lieutenant. I suggest we defer that topic to another occasion. For the moment, let me say that we are *all* so happy that you were able to make it home for the wedding—and such a grand entrance, too. You practically sailed in on the incoming tide as the ceremony began. Now that you're here, how long will you stay?"

"For a while, at least," Jamie said. "My orders are to rejoin my ship when she returns to Boston."

"When will that be?"

"She's to be relieved as flagship in March or April, so figure another six or seven weeks after that. *Constitution* may be a stout ship and the 'pride of New England,' but she is not a fast ship. It should take her that long to sail home from the Mediterranean, assuming seasonal headwinds."

"Well, then, it appears that Hingham will have the honor and glory of your presence for several months, at least."

"I doubt 'honor and glory' are the right words. But frankly, Miss Conner, I am more interested in your perspectives than in Hingham's. Might I humbly request the pleasure of your company on a ride with me to Nantasket Beach? It's something I used to do quite often with Mother and Diana, and I have sorely missed it. We can invite Will and Adele to join us, to keep everything proper, and I can catch up on Hingham gossip. I'm sure they will have a lot to contribute to *that* subject. Edna would be delighted to pack a picnic, and she packs a good one. So, what do you say? Would you care to do that? Specifically, would you care to do that some day next week?"

She tilted her head to one side and eyed him coyly. "I had heard that Navy men don't like to waste time."

"Truly, we don't," he replied. "But if you think that I am being too forward, Mindy, please tell me and I shall apologize. I've been long at sea in the company of unruly sailors. Under those conditions even a proper and well-intentioned young sea officer may forget the social niceties of requesting the companionship of a young lady of position. *Am* I being too forward with you?"

"Yes, you unbridled sweet-talker. You are being forward to the extreme."

"Then I apologize."

"Your apology is accepted," she said. "What time shall I expect you on Monday morning?"

THEIR ROUTE on Tuesday morning led them from the stables in Indian Hollow near Thomas' Pond, across Great Pasture, and onto Hull Street, an extension of East Street. When they crossed over the Weir Estuary at Mill Lane Bridge, they entered the village of Hull, a township incorporated in 1644 that comprised essentially a series of islands connected by sandbars jutting northward three miles into Massachusetts Bay. The long, thin, hooked peninsula ended at Pemberton Point, a mere five sea miles from Boston Harbor. It was from this spot that Brig. Gen. Benjamin Lincoln, who was to serve as General Washington's second in command at Yorktown in 1781 and who today, at age seventy-three, was Hingham's most famous resident, had surveyed the British evacuation of Boston in 1776.

To Jamie's disappointment, the squalls that had pummeled the area over the weekend had forced postponement of the picnic to Tuesday. The wind had shifted clockwise from the northeast to the northwest by Monday evening, a fair-weather cycle summoning in cool, dry Canadian air that felt chilly as they started out but warmed as the sun rose higher. The four young people rode at a constant walk, in deference to Adele's condition. When they came out on Nantasket Beach—a mile-long stretch of smooth, whitish-gray sand anchored on each end by craggy bluffs—they dismounted and walked together near the water's edge, their horses straggling behind.

No one spoke much at first because no one wanted to break the spell. The panorama of sparkling blue sea and sky seemed to enclose them within a different world, a retreat from the choreography of planning, postulating, and preparing that had consumed them all in various ways in recent weeks. The tide was out, increasing the size of the sandy beach twentyfold from the area available at high tide. The only other people in sight were six clam diggers halfway up the beach attacking the hard wet sand with shovels and short-handled iron rakes to pluck out the tasty mollusks residing a few inches under their feet. Gulls wheeled and mewed overhead while others stood in silent vigilance on the beach, alert for any discarded morsel tossed in their direction.

By now, the air had warmed enough to allow Jamie to doff his coat and roll up the sleeves of his white cotton shirt. As he did, Mindy gasped.

"James, let me see your arm."

"What?"

"Your right forearm. Let me see it."

He held his arm out to her, and she cradled it in her left hand as she examined the long, jagged, white scar that ran from just above his wrist to almost the elbow. "Where did you get this?" she asked, still staring at the scar.

Jamie grinned. "I jilted a girl, and she came after me with a knife."

"Be serious, Jamie," Mindy said, never taking her eyes from the scar. With her right forefinger she traced its full length, her touch so light and tender that it caused him to shudder. She looked up at him. "You got this when you were fighting in Tripoli, didn't you?"

With her solemn brown eyes locked on his, he could not lie. He nodded.

"Ah," she said, releasing his arm. Then, in a transparent attempt to restore their lighthearted banter, "I think I prefer the jilted girl with the knife."

The four of them continued on down the beach, Jamie struggling to draw logic from what had just happened. That Mindy Conner—a stylish and well-bred young woman whom he had known for years, but only as his sister's friend—was so affected by his old wound moved him in a way that was new to him—and more than a little unsettling. Until this moment his naval career had been the primary focus of his life. Everything else, including dalliances with young women, however alluring, lagged far behind in importance. But Mindy's gentle touch had made him want to reconsider that. He chanced a look at her. She was walking beside Adele, staring down at the sand before her. What was she thinking? He would give a lot to know. He was conjuring up something meaningful to say to her when Will suddenly interjected, "Jamie, do you see that building up ahead?"

He was pointing toward a sturdy wooden hut near the other end of the beach up by the low-lying scrub that grew on the narrow stretch of land between the sea side and the bay side of Nantasket Peninsula. Tilted against the front of the hut was a dory secured to the structure by a complex of ropes.

"Of course I see it," Jamie replied. "It's been there for years. It was put there by the Humane Society to help rescue shipwrecked sailors. What of it?"

"Want to race? First one past it wins."

Jamie's lips turned up in a smile. He turned to Mindy and Adele. "By your leave, ladies?"

"By our leave, indeed," Adele said. "You little boys go off and play. Mindy and I will head back to the bluffs and attend to the serious business of preparing our picnic." She gave her husband a telling look. "Do me a favor, *ma chérie?*"

"Of course," Will said, poised with his left foot in the stirrup.

"Beat the tar out of him."

"My money's on you, Lieutenant," Mindy said after Jamie had secured himself in the saddle. She smiled up at him and then stepped back beside Adele, who held up an arm for several seconds before slashing it downward. Lost in Mindy's smile, Jamie nearly missed the signal.

Heels dug into flanks and the two horses sprang forward, freed at last from the confines of paddock and tight reins. Side by side the horses careened up the beach, splashing in and out of tidal pools, throwing up clumps of wet sand from their pounding hooves, froth foaming at their mouths, every last sinew of muscle engaged in the madcap race. It was too close to call as they veered slightly inland in near perfect synchrony to avoid the clam diggers, who interrupted their backbreaking work to watch as the two brothers thundered past at a full gallop, their legs straight and their heels, knees, and shoulders aligned, balancing their weight with their feet in the stirrups, their upper bodies crouched low and forward, their hands gripping reins and pushing down on the horses' necks in ever increasing and urgent rhythms. Just before crossing an imaginary line running down the beach from the hut, Will's horse gave him one last savage spurt of speed and the victory.

"Congratulations, Will," Jamie panted as they reined in their mounts in the shadow of the bluffs at the north end of the beach and came together at an easy gait. "The day is yours."

Will was patting and rubbing his horse's neck. "The hell you say," he countered. He nudged his horse around, as did Jamie, and together they started back toward the bluffs on the distant south end of the beach. "You should still be back there with those clammers. How did a Navy man learn to ride a horse so well?"

"Mother taught me, same as you. And also a Marine private from Kentucky that I served with in North Africa."

"Well, that explains it," Will commented dryly.

"Speaking of Mother, Will," Jamie said, after they had ridden a short distance, "how does she look to you?"

Will thought before answering. "She's more tired than usual. But she seems to be holding her own. Why do you ask?"

"I'm not sure. Maybe I'm reading too much into what I see. But you have seen her often over the past three years, and I not at all. The change that I'm seeing all at once happened gradually for you. She's far thinner and frailer than she was. I'm very worried about her."

"Perhaps you're right," Will offered. "She *is* three years older than when you left. And considering what she has been through these past few months—her surgery, the trip to Barbados, capture by pirates, planning Diana's wedding—I'm amazed she's getting along as well as she is. You know Mother: she could have had all the help she wanted, but she insisted on doing everything herself. She'll improve now that the wedding is over and she can rest. Having Joseph and Uncle Hugh here helps as well."

"Yes," Jamie agreed, and let it go at that. They rode on in silence until once again they were abreast of the clam diggers.

"Who won?" one of them shouted out.

Will and Jamie each pointed at the other. "He did," they shouted back in reply, igniting grins and chuckles.

Farther on, Jamie asked, "You're still thinking of joining the Navy, Will?"

Will kept his gaze dead ahead. "I am, for one stint; but only if I can sign on as a commissioned officer. I have no intention of serving as a midshipman. I'm too old for that."

"And too experienced," his brother observed. "You've circumnavigated the globe, and very few veteran naval officers can claim to have done that. Have you discussed it with Father?"

"I have."

"And . . . ?"

"He said that he'll oblige me with a letter to Secretary Smith. He can't promise results, of course. As you know, the Navy has tightened many of its systems and procedures, and the commissioning of officers is one of them. I'll have to wait and see."

"The Navy *has* tightened its procedures," Jamie said, "because it had to. Too many qualified junior officers were denied promotions when someone *un*qualified but with the right connections stepped in to fill an open position. I never saw that happen in my ship, but apparently *Constitution* is the exception, not the rule. As a result, an officer's commission is harder to come by these days. It has to be earned. That's the way it should be, of course. I take it that Father approves of your decision?"

"He doesn't disapprove," Will replied. "He'd rather not have both sons in the Navy at the same time, but he certainly understands my desire to serve. After all, my reasons are the same reasons that led him to enlist.

He also accepts my argument that my naval experience will advantage Cutler & Sons in the future. Now that he has resigned his own commission, he will be devoting much more of his time to the family business. That gives me leave to do what I must, but I will delay until after the baby is born. Adele has asked me to wait until then, and I have agreed, barring unforeseen circumstances."

"So you've discussed this with her as well?"

"I discussed it with her first," Will said firmly. "And she's open to it as long as I don't make the Navy my life, which I have no intention of doing. But if—perhaps I should say *when*—push comes to shove and this country finds itself in a war, I don't want to be sitting on the dock twiddling my thumbs. Adele understands that."

"If so, she's a rare woman."

"That she is. And so, by the bye, is Mindy, in case you haven't noticed."

"Of course I've noticed," Jamie grinned. "But cut me some slack, brother dear. I'm just home from the Mediterranean. My sea legs still aren't used to land. And I'm not about to rush into anything. As you say, we'll have to wait and see."

Eight

Chesapeake Bay
February 1807

Young Seth Cutler peered over the rim of his mug at a table three away from where he was sitting with two companions. The four men he held under scrutiny at that table were enjoying themselves immensely, and had been for quite some time. Now that the hour was getting late and multiple rounds of frothy ale had lubricated their speech, they had become more boisterous and less guarded, so much so that other patrons in the cozy public house were casting looks of disdain and indignation in their direction. That Seth could not make out what the men were actually saying to each other did not matter. What *did* matter was that their physical characteristics fit to a tee the description of four of the six tars who had recently run from HMS *Tigress* while she lay at anchor in Lynnhaven Bay. Their accents likewise made them worthy of attention.

Seth slid his eyes over to his two companions. Robert Larkin met his gaze and gave a brief nod, confirming his suspicions. Seth had been to England only once, as a boy traveling with his father, Robin Cutler, to the family's ancestral home in Fareham, north of Portsmouth. Larkin, however, was a Devon man, a West Country man, and he knew the dialects of that region like the back of his hand. As did Kenneth Duggan, the tall, burly man sitting between them sucking contentedly on a long-stemmed clay pipe.

"Steady, lads," Larkin cautioned under his breath.

A waiter stepped up to the table and served three steaming bowls of the mutton stew that was advertised as the house specialty on the hand-written menu, which offered four other entrées as alternatives. The three men ate in silence, occasionally dipping slabs of bread torn from a freshly baked loaf into the rich brown liquid, ever keeping a weather eye on the four men at the other table, ordinary seamen judging by the cut of their cloth. Each was wearing the loose-fitting slop-chest garb preferred by both merchant and navy sailors. Seth and his companions were wearing the same garb, their rank notwithstanding.

By the time the roaring fire in the hearth had burned down to flickers of blue flame, only five tables remained occupied. Waiters began cleaning and sweeping up, the cue for those who had lingered to pay their tab and be on their way. Robert Larkin reached into a side pocket and withdrew two U.S. gold quarter-eagles, placing them on the table and indicating with a small gesture to the waiter that he expected no change.

The waiter arched his eyebrows. "Why, thank you, sir," he said earnestly. "That is most generous of you."

"Think nothing of it, my good man," Larkin asserted. "The food and the service were impeccable, and we have occupied this table for the entire evening. We'll be on our way shortly."

"Stay as long as you please, sir," the waiter insisted. "No need for you kind gentlemen to hurry off. May I offer a round of our finest ale, on the house?"

"Thank you, no," Larkin said with a smile. "That is neither necessary nor advisable. We've drunk more than our fill."

At length, the four men at the other table hauled themselves up and fumbled about in their clothing for the wherewithal to pay their tab. Coins tinkled onto the tabletop, several of them falling off and rolling along the floor. A waiter picked up the fallen coins and added them to the pile on the table. After he carefully confirmed that the total was sufficient to cover the tab and a modest tip, the four men tugged on their overcoats, giggling at each other's clumsiness, and set out unsteadily toward the front door. One of them, propped up by two of his shipmates, started bellowing an off-key sea chantey about a Spanish woman of voluptuous build, robust sexual appetite, and exotic sexual preferences. The few remaining patrons in the alehouse looked on distastefully.

As the four men were about to stumble by Seth's table, Seth stuck out his leg. Two of the three in front tripped over it and lurched forward, off balance. Kenneth Duggan was up in a flash, springing like a leopard at its prey. Before the two could hit the deck, the wide span of the boatswain's muscular arms broke their fall.

"'Ere then, mateys," Duggan said, in a gentle, soothing tone. "That was a close one, it was. You're a right sorry sight, blotto as ye are. 'Ad a merry ole time of it t'night, did ye?"

The man who had been singing had gone silent. Struggling to his feet, he looked at Duggan with glazed eyes. "That we are," he slurred. "That we did," he corrected himself. With an effort he pulled himself away, struggling for balance, suddenly embarrassed by his drunkenness. "I be much obliged to ye, good sir. Me name's Cates, able seaman. Me and me mates 'ere are bound for Havana in the mornin' and was enjoyin' our last night ashore. We best be shovin' off so's we can sleep it off." He giggled at his turn of phrase; nonetheless, he sounded a bit more sober when he said, "If you'll please excuse us."

"We're shoving off ourselves," Robert Larkin interjected in a friendly tone. "Me mates and me would be pleased to see ye to yer vessel. No telling what or who's lurking out there in the darkness, and we fo'c'sle types need to watch out for each other, eh? T'would be our honor. What say ye?"

"I say God's mercy on ye," Cates replied, a blessing echoed by his three shipmates.

After exchanging brief introductions the group set out. The route they followed in the not uncomfortably cool air of late February took them from the alehouse on Orleans Street across Eastern Avenue and then across Fleet Street, the intersection a stone's throw from the Baltimore office of Cutler & Sons, and on to Lancaster Street. From there it was an easy walk to the shipyards on Locust Point Peninsula, located adjacent to a newly constructed, star-shaped fortress named in honor of James McHenry, a Scots-Irish immigrant who, as President Washington's secretary of war, had been a leading advocate of the need for such a fort to protect the commercial hub that defined Baltimore Harbor.

Along the route, the seven men engaged in loose chatter about the sorts of things sailors of all nations found important: ships, the sea, and women. Within the half hour they reached Locust Point, where an impressive array of merchant vessels of various sizes and rigs lay nested bow-out on the quays, their yards set a-cockbill to avoid entanglement. In those thirty minutes Cates and his three shipmates had sobered sufficiently to offer firm handshakes as they bid farewell to their newfound friends. Larkin and his two companions waited until the four sailors had trudged up a gangplank onto their vessel and all was quiet along the waterfront.

"You've taken note of that snow, Duggan?" Larkin inquired. He was referring to the vessel's rig. A snow was similar in design to a two-masted brig but differed in that a square sail was furled on the lower yard of her mainmast while the gaff of her fore-and-aft trysail was secured to a shorter jack mast stepped a foot abaft the mainmast.

"That I 've, sir. Her name's *Dolphin*."

"So I see. Anything to add, Mr. Cutler?"

"Only that she's lying low in the water, sir. Whatever her cargo may be, she has it on board."

"Yes. And that cargo will slow her." Larkin had also noticed, as certainly his shipmates had, that the snow carried three guns on each side of her weather deck. But they were small guns, 3- or 4-pounders judging by their muzzles, and the threat they posed to a fourth rate was so puny as to be laughable.

"Gentlemen," he said with a smile, "let us return to our ship. Our captain is most keen to hear our report."

ALTHOUGH BRISK northerly winds propelled the single-masted, double-banked cutter at a rousing clip, it took the balance of the night and much of the next morning to cover the one hundred sea miles separating Baltimore from the mouth of the Potomac River. Speed, however, was not essential. Whatever time *Dolphin* cast off her lines, she would plot a similar course down the Chesapeake, through the Thimble Shoals Channel west of Cape Henry, and out into the Atlantic; the cutter thus had a healthy lead on her. Robert Larkin nevertheless ordered the two-man auxiliary crew who had been standing by in the cutter to snatch every breath of air possible within the taut bellies of the mainsail and jib, sheeted out wing-on-wing so far that they lay nearly at right angles to the 24-foot craft. Not long after the morning sun had risen above the low-lying eastern shore of the bay and spread its meager warmth across the light chop, Larkin ordered Seth Cutler to relieve Seaman Paulus at the tiller, just as Paulus had relieved Seaman Kelliher three hours earlier. Larkin then shifted position from the stern sheets to the bow thwart, just aft of the cutter's collapsible bowsprit. From there he kept a wary eye ahead into the widening waters between the bay's eastern and western shores.

When the cutter entered the widest part of the bay, thirty miles from shore to shore, Larkin ordered her close in toward the Virginia coast. Ahead, in Tangier Sound on the Maryland side of the bay, two French frigates lay at anchor, and these he wanted to avoid. The two third rates had been bottled up for months, virtual prisoners of a Royal Navy squadron based in Lynnhaven Bay and prowling the waters off the Virginia Capes. That America's largest and most fertile estuary had become a potential battleground for European belligerents galled Americans of every region and every political stripe. That the British squadron was based at the very doorstep of the American naval base at Hampton Roads galled the Navy Department no end. President Jefferson and Secretary of State Madison, however, had done little in response beyond registering routine diplomatic protests in Paris and London. Navy secretary Robert Smith had ordered the U.S. Navy to stand down unless American lives and property were threatened. After all, Smith had noted, the United States had invited the British to use Lynnhaven Bay as a temporary base. Or at least it had not denied them the opportunity.

In due course the three masts of a significant ship loomed into view. She was anchored a half mile south of where the Potomac emptied into the Chesapeake, and any Virginia tobacco farmer could readily identify her as a British warship even without the red-crossed white ensign flying from the gaff peak of her mizzen. Although she was more or less the same size as a U.S. Navy superfrigate and had a similar top-hamper, her two tiers of guns set her apart: twenty-two 24-pounder guns on her lower gun deck and twenty-two 12-pounder guns on her upper gun deck, plus four 6-pounder guns on her quarterdeck, three to a side, and two 6-pounder bow-chasers on her forecastle. She was a 50-gun *Portland*-class fourth rate, designed by her Portsmouth shipwright in 1776 to be a ship of the line. Today, however, the British Admiralty considered her firepower too limited to engage in fleet actions against the 100-gun leviathans she would have to face.

And unlike virtually all U.S. Navy warships, HMS *Leopard* boasted a stern richly adorned with two tiers of mullioned windows, white trim all around, a glossy blue band painted starboard to larboard beneath the lower tier, and four chaste maidens in flowing pewter-gray robes: one each at the starboard and larboard edges of the stern, and two others positioned in toward the center. It was this decorative stern that Robert Larkin and his shipmates took in after they had swept past the cruiser, come about into the wind, doused main and jib, and run out a set of oars through rowlocks cut into the cutter's top strake.

As they were pulling toward the larboard entry port, a figure wearing a fore-and-aft bicorne hat popped up at the taffrail.

"Boat ahoy!" his prepubescent voice called down. The hail of the junior watch officer was a matter of protocol only. Those on board *Leopard* had long since identified the cutter as one of their own ship's boats.

"Boat, aye!" Seth Cutler shouted up, those two words signifying that there was a commissioned officer on board the approaching boat. That he held up no fingers signaled that the officer was not of senior rank and therefore did not require a formal side party at the entry port.

As the cutter coasted in under the ship's larboard quarter gallery, Seaman Kelliher, stationed in the bow with a boathook, made ready to latch on to the mainmast chain-wale. He lunged, and the hook found its mark. Kelliher hauled the cutter up to the chain-wale, secured the bowline to the thick plank of oak jutting out from it, and then played the line out until the cutter had drifted back up beside the steps built into the ship's tumble-home. Robert Larkin was first up, in deference to his rank of third lieutenant; he was followed by Midshipman Cutler and then Boatswain Duggan. Seamen Paulus and Kelliher remained in the cutter to disassemble and stow the mast and bowsprit, and to otherwise aid the deck crew assigned to hauling the ship's boat back on board to her normal position above the main hatch.

First Lieutenant Bradford Morse met the returning officers at the entry port. "Welcome back," he said, returning their salutes. From the belfry, located at the break of main deck and forecastle, the ship's bell chimed six times in three double hits. "A fruitful sojourn, I trust?"

"I believe it was, sir," Larkin replied.

"Excellent. And how did you find the city of Baltimore, Mr. Cutler?"

"I found it interesting, sir," Seth replied.

"Yes, I thought you might. Didn't happen to run into one of your American cousins, did you?"

Seth stood at stiff attention. "No, sir, I did not."

Morse studied him a moment, then: "I imagine you three to be a bit cold and hungry. Might I suggest you go below for a change of clothes and a bite to eat? Mr. Larkin, you and I shall confer with Captain Humphreys at seven bells—unless, of course, you see a need for greater urgency."

"I do not, sir," Larkin assured him. "Seven bells will serve."

"Very well. In thirty minutes, then."

THE LOOKOUT stationed on the fighting top secured to the head of the lower mainmast was the first to make out the black hulk. It was not an easy sighting; the moon was in its dark phase, and stars and planets peeking out between scattered clouds provided the only light from the heavens above. But the mass was dark, darker than the night itself, and it was standing to the southeast and moving slowly, like a phantom, in a sea breeze that had all but died during the late evening. Once the phantom was in the seaman's sight, however, he had her cold. He had no need for a night glass. She was not far off, and the seaman could see well enough with his naked eye to determine that the rig on this vessel was similar to the rig he had been ordered to watch for.

The seaman called softly below to report his sighting. A deck officer relayed his message aft to the quarterdeck; from there a duty midshipman relayed it to the captain's after cabin located beneath the ship's poop deck. Within the minute, Captain Humphreys stepped out onto the quarterdeck, buttoning up his gilt-edged blue uniform coat and smoothing his unruly ash-colored hair before setting upon it, just so, a gilt-edged bicorne hat.

At age twenty-eight, Humphreys was tall, handsome, and lean—and highly respected both by his ship's officers and by his superiors at the Admiralty. His no-nonsense attitude and his ability to make hard decisions and get things done had won him many accolades. The third son of a vicar and his wife, Humphreys had entered the Royal Navy through the "hawser hole," not through a "wardroom quarter gallery" as was true of many of Britain's senior naval officers. He had enlisted in 1790 as an able seaman and had worked his way up through the ranks to post captain as a result of his achievements, not his pedigree or "interest" in Whitehall or Parliament. His derring-do in the North Sea and the West Indies had caught the eyes of My Lords of the Admiralty in London and, soon thereafter, the heart of a rich English heiress living in Kent. Their marriage had made Humphreys a very wealthy man, a status that seemed to suit him as perfectly as the elegant blue, white, and gold uniform he had become accustomed to wearing.

Second Lieutenant Trevor Elliot touched his hat. "Good evening, Captain."

"Good evening, Mr. Elliot," Humphreys replied. "What do we have?"

"We have sighted a two-masted vessel, sir," the senior officer of the deck replied. "She appears to be snow-rigged."

"The *Dolphin*, then."

"It would seem so, sir. Mr. Larkin and Mr. Cutler were quite specific in their description of her. We won't know for certain until first light."

"Quite so, Lieutenant," Humphreys acknowledged. He scoured the waters where Elliot had pointed. Yes, there she was: a dark shape standing in toward shore under jib, topsails, and what appeared to be a trysail. "Well, whoever she is," he said to his officer, "we shall shadow her throughout the night and in the morning see what we see. I want all running lights kept extinguished and the ship rigged for night sailing. Unless, of course, she starts to get away from us, in which case we shall have to set additional canvas to keep her close. No doubt she has spotted us, and to be safe, she will hug the shore. May these light northerlies continue. Were we to sail too far south and too far in, we should have the Hatteras shoals to contend with, and perhaps a lee shore. Be aware of that, Mr. Elliot, and please inform me immediately of any changes."

Elliot touched a forefinger to his hat. "Aye, Captain."

Early the next morning, under dark cloud cover that threatened rain or sleet or a dreary combination, the sighting was confirmed. The vessel in question was indeed a snow, and the name painted in bold black script on her stern was summoned into sharp focus by a long glass. She stood not more than a mile downwind from *Leopard*, and although the British warship was flying neither her ensign nor her jack, those in the snow clearly had recognized the British warship for what she was. *Dolphin* had pressed on all sail and was running as best she could west-southwest toward the Virginia shoreline lying low on the horizon. The officers in *Leopard* were well aware that the shoreline harbored, among other amenities, the U.S. naval base at Hampton Roads.

"She's showing us her heels, sir," First Officer Bradford Morse, newly arrived on the quarterdeck, commented to Captain Humphreys.

"Showing us her guilt is what you mean, Mr. Morse," Humphreys replied airily. "If she had no reason to run from us, *why* would she run? She knows who we are and what we're about. So, by God, we shall accommodate her. Clap on all sail."

"Aye, Captain."

Boatswain Duggan issued the order, and twittering boatswain's pipes sent sailors scurrying to their stations. On the lowest yards the main and fore courses fell into position and were sheeted home just as sugar-white topgallants sprouted above the three topsails, and royals sprouted above them. Barring the unforeseen, this race had only one possible outcome. A heavily laden merchant vessel was no match for a copper-bottomed warship that had set all plain sail to royals. Although in these light sea breezes it took nearly an hour to close the gap between the two vessels, it was evident to all concerned that the heavy cruiser would indeed close that gap before the snow could reach the safety that remained tauntingly within view. It was a question of mathematics as much as seamanship.

"Give her a hail, Mr. Morse," Humphreys said when the British warship was even with the American vessel and fifty yards upwind of her. *Leopard*'s crew lowered her royals and topgallants and raised her main and fore courses to their yard to slow her and keep her abreast of *Dolphin*.

Morse picked up a speaking trumpet and demanded that the snow douse her trysail, square her main topsail, and heave to.

Seconds ticked by with no response from the snow. Morse repeated his demands and issued a stern warning of the consequences of not responding. Still nothing happened. *Dolphin* remained on course.

"Give her a warning shot," Humphreys demanded, his dander rising.

Leopard's larboard bow-chaser barked, and orange flame and white sparks vomited forth within a swirl of acrid smoke that the prevailing breeze carried toward the snow. The ball struck the sea ahead of the snow and sent up a plume of white water.

Dolphin sailed on, as if oblivious to the vision of terrible beauty hovering so close to starboard.

"My God!" Humphreys snarled. "That ship's master either has balls of iron or he's a bloody dunderhead. What on earth does he intend?"

"If I may, sir," Morse said, his eyes fixed on the merchantman, "I believe he intends to ignore us. He's calling our bluff. He's betting that a British warship will not fire into an American merchant vessel."

"I believe you are right, Mr. Morse," Humphreys mused. "I believe you are right. The bastard's playing a dangerous game. I shall have the larboard gun ports opened and the guns run out."

"Aye, Captain," Morse said and issued the order. "Larboard ports opened and guns run out, sir," he confirmed moments later.

Humphreys considered the opportunity and the possible ramifications of pursuing that opportunity. As he saw it, both might and right were entirely on his side. He had strict orders from the admiral of the North American Station in Halifax to pursue and bring to justice British deserters from whatever hole they might be dragged out of. There was no question about the order, and no question that there were British deserters on *Dolphin*. Whitehall could not and would not tolerate desertion from a Royal Navy vessel, consequences be damned, and the most reliable safeguard against desertion was swift and ruthless punishment of those foolish enough to cross the line. If hapless bystanders were maimed or killed in the course of dispensing British justice, well, that was regrettable.

"Stand by, number two battery," Humphreys said to his first officer.

"Aye, Captain," Morse said before repeating the order to the deck officer and so on down the line.

Number two battery was located forward from amidships on the upper gun deck and consisted of four 12-pounder guns: guns 5 and 7 on the larboard side, and guns 6 and 8 on the starboard side. At the moment, the sights of the battery's two larboard guns were trained level at *Dolphin*'s starboard hull. Midshipman Seth Cutler, the battery's commanding officer, received the order to stand by from a younger midshipman acting as the captain's messenger.

With a practiced eye, Seth checked the powder and shot within the two gleaming black muzzles. After informing the individual gun captains that he intended to take charge of firing the guns, he ordered each man in the two six-man gun crews to take position. When the next order was delivered a few minutes later by the same midshipman, Seth stepped aside to position himself between the two guns, ordered his gun crew to step back away from the recoil, and seized hold of the lanyard of gun 5.

"*Firing!*" he shouted and yanked hard on the lanyard. An explosion of gunpowder thundered across the gun deck. Seth wheeled around and repeated the process with gun 7. A second explosion sent another shudder along the 120-foot deck that was instantly reinforced by the harsh rumble of a gun carriage rocketing inboard until checked by its breeching ropes. Then, all was quiet except for the distant cries of stricken men in a stricken vessel.

Seth Cutler stepped up to a gun port and peered out at *Dolphin* lying slightly astern. One round shot had punched a sizable gash in her mainmast and had sprung a mainstay. Judging by the snow's haphazard movements, Seth deemed it likely that the second shot had damaged her steering mechanism.

Leopard had heaved to, and Seth could overhear orders from the deck above to lower the ship's launch and make ready a detachment of Marines. Lieutenant Larkin was to command the boarding party, and Seth could only imagine, not without a sting of empathy, the expression on the face of Seaman Cates and his three shipmates as Larkin boarded the snow to make the arrests. Just two nights earlier they had all been friends on the walk from a Baltimore public house to *Dolphin*. Now those four sailors and perhaps others were destined for London to appear before an Admiralty court. It was a foregone conclusion that they would be found guilty: the U.S. merchant fleet had become a haven for British tars running from the harsh realities of the Royal Navy toward the higher pay, better food, and greater leniency normally found in American merchantmen. British courts of law, however, recognized neither the right of expatriation nor the principle of sailors' rights. To their mind, a British sailor born in Great Britain or to British parents remained British to his grave regardless of where he lived, whose flag he sailed under, or what naturalization papers he might possess. "Once an Englishman, always an Englishman," was Whitehall's view, and British courts of law concurred—notwithstanding the simple fact that nearly the entire population of the United

States fell within the purview of that statement. Better if Cates had died quickly from a round shot, Seth thought to himself as the launch was lowered away, than the slow death he would suffer kicking.and gagging at the end of a rope strung up over a lower foremast yard.

Regardless of his personal feelings, Seth recognized that the law was the law, pure and simple. As a warrant officer in the Royal Navy soon to take his lieutenant's exam, Seth Cutler was sworn to uphold British law and to defend the honor, sanctity, and dignity of His Majesty's empire. He would not waver from that oath.

Nine

Boston, Massachusetts
April 1807

"RICHARD? Are you with us?" The words were a distant echo barely penetrating the nightmare that had all but consumed Richard for nearly a week. Had duty not compelled his presence on Long Wharf, he would not have left her. Only his responsibility to his blood and bond had dragged him away. "Sorry, Jack," he said with a forced laugh. "I took a side trip, there. I'm back now." He shifted in his chair, aware of Jack Endicott's eyes upon him. The concern in those eyes was mirrored in those of Caleb Cutler, Agreen Crabtree, George Hunt, Hugh Hardcastle, and Richard's two sons, Will and Jamie. But he would offer no further explanation—neither to them nor to anyone else. Katherine had sworn him to secrecy. She had begged him to remain silent, and he would honor her plea.

"You're quite certain all is well?" Endicott persisted.

"Quite certain. Please continue. You were saying what about our agent in Washington?"

Endicott smiled wryly. "I introduced the subject of Mr. Shaw a few minutes ago, Richard. Perhaps I should start again from the beginning. This time around, I would appreciate everyone's full attention. The matter at hand is of considerable importance to us all."

"You have my attention," Richard said, unable to keep an edge from his voice.

"Very well, then. Here is the situation." Endicott cleared his throat. "The Royal Navy has closed European ports to American shipping— unless we first trade through a British port and pay a substantial levy on the goods we are intending to ship elsewhere. Unless we do what those meddling jackanapes tell us to do—meaning we do not attempt to trade directly with nations on the Continent—we run a considerable risk of having our merchantmen intercepted at sea, their cargoes confiscated, and our sailors impressed into the Royal Navy—even those who can substantiate American citizenship. That is bad enough, but thanks to our government's bungling efforts in dealing with England, we now run those same risks even if we *are* intending to trade through a British port. Mr. Hunt, if you would, please tell us how many of our merchantmen have been intercepted during the past twelve months?"

George Hunt made a show of consulting his notes, although he knew the tally by heart. "By the British, nine C&E vessels, Mr. Endicott," Hunt quoted as if from Scripture, "and seven Cutler & Sons vessels. According to our agent in London, five of these vessels are currently being detained in England. We have yet to be informed of their disposition. Two other vessels are being detained on the Continent by the French: one in Lorient, the other in Rotterdam. One other C&E vessel remains unaccounted for. We calculate her last position to be somewhere between Ceylon and Madagascar. She put in to Calcutta as prescribed, but not to Cape Town—at least not at the time of our last report from there. She may have been taken by pirates, although that is not likely, given her armament. We fear she may have gone down with all hands in a storm."

"Damn it all!" Endicott exploded. "Where is the profit in any of *that*? What *future* is there in *that*? If we cannot rely on our Orient trade to save us, we are indeed in dire straits." His shrill voice revealed little concern for the sailors in his employ who were presumed lost at sea somewhere in the Indian Ocean. "The net result, gentlemen, is this: every time one of our vessels puts to sea, we stand to lose both the ship and her cargo, or at best to turn a profit that hardly justifies the business risks." He held up a hand to forestall comments. "Yes, I realize there have *always* been risks in this business. But because of events in Europe these risks have never been greater than they are today."

He huffed on with hardly a pause. "Napoléon has clearly made good on his promise to seize any American ship that dares to obey these British orders in council. This he can do, of course, only when an American ship sails into a port controlled by the French. Apart from French privateers operating on this side of the Atlantic, the French and Spanish navies have not posed much of a threat since Trafalgar. The British have what's left of those navies blockaded in Toulon, Brest, and Cádiz.

"So it's the *British* who control the sea lanes and it's the *British* to whom we are most vulnerable and with whom our government must parley. And parley it *must*," he insisted. "England is *not* our enemy. Quite the opposite. If we are to survive, we must view England as our ally. I need not remind you gentlemen that the vast majority of our country's exports either go *to* Britain or *through* Britain. And most of our imports come *from* Britain. So for all intents and purposes, without British trade and succor American merchants are rudderless—and in dire peril of financial ruin."

Everyone present—everyone along Long Wharf and along every wharf on the Eastern Seaboard—had heard such statements before. Endicott, Richard understood, was simply offering a preamble to the real reason he and Caleb Cutler had summoned the principals of Cutler & Sons and C&E Enterprises to the countinghouse this morning. He waited for Endicott to continue.

"It's becoming nigh impossible," Endicott said in a voice laced with indignation, "for an honest merchant to make an honest profit—or *any* profit, for that matter—because of what other countries are doing *to* us and because of what our government is *not* doing *for* us. And we haven't yet mentioned the catastrophic effects of the sky-high insurance rates on our cargoes. As Mr. Hunt will attest, those rates are bleeding our coffers dry. And there can be no doubt that they will only go higher in the weeks and months ahead."

George Hunt nodded grimly.

"So, my friends," Endicott summed up, "here is where we stand: the vast profits you and I and other New England shipping families have earned in recent years are in serious danger of going by the boards. When war broke out in Europe after the Peace of Amiens, we seized the initiative. We increased exports to Europe tenfold. The Danes, the Russians, the Dutch, the Neapolitans: everyone in Europe was eager to buy what we had to sell, regardless of where our cargoes originated and regardless of the price we charged. As a result, the United States has become the largest neutral carrier of goods in the world, despite the best efforts by the British and the French to cripple the competition and to destroy the principle of free trade we Americans hold so dear. These past few years, however . . ." He shook his head and then continued woefully, "Gentlemen, when all is said and done, despite the challenges and threats we have had to endure, I fear we may look back on these past few years as our glory years."

Moments of silence ensued before Richard, accustomed to Endicott's flair for the dramatic, spoke up: "And your point is, Jack?"

Endicott studied him. "My point, Richard," he said softly, "is that today our situation is quite different from what it was yesterday. You have studied the books. You have seen our financial position. Not so much glory, eh? Gives you pause, does it not? Well, listen carefully, my friend—listen carefully, all of you—because what I am about to tell you will make all that seem petty. If what Bruce Shaw," referring to the company's agent in Washington, "is telling us is true—and we have every reason to trust his word—the sum total of what we have experienced in recent months will seem like child's play in comparison to what is coming. Like a summer walk on a Cape Cod beach."

Endicott's pause for effect was hardly necessary.

"Is Mr. Shaw predicting war?" Will asked incredulously. He could imagine no other possibility given the ominous tones of his father-in-law's words.

Endicott shook his head. "Mr. Shaw is not predicting anything, Will," he said. "His commission is to report the facts of what he has witnessed in Washington either with his own eyes and ears or through the eyes and ears of those in positions of power whom he trusts, and who trust him in return. This sort of information is what we pay him for—rather handsomely, I might add. No," he went on, "I am the one doing the predicting here. And what I am predicting is indeed war. But it will not be the sort of war you are imagining. *This* war will not be fought against Great Britain or France or any other country. No, *this* war will be fought against ourselves—more precisely, it will be fought against our own government."

Silence fell like a guillotine on the chamber. Richard glanced at Agreen—who as senior ship's master in the Cutler & Sons merchant fleet had both a personal and a financial stake in these proceedings—and then at Hugh Hardcastle, whose perspectives on English maritime law and Royal Navy operations had already proven invaluable to the family businesses. Hardcastle was also a man who was not afraid to speak his mind whatever the ramifications. For that attribute alone his counsel was widely respected, if not always appreciated.

Richard's gaze drifted back to Endicott. "I'm afraid I don't understand, Jack. *Who* is making war on our government?"

"In a sense, people like us. Please hear me out," Endicott said. "What I am saying is simply a summation of the inevitable consequence of what Mr. Shaw reported to me and Caleb yesterday in a special communiqué from Washington."

"And that communiqué states . . . ?"

"That communiqué states that Mr. Jefferson, with Mr. Madison's ardent support, intends to respond to what he perceives as atrocities against American maritime rights by imposing a worldwide trade embargo. Such an embargo, I need not tell you, would effectively close down American commerce overseas, and even to Canada." He looked about the room, pleased to have the rapt attention of everyone present.

"Yes, I see those words have made an impression on you. I'm glad they have. Now you better understand the gravity of our situation and the reason we are gathered here today. Should Congress ever approve such an embargo, even our China trade will be affected. And *there,* my friends, is where we make our *real* profit. I lost no time writing Mr. Van der Heyden at our office in Java to inform him of the situation. I can only imagine *his* reaction when he receives my letter. *Any* businessman with a sound mind would be appalled by this."

The men seated in the room remained silent until Agreen Crabtree asked the obvious question: "Why in God's holy name would Jefferson do such a thing? It'll cripple the economy."

"The president's reasoning is quite simple," Endicott replied, "as, unfortunately, are many of the thoughts that pass through his brain. It seems that Mr. Jefferson and his secretary of state adhere to the principle of economic coercion. If the United States stops trade with Europe and with European colonies, he believes, then the powers-that-be—in England, France, and elsewhere—will buckle under to our demands for free trade and an end to impressment. Jefferson actually believes that they will allow such demands to be rammed down their throats."

Hugh Hardcastle threw up his hands in disgust. "If Mr. Jefferson believes that," he scoffed, "then the man truly *is* the bloody idiot you Federalists contend he is. He is naïve beyond belief. Great Britain will survive quite handily, thank you very much, without American trade. And His Majesty's government will soon find other customers for Britain's exports. Those soon-to-be liberated Dago Indians in South America are perfect examples, and I can think of many more. *My* opinion? Not only will Great Britain survive an American embargo, she will flourish as a result of it. British merchants will be only too pleased to fill the void, and they will happily sing a sea chantey as they waltz their way to the Old Lady of Threadneedle Street," referring to the popular term for the Bank of England.

"*Exactly*, Hugh," Endicott heartily agreed. "That is my thinking to the letter. We should be seeking ways to mollify the British—to work *with* them, not *against* them. We most definitely should not be seeking ways to antagonize them. Imagine the effects of a trade embargo on this country! Our carrying trade is the lifeblood of our economy, and here we have a president who seeks to sever that artery and watch the lifeblood spill out. Mark my words well: if Congress approves this embargo, it is not only the New England shipping families who will suffer. Without trade to England and her colonies, where do southerners sell their cotton? Where do westerners sell their furs? All Americans, regardless of where they live or what politics and religion they happen to fancy, will be reduced to selling goods and services to each other. And damn few of us will have the money to purchase anything from anyone, anywhere. This policy would ruin us. *Ruin* us, I say." Endicott's tone had risen in pitch at the onset of his spiel, but by its end had plummeted to tones of utter despondency.

Jamie Cutler asked, "Just how imminent is this embargo, Mr. Endicott? And how much support in Washington does Mr. Shaw believe the president has?" He had a personal stake in asking those questions. If an embargo were to be enacted into law, it would fall to the U.S. Navy and a handful of revenue cutters to enforce that law.

Caleb Cutler stood up. "If I may, Jack?" Endicott nodded, sat down, and stared blankly down at the floor.

"To answer your second question first, Jamie," Caleb said, "as you heard Mr. Endicott state, James Madison supports the embargo to the letter. In fact, many in Washington believe that the embargo is his idea. And a number of others in the cabinet and in Congress support it, although I doubt most of them either understand or appreciate its full implications. I doubt the president does.

"The answer to your first question is less clear. Nothing is definite. We have not reviewed the legislation because there is as yet no legislation to review. Jefferson apparently has his proposal ready to submit to Congress but has not yet sent it. Why he hasn't is a matter of conjecture. Mr. Shaw does his job well, but of course he is not privy to Jefferson's thinking. Perhaps the president and his secretary of state are waiting for the right moment to act. What that moment might be is anyone's guess. Whatever the reason, we must assume that if and when Jefferson *does* send the legislation to Congress, it will receive the necessary votes and be enacted into law. Ever since the Republicans took control of both the House and the Senate, Congress has given the president pretty much everything he has asked for. But we won't know exactly what the proposed legislation entails, and what loopholes it may contain, until after we have reviewed the document with our legal counsel."

"It's blasphemy," Endicott muttered. "Utter madness."

Jamie said to Caleb, "I understand that, Uncle, thank you. But surely Mr. Shaw has some notion as to when the legislation will be sent to Congress?"

"His best guess is within the year," Caleb replied. "I doubt President Jefferson would want to hold a bill of this magnitude in abeyance for very long. Unless, of course, either the United States or England decides to back down."

"That won't happen," Hugh Hardcastle said adamantly. "With respect, Caleb, things have already gone too far for either side to back down with honor. But I will say this for the American president: he acts boldly when conditions warrant it. He may act foolishly, I grant you; and on this matter he is so far off the wicket he is playing on another field. But he does take action. He also understands what Jack said a few minutes ago: that despite what some members of his own party contend, America is not ready for war, especially for a war with England. That would be tantamount to national suicide. The United States would suffer a colossal defeat, and you would find yourselves back in virtually a colonial status."

"Many Americans would argue, Captain Hardcastle," George Hunt put in, "that a virtual colonial status is where we find ourselves today."

"I take your point, Mr. Hunt," Hugh conceded.

Richard listened to this discourse with growing apprehension. Like everyone present—like most people living in the five New England states—the last thing he wanted to contemplate was a further deterioration of relations with the mother country. As he and other Federalists had long contended, and as Endicott had hammered home today, England was America's natural ally. Their citizens shared the same history, the same blood, and the same aspirations for the future. Without question, England had committed any number of actions against the interests of the United States both at sea and along the northwestern frontier. Richard himself had been on a Cutler & Sons vessel that was boarded by British sailors and Marines off Bermuda, and he had watched helplessly as one of his sailors was dragged away to certain death. But he understood that the Royal Navy was perpetrating similar atrocities against its own merchant fleets in order to man the more than one thousand warships sailing under Britain's flag. He also understood that Great Britain was locked in a death struggle with France. The victor would determine the fate of England and of Europe. To Richard's mind, all bets were off and all sins forgiven when an individual or a nation was backed into a corner and forced to fight for its very survival.

He was able to retain some optimism because of his firm conviction that once the war between England and France was settled, the issues that divided Americans and Europeans would dissipate and relations would gradually be restored to normal. It was, after all, the way of history, and the alternatives were simply too mind numbing to contemplate. War with England or a trade embargo: either might well destroy his country and his future. Everything his family had worked hard to build during the previous half century would come crashing down around them. Jack was correct when he predicted that. But for Richard and Katherine—and for many other Americans—there was more. If it came to war, they would have one, perhaps two, sons engaged in combat on a U.S. Navy gun deck in a conflict from which the United States could not possibly emerge victorious. That possibility remained in a nebulous future, though. What troubled him most at that moment was Endicott's warning.

"Jack," he said, "you spoke of a war against our own government. Please explain yourself."

Jack Endicott rose to his feet, his earlier fury now replaced by resignation. He looked exhausted and years older than his actual age. "Perhaps 'war' is not quite the right word," he admitted quietly. "But of this I can assure you: Jefferson's policies and his refusal to negotiate further with England will be opposed by virtually all Federalists and a great many Republicans. Mr. Shaw is adamant on that point. If Jefferson and the Congress believe for an instant that they can impose a trade embargo without severe repercussions, they are very much mistaken. Like you, Caleb, I believe that those in power will impose the embargo regardless— and the results of doing that will be disastrous. In his communiqué Mr. Shaw offered us a clue as to what actually *may* happen as a result."

"We're all ears," Richard said into the silence that followed.

The irony in Richard's voice was not lost on Endicott. "I should hope so, Richard," he said. "Although Mr. Shaw did not name names, he has it on good authority that certain members of Congress are preparing to meet in secret. Their objective? To discuss taking New England out of the Union and establishing a separate nation."

"That's poppycock, Jack," Richard blurted out, dismissing Endicott's stunning announcement with a wave of his hand. "It's nothing more than alehouse chatter. I've heard that sort of drivel before—from people who were deep into their cups. Surely you don't mean to tell us that you take such a notion seriously."

"I *do* take it seriously," Endicott countered. "And so should you. So should we all. This Republican regime in Washington never has and never will act in New England's best interests. It is time for us to accept that and to stop hoping the tide will turn. It is time for us to stand together as a cohesive political body. This I pledge: I will do whatever is necessary— I repeat: I will do *whatever is necessary*—to prevent Washington from destroying my reputation and my business. If that means I support and help finance the creation of a new nation, then so be it. I am informed that many others of consequence believe as I do."

"Those are brave words, Jack," Richard stated in a non-confrontational tone, hoping at all costs to avoid a rift among family members. "Words to make Patrick Henry proud. I do understand your apprehension," he added sincerely. "Every man in this room understands it because we are together in the same boat, so to speak. And I understand your sense of outrage. I just don't happen to agree with your solution."

"And what, pray, might *your* solution be, Richard," Endicott asked.

"I'm afraid I have none to offer," Richard admitted.

THE MEETING over, Richard said good-bye to Will with the promise that he and Will's mother would sail to Boston soon after Adele gave birth to their first grandchild. Now that Adele was in her final month of pregnancy, Anne-Marie Endicott had insisted that her daughter and Will remain at the Endicott residence on Belknap Street on Beacon Hill with a midwife and Boston's finest physicians standing by. The demands of Cutler & Sons and C&E Enterprises, which required long hours on Long Wharf, would keep Caleb and his family in Boston as well. Jamie, too, planned to stay in Boston for another three days. He needed to report to his superiors at the Charlestown Navy Yard regarding the disposition of *Constitution*, which was soon to be relieved by *Chesapeake* as flagship of the Mediterranean Squadron. He also wanted to spend time with Will and lend what support he could to the nervous father-to-be. The next day, Hugh Hardcastle was to set sail with a cargo of oak lumber and barrel staves, his first command of a Cutler & Sons' vessel and his first visit to the offices on Fleet Street in Baltimore. So it would be just Richard and Agreen on the return voyage to Hingham.

"You're certain I can't entice you to stop by for luncheon before you leave?" Endicott inquired as Richard made ready to depart. Endicott possessed an uncanny ability to separate business and social matters, and he never allowed one to be confused with the other. The sparks of controversy so evident during the meeting had been summarily extinguished once Caleb pronounced the meeting adjourned. Others might fret and fume for hours or even days over what had been said or implied during a business session, but not Jack Endicott. It was, Richard had once said to Katherine, the most admirable and unique of Endicott's social talents.

"Thank you, Jack," Richard replied with equal bonhomie. "But I really must get back to Hingham. Perhaps later in the week?"

Endicott gave him a broad smile. "Of course," he said. "But you do realize that by deferring my invitation you are placing my well-being in considerable jeopardy. I will have Anne-Marie's wrath to contend with as soon as I arrive home and tell her that you are not coming. I believe I would do better to hide out here and not go home at all."

Richard laughed but said nothing further. He shook Endicott's hand and those of Caleb and Jamie, and reiterated his promise to return to Long Wharf three days hence. He wished Hugh fair winds and then left the countinghouse in company with Agreen.

"My love to my sister," Hugh called after them.

Richard and Agreen walked in silence along a wharf alive with the bounty and bustle of commercial enterprise. A gusty breeze and a dazzlingly bright sun enlivened the afternoon; diamonds flashed and danced upon a sapphire sea awash with white crests. The sun felt warm when they were in the lee of a building; once in the teeth of the wind, however, the brisk twenty-knot northerlies had the muscle to bite through several layers of wool clothing. At the end of the half-mile wood-and-stone structure a single-masted packet boat bobbed up and down with the wave action. A thick mat-like padding hanging over her starboard railing protected her hull from abrasion as it bumped against the wharf.

Once on board, Richard and Agreen helped the master and mate to hoist main and jib and cast off. Together they put the fifty-foot craft on a course between Long Island and Gallops Island, on a broad reach sailing for Hingham Bay.

Although the boat had a sizable cabin, Richard and Agreen chose to remain topside. The stiff April breeze became less persistent once the packet had creamed into the lee of the Boston Harbor islands and the wind was more at their back. They were quite comfortable sitting on the top of the cabin to windward with their feet on the deck and the sun full on them. And the scenery they passed by at a good clip was, as always, worthy of note.

"You know what galls me the most in all this?" Agreen said reflectively after a long spell of silent contemplation. The boat's master and mate remained aft, discreetly out of earshot beside the tiller.

"What's that, Agee?" Richard asked halfheartedly, his thoughts already ahead in Hingham. His gaze remained fixed off to larboard at the drumlin that defined Gallops Island at high tide.

"Well, as I see it, *we're* the ones sufferin' the most from what the British are doin'. I mean, it's *our* ships bein' boarded, *our* sailors bein' impressed, *our* cargoes bein' taxed and seized. We're the ones takin' it deep in the hindquarters, and yet it's the Republicans in the South and West who cry foul. Jack is right, Richard, when he says that those of us here in New England desire peace with the English. We want t' work things out with them, and why shouldn't we? Our livelihood depends on it. Besides, do you think for one minute that England wants a war with us? Hell, no. Of course not. They've got their hands full with Bonny over yonder in Europe. We're a distraction, that's all: a fly buzzin' around the lion's head. Thing is, we *could* work things out if Jefferson and his-all weren't so damn hellfire bent on twistin' the lion's tail. Jack's right about that too. And it's those Republicans who propose we build gunboats rather than frigates because if war comes, so Dearborn claims, it would be a defensive war only and therefore we wouldn't need frigates." His scorn for Henry Dearborn, Jefferson's secretary of war, reddened his face. "Now *that's* poppycock! It is t' me, at least. But then, I'm just a rube from Nowhere, Maine."

Richard looked askance at him. "You can don that hayseed cloak as much as you like, Agee," he said, "but it won't serve. You'd still be one of the smartest men I know. And the best damn sea captain I know. And the best friend I've ever had," he added with feeling.

Agreen nodded in acknowledgment and then looked away, embarrassed by Richard's overt expression of affection and praise. "So what do *you* make of all this?" he asked moments later.

Richard shrugged. "I just don't know. Two things are certain: it's bad, and it's going to get worse. Perhaps a lot worse, as Jack seems to think— and for the reasons he stated. I may find his ways annoying, Agee, but I can't deny his intellect and business insight. My family is where it is today because of three men: my father, my Uncle William, and Jack Endicott. The profits of C&E dwarf those of Cutler & Sons, and it was Jack's vision of the China trade that finally convinced my father and uncle to throw in our lot with him. So I'd be a fool not to listen carefully to what Jack has to say. And I will confess to you that what he had to say today scares the living hell out of me. If Jefferson does broadside our carrying trade, our world will turn upside down. It *is* madness, as Jack says. But I can agree with Jack only so far. I cannot for the life of me accept his notion of taking New England out of the Union. Nothing on earth could justify doing that. I love my country, and my country is the United States."

"Amen t' that, Richard."

Just north of Hough's Neck, the packet entered the twelve square miles that formed Hingham Bay. Ahead on the horizon off to starboard, in the narrow open space between the foredeck and the foot of the jib, Agreen caught a glimpse of Grape Island, its familiar low terrain marking the entrance of Hingham Harbor. In these more sheltered waters the wind had moderated considerably; the packet's former twelve-knot speed had settled into a lazier pitch and roll on the waves of a following sea. At this rate, he estimated, they would arrive at the Hingham docks within the half hour. It was now or never, Agreen decided. He drew a deep breath.

"Richard, there's somethin' I need t' ask you. It's on another subject."

"Ask away."

Agreen hesitated, then: "It's about Katherine."

Richard stared steadily northward at the distant gap between Peddock's Island and Pemberton Point known as Hull Gut. On the mainland side rose a thirty-five-foot structure that gave the end of the Nantasket Peninsula the alternate name of Windmill Point. During the early years of his marriage, that desolate but alluring spit had been Richard and Katherine's favorite destination, to walk and talk, and simply to be alone together. As he normally did whenever he caught sight of that windmill, he recalled the magic of that warm September afternoon years ago when, to his delight, Katherine had enticed him into shattering social mores by making love amid the thick shrubs and tall sea grass encircling the windmill. Richard often found himself wondering what would have happened had Rebecca Hanson or another of Hingham's gossipmongers caught sight or wind of what they had done. The thought never failed to induce a smile. "What about Katherine?"

Agreen chewed on his lower lip. "I'm concerned about her."

"Why?"

Agreen studied Richard's profile as his friend continued to gaze northward, his jaw set as if in stone.

"I think you know why, Richard," Agreen said softly. "She seems more and more withdrawn as the weeks go by. Oh, she still lights up and becomes her old self whenever Diana comes over. And she always has a smile for me, bless her. But she seems content to stay indoors much of the time. Lizzy tells me that it's hard t' get Katherine t' go out ridin' with her. You *know* there's somethin' wrong there. Before, Katherine would have jumped at almost any opportunity t' ride a horse, especially with Liz."

"Are you the one making these observations, Agee? Or is it Lizzy, through you?"

"It's us both," Agreen asserted. "We don't mean t' pry. But we can't just sit on our hands and say nothin' either. You and I, Richard, we're the luckiest of men. We've both won life's biggest prize. We married extraordinary women who, for reasons only the Almighty can comprehend, find us worthy of their love in return. Few people can claim such a union, much less understand it."

Richard nodded his agreement. "That was well put. I obviously agree."

"You and Katherine are our dearest friends," Agreen continued in a low, urgent tone. "Lizzy and Katherine have been like sisters since childhood. You and I have been like brothers since we signed on t'gether in *Ranger*. So when we're concerned about either of you, we speak up. That's what friends and family do. Lord knows, you and Katherine have done that for us. Hell's bells, you two are the reason Lizzy and I got hitched in the first place. Without your intervention and wise counsel," Agreen concluded with a chuckle, "Liz would never have had a mind t' marry me."

"I doubt that," Richard said.

"It's not only that she seems withdrawn," Agreen continued when Richard offered nothing further. "She seems frailer and thinner. Her clothes don't fit anymore; they hang on her. Lizzy and I aren't the only ones t' notice these things. I know from what Hugh has told me that he and Phoebe are concerned. So are Caleb and Joan. I suspect your children are too. Maybe they're convinced that it's all part of growin' older. But that's not the right explanation, is it, Richard."

That last sentence was not a question but a statement of fact. Richard leaned forward and clasped his hands together. For long moments he stared down at the deck and at the gush of seawater gurgling along the packet's larboard hull. When the mate walked forward on the leeward side to prepare mooring lines and douse canvas, he said, his voice gravelly and thick with emotion, "Agee, I am not at liberty to discuss this subject with you right now. Besides, we haven't the time. All I can tell you is that your concerns are noted and appreciated. And they are not without merit. I can assure you, no one is more concerned about Katherine than I am."

"So, HOW was your day in Boston, my love?" Katherine asked lightheartedly as she finished dinner preparations.

Richard was sitting at the oval teak table in the dining room off the kitchen as Katherine served their favorite dish of creamed codfish surrounded by whipped potatoes and green beans. Richard had already poured two glasses of Bordeaux. Three candles flickered in the silver candelabra placed at the center of the table; they could hear the comforting snap and crackle of birch and pine logs ablaze in the hearth in the parlor adjacent to the dining area; a strengthening northerly rattled the window-panes, accentuating the comfortable warmth inside.

"It was interesting," Richard answered as she sat down across from him. Since it was rare these days for their children to dine with them, Richard had removed both leaves of the table, contracting its size by half. Once, that would have welcomed intimacy into the evening.

Katherine took a healthy sip of wine. "How so?" she inquired. "Anything you'd like to tell me?"

He studied her in the soft glow of the candlelight. Agreen's words to him on the packet boat weighed heavily on a mind already fraught with anxiety and despair. And yet, as he gazed at her from across the table, he could almost discount that conversation. It seemed surreal, out of place. Her fetching smile was still there; her skin still glowed; her chestnut hair still curled about her face, although it was not as long as in former days. Approaching fifty years of age, Katherine Hardcastle Cutler remained a woman of extraordinary grace, beauty, kindness, and courage—to his eyes the very same woman he had married twenty-five years ago. Looking at her in the mellow, dancing light, he could neither believe not bear to accept that inside that lovely exterior her body was being viciously assaulted.

"Richard? What is it, darling?" she asked.

Richard downed a slug of wine before placing the glass gently back on the table. "Katherine," he said quietly, "I fear your secret is about to be exposed. I have not said a word to anyone, I promise you. But people are drawing conclusions on their own."

Katherine did not flinch. "You say 'people.' Who, specifically?"

"Agee. And Lizzy. This afternoon on the boat Agee told me that Hugh and Phoebe have their concerns, as do Caleb and Joan. No doubt there are others."

Katherine let out a low sigh. "Diana was over this afternoon. She asked me if anything was wrong. She said that she and Peter have been worried about me."

"How did you answer her?"

"I told her that nothing was wrong. I told her I am having some stomach ailments that I'm sure will clear up in due course. She asked me if I felt well enough to go out riding with her tomorrow. When I told her I did, she was visibly relieved. So we're meeting at Indian Hollow at ten o'clock."

"Do you think that's wise?"

"Of course it's wise," Katherine snapped. "Why wouldn't it be? Why are we even having this conversation, Richard? You know it only distresses me. Is that what you want to do? Worry and distress me?"

"Of course not, Katherine. Stop talking nonsense."

"*What*, then?"

Richard held her hard glare. "It's just that I don't know how much longer we can continue to say nothing. We know your cancer is back. Our friends and family may not know it, but they will soon assume it, if they haven't already. *I* had my strong suspicions before you told me about it last week. More to the point, Katherine, you're weaker than before. You can't deny that and you can't entirely hide it. If something should happen and you should fall from your horse . . ." He could not go on. He reached for his glass and drained it.

Katherine's eyes softened. She reached her right hand across the table. Richard took it in his. "Richard," she pleaded, "stay with me on this, I beg you. It is what I want you to do for me. People may observe all they want and draw whatever conclusions they will, but that won't change anything. I don't want their pity. I don't want to talk to them knowing that they know. There is nothing that anyone can do to treat this cancer. As good a surgeon as Dr. Prescott may be, he cannot amputate my chest." She gave him a rueful smile. "It is what it is, my darling, and we both have to accept that reality. We both have to be strong—for each other and for those we love, especially our children. They need not know about my condition for some time yet. I promise henceforth to do everything I can to appear strong and to allay concerns. I can and will endure whatever pain I must, and I promise not to take unnecessary risks.

"But in return, you must promise to stand with me. If I were to confess to everyone, as you seem to want me to do, the life I have known—the life I have loved all these years with you—would end on that day. Who knows how much longer I have? It could be many months. It could be a year or more. So let us please make the most of the days we have left together. Do not deny us the joy of seeing our grandchild. Do not give people reason to avoid us or act uneasy around us. Do not take from me this life I love so dearly one day sooner than is absolutely necessary. Don't you understand? We've been through this before."

In truth, Richard did understand. But it was the scourge of Satan for him to watch impotently while the woman he loved more than life itself suffered so in mind and body.

"I shall do as you ask," he said to her, his voice resigned. "And I shall continue to pray for God's blessing and mercy on you and on us all."

Ten

Washington, D.C., and at Sea off Norfolk, Virginia
June 1807

STEPHEN DECATUR chewed on his lower lip as he read the communiqué lying face-up on the desk of his grandly appointed study. When he had finished reading it, he lifted its upper edges and read it a second time, his eyes narrowing as he took in the very real threat couched in the polished and seemingly collegial words of a highly placed British diplomat. He cursed under his breath and banged his fist on the smooth mahogany finish. Pushing back his chair, he jumped to his feet and reached for the long velvet cord by the window drapes that would summon Martin, his orderly.

Just then, his bride of one year appeared at the open door. "What is it, Stephen?" she asked as she hurried into the room. "I do not mean to pry, but the door was open and I heard you pound your fist on the table. Why so out of sorts?"

Decatur released the cord. "It appears that our British friends are at it again, Susan," he replied stiffly. "I must confer with Mr. Smith as soon as possible."

"Whyever so?" she said, surprised at his sudden desire to see the secretary of the Navy.

He handed her the letter. As she read it, he studied her profile and her elegant features, clouded now by concern at the letter's content. Long considered a "prize of consequence" for her stunning beauty and keen intellect, before her marriage Susan Wheeler had been pursued by such notables as Aaron Burr, the man who in 1801 became Jefferson's vice president, and Jérôme Bonaparte, Napoléon's youngest bother, who had

cut quite a swath through Washington society. Ultimately she had settled her love interest on the dashing war hero born on Maryland's Eastern Shore and raised in Philadelphia. Her father, Luke Wheeler, was the
mayor of Norfolk, Virginia, and was well regarded in naval circles there
and elsewhere. He had played a pivotal role in the introduction and subsequent courtship of his daughter to the American naval officer who had led
the daring raid on USS *Philadelphia* in Tripoli Harbor. Nor had that been
Decatur's only act of heroism. He had several times risked his own life
to come to the aid of shipmates in distress, on one occasion swan-diving
off a lower yard of a frigate to rescue a waister who had fallen overboard
and could not swim.

Although no one could deny that Susan had married well, her beauty
and wit had done much to further her husband's career. "Yes, I see," she
said as she finished the letter. She handed it back to her husband and,
after a glance at the clock on the mantle above the fireplace said, "Stephen, here's a thought. Why don't I find Martin and send him off to the
Navy Yard with a note to Mr. Smith. Shall we propose a meeting time for
four o'clock this afternoon? That gives you six hours to prepare. Even if
Mr. Smith should have a prior engagement, he will certainly postpone it
once he realizes the urgency of this matter. I will be sure Martin confirms
everything with you, of course."

"That would do nicely, Susan, thank you. I shall start getting ready at
once. I want to consult with several people before I meet with Mr. Smith."

"Of course, my dear. I understand," she said and left to go in search
of Decatur's orderly.

As Decatur watched his wife leave the study, the thought again
occurred to him that what had inflamed his desire to marry this lovely
young woman went far beyond physical attraction and her intimate
knowledge of social etiquette.

By the year 1807 the District of Columbia, the seat of the federal government that had been under the jurisdiction of Congress for six years,
was beginning to take shape as a city of international renown. Designed
by the French-born American architect Pierre Charles L'Enfant, its
north-south, east-west street grid intersected by wide diagonal "grand
avenues" named for individual states had caught the fancy of domestic
and foreign critics alike. The showpiece of the city was, of course, the
President's House on Pennsylvania Avenue. But other structures were
also drawing critical acclaim, among them the Congress House, just
now finishing construction on what had become known as Capitol Hill,

and the Washington Navy Yard, built under the direction of Benjamin Stoddard, the first secretary of the Navy, and under the supervision of the Yard's first and current commandant, Commo. Thomas Tingley. The main function of the Yard was to build, repair, and outfit Navy ships of war. It also served as headquarters for the principals and staff of the Navy Department.

Stephen Decatur took scant note of Washington's many public gardens, rectangular plazas, and intricate canal systems after he left his stylish three-story red brick residence and strode toward the Navy Yard, a brown leather satchel clasped firmly in one hand. When Claude Martin had hurried back to Lafayette Square to confirm the four o'clock appointment, he had asked if Decatur required the use of his private carriage. Decatur had demurred, preferring to walk the mile or so and enjoy the cool, sunny weather that was more typical of a day in early April than one in early June. Besides, he needed to think, and he did his best thinking when strolling alone, either along city streets or, better, on a quarterdeck.

Decatur entered the Yard through a break in the white brick wall that bounded its northern and eastern perimeters. To the west, beyond the handiwork of civilization, he could see vast expanses of spongy marshes and open wetlands. To the south, the slow-moving waters of the Potomac River formed a natural boundary. The 38-gun frigate *Chesapeake* lay snug against a quay nearby. Decatur returned the salute of a Marine sentinel and was ushered inside a well-lit but slightly musty-smelling sandstone building.

A short way down the hall on the first floor, the Marine knocked on a door to the right, opened it ajar, and announced the visitor. At a word from the occupant, the Marine opened the door wide to allow Decatur entry.

"Stephen, welcome," a cordial voice said as the Marine stepped back and closed the door. A well-presented man rose from behind the room's large desk and walked over with his right hand extended. In contrast to Decatur's splendid naval captain's uniform, the man was wearing tasteful civilian garb. The two men clasped hands, their mutual affection captured in the steady gaze of one upon the other and their lingering firm grasp. At age fifty, Robert Smith was almost twice Decatur's age; in physical appearance the two men were also quite different. Whereas Decatur sported thick ebony hair and long black sideburns, Smith retained mere wisps of white hair on the top of his head and tufts of white and gray hair along the sides. And in contrast to Decatur's full, muscular frame, almost everything about Smith appeared thin and frail: his stature, lips, and fingers, even his long, prominent nose. And yet, the austere green eyes that beheld Decatur were full of promise and good fellowship—as well as respect; no one needed to remind Smith that the tall, handsome sea officer standing before him was one of America's best.

"You are well, Captain, I trust?"

"I am, sir. Thank you."

"And Susan?"

"The same."

"I am glad to hear it. I may rely on you to convey my warmest personal regards to her?"

Decatur smiled. "You may, sir."

"Excellent." Smith motioned Decatur toward an upholstered chair and then walked around and sat down behind his desk.

"May I offer you a beverage, Captain? A cup of tea? Something stronger, perhaps?"

"No, thank you." Decatur sat down on the chair and crossed one leg over the other. "Please, sir," he added quickly. "Feel free to indulge without me."

"Tempting, but no. I shall defer that until my weekly supper with Henry Dearborn at seven o'clock. No doubt he will have another round of information for me that will warrant a strong drink or two." Smiling, Smith clasped his hands together on the top of the desk and leaned in toward Decatur. "Now, then, Stephen," he said. "What's on your mind? Why all the ado?"

"Sorry to add to Secretary Dearborn's bad news, sir, but I am in receipt of this." Decatur withdrew the communiqué from his satchel and slid it across the desk. "I received it several hours ago. Why the British consul in Washington sent it to me at my home is not entirely clear to me. Mr. Erskine's message, however, is quite clear."

Smith studied Decatur's expression for a moment before putting on a pair of spectacles and picking up the official-looking letter, which he held out at arm's length. "Permit me a moment, if you would, Stephen. My vision is not quite what it used to be."

"Of course, sir." Decatur watched Smith's eyes narrow as they scrolled down to the bottom of the single page and then returned to the top, repeating the process. When he had finished reading, Smith carefully placed the letter on the desk. For several moments he sat motionless in deep thought, the fingers on his two hands forming a steeple beneath his chin. When he glanced up at Decatur, his expression was blank, as though those few moments of deep thought had produced nothing of value.

"What do you make of this, Stephen?"

Decatur shrugged. "I am not sure what to make of it, sir. Our government's policies being what they are, I don't see what course of action is open to us. More specifically, I don't see what course of action is open to *me*. As commandant of the Gosport Navy Yard, I have no jurisdiction in this matter. I cannot authorize the release of those three men to the British even had I a mind to do so—which I can assure you I do not." He stressed the last three words.

"Tell me, how did this come about?"

"Well, sir, there are facts still to be confirmed, but I do know for certain that two of *Chesapeake*'s lieutenants were out recruiting and one of them signed on the three sailors in question. *Chesapeake* is short of manpower, as you are well aware, and she is due to sail in less than a fortnight. She is already well past her original departure date, in part because of her need of repairs and in part because of her lack of crew. The lieutenants were out recruiting in Norfolk and Portsmouth. *And* at the Gosport Navy Yard, which as you read in the letter is where Mr. Erskine contends the three men were discovered hiding in a shed. Whether or not that allegation is true remains to be seen. It may explain, however, why Erskine believes I hold jurisdiction in this matter and why the letter you have before you was sent to my home. I'd wager an identical letter was sent to my office at the Navy Yard."

"And you heard nothing about those three men when you were last at Gosport? Quite recently, was it not?"

"It was, sir. I was there for two weeks and returned home three days ago. I was informed that several men had run from a British warship anchored in Lynnhaven Bay, but I heard nothing about where those men might have gone. I certainly had no notion that they might have been hiding out somewhere in the Navy Yard."

"You're quite certain of that, Stephen?" Smith remained stone-faced when he posed the question, although Decatur glimpsed what he took to be a twinkle of mirth in the secretary's eyes.

"Quite certain, sir," Decatur replied firmly.

"Then we shall leave it at that. By the bye, what are the names of the two officers who were out recruiting?"

"Lt. Arthur Sinclair and Lt. Eric Meyers, sir. You may recall that Lieutenant Meyers served as Captain Cutler's third in *Portsmouth*. He now serves as *Chesapeake*'s acting first. Mr. Butler," referring to the frigate's erstwhile first officer, "remains seriously ill with the influenza."

"So I've heard, poor man." Smith shook his head in sympathy, and then said, "Speaking of Captain Cutler, I should like to discuss his case with you at a later time. You two served together in the Mediterranean, I believe, and I know that he holds you in the highest regard."

"As I do him, sir. Both Captain Cutler and his son. James Cutler is one of the finest young men of my acquaintance. The Navy needs more officers like him."

"I quite agree," Smith said, adding, "I suspect he has learned a lot from his father. And from serving under men like you, Stephen." Smith shook his head in seeming bewilderment. "Perhaps *you* can persuade James' father to return to duty. I am not at all convinced that war with England can be avoided, despite our best efforts to avert it, and we cannot afford to lose so fine a sea officer. I have informed him that he would be up for a commodore's rank should he change his mind. I simply cannot understand what in blazes is holding him back. He is Navy through and through. Or so I thought."

"It *is* a mystery," Decatur agreed. "But unfortunately I have no explanation to offer you, sir."

"No, I didn't expect you would, Stephen," Smith sighed. "By the bye, Captain Cutler's other son has applied for a commission. His name is William and his father recently wrote to me on his behalf. Perhaps we can accommodate the young man, although you are well aware of my reluctance to promote officers on the basis of family credentials. I have assured Captain Cutler that I will make his son's availability known to our roster of sea captains. Ultimately, the decision will be up to one of them. And consider yourself so informed, Captain Decatur. If war threatens, we certainly will not leave you sitting behind a desk." Smith withdrew a handkerchief from a side pocket and blew his nose gently. "Now then, getting back to the business at hand, do Meyers and Sinclair believe the three sailors to be Americans?"

"They do, sir. The sailors claim they have papers to prove it, but as is their norm these days, the British choose to ignore those papers—*and* the fact that two of the sailors are apparently free Negroes, which almost certainly makes them Americans—or at least not British. So, yes, all indications are that they were impressed into the Royal Navy. That is why, they told Meyers, they jumped ship and ran when HMS *Melampus* put in to Lynnhaven Bay, and why they signed on in *Chesapeake*. That dastardly affair with *Dolphin* has apparently convinced them that an American frigate offers better protection to Royal Navy deserters than an American merchantman."

"Well, let us hope we do not disappoint the lads," Smith said, somewhat sardonically. "Perhaps they would have done better if they had simply returned to their homes. Or taken refuge inland."

"They are sailors, sir," Decatur said. "The sea is their life."

"Yes, quite," Smith conceded. "So it would appear that Commodore Barron holds jurisdiction in this matter. He is *Chesapeake*'s commanding officer and those three sailors are now members of his crew." The glare he gave Decatur left no room for doubt as to the importance of what he was about to say. "Stephen, the matter *must* be left there, in *Chesapeake*. Under *no* circumstances can it be allowed to advance further up the chain of command. Neither the president nor the secretary of state can become personally involved. Nor, for that matter, can either Secretary Dearborn or I. Are you absolutely clear on this?"

"I am, sir."

"There is simply too much at stake here," Smith went on, passion rising in his voice. "The American public has had its fill of Britain's arrogance at sea and machinations along our western frontier. We are sitting on a powder keg ready to explode, and God help us if it *does* explode. We will find ourselves in a war we cannot win, the skills of men such as you notwithstanding. It could mean the end of our republic."

"Yes sir. But if I may speak plainly, sir."

"Of course, Stephen. You may always speak plainly with me."

"Sir, we both know Commodore Barron. I confess to having reservations about the man, but he is a commander who will not surrender these three so-called deserters to British authorities unless he receives a direct order to do so."

"I quite agree. And he will not receive such an order."

"Then with respect, sir, where does that leave us?"

Smith gave him a ghost of a smile. "We *could* employ *Nautilus* against the British squadron in Lynnhaven Bay. That would tweak King George's nose, eh?"

Nautilus, constructed at the Perrier shipyard in Rouen, France, by an American inventor named Robert Fulton, had recently come into American hands. Compelling in design and functionality, the prototype submarine constructed of copper sheets fitted over iron ribs had caught the attention of the French minister of marine and Napoléon Bonaparte as a possible counterbalance to British sea power, especially after a mine *Nautilus* was dragging on one of its first test dives successfully blew up a 40-foot vessel. British spies soon caught wind of this invention, and the Admiralty enticed Fulton across the Channel with a cash payment of

eight hundred pounds. Although Whitehall had at first expressed interest in the 21-foot craft that could sail on the surface via a collapsible
mast and prowl underwater via a hand-turned screw propeller, Admiral
Nelson's stunning victory at Trafalgar had, in the Admiralty's judgment,
rendered such a fantastic weapon superfluous. Discouraged, Fulton had
sailed to America in October 1806 to offer his invention to the U.S. Navy.

"Indeed, I am intrigued by what Mr. Fulton has accomplished," Decatur said, his enthusiasm shining through. "I understand that *Nautilus* can
dive to a depth of twenty-five feet and remain underwater for an extended
period. And she carries multiple explosives. However, sir," he added more
darkly, "as you can appreciate, deploying such a weapon in such a manner could well bring about the war that our government is endeavoring
to avoid."

"So it would, Stephen." Smith concurred, the twinkle returning to his
eye. "So it would. You must not always take me so seriously. I was speaking with tongue in cheek." His brief stab at levity ended abruptly. "Our
agreement with Britain requires us to surrender seamen who are fugitives
from justice," he said matter-of-factly. "It mentions nothing about alleged
deserters. Of course, we cannot rely on that agreement. 'Might makes
right' as the saying goes, and the British pay that agreement no more
mind than they do any other directives of which they do not approve, even
if they are the ones who imposed them! Mr. Erskine makes it quite clear
in his instructions that if we do not cooperate, the British are prepared to
take matters into their own hands. He doesn't specify what he means by
that, although I daresay he doesn't have to. We have recent history to go
by, don't we."

"Unfortunately we do, sir," Decatur bitterly agreed. "A nation that
would defy international law by maintaining a naval squadron in American home waters in order to blockade two French warships also stationed
in our home waters will not hesitate to violate our neutrality; indeed, it
already has. What are we? A toy of Europe?"

"Calm yourself, Stephen," Smith soothed. "Remember: the British are
here at our invitation. Or if not that, at least our tacit approval."

Decatur ignored that. "Are these not the same British who fired point-
blank into an American merchant vessel just a mile offshore from our
naval base? If they had the audacity to do *that*, they have the audacity to
do just about anything else we might imagine."

"I have to agree. So to answer your original question, where this sorry
state of affairs leaves us is in what we must pray are Commodore Barron's capable hands. Whatever happens now, the mantle of responsibility

falls on him. My advice to Mr. Gordon," referring to Master Commandant Charles Gordon, *Chesapeake*'s captain, "is to get his ship ready for sea with all due haste, even if that means putting to sea short-handed. This very evening I will instruct Commodore Tingley to put every available man at Gordon's disposal. You shall see: once *Chesapeake* clears the Capes and is out into the Atlantic, the British will forget the matter and the threat will pass."

THE ROYAL Marine guard rapped purposefully on the door of the warship's spacious after cabin.

"Enter," a gruff voice responded.

Moments later, Midshipman Seth Cutler stood at attention before his captain and snapped a crisp salute. "Mr. Morse's duty, sir, and we have spotted an American frigate in Thimble Shoals Channel. She is heading for sea."

Salusbury Pryce Humphreys laid his quill pen on the desk before looking up at Cutler. "*Chesapeake*?"

"Aye, sir."

"There can be no mistake? No possible room for error?"

"No sir. She is flying the American ensign and Commodore Barron's pennant flies from her masthead."

"Commodore? Jumping the gun a bit, wouldn't you say, Mr. Cutler?" Humphreys smiled at his turn of phrase. "In my experience, one ship does not a squadron make."

"No sir," Seth agreed.

"Very well," Humphreys said, picking up his pen and dipping it into the ornate inkwell on his desk. "You may send Mr. Morse my compliments and advise him that I wish him to weigh anchor immediately and follow the procedures I have prescribed."

Seth Cutler snapped another salute. "Aye, aye, Captain."

As the senior midshipman turned on his heel and departed the cabin, Captain Humphreys picked up the dispatch he had received ten days earlier from the commander of the North American Station in Halifax, Nova Scotia. Here, in his hand, was the ultimate justification for what he was about to do. He had a direct order from a superior, and that order required Humphreys to do whatever was necessary to bring the three deserters from HMS *Melampus* to justice. Vice Admiral Sir George Berkeley had instructed his clerk to twice underline the words "whatever is necessary." I may have let down my conscience from time to time during my career, Humphreys mused as he reflected on the text of the dispatch.

That, alas, is often the fate of a post captain serving in His Majesty's Navy. But hell will freeze over and I will die a thousand deaths before I let down my commanding officer.

He noted the time and date in his log—five bells, forenoon watch, June 22, 1807—just as his steward opened the cabin door and poked in his head.

"I understand we are about to weigh, Captain," the steward said in a fine patrician accent that could rival that of the vice chancellor of Oxford. "Will you be requiring dinner at the usual hour? Or shall I expedite?"

"The usual hour will do, Langley," Humphreys said. He had already computed in his mind the logistics of time as a function of distance divided by a speed that was easily approximated in these relatively light westerly breezes. "We should not see much excitement for another few hours yet."

"Very good, sir," the steward said and set off to the captain's galley.

When evolutions for weighing anchor were completed, the 50-gun *Leopard* slipped past the 36-gun fifth rate *Melampus* and the 74-gun third rate *Bellona*, the two other warships in the British squadron in Lynnhaven Bay, and headed out past Cape Henry Light into the open sea. She was headed south-southeast on a course that followed in the wake of *Chesapeake*, which was out ahead of her by a good three to four miles. The day was cloudless and sunny, affording excellent visibility to lookouts stationed high up in the British cruiser's rigging, their long glasses trained on the stern of the Yankee frigate. Below, on the berthing deck located beneath the gun deck and above the orlop, sailors took their dinner according to their watch, the customary ration of rum having been denied to them as well as to every officer serving in the ship. It was highly irregular in everyone's memory for Captain Humphreys to issue such an order.

At four bells, halfway through the afternoon watch, First Lieutenant Bradford Morse ordered *Leopard*'s royals raised and studdingsails set aloft and alow. The extra press of canvas increased her speed by several knots and allowed her to close the distance between her and her prey. Midshipman Cutler, stationed at the base of the mainmast to relay messages aft from lookouts secured in the crosstrees more than a hundred feet above him, estimated that *Leopard* was nine, perhaps ten miles east of the Virginia Capes. His base of reference was the empty water to the west. His study of mathematics as a midshipman had taught him that the distance to the horizon at sea was roughly equal in miles to the square root of the height of the observer multiplied by a factor of 1.2. From where he was standing, the shoreline to the west had disappeared below the curvature of the earth more than an hour ago.

At five bells Captain Humphreys ordered his crew to clear the decks for action, but quietly—Marine drummers were not to beat the crew to quarters. Sailors crept through the evolutions of preparing a ship for battle and then stole to battle stations, as they had been previously instructed to do. Seth Cutler led the way down to the upper gun deck and took command of number two battery. Because at that point he did not know which side of his command would be presented first, he assumed position amidships between the four gleaming black 12-pounder guns assigned to him, two to a side, still run all the way in behind closed ports. Directly above, through the main hatchway, he could hear boatswain's mates directing sailors aloft in the rigging to prepare to furl up the main and fore courses and otherwise reduce sail to slow the ship and put her in fighting trim. He pulled his gilded watch from a waistcoat pocket and noted the time: 3:35.

Leopard slowed. Minutes ticked by. Seth could sense almost no forward motion of the ship when he heard the voice of Lieutenant Morse on the weather deck above him. He was speaking through a trumpet, requesting Commodore Barron to heave to and allow him to come on board to deliver dispatches. Such a request was not unusual. Since the Jay Treaty of 1794 had repaired damaged relations between Great Britain and the United States, American and British warships had routinely carried dispatches to foreign stations for each other. Seth realized, however, that the communications Lieutenant Morse would deliver to James Barron in the captain's after cabin were meant for Barron alone, and were communications that the American commodore would not wish to receive. There were, in fact, two communications, or so *Leopard*'s officers had been informed. One was a copy of the letter sent to Captain Humphreys by Vice Admiral Berkeley. The other was a personal message from Captain Humphreys to Commodore Barron expressing the hope that this matter could be "adjusted without undue incident" and without harming the "amicable relations that exist between His Majesty's government and the United States."

Cordial and reasonable enough, Seth had thought to himself when he heard the text of the letter read to the ship's officer corps several days earlier. But he was as convinced now as he had been then that it would not serve. At the Washington Navy Yard Commodore Barron had flatly refused to turn over the seamen in question and had stated that he would never authorize the search of a ship under his command—by the British or by anyone else. And he was known as a proud man loathe to back down from a publicly stated position.

Seth heard a ship's boat splash into the water, larboard side. That sound was soon followed by the patter of lightly shod sailors clambering down the hull into it, and followed in turn by a louder stamping of hard-bound shoes—a squad of Marines, undoubtedly—and then by the more authoritative stomp of a sea officer's boots. With the coxswain's distinct cry of "Back oars, larboard side," then "Down oars, starboard side," the ship's boat was under way toward the hove-to U.S. Navy frigate.

Again the minutes ticked by. Seth strolled up and down, back and forth, within the small square space of his command. He had his hands clasped behind his back as he conferred with individual gun captains to ensure that all was primed and ready. A deathly silence had pervaded the upper gun deck. The gun crews pricked up their ears for any telltale sound from the outside; the meager light provided by a few strategically placed lanterns and two open gun ports toward the bow of the ship and another two toward the stern cast an eerie glow of dancing light that illuminated the expression of keen expectation on the face of every man jack on that deck, from lubberly waisters to battle-tested veterans. This was history in the making. Even the dullest of the dullards among the ship's company appreciated *that*.

In too brief a span of time, Seth again heard the cry of the coxswain. "Ease all," he shouted moments before the boat brushed against the larboard hull. The process of boarding was repeated in reverse. First up the tumblehome was the sea officer, followed by the Marines and then the sailors according to rank. Seth listened intently. The shouts above on the weather deck had nothing to do with making ready the hoisting tackle on stays and yardarms that would haul the ship's boat back on board. It was left where it was, the bitter end of its tender presumably secured to the larboard mainmast chain-wale. Seth softly let out a breath, forcing himself to display no outward signs of emotion or concern over what his roiling intestines suggested would happen next. That the boat was not hauled on board meant that the three deserters remained in *Chesapeake* and that Captain Humphreys expected a repeat visit to the American frigate, this time under very different circumstances.

A tense interlude of silence intervened before Second Lieutenant Trevor Elliot, commander of the lower gun deck, and Third Lieutenant Robert Larkin, commander of the upper gun deck, clambered down the wide companionway ladder. Lieutenant Elliot continued down another companionway ladder to the lower gun deck. A minute later, in almost perfect synchrony despite standing on separate decks, the two officers shouted out, "Trice up both sides. Run out, starboard side! Make ready to larboard!"

In each of the twenty-two six-man gun crews, the assistant sponger or assistant loader assigned to the task seized the end of a thin wire line attached to a T-shaped length of iron set in above each gun. The wire led out through a small hole above the port bored through the plank with an auger, down to where it spread out into a Y, the two ends secured to a small iron hook screwed in at each end of the base of the port. When the tricing tackle was pulled inboard, the gunport creaked open on its hinges until it stood out horizontally from the hull of the ship.

With the opening of the ports, the upper gun deck was suddenly awash with sunlight and with the squeal and rumble of eleven 2-ton gun carriages being hauled out by their side-tackle until the breastpiece of each carriage bumped against the starboard bulwark and the muzzle of the 8.5-foot gun reached out as far as possible through the square hole. Belowdecks, eleven 24-pounder guns were being similarly brought to bear.

Seth peered out through the port of gun 6. His stomach knotted when he saw that the larboard gun ports of the American frigate were also opening, in response to a distant roll of drums. *Chesapeake* was beating to quarters.

After the American frigate ignored a warning hail by Captain Humphreys through a speaking trumpet, Humphreys delivered his order to the gun decks via a signal midshipman.

"Mr. Larkin," the midshipman shouted down, "captain's compliments and you may fire gun 2 across her bow!"

Gun 2 was the 12-pounder located forward by the starboard bow. At the moment its muzzle was trained directly on the bow of the American frigate lying on a course parallel to *Leopard*'s, her fore topsail similarly backed and her bowsprit pointing northward. Seth felt *Leopard*'s bow ease into the light westerly breeze. When her forward gun bore on open ocean, its gun captain called out, "Firing!" to the gun crew, who quickly stood clear. He yanked the firing lanyard, the gun barked, and as its carriage reeled inbound until checked by its breeching ropes, a plume of seawater spewed into the air fifty feet in front of *Chesapeake*.

Above on *Leopard*'s quarterdeck Seth could hear the distant order of Bartholomew Riggs, the sailing master, to the quartermaster's mates at the double wheel to come off the wind. That order was followed by another order to back the fore topsail. The two warships again lay on parallel courses a cable length apart, making scant headway, drifting, really, the guns of one trained on the other.

"The Jonathan's lips are sealed," the gunner's mate acting as gun captain of gun 10 in battery three commented grimly to Seth as the midshipman walked close by. "They're offering us no response, sir." He spoke for the entire ship's company.

"They'll be hearing from us soon enough," Seth said to the gunner. "Stand by your gun and tell your men who have one to wrap a bandana around their ears."

The gunner's mate touched the knuckles of his right hand to his forehead. "Aye, sir. Good advice, sir."

A midshipman wearing a bicorne hat appeared in the open hatchway above. In a youthful voice fraught with excitement and resolve, he shouted down, a hand cupped at his mouth, "Mr. Elliott and Mr. Larkin: you may commence firing in sequence!"

"*Fire!*" Lieutenant Larkin shouted. He clapped his hands over his ears.

"*Fire!*" The divisional commander of battery one cried out.

"*Fire!*" the gun captain of gun 2 bellowed, followed seconds later by a similar cry from the captain of gun 4, next in line.

"*Fire!*" Seth Cutler ordered his two gun captains when it came their turn. One after another, red-painted carriages jerked inboard in violent protest as shot after shot of 12-pound iron balls, keeping hot company with 24-pounder round shot fired from the deck below, rocketed toward *Chesapeake*.

"*Reload!*" Larkin shouted, and his cry was taken up by each battery commander and each gun captain on down the line of the upper gun deck.

The shouts and explosions and screech of wheels were repeated again, and again and again in five-second intervals, until gun 22 had discharged its lethal payload and a combined broadside weight of nearly 400 pounds of iron had screamed across a short span of blue ocean to slam into *Chesapeake*'s hull and top-hamper.

And then the entire process was repeated.

And repeated a third time.

Three broadsides, Seth Cutler breathed to himself. An American frigate had suffered the horrific pounding of three broadsides from a British heavy cruiser at close range without firing one gun in reply. *Not one gun!*

Then she did. *Chesapeake* fired one shot that missed its mark, its demonic screech of warning cut off when the ball plunged harmlessly into the sea. It seemed a wild shot born of desperation more than a display of naval discipline. *Leopard*'s gun crews made ready to deliver yet another vision of hell when the order resonated from the quarterdeck: "*Cease fire!*"

The order was echoed up and down the ship on both gun decks. As the guns fell silent, sailors coughed and wheezed and waved their hands in front of their faces to clear away the thick smoke that had enveloped the lower decks in white-yellow clouds with a searing stench that only gradually eased as the clouds drifted out through the leeward gun ports.

A midshipman called down. "Mr. Cutler!"

"Aye, Mr. Tilney," Seth called up, recognizing the midshipman's voice. He could not see his messmate for the smoke and the sting in his eyes.

"Your presence is requested on the quarterdeck."

"Thank you, Mr. Tilney," Seth said. He coughed hard into a kerchief, wiped his eyes with the clean side, and then stepped up the companionway. Following not far behind him were Larkin and Elliot.

Clean ocean air engulfed Seth as he emerged from below onto the weather deck. He took a moment to inhale the sweetness deep into his tortured lungs, his eyes blinking against the lingering sting of smoke and the sudden dazzling sunshine reflecting off the sea. He fought to compose himself and to look every bit the mature, unruffled sea officer as he strode aft toward the quarterdeck. He could not, however, resist a glance to starboard.

It was hard to make out much at this distance, but it was painfully evident that the 1,200 pounds of iron that had battered *Chesapeake* had torn through and sprung much of her rigging. Her sails hung in tatters, and her larboard railing and three lower masts had been whacked and chewed unmercifully. Seth could only imagine the devastation to human bodies caught in the path of a 12- or 24-pound ball impacting at a thousand feet per second.

He climbed the three steps from the waist to the quarterdeck and saluted smartly. "You wish to see me, sir?"

"Yes, Mr. Cutler," Humphreys said. "All is well belowdecks?"

"Yes sir."

"Excellent. You and your mates conducted yourselves admirably. My compliments," Humphreys said. In a tone expressing his stupefaction and regret he added, "The American frigate has struck her colors." He pointed, as if such a gesture were necessary, at the frigate's spanker gaff. The American ensign was nowhere to be seen. "This is a first in my experience, and it is hardly a victory I should wish to celebrate." He looked hard at his midshipman. "Mr. Larkin and Mr. Cartwright," referring to his third lieutenant and his captain of Marines, "are assembling a second boarding party. I should like you to be included in that party."

Although it was an order Seth did not particularly relish, he was keenly aware that his captain had just bestowed a high honor on him. "Aye, aye, sir," he said, saluting.

Humphreys touched his hat in reply and turned from Seth to confer with his sailing master.

THE BOAT that carried the first boarding party and would carry the second was the ship's pinnace, the 32-foot craft that had been bumping against the cruiser's larboard hull beneath the entry port since the first party had visited *Chesapeake.* First on board were the coxswain and the eight sailors who would man the oars, four to a side. Following close behind were six red-jacketed Marines bearing sea service muskets. They were followed in turn by Kenneth Duggan, the boatswain; Midshipman Cutler; Lieutenant Jeremiah Cartwright; and last in line, Lieutenant Robert Larkin. Seth Cutler and Kenneth Duggan sat side by side facing aft on the aftermost thwart before the stern sheets. As they settled in, they exchanged knowing glances: brothers-in-arms again, on a similar mission as before, in company with the third in their triumvirate, Lieutenant Larkin. Behind the coxswain, at the stern of the boat, the British naval ensign fluttered lazily in the gentle breeze.

The row over took place in stony silence, the only sound the creak of oars in their tholepins as the oars dipped and pulled, dipped and pulled, drawing the pinnace ever closer to the floating wreck that now defined the top-hamper of *Chesapeake.* Her hull, to Seth's observation, had sustained remarkably little damage above the waterline even though the larger guns on *Leopard*'s lower deck had fired directly into it. He noted several cracks on the wale strakes and several more on the channel wale, but, incredibly, no plank was stove in. For such minor damage a commodore had struck his colors?

"It's that Yankee oak you 'ear about," Duggan commented softly, following Seth's gaze and reading his mind. The live oak that grew only in the coastal plain of the American South was renowned as a defiantly hard wood and was saved for use on key pieces of the ship's frame. No warship constructed with this live oak had ever sustained serious injury to her hull.

"I've never seen the loike," Duggan contended. "'Ow in 'ell you can blast through it is beyond me. If a 24-pound ball ain't up to the job, I warrant that in a *real* fight we might just find ourselves in a bit of a pickle."

Seth offered no reply as the pinnace slid up alongside the hull of the frigate and the boarding party made ready to board. The coxswain and two oarsmen would remain in the pinnace, fending off.

What he found on the frigate's weather deck after he stepped through the entry port defied credulity. He counted three men dead: one with a leg blown off, another with a shattered skull, and a third who lay prone on the deck, his limbs broken and grotesquely distorted and a tip of white bone protruding through a ripped trouser leg. Streams of blood stained the deck around the dead sailors; a number of others were alive but seriously wounded. Their ghostly moans and ghastly whimpers seemed to come from a different world than any Seth Cutler had ever encountered. The Americans able to walk ignored the British boarding party standing in a cluster near the entry port and continued helping the wounded below to the surgeon on the orlop deck.

But to young Seth Cutler, born to the sea, the wounded men were not the worst of what he was seeing. Not by half. As he gazed around the slaughterhouse deck, his blue eyes opened wide. Nonmilitary supplies cluttered the deck: personal gear that had yet been stowed below, barrels and caskets and hempen bags packed not with gunpowder or anything with a military purpose, but with food and water and grog rations. Slop-chest clothing lay everywhere. Two barrels amidships had split open, spilling out what appeared to be salted meat and dried peas. Loose potatoes rolled about the deck until coming to rest against a bulwark or in a pool of blood. This unsightly mess disgraced a naval vessel under sail. Even the most benign of the merchant sea captains Seth knew would never brook such slapdash preparations for getting under way. If a Royal Navy captain were ever caught with his pants down around his ankles like this, Seth thought, by God he'd be lucky to get away from an Admiralty court with just the loss of his career. The sympathy Seth had felt for Commodore Barron and Captain Gordon just a few minutes earlier was quickly going by the boards.

When an American officer approached the British party, Lieutenant Larkin touched his hat with the left index finger of his right hand.

"I am First Lieutenant Meyers," the officer said after returning Larkin's salute.

Lieutenant Larkin bowed slightly. "Lieutenant Robert Larkin, third officer of His Majesty's Ship *Leopard*, at your service, Mr. Meyers. I am glad to see you up and about, sir."

"Thank you." Meyers said dryly. "As you can plainly see, the same cannot be said for many of my crew." He searched among the boarding party. "I take it your Lieutenant Morse did not accompany you this time around."

"No sir, he did not. Unfortunately, the time for formalities and pleasantries has passed. I have here with me Mr. Cartwright, our captain of Marines"—he indicated the red-jacketed man to his left—"and Mr. Cutler, our senior midshipman"—pointing to the blue-jacketed young man to his right. "We are here to remove the three deserters in question. I am correct in assuming we shall have no further difficulties in this matter?"

The American officer did not immediately respond, and his hard stare at Seth Cutler made the midshipman uneasy. For the life of him he could not comprehend why the American was singling him out for regard.

"Lieutenant?" Larkin pressed. "We shall have no further difficulties?"

Meyers shifted his gaze back to Larkin. "No, you shall not. *Chesapeake* has struck her colors. Commodore Barron has surrendered the ship."

"Surrendering the ship will not be necessary, sir," Larkin said tactfully. "Captain Humphreys insists that the only surrender we require today is that of the three seamen. I have orders to personally assure your commanding officer of this."

"Commodore Barron was wounded. He has been taken below to his cabin and is being attended to. Captain Gordon is with him."

"I am very sorry to learn of the commodore's injuries," Larkin said sincerely. "Nonetheless, I have my orders. I would be ever so much obliged, Lieutenant, if you would assemble your ship's company on the weather deck. Whilst you are doing that, my Marines will conduct a thorough search belowdecks that will include your sick bay and orlop. We know the culprits involved, so we should have no trouble identifying them." His lips creased in a trace of a smirk. "Especially since two of the three are Africans."

The American ignored the stab at humor. "We shall do as you request," Meyers said, resignation and disgust registering in his tone. The two officers exchanged stiff salutes.

"Thank you," Larkin said. "Now, if you will kindly have one of your midshipmen lead the way belowdecks, I should like to have a word with Commodore Barron."

As the American officer passed word for a midshipman and boatswain's mates, Larkin ordered Jeremiah Cartwright and four Marines to go belowdecks through the forward hatchway, and Boatswain Kenneth Duggan and four sailors to go belowdecks through the aft hatchway. Seth Cutler remained on deck with two Marines and two armed sailors to see to the rounding up of the American crew. When Cartwright and Duggan reemerged twenty minutes later, two Royal Marines were dragging a sailor behind them. They dumped him unceremoniously at the feet of Lieutenant Larkin, who had returned to the weather deck after a brief visit to the after cabin.

Larkin gazed down at the sailor lying prone on the deck. The man lifted his face to his captor, his lips moved wordlessly and his bloodshot eyes pleading for mercy.

"And who, might I ask, is *this* god-forsaken soul?" Larkin sniffed.

"His name be Ratfort, sir," Boatswain Duggan replied. "Jenkin Ratford. I know him. He's as English as me own blood. Ran from *Halifax*, 'e did. Found 'im cowering behind the manger."

"Good show, Duggan." Larkin gazed down with curled lips at the sailor trembling before him. "Well, Ratford, it's the hangman's noose for you if there's any justice in this world—and I can assure you there is." To Duggan: "We have Martin, Strachan, and Ware." He indicated the three wretched-looking men standing alone near the base of the assembled ship's company, their hands tied behind them and closely guarded by two musket-wielding Marines. "Our work here is concluded. You may see the men and the four prisoners into the boat."

"Aye, aye, sir," Duggan said. He saluted and set about to carry out the order.

Larkin turned to the sandy-haired American sea officer. "We shall be leaving you now, Lieutenant Meyers," he said. "Speaking on behalf of my captain and my country, may I express my deepest regret and condolences over what has transpired here today. It was certainly not our wish to fire into your ship. But we did give you fair warning, did we not?" His tone in what he said next was emphatic. "This unfortunate incident *could* have and *should* have been avoided. The policy of My Lords of the Admiralty is quite clear on the issue of desertion. It *cannot* and *will not* be tolerated under any circumstances. I repeat, sir: under *any* circumstances. Let one deserter retain his freedom and England is in danger of losing a war. It is hardly my place to lecture you, Lieutenant, but surely you and your superiors should understand by now just how seriously His Majesty's government views this issue."

"We do indeed understand," Meyers replied as the four prisoners shuffled slowly behind him, their eyes glued to their feet, unable in their despair to give their former shipmates so much as a glimpse. "And *you* should understand, Lieutenant," he said defiantly, "that the United States does not take kindly to the illegal impressment of its citizens."

"Illegal? Well, I have my doubts about that. But we shall leave it to the courts to sort it out. Regardless of the decision, the fate of these three so-called Americans was in their hands yesterday just as your fate was in your hands today. Can you possibly deny that?"

"That is hardy the point, Mr. Larkin."

"And what is the point, Mr. Meyers?"

"The point is that your ship has committed an act of war against the United States. For that, God help you."

"No, Lieutenant Meyers," Larkin said. He bowed slightly from the waist and insolently tipped his bicorne hat in a farewell salute before climbing down into the pinnace. "If it should come to war, God help *you*. And God help your country."

Eleven

Boston, Massachusetts
Summer–Fall 1807

P UBLIC REACTION to the unpro-
voked attack on a U.S. Navy frigate by a British man-of-war was
swift and violent. It was as though a towering tsunami had washed across
the American continent, leaving every citizen gasping and spluttering in a
stupefied rage.

The repercussions began soon after *Chesapeake* limped back to her
home port at Norfolk, Virginia. On the very day of her arrival, Mayor
Luke Wheeler signed a resolution denying the Royal Navy access to
provisions, water, and repair docks that formerly had been theirs for the
asking. He also made it ominously clear that American magistrates could
no longer guarantee the safety of British naval personnel who dared to
come ashore. Mayors of other major ports on the Eastern Seaboard
followed suit when word of the national disgrace reached them. Finding
themselves *personae non gratae* wherever they went, most Royal Navy
officers took Wheeler's advice to heart and remained on their ships.
Those reckless enough to venture into cities and towns often found
themselves turning tail and running for their lives in front of angry mobs
brandishing pitchforks, knives, and tree limbs—and anything else that
came to hand.

The honor of the United States had been besmirched by three British
broadsides, and Americans demanded an explanation. Commodore Barron and his officers held the keys to such knowledge, but those keys they
kept close to their vests by order of Secretary Smith, who forbade any of
Chesapeake's crew to speak publicly about the incident until a court of

inquiry had been convened and witnesses interrogated. Even the most isolated South Carolina cotton planter understood a "court of inquiry" to mean a court-martial, and the promise of its ultimate justice helped to keep the lid on a pot threatening to boil over.

More was to come. Secretary of State Madison filed a formal protest in London demanding an apology from His Majesty's government and release of the three American sailors. President Jefferson publicly urged calm while privately conferring with Secretary of War Dearborn and the governors of Virginia and Maryland. Ten thousand militia and a field of cannon were mobilized to ensure that supplies and provisions were denied to the British squadron in Lynnhaven Bay and to discourage the British from taking retaliatory measures. From the quarterdecks of their squadron, British sea officers gazed toward shore at a nation in arms watching them intently.

"Not since the British attacks on Lexington and Concord have I seen the American public so exasperated," the *National Intelligencer and Washington Advertiser* quoted President Jefferson as saying in a cabinet meeting; it was a story headlined in most other American newspapers. "And never have I seen this nation so unified."

Demands for revenge poured in from all sections of the country, including Federalist New England. Although the United States now found itself on a war footing, all but the most diehard fanatics realized that that footing lacked traction. America's military services remained ill prepared and ill equipped to go to war with anyone, least of all a superpower such as Great Britain. On this point Thomas Jefferson and the members of his cabinet suffered no doubts. Neither, of course, did the British.

ENJOYING ANOTHER delightful link in a week-long string of dazzling mid-August days—warm verging on hot ashore but cool out on the placid waters of Hingham Bay—Katherine Cutler sat on the windward side of a 40-foot sloop bound for Boston. The southwesterly breeze wafting over the cool surface waters of the bay and across the Cutler & Sons packet boat made her shiver, but she welcomed the stab of chill after the heat in the house, and the joy she felt at being under sail again trivialized all inconveniences. Her husband, nevertheless, had noted her shivering and went below to fetch her coat.

"Richard, you really needn't pamper me so," she chided him when he returned on deck and draped the coat over her shoulders. "But I love you for it," she added. He put his arm around her and she nestled in close, resting her head against his shoulder. "I sometimes wish," she murmured, "that we could sail on like this forever. Just you and me, in a boat like this, forever summer, and forever together."

Richard gently squeezed her shoulder. "We can," he vowed to the winds. "And we will."

With his typical flair for efficiency, George Hunt was waiting for them with a carriage when they arrived at Long Wharf. Richard had the distinct sense that the aging Cutler & Sons administrator had something to discuss with him, but there was no time. It was already approaching eleven o'clock, and Richard and Katherine needed to be back at the wharf in four hours if they were to return to Hingham before the light breeze died out in late afternoon or early evening, as it often did during the sultry summer months.

The distance from Long Wharf to Beacon Hill was roughly a mile. With the congestion clogging the streets near the waterfront and around Faneuil Hall, and again along Beacon Street near the Common, Richard usually found it faster to travel on foot rather than inside a hired carriage. Today, however, walking was not an option, so Richard climbed into the coach after assisting his wife on board, and together they gazed out on a city that in 1807 encompassed a population of nearly 35,000. Boston had become one of the world's wealthiest and most important trading ports, its wealth reflected on Beacon Hill in the grand homes of the social elite as well in the far simpler homes of the dockworkers living in the North End and South End who provided the hard labor to ensure that the shipping companies earned a satisfactory rate of return.

The carriage rolled to a halt in front of the familiar four-story red brick townhouse at Fourteen Belknap Street. As if poised just inside the dwelling in anticipation of this very moment, a middle-aged man dressed in formal livery and a white peruke opened the front door and strode imperiously down the flagstone walkway leading to the cobblestone street. He opened the side door of the carriage with a flourish and bowed low in European courtly fashion. Offering a white-gloved hand to Katherine Cutler, he saw her properly out and then offered the same hand to Richard Cutler, who shook his head.

"I can manage quite well, Phineas, thank you," he said in the same jovial tone he had once used with Sydney Simms, his officious yet highly competent steward in *Portsmouth*. "And a pleasant good day to you," he said, adding with a grin, "You are especially well turned out this morning, Phineas. Is that a new outfit? I don't recall seeing it before."

Phineas Chapman, Richard knew from experience, had adopted the importance and airs of the man he served. He expected social and business discourse among people of consequence to be conducted within well-defined boundaries of propriety and protocol. Idle banter and verbal jousting not initiated by his employer were to be politely ignored.

"A most pleasant good morning to you, Mr. Cutler," he said without changing his a deadpan expression. "Please allow me to welcome you and Mrs. Cutler to Boston. If you will please follow me."

Richard offered Katherine his arm, and she took it with a look as if to say, "Can you not help yourself, my dear?" But her lips were twitching as they stepped up the walkway behind Chapman.

Will, looking tired but happy, greeted them in the front hallway. "Thank you, Mr. Chapman," he said to the butler, who bowed and turned away to attend to other duties. "Mother, Father, how wonderful to see you," he said, embracing his mother and shaking his father's hand.

"How is Adele?" his mother inquired eagerly. "And how is baby Katherine?"

"As well as well can be, I'd say. They're in the nursery. Adele is just feeding her."

"Can we see them?"

"Of course!" Will laughed. "Isn't that why you're here?"

"I'll be in the study," Richard said. "When the lass has drunk her fill, I'll come up."

"I will not wait one second longer," Katherine said to Will, excitement etched on her face in anticipation of meeting her first grandchild and namesake. "Lead on, oh father my son!" The babe had been born three weeks later than the family anticipated, but the worry that caused had vanished. Young Katherine was born wailing a healthy tune. Will and Adele had long ago chosen names depending on gender, but they had refused to reveal them until after the birth. Katherine had wept private tears of happiness when a letter from Will informed her that her first grandchild had been named in her honor. As Will had concluded in his letter, there were now two Katherine Cutlers in Boston society.

The snug little room that Richard entered was one of the few rooms in the entire residence, Richard often thought, that looked as though people actually lived in it. The "downstairs study," as the room was called to differentiate it from the more spacious and richly adorned study that Jack Endicott maintained at the rear of the second floor, featured oil paintings, a teakwood desk, wingback chairs, twin camelback sofas, a thick Turkish rug, a deep-set marble fireplace, and tiers of shelves on three walls lined with leather-bound books. Richard was perusing titles embossed on the spines of the books when he felt more than heard someone enter the room. He turned, expecting to see Jack Endicott. Instead he saw Jack's wife.

"Anne-Marie," he said, smiling. "How very nice to see you."

"And you, Richard." She came up to him and embraced him in her usual manner, as always conveying a silent message by pressing her fingers briefly into his upper back and allowing her lips to linger on his cheek before drawing away. "Congratulations to you and Katherine," she said cheerfully. "You have an exceptionally beautiful granddaughter. Mother and child are doing just fine, you will be happy to learn—a great deal better than *this* grandmother. I had quite forgotten how demanding a wee one can be."

Richard grinned. "From where I'm standing," he said, "that grandmother is doing just fine as well. And congratulations go all the way around, Anne-Marie. This is a blessed event for us all. My congratulations go also to Frances and Robert. I understand that the newlyweds have returned to Boston and have taken up residence in Louisburg Square. You must be delighted to have them living so close to you."

"I am indeed. And I am pleased that so many of your family were able to attend the wedding. It meant so much to us all—to me, especially." She leaned in and said conspiratorially: "For a while there I thought it might be Jamie giving Frances away, and not her stepfather. I have never seen a young man so eager for a wedding to proceed."

Richard could not help laughing. Never before had he heard Anne-Marie acknowledge her younger daughter's long and unsuccessful pursuit of his younger son.

"You will be interested to learn," he said, "that Jamie now has a love interest of his own. I had begun to worry that he would never find a woman to meet his high standards, but she was right there in Hingham all along. Mindy has been Diana's best friend since they were children. You may recall seeing her with Jamie at Frances' wedding: the tall, slender young woman with blond hair?"

"Yes, I do recall meeting her. But I thought her name was Melinda?"

Richard nodded. "'Mindy' is a nickname."

"Well, good for Jamie. She is indeed a lovely young woman. Is matrimony in their future, do you think?"

"Nothing is official yet, and of course that is for them to decide. However it may turn out, for the moment Katherine and I are delighted. We've rarely seen Jamie so happy and we have adored Mindy for years. I believe even Jack approves of her. And as we both know, when it comes to women and the finer things in life, Jack has impeccable taste."

He meant it as a light jest and also as a compliment to Anne-Marie. Which is why he was not prepared for the dark cloud that passed over her face. She looked away.

Puzzled, Richard asked, "Is something wrong, Anne-Marie? Did I speak out of turn?"

She laughed wryly. "No, Richard, you did not speak out of turn. You *never* speak out of turn."

"What's wrong, then?"

Her eyes returned to his and she smiled. "Nothing is wrong. In fact, I have glad tidings to share with you. Will and Adele will be returning to Ship Street early next week. It is their wish, and mine, that their daughter be raised in Hingham and not here in Boston. Hingham is their home and where they need to be. Little Katherine will grow up strong and healthy there."

"That *is* wonderful news," Richard said. "Katherine will be so pleased."

"I do hope so. And if Will joins the Navy, as he has his heart set on doing, there will be many more people in Hingham to attend to Adele and the baby than there would be here."

"That's true. And those people in Hingham must include you and Jack. You can come down and visit us anytime and stay for as long as you wish. You would be such a help to Adele, and of course Adele would be happy to have you there. And remember: a Cutler & Sons packet boat is always at your disposal. Just contact George Hunt whenever the mood strikes and he'll make the arrangements. You need only show up at the dock at the specified hour. Cutler & Sons will take care of the rest."

"That is extremely kind of you, Richard. I can't thank you enough. But the fact is—" She paused, and the dark clouds gathered anew.

He placed his hands lightly on her shoulders. "The fact is what, Anne-Marie? Tell me what's bothering you."

She looked up at him, her deep blue eyes glistening with unshed tears. She turned away, walked over to close the door to the study, and returned.

"The fact is, Richard," she said quietly but forthrightly, "I'm not sure if Jack *will* be joining me. He has been corresponding a great deal with Jan Van der Heyden in Java, and he may be leaving soon to meet with him in person. If he does, he tells me, he will be gone for many months. Perhaps for more than a year, depending on where they decide to meet."

Richard shrugged his shoulders. "Is that so unusual? The Orient trade is critical to C&E, and Jack hasn't seen Mr. Van der Heyden in quite a few years. Given the difficulties we are facing today and those we'll be facing in the future, a personal meeting makes good business sense whatever the time and distance involved."

"I don't disagree," she said. "Understand: it is not *what* he is saying to me, it is *how* he is saying it. I think he is not telling me the truth about this trip. Perhaps he does not even mean to return. He is so angry now, all of the time, with me and with the government because it does not protect his ships and business. And he has so little time these days for me and his daughters. I often wonder if he is even aware that he *has* a grandchild." She raised a hand as if to stop Richard from speaking. "Yes, I know, Jack is above all else a businessman. I knew that before I married him. Truth be told, it is *why* I married him. I wanted the life and social position he could give me. But one thing I have learned in this marriage is that there is more to life than making and losing money. *People* are what matter. *Family* is the most important. You understand that, Richard, God bless you. But Jack does not. Oh, no. All I am to him these days is . . . a possession: a charming hostess when he wishes to entertain other businessmen and a person who will listen to his angry rants when we are alone. I am his wife in name only." She paused, placed one graceful hand over her mouth, and then said in a quieter tone. "I'm so sorry, Richard. *I* am the one who has spoken out of turn. I should not be troubling you like this on such a glorious day. I apologize."

"You needn't apologize, Anne-Marie," he said with a dismissive gesture. "Not to me. These are hard times, and I fear they are going to get harder. Jack is my family's business partner, and he takes justifiable pride in the commercial empire he has built. We are all the beneficiaries of his good business judgment.

"Jack is not mad at you, Anne-Marie," he continued. "Jack is scared. He can't bear to see everything he values, everything he has worked so hard to build, threatened by forces beyond his control. He has to take out his frustrations on someone, and as his wife, that burden unfortunately falls on you."

"Yes," she said simply, then: "Thank you, Richard. Thank you for saying that. I need to hear it. Still, I feel terrible placing that burden on you when you have . . . when you have your own concerns to consider."

She did not explain what she meant, nor did Richard ask.

"I believe I hear a distant wail," he said. "Shall we go up?"

"You go. This is a special day for you and Katherine, and I have no wish to intrude upon it further. I will see how dinner is coming along. Jack will be joining us, if he can find the time."

Two HOURS after the Hingham packet boat set sail for Boston, another boat, a smaller craft, cast off from the same dock and followed a more northerly course. It was clinker-built and carried a single mast with a quadrilateral sail. At its bow was a loose-footed jib whose luff was secured to a forestay that bore down from near the top of the mast to the tip of a 4-foot bowsprit. Forward, an unenclosed cuddy provided storage and shelter for supplies. Planking built in around the cockpit in the shape of a sideways U provided seating, and the polished mahogany tiller was attached to a sizable rudder bolted to the stern. Impressive enough, to Mindy, was the fact that Jamie and Will had built this beauty, but what had caught her eye the first time she had sailed in this craft earlier in the summer was its wide beam—nearly half the length of the boat at the waterline. When she had asked Jamie to explain the boat's unusual design, he had laughed.

"That's easy," he had quipped. "Girls."

"Girls?"

"Sure. Girls get scared when a sailboat heels over in the wind. So, if Will and I wanted them to go out with us, we needed a boat that doesn't heel as much. We also needed a boat that doesn't require a substantial keel so we could get in close to one of the islands, anchor, and then wade ashore for some private time."

She raised one eyebrow. "I see. The girls liked *that*, too, no doubt."

"They were lining up at the dock," he said with a mischievous grin.

"I'm sure they were." To change the subject she had asked, "You and Will really built this boat by yourselves?"

"Well, no. The shipwrights at Harrison's Boat Yard helped us out a lot. So did Father and Mr. Crabtree after they returned home from the war in the Indies. It was therapeutic for Father. It gave him something to do. He had just lost his own father."

"How well I remember," Mindy said quietly, recalling those days and weeks that had brought together the entire village of Hingham in a common bond of mourning. "It seems impossible that seven years have passed since we lost that dear man."

Mindy's heartfelt reaction to his grandfather's passing had touched Jamie deeply. "Actually, Mindy," he had confessed, "it was Father who insisted on the wide beam and sail plan. He wanted a boat that was sturdy and reliable, and that Will and I could handle on our own. I made up the stuff about the girls."

"Ah," she had said.

Almost two weeks had elapsed since their last outing together in this boat. Since early June, Jamie had spent considerable time in Boston at the Charlestown Navy Yard. *Constitution* was due at long last by mid-October, recalled home, along with *Enterprise* and *Hornet*, the last three ships of the Mediterranean Squadron, following a mutiny by members of the flagship's crew. Frustrated beyond measure by what for some sailors had been a five-year term of service, and fearful that if war with England were to break out they would be forced to remain on station for perhaps years longer, they had refused to sail anywhere unless the destination was America. Only when Capt. Hugh Campbell threatened to fire into them with grapeshot did the mutineers reluctantly return to duty. What *Constitution*'s sailing orders might be after she arrived at the Navy Yard remained a matter of conjecture, although the commandant of the yard had speculated to Jamie that the flagship would likely require a major refitting before putting to sea again. The naval dockyards at Syracuse, the squadron's base on the island of Sicily, had limited capabilities.

Meanwhile, front-page newspaper articles highlighting what the national press had dubbed the "*Leopard-Chesapeake* Debacle" continued to stoke public outrage against Britain. Although the proceedings of the court-martial were kept under wraps, those in the know were certain that Commodore Barron would ultimately take the fall. Not only was he the ranking officer in *Chesapeake* at the time, he had, by his own admission, taken his flagship to sea unprepared for battle. That Barron had no reason to anticipate a battle—and that he had a six-week cruise ahead of him to put his ship and crew to rights, and that Secretary Smith had urged him to set sail as soon as possible, and that Captain Gordon had advised him that *Chesapeake* was ready for sea—seemed not to matter. Also indisputable was the fact that *Chesapeake*'s guns were in such a sorry state of readiness, and her gun crews so ill trained to service them, that to fire the one gun that replied to *Leopard*'s three broadsides her first lieutenant had plucked a hot coal from the galley fire and juggled it in his bare hands over to a gun that was touched off for "the honor of the flag." So Commodore Barron reportedly told the five judges presiding at the court-martial, among them Capt. Stephen Decatur and Capt. John Rodgers. None of that group of five naval captains was impressed by Barron's statement about honor.

And the national press would have none of it. "*Whither the honor, Commodore?*" headlines screamed from Boston to Savannah. When it was further revealed that after a perfunctory trial in Halifax, Nova Scotia, the captured British seaman had been hanged from the yardarm of his former ship, and that the three American sailors were condemned to receive five hundred lashes with the whip—a crueler and bloodier form of execution than hanging—the cries of outrage reached a fever pitch. The public demanded punishment for those responsible, and they got what they demanded. Commo. James Barron was suspended from the Navy for five years without pay. Capt. Charles Gordon and Lieutenant Hall, captain of *Chesapeake*'s Marines, received official reprimands; and *Chesapeake*'s chief gunnery officer was dismissed from the service.

By mid-August the fires beneath the pot had begun to moderate, but the water in the pot continued to simmer. America was teetering on the brink. What threats or dangers might be lurking in the future were of minor concern to James Cutler today. The soft offshore breezes were too caressing, the scenery too enticing, and the possibilities of what lay ahead too exciting. Since their first outing together on Nantasket Beach nearly a year ago, Mindy Conner had continued to elicit perspectives and desires he had never before experienced or even believed existed.

"Take the tiller?" he said to her as they left Bumpkin Island to starboard and Peddock's Island lay ahead a half mile. "I'll get the anchor ready."

"What am I aiming for?" she said as she scooted aft toward the helm. "East End?"

"Aye. Just west of there is the sandy cove I was telling you about. Got it?"

"Got it, Commodore," she confirmed, and the little boat sailed on with hardly a flutter in her billowing canvas as they shifted positions and Mindy took command of the vessel by placing two fingers gently atop the tiller. Jamie had explained to her that applying a light touch to the helm would allow her to "feel" the small craft better and respond to its motions more effectively when on a beam or broad reach in fair winds. She had quickly grasped both the knack and the thrill of it.

Jamie checked wind and weather a final time; nothing that he could see or sense suggested a shift in conditions anytime soon. The ebb tide had turned and was on its way in. For the next six hours, both wind and tide would be in their favor. How fitting, he thought to himself, on a perfect day such as this.

When the boat entered the indent of the cove, he stood, grabbed hold of the mast, and studied the rapidly shoaling seabed beneath them. Mindy too was studying it, and when she could make out small kelp-draped rocks on the sandy bottom and a lone crab scurrying sideways, she hauled in the mainsheet, gave a warning cry of "Coming about," and pushed over the tiller and swung the boat around until her bow was pointed directly into the wind. The boat immediately came to a standstill, its two sails flapping impotently and the mainsail boom jouncing about. As Mindy secured the boom, Jamie dropped overboard the heavy block of stone that served as an anchor and paid out the anchor line, allowing wind and tide to push the boat stern-first toward shore. When he heard the shallow keel scrape against the seabed, he pulled on the line to take the boat out to slightly deeper water and tied its bitter end to a wooden cleat at the bow.

"How did you learn to handle a boat so well?" he asked as they met amidships to service the sails.

"My beau taught me," she said as she released the throat and peak halyards and lowered the gaff-rigged mainsail. Together they gathered in the canvas and secured it loosely to the boom with ties.

"Did he indeed? He must be a hell of a man."

"He'll do in a clutch," she said with a smile so beguiling that it drew him over to her as irresistibly as a moth to a light. He took her in his arms and she melted into him, her arms coming around his neck, her lips parting to duel her tongue with his. They remained entwined for long minutes until she whispered into his ear.

"Lieutenant?"

"Mmm."

"I have something very, very important to ask you."

He pressed her lithe body to his, urging her on. "What is it?" he whispered back.

"How do I get ashore without ruining my dress?"

He released her, staring at her. "Mindy!"

"What?" she asked innocently.

"Is that all you can think about at a time like this? Your dress?"

"It's an important question, Jamie," she said in tones of mock reproach. "What's a poor girl to do in a situation like this?"

He rubbed his chin as if pondering his reply. "You could remove your dress, wade ashore with me, and then put it back on—or not, if no one's around. I surely wouldn't mind."

"James Cutler, you *are* a rogue!"

"Or I could carry you ashore."

"Perhaps that would be better," she said.

He took off his shoes and lowered himself over the side of the boat, feeling for the sandy bottom as cool seawater sloshed up to his thighs. "Ready about," he said, turning, and held out his arms. When he had her safely ashore, he waded back out to the boat to collect his shoes and a small seabag stowed forward in the cuddy. This he carried back to the beach with his shoes tied around his neck. In his left hand he held a second line that he had secured to a stern cleat with a clove hitch. When it came time to leave, he would use this line to haul the boat in toward shore, dragging the smooth slab of anchor along the seabed.

"Where to?" she asked after Jamie had pulled on his shoes and wrapped the end of the second line around the trunk of a tree standing close to the beach. "I'm sorry you got your pants wet," she added contritely.

"Not to worry. They'll dry quickly in this sun. Besides," he said, "I had to get my pants wet, didn't I? Otherwise, *you* would have had to carry *me* ashore, and somehow I have a hard time envisioning that."

"So do I," she giggled. "That would hardly have been very gallant of you, would it, Commodore?"

"No, it wouldn't. It's probably something one of your former beaux would have demanded, though." He hoisted the seabag and pointed to the cliff above them. "Up we go, my sweet."

They followed a rough path winding upward through trees and thickets until they came to a clearing atop the hill that was known as East End, predictably, because it was located at the eastern end of the island. The spot offered commanding vistas of Hingham and the long, crooked Nantasket Peninsula that defined the eastern extremity of Boston Harbor. Sunlight reflected off the glassy waters of Hingham Bay and Hull Bay. Two hundred yards to the east, across the treacherous swirls of Hull Gut, rose the forty-foot-high windmill, its four vanes creaking lazily in the summer breeze. To the north, the vast reaches of the Atlantic Ocean blended with eternity.

"It's beautiful, Jamie," Mindy breathed as her gaze took in the sweeping panorama. "Do you come here often?"

"Just once before," he replied, adding pointedly, "three summers ago with Will and Adele. It was just about this same time of year, in fact. I kept worrying that Will was plotting to toss me over the cliff to give him time alone here with his bride."

"I could hardly have blamed him," she said, laughing. Then: "How many people do you suppose live on this island?"

"Not many." He set the seabag on a flat stone that he had selected to serve as a dining table. He opened the canvas bag and removed a picnic that featured, among other delicacies, sandwiches of thinly sliced chicken topped with slices of tomatoes sprinkled with fennel. Edna Stowe had insisted on taking charge of the entire meal, from gathering the tomatoes in the garden to preparing the sandwiches, and Jamie had not objected. He was glad to see her acting her old feisty self, a clear indication that while old age might be creeping up on her, it had not yet overtaken her. "Most of the land on this island is used for pasture. There are several buildings near the western end. I doubt anyone lives in them permanently."

"This island must have a romantic history," she ventured.

"Not really," he said nervously, then bit his tongue for missing the opening she had offered. "Try one of these?" He handed her a sandwich and they sat down together side by side on the stone. For long moments they sat in quiet contemplation of sun, sea, and scenery, absorbed in their private thoughts. Jamie was not hungry. He toyed with his sandwich, his mind awhirl as he tried to decide what to say next—or rather, when and how to say it. Two years ago, even a year ago, he could not have conceived of broaching this subject, of asking the question he was screwing up his courage to ask. Love, he had believed, was best left for the future, for when his naval career was assured and a wife at home would not distract him from his duty at sea. But circumstances had changed that. On the surface it seemed so natural—and inevitable, according to friends and family, and even to people in Hingham he hardly knew. Why, then, his hesitation? Because, he answered his own question, a life-defining moment was now only minutes away.

Before he could say anything, Mindy said, "I have a confession to make."

He cocked his head at her in question.

She was staring down at her own uneaten sandwich. She put it aside and then blurted, "I didn't mean what I said on the boat down there. I wasn't thinking about my dress when you kissed me, I can assure you. I couldn't care less what happens to this stupid dress. It's just that—" She hesitated.

"It's just that what, Mindy?"

She hunched her shoulders and sighed softly. "It's just that whenever I'm with you, Jamie, whenever you touch me or put your arms around me or hold my hand or just smile at me across a room, I feel as though I am no longer in control of myself. As though I cannot resist doing something I may later regret. So I resort to humor, as a defense. You do that too sometimes. I guess we all do it sometimes. Anyway, that's what I was doing on the boat. I was hiding—I was hiding from myself." She continued to stare down at her lap. She clasped her hands together and shook her head as if in denial of something.

"Please don't think me brash, Jamie," she implored. "Please don't think ill of me for saying these things. I realize it's not proper for a girl to say such things to a boy, but God help me it's the truth. You may be sailing away soon, and I don't know when I will see you again. I don't know *if* I will see you again. So there are things I must say to you. Things I need so very much for you to understand. If I have overstepped my bounds, so be it, I'll accept the consequences. But I will not apologize." Her lips quivered. She was close to tears.

His right hand went to the side of her face. Gently he coaxed her chin around until their eyes locked. "Go on, Mindy," he half-whispered to her. "I'm listening. I'm listening very, very carefully."

Emboldened by his words she said, "You know how deeply I care for you, Jamie. It's no secret. It's there for everyone to see. I can't hide it. I can't be coy. Not about something like that. I have been in love with you since that day you returned for Diana's wedding and I saw you standing next to Will in the church. In truth, I have *always* loved you, even when I was a little girl and Diana invited me over to your house and I would go, praying you would be home and I would see you there." She looked down again at her lap. "Lord, how silly all this must sound to you. How dreadfully schoolgirlish." She swiped at a tear.

Emotion clogged his throat and blocked his ability to speak. He had long known Mindy Conner to be a free-thinking and independent young woman who was not afraid to speak her mind. It was one of her most endearing qualities. But what she had just said was so unexpected, and so blatantly honest, that it momentarily caught him off guard. But the sight of her sitting there next to him in such obvious anguish at his lack of response quickly brought him back.

"Look at me, Mindy." His voice, too, quavered.

She did.

"Answer just one question?"

She nodded, swiping at another tear.

"Will you marry me?"

It was much later, when the sun was well on its downward arc and the neap tide had reached its peak, that Lt. James Cutler, USN, revealed to his fiancée what he had also brought ashore in the seabag: a bottle of the choicest French champagne that money could buy in Boston.

RICHARD CUTLER cursed under his breath when he saw the heavyset matron bustling toward him on South Street. Rebecca Leavitt Hanson was the last person he wanted to see. She was a woman of consequence in Hingham, but she was also one of the town's most notorious gossips, albeit always under the mantle of maintaining decorum within the town's polite society, for whom she considered herself the spokeswoman.

When she stepped in front of him, blocking his route, Richard tipped his tricorne hat to her. "Good day, Mrs. Hanson," he said with as much respect as he could muster.

"And a good day to you, Captain Cutler," she said congenially. "And what a delightful day it is. I have always said that September is the best month of the year. As warm as summer during the day, and yet sufficiently cool in the evening for one to enjoy the comfort of a fire in the hearth."

"Indeed," Richard agreed, preparing to move on.

"By the bye," the woman launched in, "I understand that your son James is betrothed to Miss Melinda Conner. May I offer you my congratulations."

"Thank you," Richard said.

"But I must say," the lady continued self-righteously, "that I am perplexed by the brevity of their engagement. They are to be wed next month? In October?"

"Yes," Richard confirmed.

"Why so soon, Mr. Cutler? We are all so surprised. Is there perhaps an urgent reason for the short engagement?"

When Richard's eyes narrowed and bored directly into hers, she quickly added, "I mean, my goodness, you barely have time to post the banns. And the way the two of them have been gallivanting about on their own all summer, without proper chaperones. Everyone in town is talking about it. We understand that they are in love, Mr. Cutler, and we are all so terribly fond of both James and Melinda. Which is why we are so happy for them and why nothing has been said to this point. At least by me. But people are talking and you *do* understand why such casual behavior and a hasty marriage can raise an eyebrow or two, don't you?"

Two, Richard thought to himself, is likely the exact number of eyebrows that Jamie's behavior has raised. But he said nothing.

"Oh yes, people are talking," she sniffed, undeterred by his silence and obvious anger. "I should think that you would wish to know what people are talking about."

"You have just informed me, Mrs. Hanson," Richard replied stiffly. "Now, if you will excuse me."

She made way for him. "Good afternoon to you, Mr. Cutler," she said pleasantly as he strode past her. "I trust you to remember me to your dear wife."

"Indeed, Mrs. Hanson," he said with a quick sideways glance, "I will tell her all about our encounter."

At his home a short way farther down South Street he found Katherine knitting in the parlor. "I just collided with your friend Rebecca Hanson," he called out as he hung his hat from a peg on the wall beside the front door.

"How lovely for you!" she said sarcastically as he took a chair across from the sofa where she was sitting. "What did that old windbag have to huff and puff about this morning?"

"As you would expect, she's shocked that Jamie and Mindy are getting married next month. To her warped mind, a betrothal in August and a wedding in October can mean only one thing. She was born two hundred years too late. She belongs back with the witches of Salem instead of in modern-day Hingham."

Katherine smiled. "Why didn't you just tell her the truth? That Jamie and Mindy want to be wed before *Constitution* sails?" Left unspoken was what they both realized was another reason for the brief engagement: Katherine Cutler might be unable to attend a wedding in May or June of the following year.

"Rebecca Hanson doesn't want the truth. She wants material she can use to grind through her rumor mill, the more salacious the better. What I should have told her is that Mindy is with child and they decided they had better make it legal before the baby popped out. Hell, you know that's what the old battleaxe *wanted* to hear me say. That's what she was *praying* I would say. Most likely it's what she's saying right now to her busybody friends." He threw up his hands in frustration and then noticed an unfolded piece of paper with a broken seal on a table beside the sofa. "Who is the letter from?"

"It's from Cynthia, with a note from Julia. Joseph brought it over."

"Joseph was here? I'm sorry I missed him. We haven't seen him in quite awhile."

"And we'll be seeing less of him now that classes have started up again at Derby. But that's all right. He's doing so well there, Richard. It's working out just as we had hoped. He is everyone's favorite teacher."

"He has you to thank for that, Katherine. The entire school should thank you for that. So, what does Cynthia have to say?"

Katherine handed him the letter and summarized it while he read.

"Cynthia and Julia are definitely coming to Hingham next spring for a short visit. Cynthia wants to see her son, of course, and they both want to see us. They would stay for two or three weeks. John and Robin are apparently all for it."

"And you?" he asked cautiously. "Are you all for it?"

"I honestly don't know, Richard," she said. "Joseph has asked me to respond to his mother, but I don't know what to say to her. I would so love to see Cynthia and Julia one more time before . . ." She let it go at that.

Richard refolded the letter. "Perhaps we should wait a few weeks to see how things develop," he said soberly, adding, to impersonalize what he had just said, "There is just too much uncertainty and trouble in our world today."

"There is that," Katherine had to agree.

Twelve

Hingham, Massachusetts
March 1808

I N DECEMBER 1807 the ax fell. Its blade had been hewn to a fine edge during the months following *Leopard*'s assault on *Chesapeake,* and the impact, when it hit, tore the body politic of the United States asunder. Although the vote was far from unanimous, the Tenth Congress, as expected, passed the Embargo Act recommended by President Jefferson, and he signed it into law on December 22. At the same time the government put into effect the Non-importation Act passed in April of the previous year, which prohibited the importation of many items from Great Britain, including leather, clothing, hats, and beer.

The Embargo Act was not one law but a series of laws passed in rapid succession to close loopholes in earlier iterations, especially as they related to Canada. Highly lucrative smuggling by boat, wagon, and sled began to flourish along that colony's border with Vermont and upper New York State. At its core, the Embargo Act was intended to end American foreign trade in an attempt to deny Britain and France the produce from America they so desperately needed—in Jefferson's judgment, at least—in their epic struggle, and thus force them to end impressments, seizure of cargoes, and other affronts to American law and honor. The act closed down American foreign shipping—all of it: to Europe, to the Orient, to the West Indies, to every port of call around the globe. Specifically, the act prohibited American merchant vessels from sailing into any foreign port unless authorized to do so by President Jefferson or an official customs collector. To encourage compliance, shipping companies were served notice that violations of the act would incur a financial penalty of $10,000 for each offense, in addition to forfeiture of the ship's cargo. Federalists—and many Republicans as well—viewed the Embargo Act as a flagrant abuse of Americans' liberties. The act permitted port authorities to seize cargoes without a warrant and to bring to trial any shipper or merchant who was suspected of even contemplating a violation of the embargo. Merchant vessels purportedly sailing from one American port to another American port were required to post a surety bond that was forfeited if the vessel happened to stray from its stated itinerary.

The draconian law smacked of the worst of European totalitarianism. It also flew in the face of long-proclaimed Jeffersonian principles of a limited federal bureaucracy and minimal government interference in the lives of private citizens. But on this issue the president was adamant. He would not yield an inch even though members of his own cabinet opposed him, most notably Treasury Secretary Albert Gallatin, who argued in cabinet meetings that the embargo would be ineffective and impossible to enforce. Gallatin's tune played to deaf ears. Jefferson summarily approved any and all red tape and expansion of governmental powers necessary to enforce the embargo. In coffeehouses and taverns across Federalist New England, rumblings of outrage and opposition began anew; along the shores of Lake Champlain and the coast of Down East Maine there were threats of open insurrection. The brief period of national solidarity following the *Chesapeake* affair that had brought New England back into the fold had been severed by the ax. New Englanders once again began to look to themselves to save themselves.

"At least the man had the decency to announce that he would not seek reelection," Caleb Cutler groused during a family supper at his home on Main Street in Hingham during an evening in mid-March. Outside, rain and sleet splattered against the window-panes, a mixture that in South Hingham, four miles inland and away from the warming effects of the sea, would be falling as snow. In the stone hearth a fire crackled agreeably, spreading its warmth across a dining table that seated four couples of the extended Cutler family. Diana and Peter Sprague were conspicuously absent. After the Christmas season they had moved from Hingham to a suite of rooms on Eliot Street in Cambridge near the home of Anne Cutler Seymour and her physician husband, Frederick, in order for Peter to be near his law studies at Harvard. Tonight, as had been true of many nights recently, Mindy Conner Cutler was staying with the Spragues so that she could be with Jamie when he was allowed to leave his post in *Constitution*. The superfrigate, once again under the command of Capt. John

Rodgers, was undergoing a major refit at the Charlestown Navy Yard, and her commissioned and senior warrant officers were required to be on station most days to oversee the process and to monitor progress.

"Aye, he did," Agreen said. "But ask me and I'll tell you: Jefferson's not tryin' t' do the honorable thing by limitin' his presidency to two terms as President Washington did. No sir! The man wants out; he's tired of his responsibilities. And hell's bells, who can blame him? Besides, he knows he wouldn't be reelected if he ran again."

"I wouldn't bet on that," Richard countered. "I agree that Jefferson wants out, but I suspect he'd be reelected by a good margin were he to run again. Next year the Federalists will likely nominate Charles Pinckney again," referring to a South Carolina statesman, Revolutionary War hero, and Federalist icon, "to oppose Madison, and last time around he was soundly defeated. Madison and Jefferson are two peas in a pod, as you like to say, Agee. In fact, the embargo is probably more Madison's idea than Jefferson's. Our agent, Mr. Shaw, tells us that Madison has been pulling the strings and essentially running this country for the last two years while Jefferson has been biding his time, waiting to step down and return home to Monticello."

Adele Cutler spoke up. "Like him or not, you have to admire a leader who truly believes he can achieve his diplomatic objectives through economic coercion rather than by force of arms, and thereby save lives and save his country from the ravages of war. President Jefferson may be an idealist, and I agree that in this instance his idealism may have gotten the better of him, but I say that this war-torn world needs a good deal more of his brand of idealism." She took a sip of wine and added wryly, "I realize that my stepfather would see me in a stock and pillory for uttering such blasphemy." A chorus of jovial agreement followed that remark. "Fortunately," she added, "he is not here to hear it. But it *is* a shame," she continued in a more serious tone. "Jefferson started his presidency with such hope and promise, and he is ending it in such misery and despair."

Other citizens of the United States and in the halls of Congress might disagree with those last few words, but no one at the table did. Nor was anyone at the table surprised either by Adele's candor or her eagerness to engage in verbal jousting over business and politics. It was one reason why she had become fast friends with Mindy Cutler and Diana Sprague. Well educated and well read, they shared traits that many young women of Boston society found unladylike and unbecoming.

For an extended interval the group sat in silence and ate their supper of roast venison, potatoes, and peas, the only sounds the clinking of utensils on china, the quiet sighs of gastronomic contentment, and the crackling of birch logs in the hearth. At length, Will Cutler broached a subject that was on everyone's mind but was rarely mentioned outside the inner sanctum of the Cutler & Sons' countinghouse on Long Wharf.

"Uncle Caleb," he ventured, "just how long can Cutler & Sons continue to pay its sailors with no revenues coming in?"

Caleb gave his nephew a startled look. "As long as it takes," he said immediately. "How can you even ask such a question, Will?"

Katherine Cutler glanced at her husband, who said, "What your uncle means to say, Will, is that our sailors are our lifeblood and we must keep them on whatever the cost. When they signed on with us, we made a compact with each of them that Cutler & Sons would care for them and their families, come what may. I made that very same promise twenty years ago to the crew of *Eagle* as they sat in an Algerian prison and worried about their loved ones back home. Cutler & Sons made good on that promise, even though we had far fewer resources then than we do today, and kept it throughout the ten years it took to gain the crew's release. For all those years their families never went without. We continued to pay each family what each sailor was due by contract. People wonder how we manage to sustain such loyalty among our crews. Well, there's your answer. So, we're not going to abandon our sailors now, even if that means dipping into our own family's reserves. They will continue to be paid as long as we have funds available to pay them. Sooner or later our government will come to its senses and repeal this embargo. When it does, we'll need our sailors in our employ, and we'll need their continued loyalty. That goes from Mr. Hunt right on down to the lowest-paid deckhand. We've been through this before, haven't we?"

"Yes, of course, Father," Will said. "I have always understood that and I agree wholeheartedly. My question, though, is how long can we continue to do it?"

"As long as it takes," his father said, reiterating Caleb's words in a tone that brooked no dissent.

"And bear in mind," Caleb said in a more congenial tone, "that Cutler & Sons is not entirely without revenues. You've seen the books, Will. Granted, our earnings today are not what they were in years past, but funds are still coming in. John and Robin can still ship to us, and we can sell sugar and rum to the interior of our country through our Baltimore office."

"Assuming Americans can continue to afford such items," Will asserted.

"I can't disagree," Caleb said. He left unsaid his most profound fear, one shared by every member of his family and by many of his countrymen: the effects of a prolonged embargo could devastate the fragile American economy and bankrupt the nation and nearly everyone in it. He also left unsaid the legal point that while Cutler & Sons merchant ships from Barbados were still allowed to ship goods to America under the embargo, they were not permitted to load cargo for the voyage back to Bridgetown—or to any other port. That meant they had to sail from the United States with empty holds, and *that* cut potential revenues in half and squeezed potential profits to the point of no return.

"What of C&E?" Lizzy Crabtree inquired. Earlier in the evening, she and Phoebe Hardcastle and Joan Cutler had resolved to make every effort to steer conversation away from the dangerous shoals of current affairs out toward deeper, calmer waters. But that had been like trying to contain a raging river with a fish net. Their resolve having gone by the boards before the first course was served, Lizzy was succumbing to the inevitable in asking her question.

"That is the great unknown," Caleb said. "We have long regarded the Orient as the future of our family business, but today even that business is uncertain. Although we own only a 50 percent share of C&E Enterprises, we have committed the bulk of our resources to it. To date, those investments have paid off handsomely. But with England doubling its efforts to blockade the Continent and Napoléon issuing his Milan Decree and threatening to impound any neutral merchant vessel that complies with British orders in council, C&E is in danger of losing its biggest and most lucrative market. It's also in danger of losing its crews. King George has called Jefferson's bluff and is urging the Royal Navy to step up its efforts to impress American sailors. At least we know where *he* stands on the issues of the day. So much for any lessons we hoped the good king might have learned from the *Chesapeake* affair."

"He did agree to suspend punishment of the three American sailors," Katherine pointed out.

"I don't think the good king had much to do with that decision, my dear," her brother Hugh countered. "That would have been made by the Admiralty, and I'd wager it was not motivated by any humanitarian gesture. More likely it was made in response to pressures in Parliament. Many MPs disagree with King George, and in fact openly oppose the impressment of Americans. They contend, quite correctly, in my opinion, that England has jolly well enough troubles over there without stirring up the pot over here. Of course, I may be mistaken; it has been known to happen, as implausible as that may seem. To our knowledge, the three American sailors have not yet been released, and their ultimate fate remains as uncertain as our own future prospects."

"So, you will be sailing with Jack Endicott to Cape Town, Hugh?" Joan Cutler asked. What had once been merely a business proposition from Jack Endicott to Jan Van der Heyden was about to become a reality. It had taken months to coordinate, with correspondence crisscrossing the Atlantic and Indian Oceans, but a summit meeting between Endicott and Van der Heyden had been arranged for mid-July in Cape Town, Africa, a popular port of call located roughly halfway between C&E Enterprises' New England office and its Far Eastern headquarters on Java in the Dutch East Indies.

If Jack Endicott was clear on what the two business behemoths would be discussing during their rendezvous, however, he was offering no clues, not even to Caleb Cutler. Indeed, the entire affair was shrouded in mystery. To date, Endicott had chosen to ignore the embargo, and as a result, C&E Enterprises had been fined $20,000 and two of its ships' cargoes were now in the hands of the U.S. Treasury Department. Even worse, C&E merchant ships that had managed to evade port authorities, revenue cutters, and the U.S. Navy had not netted much of a profit, certainly not enough to justify the business risks. Worse still, one of those vessels had been detained by the British and then seized by French authorities in Rotterdam because her captain had complied with British demands. Napoléon subsequently announced, tongue in cheek, that by seizing the ship and its cargo he was simply helping the American president enforce his embargo.

"Napoléon is playing Jefferson for a fool," George Hunt had commented when word of that arrived at the company's countinghouse on Long Wharf.

"Which is exactly what he is," Endicott had spat in disgust. "The United States has become the laughingstock of Europe."

Worst of all, to Richard's mind, was Endicott's flouting of the law. The Cutler name was attached to C&E, and as a former naval commander with one son currently serving as an officer in the U.S. Navy and another son aspiring to that position, his family was sworn to uphold the nation's laws, including the embargo. Richard was adamant that Cutler & Sons would play by the rules, whatever the consequences, and Caleb had agreed.

"Yes, Joan," Hugh confirmed. "We sail in six weeks. Unless, of course, Agreen has a change of mind and agrees to serve as *Falcon*'s captain. It grieves me no end to admit it, but he was Jack's first choice." He smiled at Agreen.

Agreen shook his head. "*Falcon* is yours to command, Hugh," he said. "She's as fine and fast a vessel as has ever put to sea. No one needs t' remind me of that. But I have two reasons for declinin' Jack's offer. One reason is sittin' across from me at this table, and the other reason is upstairs playin' with young Thomas. No, Baltimore is the limit for this old sea dog."

"How very fortunate for Lizzy and Zeke," Phoebe Hardcastle said sharply, either unable or unwilling to mask her sarcasm. The prospect of her husband being away at sea for many months was not to her liking, and the mention of children always seemed to underscore her inability thus far to successfully deliver one.

Hugh raised both hands. "I really have no choice, my dear," he said in a tired tone that suggested he and Phoebe had wallowed through this subject many times before tonight. "We must consider the benefits. By all accounts, money is going to be increasingly difficult to come by, and Jack Endicott is offering me a handsome wage to take him to Cape Town. He and I have handpicked a crew from the Cutler & Sons muster roll, and to ensure their loyalty, each sailor will be paid a bonus of 25 percent of his normal pay at the end of the voyage. As Agreen said, *Falcon* is a fast vessel—despite her age she is one of the fastest vessels of my acquaintance—and we shan't be tarrying long in Cape Town, I can assure you. We'll be home long before the leaves turn, and then you and I will kick up our heels like never before. We'll make Will and Adele and Jamie and Mindy look like drab, boring stay-at-homes."

"I shall be looking forward to it," Phoebe said, but there was sadness in her voice.

THE DISTANCE from the family seat on lower Main Street to Richard and Katherine's two-story gray clapboard house on South Street was only a quarter mile. Nevertheless, in consideration of the inclement weather, Caleb and Joan offered a bedroom upstairs to Richard and Katherine, with the added incentive that the room was the one that had been Richard's as a boy. Hugh and Phoebe were staying the night just down the hall in Anne and Lavinia's old room, Joan said to entice them, and in the morning the six of them could have breakfast together. When Katherine politely declined the offer, Will and Adele volunteered to accompany her and Richard home before walking the short distance to their own home on Ship Street.

The air was dank and chilly, and fog was moving in, but the mixture of rain and sleet proved to be more annoying than challenging. Winter along the South Shore and the Cape had been unusually mild this year, although the interior of Massachusetts had received its normal dose of wintry weather. Whale oil lamps hanging on posts thirty feet apart along Main Street, South Street, and North Street revealed a patchwork of dead grass, open road, and dirty mounds of slush where snow had once been piled. Without those lamps, even townspeople who had known these streets for years would have been hard put to find their way about the village on a night like this—which is why lamplighters would remain on duty to ensure that the lamps remained lit until midnight, two hours hence.

No one said much as they walked north on Main Street before turning west at the intersection with South Street. It took every bit of concentration to maintain a sure footing, and Richard kept a firm grip on Katherine's arm until they were at the front door of their home and under the protective overhang of the roof at the front stoop.

"Would you two like to come in?" he asked his son and daughter-in-law. "Your mother and I normally have a glass of wine by the fire before retiring. You're certainly welcome to join us."

A hopeful glance from Will to his wife was met with, "We'd love to, but we really must be getting back. I'm sure Edna has had her hands full with little Katherine and deserves a respite. Maybe tomorrow? Or the next day?"

"Any day is fine, Adele," Richard said, repeating his oft-used phrase: "You just need to open the door and walk in." He looked at his son. "Will, I was proud of you this evening. You must have bitten your tongue to keep from spilling the news about your letter from Lieutenant Perry."

In fact, Will had been near to bursting with excitement since receiving a letter from Lt. Oliver Hazard Perry two days ago. Richard had never met the young man, although he knew Oliver's father, Capt. Christopher Raymond Perry, who had commanded the frigate *General Greene* during the war with France. Perry's son, Richard was aware, had entered the Navy at the age of thirteen, serving first in his father's frigate as a midshipman and then serving with distinction in the war against Tripoli: in the frigate *Adams* and later as commander of the 12-gun schooner *Nautilus* in the attack on Derne. At the moment he was engaged in the construction of gunboats, although as he stated in his letter to Will, he was in line to relieve Lt. Jacob Jones as commander of *Revenge*, a 12-gun schooner attached to the North Atlantic Squadron under the command of Commo. John Rodgers in *Constitution*. The squadron's mission was to cruise the North Atlantic to enforce the embargo, and no less a personage than Navy Secretary Robert Smith had put forward Will Cutler's name to Perry.

"Nothing is definite yet, Father," Will reminded him. "I don't want to say anything about it until my appointment is approved."

"I understand. So you are firming up plans to sail to New York to confer with Lieutenant Perry?"

"I am to be there three weeks from tomorrow. The Navy is footing the bill for all expenses," he added with a sheepish grin. In former days Will Cutler would not have deemed it necessary to emphasize that point. Today he did.

His father nodded. "That will give us ample time to discuss matters before you sail," he said. "In the meantime, your mother and I wish you both a very good night."

"Indeed we do," Katherine said.

Richard opened the door for Katherine and followed her inside. After helping her off with her coat, he walked across the parlor to the hearth, lit a round of candles, and set a fresh bundle of birch logs on the smoking embers. He did the same in the kitchen and again upstairs in their bedroom. When he came back downstairs, he joined Katherine on the sofa near the now-blazing fire. On the long, low table before her she had placed a bottle of Bordeaux and two glasses next to a three-branched brass candelabra. The candles and firelight cast a cozy glow over the room as the last of the sleet and rain tapped against the window-panes.

"I shall miss Will if he enters the Navy," Katherine sighed as Richard poured out two half glasses of wine and handed one to her. "I shall miss him as much as I already miss Jamie."

"No more than I will," Richard said reflexively. An instant later the full impact of what she had just said struck him a crushing blow. When their two sons went to sea, he would indeed miss them—but their mother knew that she might never see them again. He quickly added, "We have to bear in mind how fortunate we've been to have had them so close to us during these past few months. Now they must do their duty as they perceive their duty to be, and I am proud of them both—as I know you are."

"I am," Katherine said. "And I admire Adele for handling their situation so magnanimously. Not every wife would be so supportive of a husband's voluntary leave-taking so soon after the birth of their first child. I have always said that Will and Adele make an excellent match."

"As do Jamie and Mindy. And Diana and Peter. If nothing else, my love, you and I have seen all three of our children marry well and lead the lives we would want for them."

Katherine raised her glass toward him, "We have certainly had our priorities straight when it comes to our children, haven't we." It was not a question.

Richard clinked his glass against hers. "Yes, although you deserve most of the credit for how they turned out. You did the hard work of raising them while I was often off at sea pursuing my dreams."

Katherine shook her head. "As your Aunt Emma used to say, pish posh, my dear."

The mention of his English aunt and her favorite phrase harkened Richard back to that voyage long ago, first to England and then on to Barbados, in the Cutler & Sons merchant brig *Eagle*. At their father's insistence Richard and his brother Will had signed on as ordinary seamen to learn the ropes at sea and, more important, to learn the ropes of Cutler & Sons from their uncle's perspective and those of their cousins, John and Robin Cutler. It was during their stay at their aunt and uncle's home in Fareham, England, that Richard had met Katherine Hardcastle, a close childhood friend of Richard's cousin Lizzy Cutler, now living a short way away and married to Richard's shipmate and close friend Agreen Crabtree. He marveled at how all the variables and intricacies of his relationship with Katherine had linked up, one to another, in a chain of events that had brought them from their introduction to each other at his uncle's home in Fareham thirty-four years earlier to this parlor on this night in Hingham. It must have been divinely inspired. It *had* to be.

"I remember she used to say to me in the evening, whenever I had been wrestling with a problem during the day, 'It's off to bed with you, Richard. Things will be clearer in the morning after a good night's sleep. You'll see.'" He chuckled. "Fact is, she was usually right."

"My mother used to say the same sort of thing," Katherine mused. "Except, of course, to my father. Even though she knew it wouldn't do any good."

"That's putting it mildly. When your father first realized my intentions toward you, it would have taken him more than a month of solid sleep to solve *this* problem." He pointed at himself. "No colonial rebel for *his* daughter, thank you very much."

Katherine smiled. "He had other plans for me, I admit. But in the end he came around. He actually came to like you."

"He did, but only after I had walked through hell to prove myself to him."

"No, that was not it. Father could be a cantankerous old cuss, but he *was* my father and he always had my best interests at heart. It took some doing and a few years of our being married, but when he realized how much I loved you and how very happy you had made me, he saw the wisdom of my choice. And then he began to view things a bit differently."

Richard said nothing in response. During the early years of their relationship he had indeed had his trials with his father-in-law. But Katherine was right: in the end he had come to view things differently. Back in '99, when Katherine and Lizzy had sailed with their children to visit with both sets of parents for what would prove to be the last time, Capt. Henry Hardcastle, RN, had been the quintessential loving father and doting grandfather. Katherine had often talked with Richard about that voyage during their evening fireside ritual, as she had about many of the milestones of her life as a girl living in England and then as a married woman living in New England. Those hours of fond remembrance were the ones she enjoyed most each day.

At the moment, however, she was considering not the past but the future. "Richard, we need to talk," she said, staring at the fire.

Although his heart almost stopped beating he managed a nonchalant response. "About what?"

"I believe you know," she said.

He did know, or at least he suspected, what she had in mind simply by the gravity in her voice. She had broached this topic before, on two occasions, and each time he had cut her off before she could get very far into it. He downed a healthy swig of Bordeaux and sat there, waiting.

"I understand why you don't want to discuss this. Do you think *I* do? But there are things that need to be said and resolved, so please hear me out. We must face our worst thoughts and fears, Richard," she said carefully. "The future is what it is for us all. We are *all* in God's hands. Each one of us is going to die at some point. It's the way of the world. We can only put our trust in God and in each other, and in the strength of what we mean to each other and the love we shall always have for each other. Denial does no good. I have tried it, and I assure you it does no good. We need to face this together, however much it may hurt to do so."

"Katherine . . ."

"Hush, now. Let me finish. You have no doubt been thinking about how hard all this is on me. But *I* have been thinking about how hard it must be on you, and how hard it is going to be for our children. I have often thought about what I would do if our situations were reversed, if you were the one with this dreadful disease and I was the one left behind. Honestly, I don't know how I could go on. But somehow I would have to find the strength to do it—for the many people who are near and dear to us, our children and grandchildren especially."

She paused, then took up her glass and drained its contents. Richard poured her another round and one for himself, filling both glasses to the three-quarters level.

"Where is this leading us?" he asked quietly as he gently placed the empty bottle back on the table.

"I'm not sure," she replied. "Perhaps to many places, eventually. The point for now is that we need to start talking more. We have been avoiding difficult discussions, and again, I understand why. But it's helpful to me to talk even if talking is painful and makes us sad or uncomfortable. More than anything I need to know that when I'm . . . gone . . . things will be in their proper place and that you will not be lonely."

"How could I be lonely? I have family and friends all around me. *Our* family and friends, Katherine."

"You know what I mean, Richard."

So, Richard thought, it had come around full circle for a third time to the very subject he had refused to discuss before, and would refuse to discuss now. "I do know what you mean, Katherine," he said evenly. "I know exactly what you mean, and I know exactly where you're going with this conversation. I will hear no more about it. As I have said before, I will discuss any topic you wish, at any time, except for that one. For that one the door is closed—and locked."

"Richard," she said hurriedly, "it's critical that I tell you that you have my blessing whatever may happen, whatever you may choose to do. I need you to understand that I would not love you any the less, that it would not diminish in any way what we have had together, what we will always mean to each other."

"End of discussion!" he stated emphatically. He looked at her and said, his voice breaking, "You are my wife, Katherine. You are my *only* wife. For today *and* for tomorrow."

"Till death us do part," she said quietly.

"No," he countered. "Till God in his infinite love and mercy sees fit to reunite us."

"Amen," she whispered, and closed her eyes to the night as the tears welled up.

Thirteen

The Atlantic Ocean
June 1808

WITHIN the Cutler family there was considerable debate on the course *Falcon* should follow from Boston to Cape Town. If she were to optimize prevailing winds and ocean currents, there were essentially two alternatives. The first was to sail south to where the north-flowing Gulf Stream split in two off the coast of North Carolina north of the treacherous Diamond Shoals, and follow its more powerful southern track eastward across the Atlantic to West Africa. There *Falcon* could pick up two secondary southbound currents—one leading past the Azores, the other past the Canaries—to near the mouth of the Senegal River, where the great clockwise motion of the North Atlantic Gyro veered westward back across the Atlantic toward the Indies. The voyage from the Senegal to Cape Town would potentially be the most difficult leg because the schooner would likely encounter south-easterly headwinds in collusion with the counter-clockwise motion of the great South Atlantic Gyro.

The alternate route was to avoid the Gulf Stream and other north-bound currents along the North and South American coasts and sail southward in mid-ocean until they reached the latitude of the southern coast of Brazil. From there a strong eastbound current—the southern loop of the South Atlantic Gyro—reinforced by prevailing easterly winds would take them swiftly on a direct line across the Atlantic to the southern tip of the African continent.

They would need to cross the equator on either route, and *Falcon* would be subjected to the doldrums, an area of low pressure in the low latitudes where prevailing winds are calm. Sea stories told of vessels trapped in the doldrums for weeks on end, of sailors delirious with thirst and hunger driven to commit savage acts of cannibalism. When that source of food was depleted, they succumbed to the elements, their skeletal remains bleached white on the weather deck of a ghost ship adrift on the open sea. Hugh could only pray that *Falcon* would breeze through this unfavorable stretch of ocean without undue difficulty or delay. He could not imagine living with Jack Endicott in such conditions.

Not a sailor himself and having little interest in the business of sailing, Endicott left the decision of which route to follow to his captain. Hugh Hardcastle, in turn, had conferred with his brother-in-law and also with Agreen Crabtree, the only one among them who had made this voyage. Back in 1801 Agreen had conveyed Caleb and Will Cutler in *Falcon* to Cape Town and from there to Batavia, on the East Indian island of Java, where the Cutlers had been grandly accommodated by Jan Van der Heyden and the vast resources of C&E Enterprises' Far Eastern headquarters. From Java *Falcon* had sailed east across the Pacific Ocean, south around the raging Horn, and northward off the coasts of the Americas in a circumnavigation that was completed, according to those in the know in Boston, in near record time.

Agreen recommended that *Falcon* take the first alternative, effectively shadowing the route that he and Richard had followed to Gibraltar and Algiers back in 1789. Hugh agreed. During his tenure as a post captain attached to the Mediterranean Squadron he had rarely had occasion to cruise south of the Azores. Nevertheless, he understood from his years of study of Royal Navy logs and charts that the course Agreen was recommending had first been developed by Portuguese and Spanish mariners exploring the New World and had since been refined by mariners of many nations, including, most recently, Capt. Thomas Truxtun of the U.S. Navy.

Hugh set a departure date of May 1. He had pegged the distance from Boston to Cape Town at approximately 8,000 sea miles. At an average speed of 6 knots *Falcon* would make close to 150 miles per day—twice that amount on the best days, half that amount on the worst. Allowing one full day for reprovisioning in the Canary Islands and one full week as a hedge against the doldrums and other unforeseen difficulties, Hugh put *Falcon* in Cape Town Harbor a week before the target date of July 15. If Jack Endicott were delayed for any reason, Jan Van der Heyden would simply wait for him. Van der Heyden would be sailing an equally daunting distance from Java in *China*, the largest and most heavily armed ship in the C&E merchant fleet. According to Agreen, who had toured *China* in Batavia Harbor, she looked more like a Royal Navy ship of the line than a merchant vessel.

Six weeks prior to departure, *Falcon*'s crew was hard at it. The yellow-hulled, double-topmast schooner had gone up on dry dock at the Benjamin Hallowell Shipyard in Boston, where she had originally been built, and in the process had had her bottom cleaned, her topmasts replaced, and her after cabin, normally the purview of her captain, reconfigured to accommodate a desk, a sofa, two wingback chairs, and a traditional bed for Jack Endicott, whose cabin this would be throughout the voyage. Hugh Hardcastle assigned himself the smaller albeit still comfortable first mate's cabin. Sturgis Haskins, first mate doubling as sailing master, and Paul Shipley, second mate doubling as de facto boatswain, were each assigned an even smaller cabin. A crew of twelve experienced seamen, divided equally into a two-watch bill, rounded out the muster roll. Four of these seamen, including Shipley, were well acquainted with the 9-pounder brass guns mounted on the schooner's weather deck, four to a side. Piracy loomed as a constant threat in most foreign waters, and Hugh Hardcastle was glad to have the guns. He would, he informed Haskins and Shipley, see them exercised each day during the Atlantic crossing.

A day before departure, the customs collector of Boston Harbor gave final clearance to Captain Hardcastle to sail wherever he wished because *Falcon* carried no cargo.

As YOUNG Seaman Carlson strode studiously aft, doing his best imitation of a midshipman on the weather deck of a warship, he was unable to mask a grin. "Captain Hardcastle," he announced, "Dougherty has spotted the peak of Mount Teide. She lies dead ahead, sir. *Dead ahead*," he repeated meaningfully.

Hugh Hardcastle had heard the cry from aloft and understood its significance. If *Falcon* were anywhere close to the dead reckoning that he and Haskins had plotted on the charts since leaving Boston, their first sighting of land would be of the twelve-thousand-foot-high volcano on Tenerife, the largest of the seven islands in the Canary Archipelago two hundred miles off the West African coast. Despite his inbred Royal Navy stiff upper lip and his decades at sea, Hugh could not resist cracking a slight grin at hitting Mount Teide on the nose.

"Thank you, Carlson," he said evenly. "Pray light below and inform Mr. Endicott. I should think he would enjoy seeing this."

"Aye, Captain," Carlson responded, turning smartly toward the hatch.

Presently Jack Endicott appeared on deck. Even after more than three weeks at sea he still dressed in business attire, although in these warmer climes he had left his dress coat and waistcoat below. Nonetheless, his meticulous coiffure and the quality and fit of his shoes, trousers, shirt, and silk stockings and neck stock bespoke a man who was far more comfortable in a countinghouse on land than in a vessel at sea. And yet, to Hugh's surprise and delight, Endicott had complained very little about the inconveniences and limitations of shipboard life, and he had just clambered up the companionway ladder without pause or grumble despite his considerable girth and nearly sixty years of age. What is more, Endicott freely made conversation with the two mates and with those members of the crew who were not too intimidated by him to speak, a boon that Hugh had not anticipated. He had even told Able Seaman Jeremiah Butler, the oldest and most seasoned member of the crew, that he considered Butler his equal because both men had reached the top of their chosen profession. Butler had responded to that magnanimous compliment with a blank stare.

In sum, Hugh Hardcastle had found Jack Endicott to be an agreeable and engaging companion, a pleasure to have on board despite his lubberly ways and preferences. His one shortcoming was his inability to control his frustration born of impatience. The fact that Fate had beamed on them since their first day out of Boston and that they were now considerably ahead of schedule seemed not to matter. Hugh understood that Endicott was an impatient man by nature and accustomed to instant gratification of his every wish and command, and sailing so great a distance was, by definition, a time-consuming endeavor. But there was nothing to be done about it. No sailing vessel could go faster than her hull speed, and besides, arriving too early in Cape Town simply meant that they would have to wait there for Van der Heyden. Hugh Hardcastle, for one, preferred to be out on the familiar sea, under sail, rather than ashore in a strange land, marking time.

"A most pleasant good morning to you, Mr. Endicott," Hugh said to him, using, as he always did outside the privacy of the after cabin, the formal address.

"Good morning, Captain," Endicott returned. He walked up to the helm and wheeled around to face forward. "And to you, Mr. Haskins," he said to the sailing master at the wheel. "Another fine day we have. I understand from Carlson that you have information of interest to pass on to me."

"I do. We have raised the Canaries."

"Well, that's fine, fine," Endicott said, nothing in his voice suggesting a shred of awe or a note of congratulation for what was by anyone's standards a superior feat of seamanship. "I assume that means we are maintaining our favorable pace?"

"It does. We will drop anchor off Tenerife late this afternoon. That will give us the day tomorrow to resupply. I should think you might welcome an opportunity to stretch your legs ashore. As you have heard me say, Santa Cruz is a visitor's delight."

"I have indeed heard you say it and I am sure I will agree. And I'm sure we all look forward to dining on fresh victuals. Nevertheless, Captain, we depart on Friday morning, as prescribed," Endicott insisted. "We have one day there, that is all, no matter how enticing the women, no matter how delectable the food. We have no time to dilly-dally."

Hugh Hardcastle suppressed a smile. "One day will suffice, I should think."

THE AREA around what was now called Santa Cruz was indeed a visitor's delight, as voyagers from Phoenicia, Greece, Carthage, and Rome had discovered more than two millennia earlier. Formerly a tiny fishing village tucked within the rugged cliffs and black sand–pebble beaches of Tenerife's northeastern coast, the village of Santa Cruz had come into its own after a volcanic eruption in 1706 destroyed Garachico, a town cross-island that in 1700 was the major seaport of the Canaries. Since then, Santa Cruz de Santiago de Tenerife had become, together with Las Palmas, a key port of the Canary Islands—a name derived not from the renowned songbird but from the Latin for an indigenous breed of fierce dogs first encountered by ancient seagoing Romans—and a preferred way station between the Old and New Worlds. It was also a town that held emotional significance for Hugh Hardcastle. It was here, a decade earlier, that his lifelong friend, onetime shipmate, and longtime commanding officer Horatio Nelson had lost his right arm to a cannonball during a failed British attempt to wrest Tenerife from the Spanish, who had themselves wrested the island from aboriginal Berber chieftains in 1495.

Following a day of taking on fresh supplies of water and hogsheads of onions, bananas, tomatoes, grapes, and salted fish and meat, *Falcon* cast free her lines and set sail on a modified course that would now take her into the heart of the great South Atlantic. It was a considerably longer route than sailing straight down the African coast would have been— from Tenerife *Falcon* would sail southwestward for more than a thousand miles before turning eastward toward Cape Town—but Hugh Hardcastle was convinced that this revised course would prove quicker and more comfortable. Rather than tacking back and forth against strong headwinds and currents, *Falcon* would set out on a beam reach, one of her fastest points of sail, before bringing the wind full on her back for the final eastward push to the southern tip of Africa.

On the first evening out of Santa Cruz, Hugh Hardcastle laid a chart of the South Atlantic on Jack Endicott's desk in the after cabin and explained the logic and logistics behind his decision. He used as a base of reference a large right triangle that he had drawn on the chart. Its apex was at the intersection of the equator and the bulge of West Africa, and its right triangle ran due south from that point to near Cape Town. He slid his forefinger along the hypotenuse, on which they were now sailing. Hugh had contemplated this change in sailing plan while crossing the Atlantic and had settled on it after talking with local mariners and pilots in Santa Cruz. Endicott, Hugh presumed, would be opposed to the plan for the simple reason that it involved considerably more sea miles than the original route. Points of sail and maximizing wind power were concepts foreign to Endicott. To his mind, the quickest and therefore most efficient course for a sailing vessel to follow to get from here to there was along a straight line, other factors being of secondary importance.

They were in the after cabin in what had become a frequent evening ritual of sharing a glass of spirits before Endicott retired for the night and Hugh went back on deck to make sure the schooner was properly tucked down for night sailing. As Hugh had expected, Endicott gave the chart but a cursory glance; he showed more interest in the local wine he had purchased in Santa Cruz than in the information Hugh Hardcastle had laid out before him. He shrugged and said merely, "If you think it's best," and then returned to his chair. Relieved, Hugh rolled up the chart and sat down in the other stout wingback chair. For a while they sat in comfortable silence, feeling the almost imperceptible sway of the schooner as she approached the equator. It was Hugh who ultimately broke the silence.

"Jack," he said, "I would like to ask a question that has been long on my mind."

Endicott glanced up. "Ask it."

"Thank you." Hugh crossed his right leg over his left and brushed a speck of dust from the knee of his trousers. "I am wondering what you hope to accomplish in Cape Town. I realize that we have discussed this topic before. But with respect, each time we do I sense we are not addressing the real issues. I rather sense that you are holding something back from me, that there is something you do not wish to share. If that is so, and if that is your wish, then so be it. It is not my place to intrude."

"Why, then, intrude?" Endicott inquired. His tone and expression showed no anger. To the contrary, Hugh detected a glint of humor in Endicott's eyes.

"Curiosity, of course. But more than that—I need to know. Since arriving in America, Phoebe and I have grown quite close to the Cutlers. We feel we have become an integral part of their family, and not just because Katherine is my sister. Since those early days in Barbados when Richard and Katherine were newlyweds and I had numerous occasions to get to know Richard, I have come to think of him not as my brother-in-law but as my blood brother. So naturally I have their best interests at heart. I would do anything for either of them. And of course I am very much aware that much of the family's future hinges on the outcome of your discussions with Mr. Van der Heyden, whatever may be the purpose of those discussions."

Endicott contemplated that. "Your words are admirable, Hugh. And indeed, my own observations tell me that you and your lovely wife have become welcomed additions to the Cutler family. I understand what you are saying, and as always I find you to be a most perceptive and straightforward fellow." He paused for a moment, then: "What you said is quite true. I have not been as forthcoming about my plans as I might have been, either to you or to any of the Cutler family. Or to my own wife, for that matter." He held up a hand to ward off interruption. "Now, may I ask you in turn, Hugh, if concern for the welfare of the Cutler family is the *only* reason you raise your question? I grant you, it's reason enough."

Hugh replied without pausing. "No, it is not the only reason, Jack. During this cruise we have come to know each other quite well. You have shared much about your life, and I am grateful that you have. I greatly respect what you have accomplished. You have also been most kind and forthcoming in sharing your personal views and philosophies of business and of life. As a result, I am learning a lot from you."

"I am pleased to hear it. And so . . . ?"

"And so now I consider you more as a friend than as my employer or business colleague. I am hoping you might consider me in the same light."

Hugh's words seemed to jolt Endicott. He averted his eyes and gazed aft across his desk to where stern windows were hinged open to the sultry night air. "Thank you for saying that, Hugh," he murmured at length. He continued to stare aft. "Thank you very much. I appreciate what you just said more than you might suspect. Very few people have been so open with me. Most of what I hear is something quite different—assuming I hear anything at all. And so it has been as far back as I can remember. I have a talent for making money but none for making friends. In the end I always seem to put people off." He heaved a sigh as Hugh sat in silence, amazed by Endicott's revelation of personal weakness. Then, in a less apologetic tone, as if pushing sentiment aside and returning to the matter at hand, Endicott continued, "But we are getting off subject, aren't we? You have a question to ask me."

"I have already asked it," Hugh replied, "and we are not off subject, Jack. I realize how much pressure you are under. You have staked all of your resources—and much of the Cutlers' as well—on your company, and now your company is at risk. I want you to know that if there is anything I can do to assist you, if there is anything of value in my own experience that can be brought to bear on your behalf, I will do whatever I can for you. Just as I would do for any member of the Cutler family."

Again Hugh's words seemed to jolt Endicott. He ran his short, stubby fingers through his thinning pewter-gray hair and asked with a wry smile, "So you deem me a man in need of assistance?"

"Every man has that need at some point in his life, Jack. No man is an island unto himself. Lord knows I am no exception. Just ask my wife."

Endicott's smile turned rueful. "Yes, well, perhaps it's best not to ask *my* wife." He fell silent, his face grave, as if whatever had seized hold of his thoughts caused him great remorse. Hugh drained his glass and waited. Minutes ticked by. After too many silent moments had elapsed, he gathered his tricorne hat from a side table and was preparing to return topside when Endicott said, in a distant but firm voice, "Don't leave, Hugh. I beg of you, don't leave. Please, sit down. Join me in another round. I have some explaining to do."

Hugh complied and cast Endicott a questioning look.

"What you are really asking me," Endicott said to Hugh without looking at him, "is why I chose to travel sixteen thousand miles when Herr Van der Heyden and I could just as easily have discussed world affairs and revised our business strategies in written correspondence, thereby saving both of us time and saving me a considerable amount of specie. Is that a fair summation?"

"I would say so, yes," Hugh replied carefully. "But Jack, as I said, I have no wish to intrude. If you prefer to leave things as they are, then so be it. I am merely asking as your friend. I have no personal stake in any of this."

"Ah, but you do," Endicott said mysteriously. "And since you ask as a friend, I shall answer as a friend." Endicott settled down into the comfort of his yellow-on-blue-upholstered chair. "I doubt that what I am about to say is what you are expecting to hear. Or what Caleb or any member of the Cutler family would expect to hear. Quite simply, Hugh, I am sailing to Cape Town to offer to sell C&E Enterprises to Jan Van der Heyden."

"*Sell your company?*" Hugh exclaimed, aghast. "Why on earth would you do such a thing, Jack? Is it because of the embargo?"

"Yes, but again, perhaps not for the reason you might suspect. So far, C&E has been able to absorb the losses it has suffered as a result of the embargo. Cargoes are routinely lost at sea—to pirates and storms, and to belligerent nations. To a merchant shipper such as I, lost cargoes are part of the normal costs of doing business. But our current state of affairs cannot endure for very much longer. We are suffering far too many of those losses. They are mounting, and soon they will begin eating into our reserves. As no doubt you are aware, when that happens, financial disaster looms. I have walked to the edge of the cliff to see how far down is down, and what I see there does not bode well for our nation's future. What is more, I am convinced that what we have suffered to date is but the tip of the iceberg. I believe that much worse is yet to come. I am, in fact, convinced that if Jefferson's policies are not quickly reversed—and they won't be, the man is much too stubborn to admit to failure—the United States will teeter on the brink of that cliff and will eventually fall into the abyss, taking with it every American who is engaged in overseas trade.

"Do you want to know what I see when I look over the edge of the cliff?" he asked rhetorically. "I see ships rotting in ports. I see cargoes going to ruin in warehouses. I see thousands of out-of-work sailors sitting hungry on the beach and on the docks. And I see vast family fortunes such as my own dwindling to naught. Are you getting the picture?"

"Vividly, I'm afraid. But . . ." Hugh's mind whirled. "But what could Van der Heyden do better than what you would do, should he own the company? How could he protect himself any better than you would try to do?"

Endicott shrugged. "Who's to say? Herr Van der Heyden is no man's pawn. He is an excellent man of business, and he has made a great deal of money in his own right. He knows as much or more about shipping and the Orient trade as I do, which is why I was so keen to hire him as director of C&E's Far Eastern operations. Were I he, and I owned C&E, the first thing I would do is convert its merchant fleet to Dutch registry, which of course he *could* do as the owner. It is something I obviously cannot do as an American. Dutch registry would allow him open access to most European ports, assuming his ships are able to evade or outrun—or outgun—the Royal Navy. The point is, whatever he may decide to do with

C&E Enterprises would no longer be my concern. And quite honestly, the burden of that concern is destroying me."

"Does Van der Heyden understand the realities of the embargo? The effect it is having and the effect it is going to have?"

"He certainly knows about the embargo. I have written him in detail about that, and he has other sources of information as well, of course. But I doubt he fully understands its current or future implications. How could he, being so far removed from Washington?"

Hugh frowned, a question nagging at him. Was Endicott simply proposing to sell C&E to his Far Eastern director? Or was he proposing to sell him out?

"What will you tell Van der Heyden is your reason for selling?"

"I will tell him the truth, that I now wish to invest my available resources in textiles."

"Textiles? You mean, as in manufacturing?"

"Precisely. There is a significant business opportunity brewing in manufacturing, thanks to the embargo and to recent developments in production, and it comes with much less financial risk. We Americans have always depended on Great Britain for our manufactured goods, especially for our shoes and clothing. And who benefits from that? Not us, by God! America claims to be a sovereign nation, but the English continue to make a pretty penny off what is, essentially, a captive market. It's time for enterprising Americans to claim those profits for themselves. I can produce as functional a shirt, as durable a pair of trousers, or as fashionable a hat as the British can. And I can sell it in America at a considerably lower price than American consumers are now forced to pay. Jefferson will actually *help* me accomplish this. His embargo and Non-importation Act are keeping many British-made goods out of America, and I pray that will continue long enough for me and others like me to establish our roots. Mind you, I am not the only New England shipping merchant to be thinking along these lines. I know from personal conversations with some of Boston's most enterprising families that they are aware of the opportunity and are preparing to act on it.

"If my vision is correct—and I am certain that it is—textile manufacturing will flourish not only in Massachusetts but throughout New England. We have the rivers to power the mills, and we can purchase the cotton, flax, and wool we need from our fellow countrymen. Eli Whitney's cotton gin has already revolutionized the cotton industry. Why ship all that precious cotton to England? Why not ship it to Boston in the hold of a Cutler & Sons vessel? Perhaps in the hold of this very schooner? In my vision everyone wins—our families, New England, and Americans throughout the nation. And a business principle you must never forget is that when everybody wins, you have the basis of a sound business transaction. With manufacturing thriving in America, and with Americans selling profitably to each other, we will no longer be dependent on Great Britain or on any other country in Europe. We will be dependent on ourselves, and good Christ Almighty that's the way it *should* be! My goal is to be among the first in, and the sale of C&E Enterprises will provide the funds to ensure ultimate success."

"Fascinating, Jack, but what if Van der Heyden doesn't buy it?" Hugh meant that in both a figurative and a literal sense.

"I am sure that in a face-to-face dialogue we can arrive at a mutually agreeable price. Which answers your question of why meet face-to-face. That sort of negotiation cannot be effectively accomplished by passing letters back and forth halfway around the globe. And the selling price, of course, is the key to everything. We need to sit down together, review the books, have some back and forth, and hammer out the terms. I see no viable alternative."

"What if you cannot agree on a price?" Hugh persisted.

"That will not be a problem. My position is unassailable. I shall inform Herr Van der Heyden that if he does not buy C&E Enterprises, I shall cut my losses and conserve my capital by closing the business, putting every sailor, every ship's master and mate, and every director out of work. Under that scenario, Herr Van der Heyden would walk away from C&E with nothing in his pocket, and I can assure you that he is much too savvy a businessman to allow *that* to happen. After all, under the right circumstances C&E Enterprises is a company with a bright future, and its future is bright largely *because* of what Jan Van der Heyden has already accomplished. No, he'll come to terms; no doubt about it," Endicott concluded confidently.

"What of the Cutlers? What of their position in the company? They own half of it, do they not? And yet you have not discussed this plan with Caleb and Richard?"

"The Cutler family owns half of the company's shares. But by my agreement with them I hold the controlling interest in C&E. Because I do, this decision is mine alone to make. Of course, when Jan and I agree on terms, the Cutler family will receive half of the proceeds. Unless, of course, the Cutlers decide not to sell their interest in C&E. In that case, Van der Heyden would pay only half of the negotiated price, to me, and he and the Cutler family would go forward as partners on terms that *they* agree upon. I strongly suspect, however, that the Cutlers will be only too happy to sell their interest. Caleb is worried sick about finances, as well he should be. His commitment to his sailors and staff is admirable, but in my estimation it is foolish to the extreme. It is not what I would do, as I have just indicated. Caleb, however, is Caleb, and he always makes good on his promises; I will give him that. The proceeds of the sale should provide the necessary reserves for the Cutler family to weather the storm until the embargo is repealed—which it will be because Congress and the American people will eventually come to realize that it is a suicidal piece of legislation. And that is why time is of the essence and why the time elapsing here at sea weighs so heavily on my mind."

As he listened, Hugh felt a new admiration for Jack Endicott. He seemed to have considered every angle of the proposed transaction, and the odds were better than even, it seemed to Hugh, that at the end of the day everyone involved would indeed benefit from it. And while Hugh was a mariner and not a businessman, he could not deny the opportunity Endicott saw in textiles. He had but one final question, and as if reading his mind, Endicott answered it before he could ask it.

"I haven't told any of this to anyone before this evening, Hugh, because I didn't want anyone second-guessing me. I said nothing even to Anne-Marie, although I did leave a letter with my attorney detailing my intentions. I have instructed him to share that letter with her before the reading of my last will and testament should anything untoward happen to me on this voyage. She is then to share it with Caleb.

"Another business principle I have always adhered to," Endicott continued, "is that when you are convinced you are right about something, be bold, make the tough decisions, and deal with the consequences later, as they arise. That principle has served me very well over the years." He stretched out his arms and yawned. "Whether you meant to or not, Hugh—and whether you agree with me or not—you have taken a considerable weight off my shoulders this evening. I believe I will sleep quite well tonight thanks to you."

POSEIDON CONTINUED to smile, and *Falcon*, a sleek and sturdy vessel, pottered through the frustratingly light winds of the doldrums, making some headway each day and rarely becoming becalmed for more than an hour. Once free of the horse latitudes she sprang free like a bird released from a cage. Her two large fore-and-aft sails, two topsails, and two fore staysails and jib were drum-taut as she raced through the southern seas, her hull encased in foam as she creamed down one great Atlantic swell after another. By day, *Falcon* sailed under a torrid yellow sun, powder-blue sky, and high scudding clouds. By night, she sailed under a star-spangled dome highlighted by the Southern Cross and the two Magellanic Clouds, dark galaxies in the Southern Hemisphere first noted by ancient Persian astronomers and first recorded in detail by Italian stargazers accompanying Ferdinand Magellan on his sixteenth-century circumnavigation. The exhilarating blend of waves, wind, and sunshine enticed Jack Endicott on deck more frequently. He smiled more often as well now that they were making encouraging progress toward their destination, albeit on an indirect southwesterly course. The distance between *Falcon* and the African coast would continue to expand until she hauled her wind for the final sprint eastward.

It was during the third week out from the Canaries, sometime in the wee hours of June 14, that Hugh awoke with a start in his bunk. He pricked his ears and listened, his body tensed in anticipation. Then he heard it: the sudden hard splatter of rain on the weather deck above him just as the schooner pitched and yawed as if Poseidon's fist had shoved her sideways. He was up and pulling on his oilskins seconds before the after hatch scraped open and a seaman yelled down, "*All hands ahoy!*"

Hugh leapt for the companionway as the off-duty watch lumbered aft from their hammocks in the forecastle. Hugh was first up the ladder. When he emerged through the square opening, the wind hit him with such fury that it tore his oilskin hat from his head and sent it tumbling out to sea.

He pulled himself up through the hole, waited until the six sailors behind him were out, and then secured the hatch cover and worked his way slowly aft, bracing himself against the fierce wind. He kept his head down and held his right hand above his eyes to shield them from the stinging rain. "What do we have, Sturgis?" he fairly shouted at his first mate when he reached the helm.

"We're in for some weather, sir," Haskins shouted back. He wore no oilskins; there had been no time to don them. His clothes were soaked through and clung to him like a second layer of skin, and his shoulder-length brown hair had blown free of its queue and whipped about his face. "It came up sudden-like, Captain. Our only warning was the glass. I checked it at four bells and again at five bells. It had fallen. Faster than ever I have witnessed. I ordered the watch to prepare for foul weather, and then the squall hit us."

"Looks to be a bit more than a squall," Hugh shouted out.

As if to underscore his observation, a cresting wave thumped against *Falcon*'s larboard hull and shoved her sideways. Water streamed over the larboard railing, washed across the deck, and flooded out the starboard scuppers.

"Is the forward hatch battened down?"

"Aye, sir. With a tarpaulin."

"What about the guns?" Hugh yelled.

"Paul saw to them first thing, sir. By God's grace he was on deck at the time. They're bowsed up tight as can be. The Devil himself couldn't budge them, he says."

"Very well." Hugh peered up through the rain at the rigging. It was hard to see much in the murk; thick glass lanterns set amidships and near the helm swung eerily back and forth in wide arcs, adding a ghostly element to the wailing wind. He noted with satisfaction the two topsails tightly furled to their yards, standard procedure for night sailing. At least, he thought, no one would have to climb up the ratlines in this mess to reef or take in those sails. Some unlucky soul, however, would have to crawl out on the jib-boom to douse and stuff the jib.

At the foremast, sailors bent over the boom like jackknives clawed in sodden canvas as the halyard was slowly released and the loose folds of the giant fore-and-aft sail were gathered in, thundering and snapping in protest. At the mainmast, Second Mate Shipley directed a crew fighting to shorten sail by taking in a reef at the second reef point above the foot of the sail and lashing the loose canvas to the boom with gaskets. It was a hard task in the best of conditions; these were among the worst of conditions. One sailor, Hugh could not identify him in the darkness, lost his footing, either from the crash of a wave or from the flailing canvas, and slid pell-mell across the slippery deck on his stomach, his cry of anguish when his head whacked against the starboard bulwark quickly drowned out by the howling wind. When he struggled to get back up, his knees buckled and he collapsed onto the deck. He lay still, face up, as seawater swirled around his body. None of his mates came to his aid. No one could; they had all they could do waging war against wind and sea.

"I have the helm!" Hugh cried. "Lend a hand up there and get that sailor below to my cabin. Have him strapped into my bunk. And I'll have the fore stays'l doused. Advise the men to stand by to take in all sail. Got it?"

"Aye, Captain," Haskins shouted.

"I'm going to bring her off two points, Sturgis," Hugh added, his mouth close to Haskin's ear. "She's taking too much punishment. We'll take stock at dawn when we can see what's what."

The first mate nodded and set off.

Bringing her off two points brought the wind from her beam to her quarter and allowed *Falcon* to better flee before the raging gale. But it was a course, Hugh realized, that took her toward Cape Horn, not Cape Town. He prayed that daylight would bring with it an easement of wind sufficient to allow her to lie to under a backed storm jib and a trysail secured abaft the mainmast. To set those sails they would need to bring her about into the wind and keep her there until the heavy canvas could be bent on. To attempt such a maneuver now, in the heart of darkness and without a clear view of what was coming at them, might cause the schooner to veer to windward and broach, her vulnerable broadside exposed to the raging sea.

Dawn revealed a gray world of ugly low-lying clouds and menacing twenty- to thirty-foot waves capped with white spume whipped up by what had intensified into near hurricane-force winds. The entire surface of the ocean, as far as the eye could see, was flecked with white foam. Each time *Falcon* rode up a towering wave and hesitated briefly at the crest, Hugh scanned to windward, hoping against hope to catch a glimpse on the distant horizon of anything that might indicate a change of weather. But he saw no horizon. Each time, before *Falcon* plunged down into a deep watery canyon, he saw only dark skies and white seas. And the barometer continued to fall. And the wind continued to intensify.

The moments down in the trough between two towering waves, where there was no wind and all was eerily quiet, were among the most dangerous. Without the stabilizing effect of the topsails, which, had they been set, were tall enough to draw a breath of wind even at the lowest depths, the schooner slewed about as if trying to escape before the next dreadful climb into the shrieking wind that drove rain into raw flesh as though it were a torrent of pricking needles. Hugh needed all his skill, instincts, and endurance to keep *Falcon*'s bowsprit in line with the mammoth westward-rolling waves.

On and on they plowed over the swells, sea mile after sea mile. In the meager light of day Hugh ordered all remaining wisps of canvas taken in. They were now running for their lives under bare poles.

Paul Shipley slogged his way aft along the starboard bulwark, seawater sloshing up almost to his waist. The starboard scuppers were no longer able to keep up with the weight of seawater swirling against them. "I've sent the first watch below, sir," he shouted, "to snatch what rest and food they can. I'm here to relieve you, sir," he had to almost scream to make himself heard.

"Very well, Paul," Hugh shouted. He could not deny the bone-weary exhaustion consuming him. His efforts to hold the helm had left him weak and shaking. The wind was pushing his eyeballs back into their sockets and forcing tears from the corners of his eyes. "You, Sturgis, and I will alternate at the helm. From here on, it's one-hour shifts until this bastard has had its fill of us, one way or the other. Understood?"

Shipley acknowledged and took command of the helm.

Hugh turned his back to the wind and brought his mouth up to his mate's ear. "I'm going below to check on Pearson," he shouted through cupped hands, referring to the injured sailor who was strapped into Hugh's bunk, "and Mr. Endicott."

Shipley nodded, his gaze steadied forward.

Below, out of the wind, the jerks and yaws of the schooner forced Hugh to walk gingerly, holding onto or leaning against something at all times lest he be thrown onto the deck. He began to peel off his soaked oilskins and then decided not to bother; he'd be returning topside shortly. When he ran a cold hand over his face to brush away the droplets that still covered it, he tasted salt. And he still felt the sting of salt in his eyes.

"Sweet Jesus in heaven," he muttered to himself. He had ridden out storms in the Caribbean, but in all his days at sea—in service first to the Royal Navy and then to Cutler & Sons—Hugh Hardcastle had never known the raw fear that coursed through him now that he had time to actually think rather than just react. As he inched along the bulkhead, his back against the outer side of Haskins' cabin and then his own, tossed about by the haphazard motions of the schooner, the thought came to him that many an experienced sailor had died at sea in such conditions.

At the after cabin door he knocked once, twice. When there was no reply, he opened the door and stepped inside. In the dim light admitted by the thick wooden shutters secured over the stern windows he saw the two wingback chairs lying upended against the starboard bulwarks amid papers, files, books, and broken glass and china. The sudden shock of a wave smashing against the hull sent him lurching and reeling like a drunken man. He grabbed hold of the back of the sofa just in time to break his fall. On the bed nearby, Jack Endicott lay on his right side with his back to Hugh and his knees drawn up into fetal position. The stench of vomit filled the stale air. Although the after cabin contained its own private head emptying directly into the sea, Endicott had not made it there. Or, Hugh suspected, had not tried to make it.

"Jack?" Hugh called out tentatively. No response.

"Jack!" he said in a louder voice.

Endicott emitted a low guttural groan.

"Anything I can do for you, Jack?" Hugh did not expect an answer. There was nothing he could do for Endicott.

Endicott responded with two weak backhanded motions of his left hand. His message was clear: Get the hell out and leave me alone.

"Right," Hugh said with forced good cheer, his own innards roiling from the rank odor. "I'll check back later. Chin up, Jack. We'll soon be out of this slop."

Hugh sidestepped from the after cabin to the door of his own cabin, where he braced his legs and waited. During the brief lull at the bottom of a trough he quickly opened the door and lurched in.

He had to pause a moment to allow his eyes to adjust to the darkness. Unlike the after cabin, the first mate's cabin had no windows or portholes to shutter, and the aft hatchway was closed tight, permitting only drips of water to ooze through. The only other light normally available belowdecks passed through a scuttle, also used for ventilation, secured into the deckhead above. But the scuttle had been covered with a deadlight to prevent water from sloshing below. In the darkness, with the violent pitching and rolling of the schooner and the otherworldly creaks and groans of her timbers as she took one harsh blow after another, *Falcon*'s main deck seemed like a Stygian realm of the dead and dying rather than the well-designed interior of a graceful schooner.

"Captain," Hugh heard Pearson weakly rasp. He made his way over to the bunk and dropped to a knee, clutching the retaining edge of the bunk as a handhold. "How are you doing, Nate?"

"Fine, sir," Pearson replied, but even in the poor light Hugh could see that was not so. The sailor's face was as white as the pillow his head rested on—the part of it that was not splotched in red—and the brown hair on one side of his head was matted in blood. Hugh grabbed a shirt of his that had fallen from its peg onto the floor and crawled over to the wide-bottomed barrel containing fresh water, which surprisingly had remained upright. He soaked the shirt in the water and then half-filled a cup whose handle had been attached to a hook secured to the tub. He crawled back to the bed, snaked his arm under Pearson's neck, and gently lifted his head. "Drink," he said.

Pearson brought both hands to the cup and drank greedily before a hard roll of the schooner wrenched the cup from his grasp. "Thank you, sir," he said as Hugh laid his head back down. "That did the trick."

Hugh dabbed at Pearson's bloody head with the wet shirt. He could not determine the extent of the wound, only that the cloth had absorbed fresh blood. He withdrew a small sailor's knife from its sheath at his belt and cut away a sleeve. This he wrapped around Pearson's head, over the wound. As he rose carefully to his feet, Pearson again mumbled, "Thank you, sir."

"You're welcome, Nate," Hugh said. "Rest easy. I'll be back," he added before working his way out of the cabin. Just as he reached the companionway leading up to the weather deck, *Falcon* slewed hard to leeward. Stumbling forward, Hugh seized a lower rung of the ladder and hung on for dear life until the schooner had gone over as far as she would and slowly began to right herself. When she was back on an even keel, more or less, he pulled himself laboriously up the ladder.

On deck, his first impression was that the wind had eased a knot or two during his stint belowdecks. Paul Shipley, still at the helm, confirmed that impression.

"I think we've seen the worst of it, sir," he said. "She's beginning to moderate. The wind, that is, not the sea. And sir, the garboard strakes are leaking. Patten went down in the hold for a look, and he reports we're taking in water. Nothing to be overly concerned about yet, I should think."

"Shit," Hugh cursed aloud, although he was not surprised by Seaman Patten's report. The garboard strakes were the first planks rising from the keel and were the hardest to caulk. If seawater were to seep into a vessel during a bad storm, every sailor worth his salt knew it would likely be through the garboard strakes.

"We've manned the pumps?" Hugh asked, already knowing the answer. He had heard the clanking amidships when he had been below.

"We have, sir. Sturgis is down there now seeing to it and assigning shifts. We're holding our own, I believe. We can recaulk in Cape Town— Hang on, sir!"

Falcon, riding the cusp of a wave, took a sudden sharp dive, careening down the wave's leeward slope toward the trough. Hugh lunged for the railing and hung on with one thought in mind: *Falcon*'s hull. She could not many more times run bow-on down a wave like a lone lancer charging a Mongol horde and survive. He dared not contemplate how long the schooner could continue this fight, especially now with water coming in.

"I've got the helm, Paul," he said in the lull. "Your hour is up. Go below and advise Sturgis that he's next. I'll hear his report when he comes on deck."

Shipley nodded. When the wheel was firmly in the grip of his captain, he waded forward toward the aft hatchway, keeping a hand on the starboard railing for balance. Hugh watched him disappear below and then peered forward at the next wave in battle array. It seemed considerably taller and steeper than the others, more ominous; and something else was different, too. Unlike previous ones, this wave towered so high that it seemed primed to collapse under its own crushing weight. Now on the high upward roll, Hugh faced a nearly vertical slope with grayish-white spume dancing on its cap, as though challenging the impudence of the puny block of wood bobbing up and down like a cork on the endless expanse of angry gray water and white foam.

Alone on the weather deck, Hugh felt a chill run down his spine. "Come on, you beautiful bitch," he muttered, urging *Falcon* to Herculean efforts. He hunched over the wheel and gripped its spokes with all his might, fighting to keep the bowsprit dead-on in line with the wave's monstrous roll, painfully aware that one small error at the helm could spell instant disaster. Up, up the schooner climbed, until at the very peak of the wave she hesitated, giving her captain a quick sweeping vista of the South Atlantic and a glance to windward that disclosed a brighter sky on the far eastern horizon and thin shafts of golden sunlight streaking down through breaks in the distant grayish-black clouds.

Mesmerized by the sight, Hugh's attention was jolted back when he felt *Falcon*'s bow tip downward, toward the abyss, and heard the ferocious thundering roar that came at her from behind, a gargantuan wash of foaming-mad seawater that sounded like every demon in Hell was shrieking down upon them. The cresting wave crashed over the schooner's stern in a cascade of water so powerful that it plucked Hugh Hardcastle from his place at the helm as though he were a twig and propelled him down the full length of the schooner, his body ricocheting off masts sprung from their shrouds and stays and snapped off like matchwood. Hugh slammed hard against the forward larboard bulwarks, and from there was carried up and over her forecastle and bow, feet-first as though spurting from a colossal spigot.

Underwater for what seemed like hours, his bearings utterly askew, Hugh managed to claw his way upward. He broke the surface gasping, thrashing, sputtering, drawing air deep into his tortured lungs. He spotted a broken mast floating nearby and sidestroked over to it, pain searing through his body with each stroke. Draping his left arm over the spar, he treaded water as best he could and searched wildly for *Falcon* to shout out a cry for help. He found her, lying over on her beam-ends, a crippled gull shorn of its wings, and nary a soul visible anywhere on her or around her. As Hugh watched in abject horror, *Falcon* gradually settled into the foaming sea, water pouring into her from every quarter, until her bow lifted, drawn down by the weight of water filling her spacious after cabin. For brief, agonizing moments her bowsprit remained, pointing skyward as if in silent tribute or final farewell. Then, on a steep uproll, a wave washed over the bowsprit and it too slipped from view, leaving Hugh Hardcastle adrift and forlorn upon a cold, desolate sea.

Fourteen

Hingham, Massachusetts
June 1808

O N THE DAY BEFORE the Atlantic claimed *Falcon*, Katherine
Cutler took a bad spill on the
front stairway in her home on South Street. Richard heard the sickening
thuds and rushed to her side. After first checking for broken bones and
finding none, he cradled her in his arms and carried her, barely conscious,
to the four-poster in their bedroom. When he was satisfied there was
nothing more he could do for her, he raced down the stairs and out the
front door in search of Dr. Prescott.

Two hours later Dr. Prescott found Richard Cutler in the parlor,
slumped over in a chair with his head in his hands. "She is resting comfortably," he said, sinking into the chair opposite Richard's. After a moment
he added quietly, "I fear she cannot last much longer, Richard. She is of
stout heart and mind, but the human body is not designed for immortal-
ity, not on this earth."

Richard glared into the physician's somber gray eyes, as though his
anger might spur the doctor to greater efforts. "Is there *nothing* that can
be done?" he whispered."

Prescott shook his head. "Nothing, I'm afraid. The cancer lies deep
within her, and by now it has certainly infected vital organs. In point of
fact, there was nothing that I or anyone else could have done for her after
the surgery. She was in God's hands then, and she is in God's hands now.
The miracle is that she has lived such a healthy life since then, and for
so long. I frankly did not expect her to survive for three years. To judge
by her outward appearance she seems to be in relatively good condition.

When I examined her today I found no dark color around her eyes or blotches on her skin, or any of the other signs of illness and deterioration that one would expect to find. She is thin, of course, because she has no appetite. But her skin still glows and her hair remains thick and healthy. That in itself is a miracle, I can assure you. I have never seen the like."

"What of the pain? Can we treat that, at least?"

"I offered laudanum, but she refused to take it. She insists that she is experiencing no pain."

Richard nodded knowingly. "She tells me the same thing, although I know she is lying to spare me. I have asked her many times about the pain, hoping that she would allow me to tell you that the cancer had returned. But each time I did, her answer was the same. Pressing the issue only made her angry—for a short while, anyway." He smiled ruefully. "We could never remain at odds with each other."

Prescott shook his head. "Of course she experienced pain; I knew that. I can only imagine its degree and extent. But she was determined not to let on. I have rarely witnessed such courage. Do you know why she refused help?"

"I do. It was for the same reason she didn't want to tell anyone the truth about her cancer. She wanted to live out the balance of her life as normally as possible, free of pity and sparing her family the suffering and sorrow that knowledge would have brought."

"That's Katherine Cutler for you. Always thinking of others; never of herself. When did she tell you that she suspected the cancer had returned?"

"Last spring, a year ago."

"My word. She confided in no one else? Just you?"

"Just me. And Reverend Ware. She called on him a number of times during the past year for spiritual guidance and counsel. Like you, he is a dear friend of our family and a man we trust completely."

"But surely your children and others of your family must have realized that something was . . . *different*?"

"Our children have been away in recent months and very much involved in their own lives. Will has joined the Navy. Jamie is also away at sea, and Diana and Peter are living in Cambridge. We hardly ever see Joseph. Others here in Hingham may have had their suspicions—Katherine was losing weight, as you say, and she has not been out in town as often as she once was—but they rarely confronted either of us with their concerns. Agee tried once or twice, but I could not tell even him. Katherine had sworn me to secrecy, and I was determined to honor her request. Besides, it was hard even for me to think that anything was seriously wrong with her, for the very reasons you just mentioned. And her disposition has remained as bright and cheerful as always."

"I understand," Prescott said as he removed his spectacles. He wiped the lenses with a handkerchief, held them up for inspection, and then tucked them into his coat pocket. "As I am sure Reverend Ware would agree," he said devoutly, "God has blessed your family, Richard. He has blessed you all through her. I wish there was something more I could do for her."

"I realize that, Doctor," Richard said. "I know you care deeply for Katherine. More to the point, she knows it too." He looked away, biting his lower lip, and then returned his gaze to Prescott. "How long does she have?"

"A week or two, I should think," Prescott replied. "If pneumonia sets in, less; if she slips into a coma, it could be more. These are just estimates, of course. Each body responds in its own way, and no one can accurately predict what will happen and when. Because that is so, I urge you to gather your family together as soon as that can be arranged. I further urge you to say whatever you want to say to her now, while she remains lucid. I realize how terribly difficult all this is for you and your family. But in the future, none of you wants to regret lost opportunities to say your farewells. I will monitor her closely each day, and I will do my best to keep you and your family informed of where matters stand."

"Thank you, Doctor." His eyes bright with unshed tears, Richard asked, "Does Katherine know . . . all this?"

"She does. She asked me for the truth, and whenever a patient asks me for the truth, I tell the truth as I understand it to be. We talked awhile and I can tell you without equivocation that she is grateful to the Almighty for every day of her life. She accepts her fate, Richard, and it's imperative to her that you understand that. It's certainly not a fate she would have chosen, and certainly she has no desire to leave you and your children. But please understand that she is at peace with herself and with God. What she wants now is to be allowed to go quietly into the night without a lot of fuss and bother."

Richard looked around the parlor as if seeking answers to unanswerable questions. "What can I do to make this easier for her?" he managed.

"Just be there. She is sleeping now. She'll likely sleep more and more as time goes by. That fall took the fight out of her, and she is no longer able or willing to defer the inevitable. But sleep is a blessing. Think of it as God's way of keeping her oblivious as her body gradually shuts down.

She will not want to eat much, if anything, but make certain she has as much water as she wants. And be sure to move her position on the bed every few hours. To avoid bedsores, you understand.

"I'll check back tomorrow morning. Perhaps we can convince her then to take some laudanum." He rose to go. "Is there any other service I might perform for you?"

Richard fought through the daze settling over him. "Yes, Doctor, there is," he said. "If you would, please drop by Caleb's house and ask Joan to come over as soon as she can. And Phoebe, if she's there. You might also check in on Edna. She hasn't been feeling herself this past week."

"I will see to it immediately," Prescott said, adding, with a touch of a smile, "although I doubt Edna will want anything to do with me and my medicine. She is the orneriest woman I know—and one I admire very much." He offered Richard his hand and then picked up his black leather medical bag and left the house, closing the door softly behind him.

JOAN CUTLER and Phoebe Hardcastle arrived within the half hour. To Richard's surprise, neither woman seemed overwrought by his news. They sat quietly, watching him pace like a caged lion and listening to his agonized announcement. They nodded as though they had long ago accepted as fact what he had expected them to hear as a surprising revelation.

"I must contact everyone," Richard concluded in the same firm tone he had once used on a quarterdeck, as if taking decisive action and issuing commands might blunt or defer the pain: "Anne and Frederick, and Lavinia and Stephen, and Diana and Peter, of course. Let's see: Mindy is living here, with her parents, and Caleb—when is Caleb planning to return from Boston, Joan?"

"On Friday, Richard," Joan said.

"Very well. We'll arrange for a packet boat to be standing by on Long Wharf on Friday morning. Shall we say at ten o'clock? That leaves Adele, who is here in Hingham with her mother, and Agee and Lizzy and—oh my dear Lord, Will and Jamie." At the harsh realization that their two sons would have no chance to say their good-byes, or even know that their mother was dying, he gave an anguished sob.

Phoebe was up in an instant and took him in her arms, clasping him tightly to her.

"I'm sorry," he rasped.

"Don't be," Phoebe soothed.

"I mustn't do that," he insisted. "I cannot break down. I need to be strong—for her and for our family."

"You will be," Joan said, coming up and wrapping her arms around Richard and Phoebe. "You will find the strength you need. Phoebe and I will see to everything," she added firmly. "And I mean *everything*. We'll enlist Agee and Lizzy's help too. Knowing them, they'll want to come right over, if that suits."

"Of course it suits."

"Good. I'll tell them that. At least one of us will be here to help at all hours. We have plenty of room for houseguests, so don't worry about that. Edna hopes to be over later today to help with meals. She wants to be here for you and Katherine. If it turns out she is unable to come, we'll take care of meals as well. You are not to concern yourself with such things."

"You have but *one* concern, Richard," Phoebe seconded, "and that is to give your full attention to your wife."

"Thank you," Richard said quietly. "Thank you and bless you both."

AFTER JOAN AND PHOEBE LEFT, promising to return shortly, Richard went upstairs to the bedroom he had shared with Katherine since their earliest days in Hingham. She lay supine with pillows propping her up in a half-sitting position. A bedsheet was drawn up to her waist, and a light cotton blanket to her knees. The heavy dark blue drapes that covered the two east-facing windows had been drawn apart and tied off; the two windows were open, and a warm summer breeze stirred the white lace inner curtains. Richard heard the gleeful chatter of children at play and dogs barking excitedly in the distance. The sounds belonged to another world.

He sat down on a chair pulled close to the edge of the bed on Katherine's right side and took her hand in his, gently massaging the palm with his thumb, his gaze fixed on her beautiful face. A hundred memories spanning thirty-four years swept through his mind, each brush of memory combining with the others to create a portrait of a marriage well lived and well loved. He dared not, could not, consider the future. His context was in terms of yesterday and today, never of tomorrow. Since he had first met Katherine Hardcastle in England as a boy of fourteen, his life had been inexorably tied to that of the dear soul who lay dying three thousand miles away from her birthplace and birthright. He could not imagine, let alone accept, what his life would be like without her.

At length she opened her eyes. For several moments she stared vacantly at the ceiling, as if to get her bearings, perhaps to cross the gap between dream and reality. She looked to the left and then down at her right hand.

When her gaze rose to meet Richard's, she smiled weakly. "Hello, my darling," she whispered.

In reply, Richard raised her hand to his lips and kissed the cool, silken flesh.

"What time is it?" she asked, sounding a little stronger.

"Coming on four o'clock."

"I've been asleep for a while."

"For a while." He noticed her wetting her lips with her tongue. "Are you thirsty? Let me give you some water."

"In a minute, perhaps." She knitted her brow. "Dr. Prescott was here, wasn't he?"

"Yes, he was. Seven hours ago. He'll check back tomorrow morning. He told me that you two had quite the talk."

"We did. I admire him so much. He's such a kind and caring man." She gave Richard's hand a light squeeze. "Very much like my husband."

"Katherine . . ." He looked down, battling his emotions.

She gave his hand another gentle squeeze. "It's all right, Richard. It's really all right, my love. Everything is going to be all right, I promise you."

Richard's laugh came out more as a sob. "Good Lord, Katherine, *I'm* the one who should be telling *you* that."

She smiled faintly and then lifted her gaze back to the ceiling. "I do so wish," she said longingly, "that I might have the opportunity to say good-bye to the many people who are dear to me. I have said my good-byes to Will and Jamie. I have written each of them a letter to read when they return home. They are in my right top drawer. But there's Julia and Robin, and Cynthia and John, and Jeremy and dear Hugh . . ."

"I'll take care of all that," Richard assured her. "Cynthia and Julia will be here next spring. If it turns out they cannot come, I have told Joseph that I will take him to them next summer for a visit."

"Yes, we have talked about you doing that," Katherine said. "I do hope you can go there soon, regardless. Barbados holds such special memories for us."

Richard again brought her hand to his lips. "I have special memories of every day I have known you."

From downstairs they heard the front door creak open and familiar voices in muffled conversation. Lizzy Crabtree called out once; then all was quiet. After placing Katherine's hand back on the bed, Richard clasped his own hands together and for long moments stared down at them as if in silent prayer. The feel of her fingertips tenderly touching his cheek brought him back. She reached up to stroke his hair.

"Richard . . . ?"

The blue of his eyes captured the hazel of hers. She was smiling at him, broadly, and for one unforgettable instant he saw the beautiful laughing girl of irresistible charm who had so transfixed him as a youth and so impassioned him as a man.

She held his gaze for several dreamlike moments, and then said: "I have always been in love with you, Richard. I loved you even before I met you, when I was a little girl growing up in Fareham. I loved the promise of you coming into my life. It's a promise you have never failed to keep."

Her words sent a torrent of grief and unspeakable loss coursing through him. He felt the tears well up and again fought to stem the flow. But this time it was to no avail.

WHEN DIANA CUTLER SPRAGUE received Phoebe Hardcastle's letter at her residence on Eliot Street in Cambridge, she insisted that she and Peter depart immediately for Hingham and not wait two days for the packet boat on Friday. Peter agreed and set out to hire a coach-and-four.

Five hours later, after traveling as fast as safety allowed on dirt roads recently rutted by rainstorms, the coach drew to a halt at her parents' home. Diana did not wait for the groom or her husband to help her out of the coach. She opened the door herself, jumped down, and ran up the walkway toward her childhood home. The front door opened and Lizzy Crabtree was there to greet her.

"Aunt Lizzy!" Diana cried, pulling away from her aunt's embrace. "Where is Mother? I must go to her!"

"She is upstairs in her room. Your father is with her. Wait, child," Lizzy soothed, holding Diana's arm when Diana made to bolt past her toward the stairway. Peter stood behind them, framed in the open doorway. "She is sleeping now, thank God. Let her be. She needs her rest. There will be time soon enough."

Peter stepped up and placed his hands on his wife's shoulders. "Come, darling," he said. "Aunt Lizzy is right. We must be patient."

Reluctantly Diana turned and melted into her husband's arms, then wrenched around at the sound of footsteps in the hallway above. "Father!" she cried when she saw him on the top landing. In an instant she was bounding up the stairs and into his embrace.

"Father!" she wailed again, her tears running freely.

Richard clasped his daughter close. "There now, Poppet," he said, using the pet name of her youth. "There now." He drew out a handkerchief and dabbed at her eyes and cheeks. "Let's go down to the kitchen together, shall we? You'll want some refreshment after your trip, and I want to talk with you and Peter. When your mother awakens, you will be the first to see her, I promise."

MEMBERS OF THE CUTLER FAMILY continued to arrive in Hingham over the next several days. Lavinia and Stephen Starbuck rode up from Duxbury, a scenic seaside town north of Plymouth where Stephen had for years been a noted apothecary. Anne and Frederick Seymour and their two teenaged sons joined Caleb on the packet boat sailing from Long Wharf. The mood was somber not only in Cutler family homes but also, it seemed, throughout Hingham. Word of Katherine's sudden relapse had spread quickly without the assistance of local gossipmongers such as Rebecca Leavitt, and as had been the case following Katherine's surgery nearly three years earlier, citizens stood outside on South Street, maintaining a respectful distance from the Cutler residence, some holding candles well into the summer nights.

At Diana's most earnest request, she and Peter stayed in a bedroom down the hall from her parents' room on the second floor. Anne-Marie Endicott had invited them to stay with her and Adele and baby Katherine at Will and Adele's home on Ship Street, but Diana politely declined. She wanted to be near her mother at all hours of the day and night, to tend to her needs. Mindy Cutler was often at her side, as was Adele Cutler. The inseparable friendship that joined the three of them was to Richard's mind a godsend. It made it easier for Diana to cope—and thus for him to cope.

At midmorning on July 2 Richard entered the bedroom to find Diana asleep on the chair next to her mother. Katherine was stirring in sleep, her chest rising and falling irregularly. For several moments he stood silently watching them, the one the mirror image of the other. It amazed him even now that Katherine had somehow passed on her very essence to her daughter, as though in testament to her own earthly existence. Their hair was of similar color and length, their features at once both delicate and determined, their physical frames the embodiment of grace and femininity. Just as he counted himself among the most fortunate of men, Richard thought at that moment, so did he count his son-in-law, Peter Sprague. He prayed that the call of duty or adventure would never take them far away from him. It would be a separation difficult for him to bear.

He gently shook his daughter, and she snapped awake, her gaze going first to her mother, then to her father. "What is it?" she asked.

"Everyone is downstairs," he said. "We need you there."

"But I can't leave Mother. She's waking."

"I can see that she is. That's why I need you downstairs."

Reluctantly Diana arose from the chair. After giving her mother a quick glance, she followed her father down to the parlor where the family had gathered. For Richard, as for many of them, the scene was reminiscent of one in Caleb's house three years earlier, on the day of Katherine's surgery. This gathering was for the same purpose: to say what had to be said. After Richard bade everyone sit, he faced them and spoke in an even tone that could not hide his anguish.

"I'm afraid the time has come," he said softly. "Dr. Prescott was in to see Katherine early this morning, and he reports that she is showing signs of rapid decline. He believes the end is near. By God's grace she has not slipped into a coma. She remains aware. So, please, those of you who have not already done so, now is the time to say good-bye."

Although Richard's words came as no surprise to anyone present, for several moments no one stirred, as if by refusing his request they could deny his words. They stared vacantly at him or silently at each other. Then, as if by an unspoken cue, they rose and began embracing each other, stricken family members all. Sounds of quiet weeping filled the parlor.

"Please," Richard urged, "we may not have much time."

Lizzy Crabtree strode stoically toward the stairway. Phoebe Hardcastle followed a minute later, and Anne Seymour stood by the door to await her turn. One by one, Cutler family members steeled themselves to do the impossible, to accept the unacceptable.

"I won't go up, Richard," Anne-Marie Endicott said to him softly. "I don't think it is appropriate. I am not sure it is appropriate that I am here at this moment, although Lord knows I am sickened with grief."

"Of course it's appropriate, Anne-Marie. You are Will's mother-in-law. You and Adele are standing in for him as well as for yourselves."

"Yes," she said, and she kissed him on the cheek. "We all love you, Richard," she whispered in his ear. "I love you. You are not alone in this."

Quickly she took her leave, yielding to Agreen Crabtree.

"Hard times," Agreen said, because he didn't know what else to say.

"The hardest," Richard said. He heaved a sigh. "I've been dreading this day for such a long time, Agee. For every hour of every day for the past year I knew this day would eventually come. My heart prayed for a miracle, but my mind told me there were no miracles left." His voice faltered, but he forced himself to continue. "It was never my wish to hide the truth from you and Lizzy, Agee. I hope you understand that."

Agreen clapped a hand on his friend's shoulder and looked him square in the eye. "Of course I understand that. Hell's bells, Richard, we *all* understand that. You did what was right by your wife. That's all that matters. Trust me, mate: I would've done the same thing, was it Lizzy who was ill."

Richard nodded. "I have always trusted you, Agee. In this as in everything else."

Eventually it came down to Richard. He ascended the stairs slowly; in a daze of memories of two lives lived as one he walked down the hall and into his bedroom. Diana was there, being consoled by Peter on her right and by Mindy and Adele on her left. Richard's two sisters and brothers-in-law were also there, as were Caleb and Joan, Lizzy and Agreen, Phoebe and Joseph. They stood in a cluster at the back of the room against the wall and said nothing to Richard as he passed. He pushed aside the chair, sat down on the edge of the bed, and took Katherine's cool hand, now a bluish color, in both of his.

Her eyelids were closed and her breathing came in quick, shallow spurts, with pauses in between that increased in length as the minutes ticked by. He felt the souls of his family and ancestors upon him as he placed his left hand on Katherine's brow and kissed her parched lips.

Her eyelids fluttered open. "Richard . . ."

"I'm here, my love," he said.

"Richard," she whispered again, pleading as much with her eyes as with her voice. She had hardly the strength to speak.

"I'm here, Katherine," he said again. "I will *always* be here."

"Richard," she said, this time so softly he had to lean in close to hear her. "I love you, my darling, but I must go to sleep now. When I awaken, I will still be with you."

"And I with you, Katherine," he vowed to her. "Forever."

She gave him a ghost of a smile. Slowly, ever so slowly, as though reluctant in these final moments to ascend from a world so benevolent and loving, she closed her eyes. He sat there on the edge of the bed for a span of time that could have been minutes or hours, and he held her hand close to his heart as he gazed down upon her and watched her life ebb away.

Glossary

aback   In a position to catch the wind on the forward surface. A sail is aback when it is pressed against the mast by a headwind.

abaft   Toward the stern of a ship. Used relatively, as in "abaft the beam" of a vessel.

able seaman   A general term for a sailor with considerable experience in performing the basic tasks of sailing a ship.

after cabin   The cabin in the stern of the ship used by the captain, commodore, or admiral.

aide-de-camp   An officer acting as a confidential assistant to a senior officer.

alee or *leeward*   On or toward the sheltered side of a ship; away from the wind.

amidships   In or toward the middle of a vessel.

athwart   Across from side to side, transversely.

back   To turn a sail or a yard so that the wind blows directly on the front of a sail, thus slowing the ship's forward motion.

back and fill   To go backward and forward.

backstay   A long rope that supports a mast and counters forward pull.

ballast   Any heavy material placed in a ship's hold to improve her stability, such as pig iron, gravel, stones, or lead.

Barbary States   Morocco, Algiers, Tunis, and Tripoli. All except Morocco were under the nominal rule of the Ottoman sultan in Constantinople.

bark or *barque*   A three-masted vessel with the foremast and mainmast square-rigged, and the mizzenmast fore-and-aft rigged.

bar-shot   Shot consisting of two half cannonballs joined by an iron bar, used to damage the masts and rigging of enemy vessels.

before the mast   Term to describe common sailors, who were berthed in the forecastle, the part of the ship forward of the foremast.

before the wind   Sailing with the wind directly astern.

belay   To secure a running rope used to work the sails. Also, to disregard, as in "Belay that last order."

belaying pin   A fixed pin used on board ship to secure a rope fastened around it.

bend   To make fast. To bend on a sail means to make it fast to a yard or stay.

binnacle   A box that houses the compass, found on the deck of a ship near the helm.

boatswain   A petty officer in charge of a ship's equipment and crew, roughly the equivalent in rank to a sergeant in the army.

bollard   A short post on a ship or quay for securing a rope.

bower   The name of a ship's two largest anchors. The best-bower is carried on the starboard bow; the small-bower is carried on the larboard bow.

bowsprit   A spar running out from the bow of a ship, to which the forestays are fastened.

brace   A rope attached to the end of a yard, used to swing or trim the sail. To "brace up" means to bring the yards closer to fore-and-aft by hauling on the lee braces.

brail up   To haul up the foot or lower corners of a sail by means of the brails, small ropes fastened to the edges of sails to truss them up before furling.

brig   A two-masted square-rigged vessel having an additional fore-and-aft sail on the gaff and a boom on her mainmast.

Bristol-fashion   Shipshape.

broach-to   To veer or inadvertently to cause the ship to veer to windward, bringing her broadside to meet the wind and sea, a potentially dangerous situation, often the result of a ship being driven too hard.

buntline   A line for restraining the loose center of a sail when it is furled.

by the wind   As close as possible to the direction from which the wind is blowing.

cable   A strong, thick rope to which the ship's anchor is fastened. Also a unit of measure equaling approximately one-tenth of a sea mile, or two hundred yards.

cable-tier   A place in a hold where cables are stored.

camboose   A term of Dutch origin adopted by the early U.S. Navy to describe the wood-burning stove used in food preparation on a warship. Also, the general area of food preparation, now referred to as the galley.

canister shot or *case shot*   Many small iron balls packed in a cylindrical tin case that is fired from a cannon.

capstan A broad, revolving cylinder with a vertical axis used for winding a rope or cable.

caravel-built Describing a vessel whose outer planks are flush and smooth, as opposed to a clinker-built vessel, whose outer planks overlap.

cartridge A case made of paper, flannel, or metal that contains the charge of powder for a firearm.

catharpings Small ropes that brace the shrouds of the lower masts.

cathead or *cat* A horizontal beam at each side of a ship's bow used for raising and carrying an anchor.

chains or *chain-wale* or *channel* A structure projecting horizontally from a ship's sides abreast of the masts that is used to widen the basis for the shrouds.

clap on To add on, as in more sail or more hands on a line.

clewgarnet Tackle used to clew up the courses or lower square sails when they are bring furled.

close-hauled Sailing with sails hauled in as tight as possible, which allows the vessel to lie as close to the wind as possible.

commodore A captain appointed as commander in chief of a squadron of ships or a station.

companion An opening in a ship's deck leading below to a cabin via a companionway.

cordage Cords or ropes, especially those in the rigging of a ship.

corvette or *corsair* A warship with a flush deck and a single tier of guns.

course The sail that hangs on the lowest yard of a square-rigged vessel.

crosstrees A pair of horizontal struts attached to a ship's mast to spread the rigging, especially at the head of a topmast.

cutwater The forward edge of the stem or prow that divides the water before it reaches the bow.

daisy-cutter Another name for a swivel gun.

deadlight A protective cover fitted over a porthole or window on a ship.

dead reckoning The process of calculating position at sea by estimating the direction and distance traveled.

dogwatch Either of two short watches on a ship (1600–1800 hours and 1800–2000 hours).

East Indiaman A large and heavily armed merchant ship built by the various East India companies. Considered the ultimate sea vessels of their day in comfort and ornamentation.

ensign   The flag carried by a ship to indicate her nationality.

fathom   Six feet in depth or length.
fife rail   A rail around the mainmast of a ship that holds belaying pins.
flag lieutenant   An officer acting as an aide-de-camp to an admiral.
footrope   A rope beneath a yard for sailors to stand on while reefing or furling.
forecastle   The forward part of a ship below the deck, traditionally where the crew was quartered.
furl   To roll up and bind a sail neatly to its yard or boom.

gangway   On deep-waisted ships, a narrow platform from the quarterdeck to the forecastle. Also, a movable bridge linking a ship to the shore.
gig   A light, narrow ship's boat normally used by the commander.
grape or *grapeshot*   Small cast-iron balls, bound together by a canvas bag, that scatter like shotgun pellets when fired.
grapnel or *grappling hook*   A device with iron claws that is attached to a rope and used for dragging or grasping, such as holding two ships together.
grating   The open woodwork cover for the hatchway.

half-seas over   Drunk.
halyard   A rope or tackle used to raise or lower a sail.
hawser   A large rope used in warping and mooring.
heave to   To halt a ship by setting the sails to counteract each other, a tactic often employed to ride out a storm.
hull-down   Referring to another ship being so far away that only her masts and sails are visible above the horizon.

impress   To force to serve in the navy.

jack   The small flag flown from the jack-staff on the bowsprit of a vessel, such as the British Union Jack and Dutch Jack.
jolly boat   A clinker-built ship's boat, smaller than a cutter, used for small work.

keelhaul   To punish by dragging someone through the water from one side of the boat to the other, under the keel.

langrage   Case shot with jagged pieces of iron, useful in damaging rigging and sails and killing men on deck.

larboard   The left side of a ship, now called the port side.

lateen sail   A triangular sail set on a long yard at a forty-five-degree angle to the mast.

laudanum   An alcoholic solution of opium.

lee   The side of a ship, land mass, or rock that is sheltered from the wind.

leech   The free edges of a sail, such as the vertical edges of a square sail and the aft edge of a fore-and-aft sail.

lighter   A boat or barge used to ferry cargo to and from ships at anchor.

loblolly boy   An assistant who helps a ship's surgeon and his mates.

manger   A small triangular area in the bow of a warship in which animals are kept.

muster-book   The official log of a ship's company.

ordnance   Mounted guns, mortars, munitions, and the like.

orlop   The lowest deck on a sailing ship having at least three decks.

parole   Word of honor, especially the pledge made by a prisoner of war, agreeing not to try to escape or, if released, to abide by certain conditions.

petty officer   A naval officer with rank corresponding to that of a noncommissioned officer in the Army.

pig   An oblong mass of metal, usually of iron, often used as ballast in a ship.

poop   A short, raised aftermost deck found only on very large sailing ships. Also, a vessel is said to be "pooped" when a heavy sea breaks over her stern, as in a gale.

post captain   A rank in the Royal Navy indicating the receipt of a commission as officer in command of a post ship; that is, a rated ship having no less than 20 guns.

privateer   A privately owned armed ship with a government commission authorizing it to act as a warship.

prize   An enemy vessel and its cargo captured at sea by a warship or a privateer.

purser   An officer responsible for keeping the ship's accounts and issuing food and clothing.

quadrant   An instrument that measures the angle of heavenly bodies for use in navigation.

quarterdeck   That part of a ship's upper deck near the stern traditionally reserved for the ship's officers.

quay   A dock or landing place, usually built of stone.

queue   A plait of hair; a pigtail.

quoin   A wooden wedge with a handle at the thick end used to adjust the elevation of a gun.

ratlines   Small lines fastened horizontally to the shrouds of a vessels for climbing up and down the rigging.

reef   A horizontal portion of a sail that can be rolled or folded up to reduce the amount of canvas exposed to the wind; the act of so rolling a sail.

rig   The arrangement of a vessel's masts and sails. The two main categories are square-rigged and fore-and-aft rigged.

rode   A rope securing an anchor.

round shot   Balls of cast iron fired from smooth-bore cannon.

royal   A small sail hoisted above the topgallant that is used in light and favorable winds.

scupper   An opening in a ship's side that allows water to run from the deck into the sea.

sheet   A rope used to extend the sail or to alter its direction. To *sheet home* is to haul in a sheet until the foot of the sail is as straight and as taut as possible.

ship-rigged   Carrying square sails on all three masts.

shipwright   A person employed in the construction of ships.

shrouds   A set of ropes forming part of the standing rigging and supporting the mast and topmast.

slops   Ready-made clothing from the ship's stores, or slop-chests.

slow-match   A very slow burning fuse used to ignite the charge in a large gun.

stay   Part of the standing rigging, a rope that supports a mast.

staysail   A triangular fore-and-aft sail hoisted upon a stay.

stem   The curved upright bow timber of a vessel.

stern sheets   The rear of an open boat and the seats there.

studdingsail or *stunsail*   An extra sail set outside the square sails during a fair wind.

swivel-gun   A small cannon mounted on a swivel so that it can be fired in any direction.

tack   A sailing vessel's course relative to the direction of the wind and the position of her sails. On a "starboard tack," the wind is coming across the starboard side. Also, the corner to which a rope is fastened to secure the sail.

taffrail　The rail at the upper end of a ship's stern.

tampion　A wooden stopper for the muzzle of a gun.

tholepin or *thole*　One of a pair of pegs set in a gunwale of a boat to hold an oar in place.

three sheets to the wind　Very drunk.

top　A platform constructed at the head of each of the lower masts of a ship to extend the topmast shrouds. Also used as a lookout and fighting platform.

topgallant　The third mast, sail, or yard above the deck.

top-hamper　A ship's masts, sails, and rigging.

topsail　The second sail above the deck, set above the course or mainsail.

touchhole　A vent in the breech of a firearm through which the charge is ignited.

tumblehome　The inward inclination of a ship's upper sides that causes the upper deck to be narrower than the lower decks.

waist　The middle part of a ship's upper deck between the quarterdeck and the forecastle.

wardroom　The messroom on board ship for the commissioned officers and senior warrant officers.

watch　A fixed period of duty on a ship. Watches are traditionally four hours long except for the two dogwatches, which are two hours long.

wherry　A rowboat used to carry passengers.

windward　Facing the wind or on the side facing the wind. Contrast *leeward.*

xebec　A three-masted Arab corsair equipped with lateen sails. Larger xebecs had a square sail on the foremast.

yard　A cylindrical spar slung across a ship's mast from which a sail hangs.

yardarm　The outer extremity of a yard.

About the Author

WILLIAM C. HAMMOND is a freelance editor who lives with his three sons in Minneapolis, Minnesota. A lifelong student of history and a longtime devotee of nautical fiction, he sails whenever possible on Lake Superior and off the coast of New England.